Home Field

Home Field

Hannah Gersen

𝔀𝓜
WILLIAM MORROW
An Imprint of HarperCollins*Publishers*

HOME FIELD. Copyright © 2016 by Hannah Gersen. All rights reserved. Printed in the United States of America. No part of this book may be used or reproduced in any manner whatsoever without written permission except in the case of brief quotations embodied in critical articles and reviews. For information address HarperCollins Publishers, 195 Broadway, New York, NY 10007.

HarperCollins books may be purchased for educational, business, or sales promotional use. For information please e-mail the Special Markets Department at SPsales@harpercollins.com.

FIRST EDITION

Designed by Diahann Sturge

Library of Congress Cataloging-in-Publication Data has been applied for.

ISBN 978-0-06-241374-1

16 17 18 19 20 OV/RRD 10 9 8 7 6 5 4 3 2

For M.G.A.

Home Field

Prologue

June 16, 1996

At the edge of the creek a willow's tapered leaves floated on the gentle current. The water was cloudy with mud from the previous day's rain but Stephanie's horse, Juniper, drank thirstily. Her father's horse watched from a distance. Nearby there was a small pebbly beach where Stephanie and her younger brothers could launch canoes and inner tubes. Stephanie sometimes even went swimming, although yesterday she'd had a bad scare, one that she hadn't been able to shake off. She had come down to the creek by herself, riding Juniper without a saddle. It had been hot, in the nineties, and the water was so clear she could see straight to the bottom. She didn't have her suit with her so she went in wearing her clothes, a lightweight T-shirt and shorts. The swim was as refreshing as she'd imagined, but when she mounted Juniper, he reared up in surprise at her wet clothes and then bolted toward the woods, trying to throw her. It took less than a minute to subdue him, but as Stephanie realized what a fragile thing her body really was, time slowed down in a way that seemed almost supernatural, the seconds stretching to accommodate her fear. She didn't tell her parents what happened, afraid they would stop letting her go for solo rides. She loved to go out on her own, loved the calm that descended as she meandered along the wooded trails that surrounded the farm.

But it was also nice to be with her father, to have him to herself for a while; it felt like it had been months, maybe years, since they'd spent time together, just the two of them. Stephanie had deliberately distanced herself, wanting to become more independent, *needing* to be more independent, in light of her mother's dependence on her. She'd thought her father would take over after she left for college, but instead it seemed that Robbie would. He was at that age—the age when you begin to look offstage, to wonder what's going on behind the scenes of family life.

Her father rode one of the newer horses, a palomino whose sandy silver mane matched her father's graying blond hair. Beneath the black dye, Stephanie's hair was as light as her father's, though technically he was her stepfather; he had married Stephanie's mother when Stephanie was four. Every once in a while it would occur to Stephanie that she and her father were not related and she would wonder what her life would be like if her real father had lived. But her real father was not so real to her. He was a man in a posed photograph in her mother's frilly wedding album.

"That tree's going to fall soon." Her father pointed toward the willow whose trailing branches hung over the water. "It's going to stop up everything." Its trunk leaned at a forty-five-degree angle, the roots clinging like fingers to the banks.

"Robbie and Bry will like that," Stephanie said. Her younger brothers loved to build dams on the little stream that ran through their backyard. It seemed to her a distinctly boyish thing: to want to manipulate the landscape. When she was their age, she made boats from feathers and bark and watched them float away. She would make wishes on the boats. How many dozens of boats had she sent downstream when her mother was pregnant, wishing that Bryan would be a girl? Sweet, gullible Bry. Her other wish, the one she'd chased with fleets of twig and leaf, was for her mother to feel better. To forget whatever special torment distracted her from life. There were months, even years, when that wish seemed to come true. But just when Stephanie would begin to relax, to believe that her mother had finally paid off her debt of sadness, it would return.

Stephanie was always the first to notice. It would take her father weeks to catch up. Sometimes Stephanie loved him for his obliviousness and sometimes she hated him for it. She was relieved to be going away to college. When she got her acceptance letters, her father told her about winning a football scholarship when he was her age, how proud and surprised he'd been that his hard work had actually paid off. He hadn't grown up in an athletic family; no one had encouraged him to play sports or to spend his free time lifting weights and running laps around fields of grazing horses. Once, Stephanie asked why he hadn't learned to train horses, like his father, but he only shrugged and said he wasn't a horse person. Stephanie wasn't a horse person, either, but she liked visiting her grandfather's farm in Pennsylvania, liked being far from Willowboro, Maryland, where everyone knew her as the coach's daughter.

Her mother seemed freer here, too. All week long she'd had energy for everything: for cooking, for riding, for hiking. Even for minigolf, which she typically hated because it reminded her of the country club where she worked.

"We should probably get back," her father said. "Do you want to lead the way? Otherwise you're stuck looking at a horse's ass."

"Dad, you shouldn't be so hard on yourself."

He laughed and Stephanie smiled at how easy it was to make her father laugh—she barely had to attempt a joke—and how good it felt anyway.

The ride home was quiet and still, with just the sound of the horses' hooves clopping on the mud-packed ground. The trees arched over the trail, the leaves glowing green in the summer sun. Stephanie thought dreamily that it was like the end of *Sleeping Beauty*, when the thorns that surround the castle magically rearrange themselves to form a tunnel directly to the castle door.

"Do you hear that?" her father asked. "Sounds like an ambulance."

"I thought it was cicadas."

"It sounds close, like it's on the drive. I hope Grandpa's okay."

"What's the matter with Grandpa?"

"Nothing. He's just getting old. I get nervous, the way he climbs the rafters. I have to remind him that he's almost seventy. But he doesn't want to hear that."

The mew of the sirens got louder and then stopped. Was that good or bad? Juniper picked up the pace.

The creek trail was a loop that began and ended at the far corner of the fenced-in pasture adjacent to the stables. The pasture was a long, narrow rectangle, the length of two foot-

ball fields, at least. Stephanie came out of the woods and approached the wooden gate. She could see a white ambulance
in the distance: it was parked outside the barn, the back of the
vehicle pulled up to the door.

"Oh my God." Her father dismounted to unlatch the gate
and then climbed back onto his horse and galloped ahead without waiting for her or even looking back. Stephanie was so surprised by his wordless departure that she stood at the gate for a
moment, uncertain of what to do next. The peaceful mood of
the walk was gone, but her body hadn't gone into panic mode,
not like her father's. He was acting on instinct; he was going
after his father. Or her brothers. Oh God, her brothers. She
thought of how reckless Robbie could be. How he would swing
so high on the rope swing and then leap off to land on the
gravel lane, instead of into the hay. Her mother was always
telling him to stop, that he was going to hurt himself.

Stephanie led Juniper through the gate, trying not to startle her. But there was fear in the horse's black long-lashed eyes.
Stephanie wished for her grandfather's gentle presence. What
if he had fallen or had a heart attack? Dread rippled through
her body.

Juniper raced across the field, going almost too fast for
Stephanie, who had to lean forward and squeeze hard with her
thighs to keep her balance. Her father had left the front gate
open and Juniper slowed at its entrance but ran up to the barn,
which was on a slight rise. Stephanie pulled hard on the reins.
The ambulance was driving away. Her father and grandfather
stood in the barn's doorway, her grandfather holding on to the
palomino's bridle. Robbie and Bry were nowhere to be seen.

"What happened?" She was looking down from her perch

atop Juniper's saddle, and they were looking up at her with naked pain. Stephanie felt time slow down the way it had the day before, when Juniper tried to throw her.

"I need you to go to your brothers," her father said. "They're up at the house. The police are coming and I have to go with them to the hospital."

"What happened? Please, you have to tell me what happened."

"Your mother . . ." His face contorted. "She hanged herself with the rope swing. Robbie found her."

Her grandfather just kept staring at her.

Stephanie pressed her face into Juniper's mane, which smelled like the muddy creek and the warm sun and the rich animal murk of farm life—a beautiful, decaying perfume.

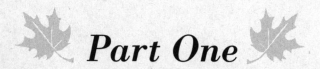

Part One

Chapter 1

The boy cried helplessly in Dean's office. He wiped his face with his scrimmage jersey, but it was too sweaty to be of any use to him. Even without his pads, the boy's shoulders were unusually square and broad. He looked like a grown man, with dark stubble already arriving in the late afternoon. Dean remembered scouting him from eighth-grade Field Day. He was big even then, uncoordinated but strong, his thick black hair growing as wildly as his body and long enough for a ponytail. He threw the shot put like it was nothing much, something slightly heavier than a softball. His name was Laird Kemp. Dean stood on the sidelines and watched him, writing a summer conditioning regimen on the blue index cards he always carried in the side pocket of his windbreaker. He gave it to the boy and told him to try out for junior varsity football in the fall. Four years later, Laird was their middle linebacker, the linchpin of their defensive unit. And he was telling Dean that he was sorry, but his family was moving in two weeks. His dad's company—Mac Truck—had transferred him to another one of their corporate offices.

"I'm sorry, Coach. I know I should have told you sooner. I don't know why my dad has to take this job."

"I'm sure he has good reasons." Dean knew Laird's parents fairly well. Like Dean, they weren't originally from Willowboro, which was a significant line of demarcation. They were also better off than most and lived in one of the nicer suburbs outside of town. They liked football as much as anyone and gave generously to the Boosters, but it wasn't their priority. They probably wanted Laird to spend his senior year preparing for college.

"I don't want to go to a new school," Laird said. He took a deep breath to steady himself. "I'm happy here. Things are good for me."

"Things will be good for you in your new school," Dean said. "I'll give a call to that coach over there. I'll tell him how lucky he is to have you joining his team."

Garrett Schwartz, the assistant coach, appeared in Dean's doorway. "You're leaving? You can't leave! We need you!"

Typical Garrett: awkward, blunt, and easily excited. He was the athletic director in addition to his role as assistant coach. His slightly built figure was a familiar sight at the beginning of every game as, clipboard in hand, he checked to make sure the facility was clean, the scoreboard turned on, the bleachers pulled down, and the soda and snack machines stocked and lit. He checked in with the cheerleaders, the Boosters, the refs, the coaches, and anyone else he recognized. He always had a whistle and a stopwatch around his neck, the stopwatch strung on a gimp lanyard that the cheerleaders had made one year for Spirit Week. Dean had given his lanyard to Stephanie.

"Don't worry about us," Dean said to Laird. "Go and shower. We'll tell the team tomorrow."

"I can come to practice tomorrow?"

"Of course."

Garrett began to brainstorm ideas for a replacement as soon as the kid was out of earshot. No one was as built as Laird—or as aggressive. That was the thing about Laird; even though his temperament was mellow, almost timid, he was ruthless on the field. Dean had a theory: Because Laird had always been big for his age, he'd had to learn how to be gentle, or risk hurting littler boys. When he played football, he could show his true strength.

"What about Jimmy Smoot?" Garrett asked. "He bulked up over the summer."

"He's fast," Dean said. "He's got a sprinter's build. You don't let that kind of speed go."

"I'll put him down as a question mark," Garrett said. "All the Smoots are linebacker material. It's in their genes. I went to high school with Jimmy's cousin. His nickname was Bear."

Garrett knew everyone in Willowboro. He had lived in the area all his life. Dean had arrived when he was twenty-six. Even after fifteen years of coaching and a half-dozen championship teams, he still felt he was regarded as an outsider.

"Okay, here's an idea," Garrett said. "I've actually been thinking of it for a while, but I sat on it because I know you don't like to poach from other teams."

"That's a firm policy of mine," Dean said.

"I know, but there's this pitcher on the baseball team, a junior, and he's a big guy, okay? Kind of a gut, maybe, but we can work with that. He's got a really fast pitch. He's already being scouted. His name's Devlin, Mark Devlin."

"I know Devlin. He takes gym every year," Dean said. "I don't want him getting injured."

"But he wouldn't necessarily," Garrett said. "And I think if we leaned on him, he would play."

"You asked him already?"

"I ran the idea by him in the spring. I was at a game. He said he didn't see himself as a football player, but you should see him pitch, he's an animal. He'll hit the batters if he has to."

"If he doesn't come here voluntarily, I don't want him," Dean said. "Remember Tyler Shelton? He ruined his knee playing football. Lost a basketball scholarship because of my dumb sales pitch. Trust me, you don't want that kind of guilt."

The phone rang and Dean picked up right away. It was Stephanie, reminding him in a sour voice to be home by four.

"I have a dinner shift, okay?" she said. "So please don't be late again."

"You know I can't get home early on double days."

"You're going to have to figure something out, because I'm only here one more week. Or did you forget that, too?"

The line went dead, but Dean said good-bye before hanging up. Garrett made a show of flipping through the papers on his clipboard.

"Everything okay?" He glanced at Dean quickly.

"I have to get home," Dean said, ignoring Garrett's half-assed attempt at meaningful conversation. Garrett didn't really want to know. No one did. "Would you mind taking a look at the playbook? Find all the ones that we wrote for Laird. We're going to have to change things up."

"I'll mark it and make a copy for you."

"You don't have to do that. We can compare notes tomorrow."

Dean left, grabbing his cap on the way out. He'd worn his

oldest one today, with the retired logo: a sunrise between two mountains with a small bird gliding in the corner. Now the bird—an eagle—was front and center, the mountains in the background. The sun had been removed.

Outside there were piles of grass clippings everywhere, but no mower in sight. The groundsman liked to start and finish his days early and was probably already at home on his deck, enjoying a cold one. When Dean first started coaching at Willowboro, it had been up to him to maintain the football and practice fields, a side duty he had thoroughly enjoyed, riding atop the whirring mower in the early evenings, feeling at once productive and leisurely as the sky above turned orange and then pink and then violet. He'd lime the sidelines in the dusky light and they would seem to glow. The next morning it would all be waiting for him in bright primary colors.

Dean always felt as if he needed August, as if these long days of practice, unfettered by academic or familial demands, were an interlude that restored him in some way, a time of simple feeling and nostalgia that connected the man he had become to the boy he had once been. It was the time of year when he felt that he knew who he was.

But this year that clarity was gone.

Don't try to get to the end of your grief. That's what his mother-in-law had told him. She had moved in with them for a few weeks over the summer, and Dean still missed their late-night conversations.

Two teachers waved to Dean from the other end of the lot. Dean waved back vaguely. He didn't know the other faculty that well. He was sequestered in the east annex, where his office, the weight rooms, and the locker rooms bordered two gyms, one large and one small. The teachers' lounge was at the other end of the school. That was fine with him. Although he taught PE, Dean didn't think coaching had much to do with teaching. He was more like a mechanic, or a horse trainer, like his father. The point was, he didn't consider his work to be intellectual. He'd never thought this was unusual, but Nicole had seized on it on one of their first dates.

"But the kids learn so much from you," she'd said. "Of course you're a teacher."

"All I care about is winning games. If they happen to learn something in the process, that's just a by-product."

She'd laughed, but he wasn't going to be one of those men who claimed that football was "character building." It wasn't a civilized sport. The training could be brutal. The players were often crude. He could think of few lessons that would serve anyone for a lifetime. It was a moment-by-moment kind of game. That was why he needed it now. All summer long he had been living "one day at a time," as everyone advised. It was an act of will not to look ahead, not to think about all the ways his future had been destroyed. He tried not to look back, either, but that was harder. Everyone said he couldn't blame himself, but Dean knew they were all thinking the same thing, that it would never happen to them, that they would never *let* it happen. And at the same time everyone told him how shocked they were, how they had *no idea*, how they never would have guessed that someone like her, a woman so, so, so . . . they always struggled to say what had fooled them. So normal, perhaps. Or maybe: so undefined. So easy to project happiness onto.

Maybe they all just had crushes on her. Dean got notes of

condolence from her country club clients, most of them male, all of them recalling Nicole's sunny nature. *She always had a smile for me*, one wrote. *As if that meant anything*, Dean thought bitterly. He hated how grief made him cynical. The world, for him, was now full of shortsighted, awkward idiots.

Dean drove down Main Street, which was actually Route 40, an old road you could take west all the way to Utah. Or east to Baltimore. Dean could still remember learning the roads in the area, before everything became rote, before he met Nicole. There had been a time when he wasn't even sure he'd stay very long in this particular corner of western Maryland, this tiny town tucked into the skinny arm of the state. Even though it was several hours from his father's, it had seemed too close to where he'd grown up. Or maybe it had just seemed too small.

Willowboro had never been prosperous or historically significant. Unlike other nearby towns, which had hosted Civil War battles and bunkered generals, Willowboro's wartime role was to receive the bodies of the dead after the Battle of Antietam. This ghoulish task had taken place in the town's livery stables, now the site of Weddle's Nursing Home. The place gave Dean the creeps, but he had to visit it every October with his players. They would sing fight songs, and then Dean would give an overview of the season, with slides. It was called "A Night with the Coach," and it was open to the whole town. The point was to get people to visit their infirm relatives, and it worked. Only Christmastime was busier.

Dean turned right at the stoplight, driving past the four businesses that were the cornerstones of Willowboro's social life: Asaro's Pizza, Mike's Video Time, Jenny's Luncheonette, and the post office. Willow Park was tucked behind them, a small but quaint landscape with arched stone bridges, wooden pavilions, playgrounds, and, of course, willow trees—the grandchildren of the original trees, planted at the turn of the century. Before it was called Willowboro, the town was called Weddle, for its founding brothers. Dean thought that the dopey, sleepy-sounding "Weddle" was more fitting.

Willowboro was bounded by two stoplights, and the town quickly thinned out on either side of them, the sidewalks petering out to accommodate the shoulders of wider roads. The Legion Hall, with its beige siding and sloping black roof, marked the edge of town. The football banquet, homecoming dance, and prom were held there every year. A half mile past the Legion Hall was Shank's Produce, which was owned by Dean's sort-of in-laws, Vivian and Walter Shank. The Shanks were the parents of Nicole's first husband, Sam. Sam was buried ten miles from here, and after the Shanks moved away, they talked about getting him exhumed to a cemetery closer to them. Nicole thought they said things like this to get under her skin, but Dean thought they were just odd people. Stephanie liked them, though. And they were a good influence. He doubted she'd be going to a college like Swarthmore if they hadn't pushed her to apply.

The new Sheetz loomed ahead, bright red and yellow and simple in design, like something a kid would make with Legos. Dean stopped to fill up and then decided to go ahead and get some subs for dinner. It was the third time this week they'd had them, but it was the only thing the boys ate with any kind of appetite.

He ran into Jimmy Smoot in the parking lot. He was with a girl Dean didn't recognize and drinking a mouthwash-blue

Freeze. His Adam's apple bulged in his skinny, razor-burned neck and Dean thought that Garrett was wrong; this kid was not going to bulk up, not ever.

"Hey, Coach," Smoot said. "You tried these? It's team colors."

"You should drink chocolate milk after practice. You need protein with your carbohydrates."

The girl crossed her arms. "Plus milk doesn't give you Smurf lips."

"This is my sister, Missy," Smoot said. "She's going to be a freshman this year."

"*Melissa*," the girl corrected. She was tall, like her brother, and had his rangy, broad-shouldered frame, which she accentuated by wearing oversized clothing: baggy jean shorts and a black T-shirt with the word HOLE on it. Layered over the T-shirt was a short-sleeved button-down, also oversized. The ensemble was intensely unflattering, but Dean recognized it as "alt style." Stephanie had explained this term to him when she began to dress in the same way.

"Are you an athlete, like your brother?" Dean asked her.

"Missy's going out for cheer squad," Smoot said. "She can't help herself, she just has to cheer me on—oh, shoot! Brain freeze!" He pressed the heel of his palm to his forehead and squeezed his eyes shut, as if it was the worst pain he'd been in all day.

"You drink those things way too fast." Melissa turned to Dean. "I don't play sports. I'm not coordinated."

"Maybe you just haven't found the right sport."

"Maybe." She nudged her brother. "Come on, you said you'd drop me off."

"Yeah, okay. See you Monday, Coach."

They waved guilelessly, completely absorbed by the logistics of their evening and the politics of siblinghood. They couldn't see Nicole's ghost, and for that, Dean was grateful. Both the best and worst thing about working with kids was that they had almost no ability to imagine life beyond the age of thirty.

Dean turned on the radio for the ride home, searching for WINQ, the oldies station he and Stephanie used to sing along to together. Once, they had been buddies, best friends. She had tagged along to every game, and sometimes even to practices, doing homework in the stands. She'd been three years old when he met Nicole, the young widow no one wanted to date—or maybe, the young widow everyone wanted to date but was too cautious to approach. Dean had no idea of her previous marriage. And neither did Stephanie. As far as she was concerned, Dean was her new father. He'd never pictured himself marrying a woman who already had a child, but after their first week together, he was already sitting next to her in a church pew, unwilling to be apart from her for any part of the weekend. He'd never fallen for someone so quickly, and it was exhilarating. When he and Nicole broke the happy news to Stephanie, she seemed confused. It took them a while to realize that she thought they were already married. They let her pick the wedding cake, and she chose to have it decorated with pink and purple flowers. She wore a ruffled pink-and-purple dress to match.

Now Stephanie was a different kind of girl altogether. She didn't fantasize about wedding cakes and she never wore pink. She had gone to her junior prom wearing a torn slip and a man's blazer, her date a boy who was not the least bit interested in girls—a fact that unsettled Dean, though he was careful not to say so. Nicole was even more disappointed than he was. Stephanie had started high school on her mother's path: a cheerleader, a churchgoer, a smiling girl with smiling friends. But she started to change at the end of ninth grade. Nicole noticed before Dean did; it began with her clothes. Stephanie stopped shopping with Nicole at the mall and instead went to thrift stores to find items that no one else had. New clothes led to new friends; that was how it worked with girls, apparently. The new friends weren't bad—they were smart and polite—but they mystified Dean with their dark clothes, their dark looks, and their dark under-the-breath jokes. What did they have to be depressed about? There had been a war going on when he was in high school. He blamed the culture, the muddy-sounding music. He would watch MTV with Stephanie to try to figure it out. One of the singers mumbled so badly that his lyrics were put up on the screen, like subtitles. This guy wore a dress onstage. When he killed himself, Stephanie wanted to take a day off from school. An absurd request, Dean thought, not even worth acknowledging, but somehow it turned into one of her and Nicole's bigger fights. Sometimes it seemed as if the two of them could not even breathe the same air. Dean's policy was impartiality. Nicole thought he was taking Stephanie's side.

Dean turned onto Iron Bridge Road, a lane divided into two sections: one old, narrow, and badly paved, and the other new, wide, and smooth as a highway. Dean lived in the old section, where the road's namesake, a wrought-iron bridge, had once stood. It was demolished in the late seventies and replaced by a plain cement structure with thick safety rails made of corrugated metal. Dean might have seen the original if he'd arrived in Willowboro just a couple of years earlier. He was genuinely sorry to have missed it. He'd had a fondness for Iron Bridge Road even before he lived on it. When he first moved to the area, he would take long bike rides in the country, lacking anything better to do. He remembered discovering the old part of Iron Bridge Road and thinking it would be a good place to build a house. He had been surprised, later, when Nicole agreed. Her family all lived close to one another on a farm on the outskirts of town. He assumed she would want to stay near them. But she had wanted a change.

They ended up buying an old house and constructing an addition, instead of building something new. It was a simple two-story stone house, similar to others in the area, made from gray limestone and white mortar, with small square windows, evenly spaced and white-silled. The house's selling point was a double-decker side porch, a real Maryland porch. In the summer, the boys liked to spend the night there, dragging their sleeping bags right up against the window. Mornings they'd come downstairs with imprints of the screen on their cheeks. Their real bedroom was downstairs, in the addition. Robbie had been planning to move into Stephanie's upstairs bedroom after she left for college, but he hadn't mentioned it recently. The boys had once complained about having to room together; now they seemed pleased to have a shared retreat, a reason never to be alone.

Dean didn't see Stephanie's car in the driveway as he approached his house. He pulled in and saw that it wasn't parked in the shady side yard, either.

He cursed aloud. He had wanted to say good-bye before she left. He was becoming superstitious.

There was no note in the kitchen and the boys weren't in their usual spot, playing Nintendo in the living room. He checked their bedroom, but it was empty.

He went to the back porch and called for them in the yard. "Robbie! Bry!" Then he went upstairs to check from his bedroom window, where he could see into the backyard and surrounding fields. His door was closed, which was odd, since he usually left it open. Nicole was the one who would close it—a signal to him to leave her alone. Had he left her alone too often? Not enough? It was impossible to know in retrospect.

With Nicole so strongly in his mind, Dean wasn't surprised, at first, to see her clothes strewn across the bed. It was a sight that had greeted him many mornings when he emerged from the shower. "What's the weather like?" she would ask, as if their bathroom was a portal to the outdoors. He always said, "Partly cloudy." One day he added, "with a chance of hail," and that stuck for years, becoming funny for no good reason. At some point she stopped asking.

He gazed at the clothes, the layers of patterns clashing with the bedspread. Florals, bright colors, lots of blue—to bring out her eyes. Stephanie must have been going through them to see if there was anything she wanted to bring with her to college. He'd told her to take a look in the closet before he gave them away, but he didn't think she actually would. He began to pile the clothes into the hamper. They rustled and he thought he heard whispering. "Nic?" he said aloud, involuntarily. The room was silent. He didn't believe in ghosts. He didn't even try to talk to Nic in prayer. Still, he felt that someone was in the room with him.

"Boys?" he called.

He heard the whisper again. It was coming from underneath the bed.

"Boys?" Dean knelt to lift the duster. There they were, squeezed together, their eyes bright like little animals'. "What are you doing?"

"Playing hide-and-seek," Robbie said.

"Who are you hiding from?"

"Steffy."

"She said to tell you she went to work," Bry added.

"No, she *didn't*."

"She did so—ow!"

Dean stood up. "Look, I don't care, just get out from under there."

"Can you go down to the kitchen and we'll meet you there?" Robbie asked.

"No," Dean said, sharply—too sharply, he knew, but he was losing patience. They were hiding something, obviously, something that was probably nothing, but in their kid brains it was worth lying about.

"*Please*," Robbie said.

"Hurry up," Dean said. "I'm waiting."

There was no movement, and Dean thought he was going to have to lift the box spring off the frame, but then Bry began to wriggle out on his stomach. At first, Dean noticed nothing unusual about his eight-year-old son's appearance. His dark-blond hair was its usual cowlicked mess, his cheeks flushed, his fingernails dirty. It wasn't until Bry's torso was completely exposed that Dean realized his son was wearing a woman's white blouse. Nicole's blouse. He was wearing a skirt, too. It was green with tiny yellow polka dots. The skirt, which had been knee-length on Nicole, hit Bryan midcalf. Dust bunnies clung to the hem.

"Daddy—" Bry began.

Dean held up his hand. "Robbie! Did you put your brother up to this?"

"Why do you always blame me?"

"Get out from under there right now."

Robbie rolled out at the foot of the bed. He was wearing one of Nicole's dresses, a pale blue one with buttons down the front. On his feet he wore a pair of her heels, with bows. Everything feminine about his older son—his shaggy overgrown hair, his long-lashed and expressive eyes, his slender neck and arms—was brought into relief.

"Steffy was trying things on—" Bry said.

"Never mind! I don't want to hear it. Just get back in your regular clothes."

Bry began to cry. He was always the first to do so; sometimes he seemed to be the family's designated mourner, tearing up whenever his mother's name was mentioned by some sympathy-wishing stranger. "I'm sorry," he said, wiping his nose with Nicole's ruffled cuff.

"I'm sorry, too," Dean said. "I'm sorry I had to see this."

"It's not that big a deal." Robbie tossed his head to get his hair out of his eyes. Dean had to look away, but when he averted his gaze, he caught his sons' bizarre image in Nicole's vanity mirror.

"Just change back into your clothes, all right?" Dean said.

"Steffy said you told her to try things on. So can't we?"

"Don't be smart with me. You know the answer to that question."

"Why didn't you just get rid of them?" Robbie said. "Stephanie already has a ton of dead-lady clothes from Goodwill."

"Don't talk about your mother that way."

"What, that she's dead?"

"We're not a family that just dumps things at Goodwill."

"What kind of family are we?"

"I don't know, Robbie! Will you get out of those clothes?"

Bryan was still crying. "I'm sorry, Daddy! I didn't know you would be so mad."

"It's okay," Dean said. He glared at Robbie over Bryan's head. "I'm going downstairs. I want you down there in five minutes, in your normal clothes. Got it?"

Bryan immediately began to unbutton Nicole's ruffled blouse. Dean hurried out, not wanting to see his scrawny chest beneath. In the kitchen, he got a beer and downed it quickly, and then opened a second can and poured it into a glass, like he was a civilized person having a drink at the end of the day. Everyone had told him this would happen, that his boys would "act out," but Dean had steeled himself for something quite different. He thought they would pick fights, punch walls, break things. Instead they had become quiet. They never talked about their mother, except when Dean brought her up, and even then, they said very little. He never had any idea what they were thinking. And now this. He couldn't even tell anyone about it. There was a sexual element that disturbed him.

"Boys!" he called.

They came downstairs together. It was such a relief to see

them in their T-shirts and shorts that Dean immediately apologized.

"Let's go out to dinner, okay?" he said. "We can go to the Red Byrd and surprise your sister."

"But you got subs," Robbie said, pointing.

"We can have them tomorrow," Dean said. "Come on, don't you want to get out of the house? You've been stuck here all afternoon."

Only Bryan nodded, but that was enough for Dean.

The radio came on loud when Dean started the car, startling the boys, but somehow it cleared the air.

"Steffy's leaving next week," Dean said. "We have to figure out something for you to do when I'm at practice."

"I don't want to go to Aunt Joelle's," Robbie said.

"You don't like playing with your cousins?" He wasn't eager to leave them with Joelle, but there was no reason for them to know that.

"She has Bible verses taped up everywhere," Bryan said. "And she makes you say one before she gives you a snack."

"It's good exercise for your brain to memorize things," Dean said, trying to find the secular virtue. Joelle's fundamentalism was getting harder to ignore. It had started before Nicole's death, but then he'd had Nicole as a buffer. Or maybe it was that Joelle had spent her energies trying to convert Nicole instead of him. She thought love of Jesus could cure Nicole, that modern psychology was a crock. Dean was no big fan of psychology, either, with all its doped-up promises, but he thought Joelle's minister told bigger lies, with his shiny face and his PowerPoint "teachings." Nic had gone to Joelle's church one Sunday and returned confused. "They actually think they're talking to God," she said. "Can you understand that?" Dean's answer had been no, he couldn't. He assumed that God had more important people to talk with.

"What if we went to Grandpa's?" Robbie said.

"Grandpa lives too far away," Dean said, carefully.

"We could stay overnight," Robbie said.

"All week? No, that's not going to work." He couldn't believe they wanted to go back there.

"Maybe Grandpa could come live with us," Bry said.

"Grandpa would never leave his horses," Robbie said.

Dean had long since accepted that his father preferred horses to people, but it was still jarring to hear Robbie say it. At Nicole's memorial, his father talked about how good she was with the horses, and how much they would miss her. It was as if he could only understand the loss by imagining the animals' response.

The Red Byrd was up ahead, with its row of cardinals perched on the roof and its old-fashioned marquee promising the best red velvet cake in Maryland. The parking lot was already crowded with cars. Dean snagged one of the last shady spots, next to a car with a bumper sticker that read MY CHILD IS AN HONOR STUDENT AT WILLOWBORO HIGH. They had four of those stickers at home, but Stephanie forbade their display.

Inside the restaurant, the atmosphere was noisy and friendly. Dean eyed a corner booth and asked the hostess if it was in Stephanie's section.

"Steph's not working tonight. I think she's on tomorrow night."

"Are you sure?" Dean asked.

"I can double-check the schedule—"

"No, it's all right. I must have gotten mixed up. We'll just take the booth, if it's free."

They followed the hostess across the dining room, past a couple of people Dean knew from the Boosters Club. He nodded in their direction. He knew he should stop and chat, but he didn't.

"Steffy lied?" Bry said.

"Obviously," Robbie said.

Dean gazed at his placemat, seeking solace in its usual lists of presidents or cocktail recipes, but instead found himself staring at last year's football stats, a nearly undefeated season. The Red Byrd had printed these placemats after they won the state championship—a triumph dampened for Dean by Nicole's depression and Stephanie's disdain. Neither of them had gone to many games last fall. As Dean read the old scores, numbers he could have recited in his sleep, he had a sudden, fervent wish for Nicole to return, to sit here beside him and put her hand on his leg. The wish radiated through him, through the whole of his day. Through every day.

A waitress appeared, greeting him by name. "You like our placemats?" she asked. "We're going to have to make another batch this year, I bet."

"I sure hope so," Dean said, forcing a smile.

"You boys ready to order?"

Robbie and Bryan stared at her silently.

"I think we're going to need some more time," Dean said.

It was still light outside when they got home from the Red Byrd, so Dean suggested a walk through the meadow behind their house and down to the creek. The boys agreed, picking up walking sticks in the backyard. They had been shy with him all through dinner, but by dessert they'd relaxed. Dean blamed himself for yelling at them earlier, but he blamed Stephanie, too. Her absence had put them all on edge. They were so fragile right now that any little thing worried them. Stephanie was a mother figure, whether she liked it or not. Dean thought she liked it, but it was hard to tell. Sometimes Dean got the feeling she was putting off her grieving until she was away at college, where she could be alone. Other times he thought she had decided to just put her mother's death out of her mind, something to be dealt with later. It hurt him that she would not admit her sorrow to him; it hurt him even though it had been years since she shared anything *true* with him. He was accustomed to being shut out from her world.

Down by the creek, the air was cooler. Robbie and Bry took off their shoes and socks and waded into the water. The creek was narrow here, no more than twenty feet across, and shallow, littered with hundreds of smooth, baseball-sized stones that created small disturbances in the current. The boys had spent much of their summer down here, industriously piling small rocks into dams, only to find them dismantled the next time they visited. But they didn't seem to care about their progress—or at least, Robbie didn't. At eleven, he wavered between adult interests and childish ones, capable of discussing current events and football strategies with Dean, but also still interested in building Lego cities or cuddling with his stuffed animals, which he arranged on his bed every morning, in a particular order. The image of Robbie in Nicole's pale blue dress flitted through Dean's mind before he could dismiss it. He could accept the behavior if it had been instinctual, if

Robbie hadn't really thought about it, if it was an act of grief, of confusion—not pleasure. But what if Nicole's death had perverted him in some way? Dean was angry with Nicole for not thinking of this; he had to believe she hadn't been able to fully imagine the consequences of her actions.

He had to believe it, and yet he couldn't.

Dean tried to recall some of the strange things he'd done after his own mother left. But it wasn't the same because his mother hadn't died; she'd just married another man, a salesman she'd met in the hospital where she worked as a nurse's aide—*not even a nurse*, Dean used to think, when he wanted to think ill of his mother. He'd taken his father's side, calling his mother a self-loathing snob. He assumed she left because she was tired of being married to a borderline servant. His father had worked on a bigger farm then, and they'd lived in a small house near the training grounds of a pristine estate surrounded by white fences that were painted every spring. The farm was owned by one of the oldest horsing families in the state, not that Dean's father would ever describe his employer that way. It was the horses Dean's father admired, not the lavish properties, not the races, not even the status that went along with being the kind of person who stabled such beautiful animals.

There were dozens of people like Dean's father, people who humbled themselves in moneyed society in order to be close to horses. Why were all these men and women, possessed of beautifully calibrated efficient muscle and bone, wistfully gazing at horses as if their strength were somehow more mysterious? The one time Dean had felt close to his father's horses was when he was in training for his first varsity season. He was out for a jog and the grazing horses broke into a run toward him, as if to say, *It's easy, don't you see?* As a teenager he'd seen his father as a weak person, a minor failure, not because of his job but because his mother had cheated on him. After she left, Dean's father stopped working with racehorses, taking a more low-key job at the farm where he now worked. It was for Dean's benefit, but Dean resented it. He did everything he could to be different from his father, starting with his body.

In the summer between ninth and tenth grade, Dean bought a pair of running shoes and a set of dumbbells and got a book from the library called *Speed, Strength & Agility*. He did every workout in the book, marking each one with a penciled checkmark. Every two weeks he had to renew the book, and he would run the 4.7 miles to the library in town, carrying it in a backpack. It was easier each time, his muscles a little less sore afterward. In the barn, in one of the unused stalls, he set up a makeshift weight room. The barn was hot, a dry and dusty heat. The smell of hay and horseshit—sweet and fetid— seemed to make the place even hotter. Dean kept a canteen of ice water next to him, his reward between sets. Water never tasted so good. Cold never tasted so good. In the evening he took baths, his muscles aching and expanding. Sleep came immediately; it was like going into a dark cave. Dean doubted he'd ever been healthier. Whenever he got on a self-improvement kick, when he dieted or tried to get "back in shape," it was this elusive time that he was chasing.

Dean's mother was athletic, and Dean would begrudgingly admit that he owed his love of sports to her. He remembered watching the 1964 Olympics with her when Billy Mills won the 10,000 meters out of nowhere, upsetting the race, the announcer screaming, "Look at Mills! Look at Mills!" and his mother jumping up and yelling, "Go! Go! Go!" It was rare for her to show that level of excitement. He saw now that she was an unhappy person, perhaps wanting to escape her marriage for a long time before she actually did. On weekends she would take Dean for hikes on the Appalachian Trail, smiling back at him sometimes but mostly keeping her gaze ahead, fixed on the trail. Dean wondered now why his father had not joined them. His mother taught him how to swim, and she liked to tell a story about the time a diving instructor singled her out at a public pool and said she should train professionally. But her high school didn't even have sports for women. At his most charitable, Dean imagined his mother had been born at the wrong time, unable to make use of her strong, muscular frame. She'd had so much energy. That was her best quality. She'd died of a heart attack while she was out picking up trash alongside the road. It was something she did every morning, walking three miles after breakfast. A state trooper had seen her collapse, with her garbage bag full of bottles and cans and fast-food wrappers. Dean had to explain to the police it was her Good Samaritan hobby, that she wasn't some homeless person.

He felt relieved after she died, like he had one less person to worry about. But he knew he wouldn't feel that way when his father passed away. He still needed his father. He didn't think of him as weak anymore. His father had been the one to cut Nicole down. Dean didn't ask him how he'd done it, but he had seen the standing ladder and the hay bales next to it, draped with a horse blanket. He must have laid her body down on the bales. He must have done it fast. Maybe the ladder was already in place. It must have been. But it would have been hard to carry her down alone. Adrenaline must have flooded his body; Dean knew what it felt like to want to protect your children.

His father came with him to the hospital, and he stayed up with him that night. They'd watched a baseball game because what else were they supposed to do? Stephanie came into the room in the middle of it, and the expression on her face was one of such pure disgust that Dean got a jolt back to his own adolescence, remembering those sharp, hot judgments that would seem to burn inside him. He hadn't thought she would hold on to her resentment the next day, but he had been wrong. She held on to it all summer. After a while, he'd realized she was blaming him the same way he'd blamed his father after his mother left.

Bry called to him, pointing, and Dean saw a heron standing calmly on the opposite shore, one leg drawn up. The bird had something of Stephanie's stern regarding manner, the affect she'd adopted when she began to change in high school. After the new clothes and the new friends, she'd started quitting things: cheerleading, choir, student council, and even church. Her reasoning, that she wanted to concentrate more on academics, was foolproof. And she had the grades to prove it. How could they complain? Dean thought he understood, having pulled away from his own parents, but Nicole didn't get it. She'd never left the town where she'd grown up. She'd married her high school sweetheart. College was her big adventure, and she talked about it like it had been a visit to a faraway place, even though she'd gone to a Christian school just an hour away. Sam had been at the same school, recruited to play football for their no-name team. Nicole remembered him as a big star, though—the whole town did. Sometimes Dean got annoyed and wanted to point out that he couldn't have been that great if he ended up at a Division III program.

He hated to think of the stories people would tell about Nic: the girl who was widowed too young. The girl whose broken heart had never quite healed. The girl who tried in vain to replace her football star husband with the high school football coach. People were already acting as if she were destined to be some perfect ghost, putting her alongside Sam in heaven, under the banner of First Love. It was offensive to Dean, the way it overlooked his and Nicole's fourteen years of marriage—somehow four years with Sam surpassed that. People were invested in Sam because they'd watched him grow up. Dean understood that. But he'd thought that the town was invested in him, too. He'd become a father to Sam's daughter, he'd taken care of Nicole, he'd coached a championship team. Everyone had seemed so grateful; he had *felt* so grateful. Those early years were easy, busy years. He could still remember the piles of gifts when Robbie was born: the baskets of food, the bouquets of flowers, the boxes of homemade fudge. He felt as if people were paying him homage, as if he were a minor king.

The heron was still standing there, glowing more whitely now that the light was fading. Dean called to the boys, and they started, as if they'd forgotten he was with them. The heron was startled, too, and stretched its wings. Suddenly it was in flight, sailing low, just a few feet above the water. Its white form was like a streak of fresh paint against the muddy creek.

Robbie and Bry waded back to shore, where their shoes and socks were waiting for them. Together, the three of them climbed the steep bank and walked across the meadow that led to their house.

There was an aluminum-foil-wrapped pie pan sitting on their front step. People were still dropping off baked goods. Dean didn't know how to make it stop.

"Peach," said Robbie, sniffing.

"I wish it was chocolate cake," Bry said.

Dean brought it inside and found a note tucked beneath the foil. It was from Julie Frye, a woman from church. Most of the baked goods he received were from church ladies. Joelle said they were "on the prowl." Dean couldn't help thinking that each of these little offerings was meant to make him feel guilty for skipping services, week after week. He stuck it in the fridge with all the other leftovers, wedging it so tightly that he ended up knocking over something in the back. It was one of Nicole's bottles of sunscreen. She liked it to be cool when she put it on her face. He gazed at the white bottle with its orange cartoon sun, little bits of the sun's rays chipped off with use. The boys were staring up at him.

"Can we watch TV?"

"If you get ready for bed first," Dean said.

"But it's still light out!"

"Just do it." Dean chose not to remind them that they fell asleep every night in front of the TV, a habit he hadn't meant to foster but had stopped trying to resist. TV, along with snacks, worked like a sedative to get them past the precarious border between waking and dreaming. It worked for Dean, too, although his snack was beer or bourbon.

"Can we have microwave popcorn?" Bryan asked.

"Sure, sure," Dean said. Outside, someone was pulling into his driveway. His first thought was Stephanie, but when he checked the kitchen window, it was Garrett's shiny white Geo. He probably got it washed every week.

"Garrett," Dean said, meeting him at the side door.

"Hey, Coach. I just wanted to drop off the playbook, like I said." Garrett held up a manila envelope.

Dean opened the envelope and flipped through the book. There were notes on almost every page. Dean couldn't believe so many plays were going to be affected by Laird's departure.

"I got a little carried away and ended up staying late," Garrett said. "And then Brett Albright stopped by."

"What did he want?" Albright was his QB and team captain. He was one of Dean's favorites, a smart kid who had learned the game from his older brother, borrowing his playbook and memorizing it for fun. Dean had taken him out of JV his sophomore year even though he wasn't quite physically ready.

"His right shoulder is acting up, but we can talk about it later. I gave him some stretches. And, uh, I told him about Laird. I told him not to mention it."

"Okay." Dean didn't really feel like being annoyed with Garrett. "You want to come in for a beer?"

"I would," Garrett said, "but I have plans with Connie."

In the spring Garrett had begun dating a tennis instructor, a woman Dean had inadvertently introduced him to when he gave Garrett free passes to the country club where Nicole worked. Secretly Dean felt that Connie, who was fit and young and innocently pretty, was out of Garrett's league.

"Another time," Dean said. As he watched Garrett leave, he felt jealous, not only of Garrett's night ahead, but for the entire phase of life that Garrett was in—the beginning phase, when everything was still unknown, but your goals were clear. If someone had told Dean last fall that he would be envious of his excitable assistant coach, Dean wouldn't have believed it. But here he stood, in his own yard, wishing he were the one driving away in that spotless little white car.

STEPHANIE STARED UP at Robert Smith, tacked to Mitchell's ceiling. His pale face seemed to glow in the dim light of the room. Mitchell's room was always dark and gloomy, the windows draped with layers of gauzy scarves from Goodwill and the lights turned down low. When Mitchell's parents were gone, he burned incense and played music that his father did not approve of, bands like Nine Inch Nails and Nirvana and, if Stephanie was visiting, Tori Amos. The incense was purely theatrical; Mitchell wasn't trying to cover the smell of anything. He didn't smoke pot or drink, although everyone assumed he did, with his laid-back persona and baggy, patchouli-drenched clothes. It used to be that only Stephanie knew how smart and driven he truly was, but getting into MIT had changed that. Now everyone called him Doogie Howser.

"You going to take all your posters with you to school?" Stephanie was trying, for what seemed like the tenth time, to get a conversation going. They usually talked easily, but they were having trouble tonight.

"Nah, I'm starting fresh," Mitchell said. "Maybe I'll be a minimalist."

"Yeah, right." Stephanie nodded to his dresser, crowded with a zoo of Tetley tea animals he'd inherited from his grandmother. Hung above them was his collection of black velvet paintings, scrounged from yard sales. "You're like the king of kitsch in here."

"And you're the queen in that dress."

"It was my mother's," Stephanie said, with an awkward laugh. Her dress *was* kind of Holly Hobbie–ish, but she liked the simple print of yellow sunflowers on a black background.

"Sorry," Mitchell said. He looked at her dolefully but without pity. He was the only person in her life who hadn't treated her like a fragile flower after her mother's death.

"You think it's strange that I'm wearing her dress?"

"A little," Mitchell said. "So what? You should do more strange things."

Stephanie took this as a jab at her conventionality—one she would have welcomed before her mother's death, but which now felt like a criticism. Lately she felt overly sensitive. She couldn't handle Mitchell's or anyone's wisecracks; it was as if they put real cracks in her.

"It's a little bit long," Mitchell said. "Maybe you should shorten it."

"You think so?" She and Mitchell often altered items they bought at thrift stores, usually with help from Mitchell's mother. But this wasn't the same thing, exactly.

"Definitely. I'll go get my mom's scissors."

He left the room before Stephanie could protest. She had the sense he'd been looking for an excuse to leave.

Lying back down on his bed, she returned her attention to his collaged ceiling. Next to Robert Smith was Tuesday Weld, peering out from beneath a fur-collared coat, which was draped over her head, as if she needed to hide from something just out of frame. The photo was from the cover of Matthew Sweet's album *Girlfriend*—Stephanie's favorite album, at one time. Mitchell just liked the cover—the romance of it, the lavender light, the borrowed glamour. He'd told Stephanie that her mother reminded him of Tuesday Weld. Stephanie couldn't see the resemblance, but one day when Mitchell was over, they got out her mother's old yearbooks and looked at pictures of her as a teenager. Then Stephanie got it: the bright blond hair, the delighted smile, the little nose and teddy-bear eyes. Her mother was a dream. Looking at those photos, Stephanie felt cheated. What happened to that buoyant girl? And at the same time she wanted nothing to do with that kind of femininity. It was no coincidence that Stephanie had decided to dye her hair after looking at those yearbooks, and no coincidence that she began to distance herself from her best friend, Bethany, who was on the junior varsity cheer squad and wore silk ruffled shirts and Red Door by Elizabeth Arden perfume and whose goal in high school—if not explicitly stated—was to like and be liked by absolutely everyone.

Her father, Sam, was in those photos, too. He seemed like a nice person. And also exactly the kind of guy she had grown weary of. She and Mitchell had a love-hate relationship with the football players at their school. They were so banal and clueless, so spoiled and doted upon, and yet physically, they were rather outstanding. There was one player in particular, Brett Albright, who was so attractive that Stephanie had to look away when she saw him in the hallway. He was always tanned, no matter what the season, and he wore his sandy-brown hair cut very short, almost a crew cut, which highlighted his sharp, grown-man's jaw. According to her father,

Brett was small for a football player, but Stephanie thought his body was perfect: his torso a classic inverted triangle, and his arms and legs thick with muscle—but not too thick. His only flaw was the oily patches of acne on his forehead and sideburn area, but even this seemed a piece of his masculinity. Once last spring he came to her house for dinner, and Stephanie spent the whole meal thinking of what it would be like to run her fingers along the stubble at the back of his neck. When she told Mitchell that later, he said he would have thought of running his fingers along something else.

Stephanie wondered if Mitchell had ever fooled around with any of the boys at her school. She thought not, because he would have told her, but then again, maybe he wouldn't have.

The one person she thought she knew best in the world, her own mother, had it within her to shorten a rope, fashion a slipknot, and climb a wooden stepladder. But Stephanie could not actually imagine that moment in her mother's life. And when Stephanie looked back on her childhood, she sometimes felt as if her mother had not really lived with their family at all, but instead had wandered in and out of their lives, like a visitor. It was as if they were on the road, and her mother was walking in a field beside the road, a wide field of tall grasses, or maybe corn, so that sometimes you got a glimpse of her, but mostly you did not see her, you could only sense her presence behind the screen of wild growth.

And yet even from this distance her mother was perceptive. It was her mother who had first noticed Mitchell's proclivities. "Well, he's different, isn't he?" was how she put it, after his first visit to their house. "Different how?" Stephanie asked. And as soon as the words were out of her mouth, the pieces came together and she saw it, too: he liked boys, not girls. In that instant all of Stephanie's fantasies were blown away. She had thought she was in love. She had thought being in love was easy, like having a best friend.

Now it was funny to remember that she had ever thought Mitchell was straight. She had been so naive when she started high school, a lamb of a girl who believed her football-coach father was beyond reproach and that her mother's blue moods were normal, the price of motherhood. It was Mitchell who taught her to examine her family, to see them as an outsider might. The two of them had formed their own little unit of judgment. They practiced being smart together, training their newly acquired analytical skills on everyone, especially their families. They were both obsessed with their parents. Mitchell's father was a preacher who thought AIDS was a message from God. He had no idea his son was gay. Stephanie thought he had to have figured it out by Mitchell's senior year, when it was obvious that her and Mitchell's four-year friendship had never evolved into a romance; but on prom night, when she and Mitchell posed beneath the cherry tree in Mitchell's front yard, both of them wearing ragtag looks inspired by Courtney Love and Kurt Cobain, he made a remark about the importance of chastity. They had laughed hard about that, harder than they laughed when Stephanie's mother, upon seeing her ill-fitting baby doll dress said, in a completely befuddled and nonbitchy way, "Is it the style not to look pretty?"

"My mom thought you might be hungry." Mitchell stood in the doorway brandishing a pair of yellow-handled scissors. In his other hand was a plate of chocolate-chip blondies, cut into neat triangles.

Stephanie reached for one, though after months of front porch offerings, sweets no longer felt special. By some miracle, she had not gained a pound. It was working at the Red Byrd, she decided. Or maybe it was like people said: she was young, she could eat what she liked. Stephanie had always had a hard time remembering that she was young.

"All right, off with your dress," Mitchell said. He tossed one of his T-shirts her way so she could cover up. Stephanie stepped behind his open closet door to change, realizing half-way through that her backside was reflected in Mitchell's full-length mirror, which hung on the opposite door. But he wasn't even looking! In moments like this Stephanie thought Mitchell's mother must have some inkling of his sexuality. Why else would she let them stay up here by themselves for hours?

Mitchell flattened the dress across his desk and held it in place while she cut it. She didn't bother to measure and mark it; she just let the sharp blades slide quietly through the fabric. She thought of her mother's clothes on her father's bed. She'd left them there on purpose, wanting him to be disturbed by their presence. *She* was disturbed by his weird suggestion that she take them with her to college. They weren't even her style.

"That's pretty short," Mitchell said, examining the new hem.

To Stephanie's oversensitive ears, this sounded like criticism, but she tried not to take it the wrong way. She wondered if Mitchell was sick of hanging out with her. She should have just gone to work. She liked waitressing because any awkwardness with customers or coworkers was dispelled by the fast pace of the dinner rush. And the exhaustion she felt at the end of the night was a satisfying distraction. Before she drove home she would sit out back with Jon and Becky, the line cooks, listening as they bellyached over their shift drinks. Once she asked for a cigarette and they admonished her, telling her never to start, that it was the filthiest habit. And even though that had been annoying, she felt protected. They were constantly telling her she was "a strong young lady" and somehow that felt like an expectation that she had to fulfill. She found she liked having an expectation—or at least she liked it when it came from Jon and Becky, whose ideas about her were based on observation, rather than, say, her father's stoic ideal.

She put the dress back on. The new hem hit midthigh, and it was jarring to see her mother's dress so radically changed. As always, Stephanie thought her knees looked bony and overly large. Her father said they were *strong, athletic knees*, the kind that wouldn't blow out. Everything came back to sports for him.

"Looks better now," she said, pulling on her jean jacket. She put her hands in the pockets and found the half pack of cigarettes she'd scrounged from one of the booths. She held up the rumpled package. "Want one?"

Mitchell frowned, his long features turning dour. He had a haunted, thin face, one that had always reminded Stephanie of photos from the Civil War, the daguerreotypes of teenage soldiers. She remembered, with a twinge, the intensity of her old crush on him.

"You think you're going to look like Marlene Dietrich with a ciggie in your hand? Please, you're Rebecca of Sunnybrook Farm."

This time she was sure she wasn't imagining the irritation in his voice. "Why are you being so mean?" she said. "All night long you've been acting like you don't want me here."

"Sorry, I'm just stressed," he said. "I'm supposed to go to school next week and now my dad's saying I can't even bring my car. He's still pissed I'm not going to Frostburg. I have to take the bus from Hagerstown. It's going to take, like, ten hours."

"You can't take the bus to college! Let me drive you. My dad's not coming with me. It would just be the two of us."

"Your dad isn't taking you?"

"It's one of his double practice days. I mean, he offered, but I could tell he didn't want to. And we would have had to take two cars with my brothers coming along and all my stuff. But there's room for you."

"I couldn't. It doesn't even make sense. Boston is so far out of your way."

"So what? Come on, how much fun would we have?"

"No, it's okay. I might not have to take the bus. My mom is looking into Amtrak. It will be good. I have too much shit anyway. Fresh start."

"Yeah, I get it," Stephanie said. But she was surprised that he would turn her down so quickly—surprised and hurt.

"So what are we going to do tonight?" Mitchell said.

"Sarah's having a party," Stephanie managed to say. It was dawning on her that Mitchell was really going to leave. She could see it now, she could imagine him waiting on a brick platform, wearing his long black coat and one of his mother's crocheted caps, carrying his big duffel and maybe a backpack. And then he would board a silver train and be whisked up the Eastern Seaboard to Boston, a city full of students, a city full of people as smart as he was. He was just a few days from starting a whole new life. And she was happy for him. But she was sad for herself. She no longer felt optimistic about leaving Willowboro. It felt like some other girl had decided to go to Swarthmore, and now she wasn't confident she could fulfill that girl's fancy private-school ambitions. She wasn't even sure that girl would ever return. If it was just a matter of keeping the ambitious girl's seat warm, of biding her time in sadness, in grief, then she could do that. But the more Stephanie thought about it, the more ludicrous that idea seemed. You couldn't "sub in" for yourself, waiting for some previous happiness to return. Because you would never forget the sad shit that went down. It got engraved onto your brain. Stephanie pictured her mother's brain, intricately engraved, like some Roman sarcophagus.

"I don't want to go to Sarah's," Mitchell said. "It's just going to be a bunch of football dudes. And everyone's probably already drunk by now. Let's go to the dollar theater."

"Not everyone will be drunk," Stephanie said. "Dan will be there. He doesn't drink."

"Because he's Mormon," Mitchell said.

"That's basically why you don't drink."

"I'm not Mormon!"

"No, but you come from a religious family."

"You think that's why I don't drink?" Mitchell asked. He seemed genuinely curious, open to the fact that he might not know himself as well as he thought. It was this sincerity that Stephanie had first noticed about Mitchell, even before she knew anything about him, when he was just an interesting-looking boy in her freshman geometry class, a boy who always finished his in-class assignments early and used the extra time to read the Jean M. Auel novels forbidden in his household.

"I don't know," Stephanie said. "Maybe you've absorbed certain puritanical attitudes."

"Well, look at your family," Mitchell said. "The attitudes you've *absorbed*. I mean, your dad?"

"What about him?"

"Um, hello? He basically presides over a kingdom of 'roided-up homophobes."

"No one on my dad's team uses steroids!" Stephanie wasn't going to touch the homophobia. She and Mitchell had never talked about the fact that her father was obviously uncomfortable around him. They had never talked about it, because what was there to say?

"This isn't even coming from me. You're the one who's been complaining. Didn't you just tell me he was going to coach a practice instead of taking you to college?"

"One thing doesn't have anything to do with the other," Stephanie said, even though she was as hurt by her father as she was by Mitchell. Her mother hadn't hurt her in this way; even at her most spaced out and distant, Stephanie always felt her mother was with her in spirit.

"Hey, what's the matter?" Mitchell said. "Your dress doesn't look that bad."

"I'm just sad because we're leaving in a week, you know? I don't want to say good-bye."

"You say it like I'm dying!" Mitchell joked. And then realized his mistake. "Oh, God. I'm sorry."

"Don't be sorry," Stephanie said. The problem was that Mitchell was excited to go away to college and she wasn't, and he knew she wasn't, and he'd been trying to conceal his own excitement out of courtesy, but now he was getting tired of hiding his true feelings. And Stephanie felt guilty, but at the same time, she felt jealous, because it was like Mitchell got to go away to school and assume some fabulous new identity while she became—what? She didn't know. And it scared her that she didn't know, and it scared her that she didn't know if this rift between them—if that's what it was—was occurring because they were naturally growing apart, or if it had to do with her mother's death. She couldn't see her life clearly anymore, and clarity was the most important thing to her; it was her secret power. Her mother had taken that from her.

"Let's just go to the party," Mitchell said. "You can smoke your filched ciggies, and I'll have pretzels and lemonade with Dan. It'll be positively thrilling for all involved."

"Don't do me any favors," Stephanie said. "I can go by myself."

"No, no, no," Mitchell said, shaking his finger. "Friends don't let friends go to the suburbs by themselves. If worse comes to worst, we can always *cruise the dual*."

"Cruising the dual" meant driving on the dual highway outside of town, driving but never exiting, just going around and around in circles and taking in the sights of the commercial strip. It was a "classic" Willowboro activity, so classic that Stephanie and Mitchell had never bothered to try it, although they'd always said they would do it before they left for college. Tonight would be the perfect night to give it a whirl—or it *would* be the perfect night, if only Stephanie could be the girl she used to be, the impatient overachiever who liked nothing better than to view her hometown from a certain ironic distance.

DEAN COULD TELL from the way Stephanie moved that she'd been drinking; she'd lost her specificity, all the micromovements and small gestures that made her special to him. Her dark hair was in a low ponytail at the nape of her neck, with a few long strands left loose. She came in through the side door and headed straight to the refrigerator for a glass of orange juice.

"Stephanie," he said quietly, so she wouldn't startle. He was sitting at the kitchen table, waiting.

"Dad!" She turned around, surprising him with a warm smile—an intoxicated smile, but still.

"Late night at the Red Byrd?"

"Yeah, and then I went out." She sat down at the table to drink her juice. "Sorry, I should have called. I feel bad, you waited up."

Her lie was so transparent that he was reminded of the fibs she told when she was a little girl, how obvious they were, and how stubbornly she clung to them. Lying, in small children, was a sign of intelligence.

"Steph, the boys and I went to the Red Byrd for dinner."

"You came to check up on me?"

"I wanted to see you," Dean said. "And the boys did, too. You left them alone."

"It was only for, like, fifteen minutes."

"They're little kids."

"I'm sorry." She got up and poured herself some more juice. "Mitchell called and he really needed me to come over—he's going through a hard time—so I got Katie to cover my shift. And I didn't tell you because I didn't want it to be some big thing. But I had to go, he's my best friend."

It bugged Dean that Mitchell was her designated "best friend." Why couldn't she be best friends with another girl, a typical girl, a girl who was happy, who didn't view high school as one big hard time?

"How much have you had to drink?" Dean asked.

"I wasn't driving," she said. "Mitchell dropped me off."

"So where's your car?"

"It's parked at Sarah Auerbach's. She had a party, okay?"

He noticed now that she was dressed up, wearing a flowered sundress. It was the kind of modest, feminine dress Dean preferred for her to wear—or would have been, if Stephanie hadn't cut it short, leaving the edges ragged.

"Is that one of your mother's dresses?"

"Yeah." Stephanie tugged at the hem of her skirt, pulling on a loose thread. "It's not like Mom cares. She's gone. The dead don't care, that's what Mitchell says."

Robbie's phrase, *dead-lady clothes*, came into Dean's mind. Along with Robbie and his flushed cheeks, Nic's pale blue dress.

"I don't care what Mitchell has to say," Dean said.

"You've always been hostile toward him. What's that about? He's really smart. He's probably the smartest person I've ever met. Just because he doesn't care about football doesn't mean he's not worth your time."

"Steph, I don't want to talk about your friend right now."

"I'm just trying to have a conversation," she said, slurring as she navigated *conversation*'s four syllables. "But if you just want to walk around all stoic, that's fine, we can pretend everything's okay. Just like we did with Mom."

"That's something, coming from the girl who barely spoke to her mother for a year."

Stephanie got up and put her juice glass in the sink. She stood there and Dean could tell by the way her shoulders were hunched forward that she had begun to cry. It had been so long since he had seen her cry that he was almost heartened by her tears, by their intimacy. But then, seeing her pale face reflected in the darkened window above the sink, he felt as if she had eluded him yet again, as if the cheerful girl he had once known—the girl he hoped would be restored to him at the end of adolescence—had been displaced by this ghost of a girl.

"Sweetheart, I'm sorry, I've had a rough day. I lost one of my best players, a linebacker, and we don't have a good replacement. I have to rethink everything."

"That sounds pretty stressful," she said drily.

"I'm sure it doesn't seem like a big deal to you, but if you knew about football—"

"I *know* about football. I just don't find it especially interesting."

Dean turned away to gather up his notes, as well as Garrett's. He was tired; his eyelids burned. He couldn't understand why his kids were giving him so much grief. He wasn't the one who'd left them.

"Where is it written that I have to like football?" Stephanie said.

He faced her again. "Look, I don't expect you to care about the holes in my playbook, I really don't. But I *do* expect you to give a shit about your younger brothers, who really need you right now."

"I'm so sick of this. I go out, I let loose for one night, and you make me feel guilty. I've been babysitting them all summer long." Stephanie swiped at her eyes, smearing her already smudged makeup. "Aunt Joelle says I'm the one holding this family together."

"Don't bring Joelle into this."

"Why shouldn't I? You're just going to dump Robbie and Bry on her when I leave."

"I'm working on getting a sitter," Dean said, straining to keep his voice even. "I was going to ask around at church tomorrow. I was hoping you'd come with me."

"I'm supposed to help with Aunt Joelle's barbecue."

"So am I. We can go after."

"I thought you didn't want to go."

"That doesn't mean I'm not going."

He matched her stubborn gaze. She didn't like church; he didn't like Joelle. He had her in a bind. She couldn't say no without making him look like a better person.

"Fine, I'll go."

She turned the lights off as she left the kitchen—out of habit or spite, Dean couldn't tell. The darkness was a relief. Cool air came through the window above the sink, a hint of autumn. It was something Dean noticed every August, that unexpected hint of crispness, like a pocket of cold water in a sun-warmed lake. Dean had met Nicole in August, just a few weeks after he'd moved to Willowboro. He'd gone to the country club to inquire about membership, and she had been at the front desk. The club was in the midst of a renovation; it was being changed from a small, family-run golf course to an "outdoor recreation facility" with a pool, tennis courts, driv-

ing range, and, for the winter months, a small gym with rac-
quetball courts and a sauna. With her fresh, makeup-free face
and her optimistic smile (a willed optimism, Dean realized
now), Nicole seemed a part of that transformation. She seemed
like the future of this new place that he had moved to. Later he
told people that he knew he wanted to marry her at first sight,
because that was what people said about their brides, but the
truth was, his wish on that night was just to be near her again.
It was unbelievable to him that she was single; later he learned
that everyone still thought of her as Sam's girl. People warned
him to be careful, that she was on the rebound. She came to
every game; she knew about football. Dean didn't care how
she'd learned it. All that mattered was that she seemed happy
when she was with him. She had been so sad when they met;
she had been sad and he had made her happy. Dean couldn't
understand why he was never able to do it again.

Chapter 2

The sun felt like an assault when Dean woke up the next morning. He had slept through his alarm. Downstairs, he found Stephanie making breakfast for the boys, without a trace of the night's excesses on her pale face. *Youth.* His players displayed the same imperviousness.

Everyone needed a shower, and by the time they left the house they were late. They arrived at church midway through the opening hymn, and Dean felt self-conscious as he walked down the side aisle, looking for space for the four of them. On the way in, he had noticed a sign-up sheet in the foyer that said, "Support for the Renner Family"; beneath it was a list of the foods that had appeared on his doorstep over the past two months. He wanted to take it down but knew he should go through the proper channels, whatever they were. Church politics had always been Nicole's domain.

They filed into a pew in a hurry, without noticing who was sitting nearby. As the hymn ended and everyone got resettled, Dean tried to guess his neighbors by looking at the backs of their heads. The family in front of them was most definitely the Schaffers, and to the right of them, the Hochstedlers. To the left was the Ashbaugh family, the dead giveaway being

Roger Ashbaugh's moon-white bald spot, ordinarily covered by a baseball cap. He was a short, round-shouldered man, while his wife, Susie, was angular and tall, with aggressively permed hair. Dean and Nicole used to joke that she looked like a poodle, which was funny because Roger was a dog trainer.

A few rows ahead, a woman's long neck caught his eye. Her hair was drawn up into a messy bun, and he could see the backs of her dangling silver earrings. His first thought was *Laura*, but that was impossible. Laura didn't go to church. He kept staring at the back of her neck, trying to convince himself that it wasn't her. But then she turned to whisper something to the man sitting next to her, and he saw her familiar profile: her long, almost pointed nose; her smooth brow; and that warm, wry half smile. It was Laura, all right. *Ms. Lanning* to the boys at school. *Miss Laura* to him, at first. Then, when they got to know each other better, when he could finally stop teasing her, could finally stop making up excuses to see her, when she was part of his routine, when she was his friend, she was just plain Laura. But not plain, never plain. What was she doing here? Was she dating the man next to her, the tall guy with a sunburned neck? Was this the inconstant Tim, the young man whose employment as an elementary-school teacher had some-how made him desirable instead of emasculated—so desirable that he'd needed to take some time off from Laura to *play the field*? (What *field*?, Dean had wondered when Laura tearfully repeated the callow phrase to him during one of their morn-ing chats. Did Mr. Timbo honestly think he was going to find anyone better than Laura in Willowboro?)

Dean glared at the back of Tim or whoever's head and tried to convince himself that he wasn't jealous. He had worked so hard to forget Laura. And now his memories were all tumbling out, not forgotten but merely stored behind a door. So much mental energy had been devoted to her. He could admit that now. Last fall, he'd organized his days around her comings and goings like a schoolboy. He had, in fact, first heard about her from the boys on his team. They were all wannabe Lotharios, boasting loudly of the girls they'd like to claim. One day he heard them discussing a certain Ms. Lanning. At first he thought it must be an especially prissy girl, but then they began to guess her age. Thirty, one said. No way, said another. Twenty-five, tops. They began to discuss her body, which she apparently tried to disguise with modest clothing. But they were not fooled by her turtlenecks and blazers. She taught honors English and one of the typing electives. Most of Dean's players knew her from typing.

Dean had felt the need to investigate. He searched for a Ms. Lanning in the staff directory and found none. Then he checked the database on the library's computer, which was more up to date, and found her name, but not her photo, under the list of long-term subs. But he couldn't figure out whose class she had taken, and other than wandering around the English department or the computer lab, places he had almost no call to be, he didn't know how to find out.

They finally met at the October faculty meeting. By then, it felt like he'd been waiting a long time, although it had only been a couple of weeks. He immediately saw why his players liked her; she had a young, girlish way about her, although she kept a straight face. Her slim wrists and ankles gave her away, as did her bright eyes, and the vigorous way she walked down the hallways. When Dean first approached her, his excuse was that he was trying to recruit some new female staff to help with the girls' athletic program. But the only thing she'd ever played was field hockey, a sport Dean associated with preppy girls. As it turned out, her previous teaching position had been in New Hampshire, where she was originally from. "How did you end up down here in the boonies?" he asked her.

"Love," she said.

"Who's the guy?"

"How do you know it wasn't a woman?" Laura asked, with a half smirk that Dean couldn't read.

And then he had started backtracking, embarrassed mainly because he had just attended a mandatory schoolwide workshop about sexual harassment and gender-neutral language, a workshop that scared the crap out of him because he did not always—or, honestly, ever—use the most neutral language when speaking to his players, and in the midst of this backtracking, of cursing himself for even asking about her personal life, she started laughing.

"Relax! I'm just messing with you!"

She smiled widely, delighted with her joke. She hadn't realized that he was the football coach, the high school's number one authority figure after the principal, and that no one messed with him. But he found that he liked being messed with, that it felt good to relax his grip.

"*The guy*," she said, sarcastically, "wanted to be an organic farmer. We moved here so he could work on a raspberry farm—you know, Schulz Acres? But he didn't like farming after all. So he left."

"But you stayed," he said.

"I got this job. It's only subbing, but still. Good teaching jobs are hard to come by." She shrugged. "It's beautiful here, too. You've got the Appalachians. I like mountains."

By coincidence—and it really was coincidence, at first—he talked to her the next morning in the cafeteria, where he occasionally went for coffee. She called to him, and when he saw her standing by the tall cafeteria windows, the morning light shining on her hair and through her skirt to reveal long, slender legs, he realized it had been fourteen hours since they'd met and he hadn't stopped thinking about her.

Over the next few weeks, and then months, they got to know each other. Dean began to stop by the cafeteria in the mornings, where Laura monitored the kids who qualified for free breakfast. No one who got free breakfast wanted to draw attention to that fact, so he and Laura were left undisturbed. At first Dean only stayed for a few minutes, chatting with her on his way out after buying a cup of coffee. But when he felt confident that she enjoyed his company, he began to stay for longer periods. He sympathized with her because he was attracted to her, but also because she, like him, was not originally from the area. He liked hearing her impressions of the town and the people she met, and she liked to pry bits of gossip from him. He surprised himself by how much he knew and by how opinionated he was. No one had ever really asked him what he thought of local politics and personalities. People only wanted to know what he thought about football: his analysis of last night's game, tomorrow's scrimmage, next year's recruits, so-and-so's college prospects. Laura wanted to know about him.

He felt guilty about visiting her, but not guilty enough to stop. As their friendship developed, he decided his motives were less questionable. Sometimes he even thought of himself as Laura's mentor, because of their age difference, but also because she seemed lost. He had the sense, when he talked with her, that she wasn't going to stay in Willowboro forever, that the town was just a way station, a place for her to organize her ambitions. Still, he never mentioned her to Nicole. Looking back, he saw that he was lonely in his marriage. Nicole had distanced herself from him—no, that wasn't fair. She had been distracted. Stephanie, who had already rebelled once, with her black clothes and her oddball friends, went through a second rebellion, what Nicole called an "identity crisis." To Dean it looked like a drama concocted for the sole purpose of upsetting her mother.

In the fall of her senior year, around the same time Dean met Laura, Stephanie wanted to know more about her father's death. Nicole obliged her, going to the attic and bringing down a box of Sam's mementos that Dean had never seen before. It was full of papers, mostly newspaper clippings documenting his athletic career, but there were also letters and medical records. Stephanie stayed up all night, reading every word. When Dean and Nicole came downstairs the next morning, they found her asleep among the papers. Dean couldn't resist stroking her cheek, the way he used to do when she was a toddler. Her makeup was faded, her face soft and calm. She seemed at peace.

But for weeks afterward, Stephanie hounded Nic, asking the questions she couldn't have formulated at the time of Sam's death. She wanted to know why Nicole hadn't taken her father to an oncologist right away. And, why, after getting surgery, hadn't they gone to Johns Hopkins or D.C. or wherever it was that people went to get the best treatment? Why, in short, had

Nicole let her father die? And what about her grandparents, the Shanks? Why weren't they a bigger part of her life? Was Nicole trying to erase her father? Nicole promised that she had never tried to do any such thing; that, in fact, she had often asked the Shanks to visit. But the Shanks had moved shortly after Sam's death. They'd used the excuse of their business; they were expanding beyond Shank's Produce, they had invested in a gourmet grocery franchise, the kind of store that was popular in well-to-do suburban areas but not in small towns. Nicole had felt abandoned. And then, when she'd announced her engagement to Dean, they'd told her, in no uncertain terms, that they thought it was too soon. That hurt, it hurt a lot. Nicole stopped making an effort.

Sam's illness had taken everybody by surprise. It was hard to convey to Stephanie just how young her father had been. To her, twenty-seven sounded like someone well into adulthood. But Sam hadn't even settled into a career, other than managing his father's stores. And the symptoms of this particular cancer, fatigue and muscle soreness, were so common for athletes that he had overlooked them for months. And then it was too late. The disease had spread too far.

It was impossible to say whether or not these answers helped. Sam's box went back up to the attic, and Stephanie's interrogation of her mother ended. Her anger seemed to dissipate, and she began to concentrate on her college applications. The only change was that she got in touch with the Shanks and began to visit them on her own. They never came to Willowboro, despite Nicole's renewed invitations. Sometimes Dean worried that he was the reason for their absence, that they just didn't like him, but mostly he was grateful for their influence on Stephanie. She opened up to them about her plans for the future—she wanted to be a doctor, maybe—and they encouraged her to apply to schools that her teachers wouldn't have thought to mention.

Nicole wasn't as grateful. Stephanie's rummaging had sparked something deeper than passing melancholy in his wife. She became restless, staying up late to pore over old photos of Sam from high school and college. In the mornings she would sleep in, and Dean wouldn't see her until dinnertime. She started taking weekend shifts at the club even though she was management and didn't have to. She said it was to make extra money for Stephanie's college tuition—money they wouldn't need, since the Shanks had volunteered to pay whatever Stephanie's financial aid package didn't cover. Dean knew Nicole was avoiding him and the kids. He tried to be patient. When she got depressed, sometimes it helped if she stayed busy. Then he turned forty and it struck him as unfair that Sam got to stay young and perfect in her mind, the athlete extraordinaire, while he aged like an ordinary man.

Talking to Laura made him feel younger. She was dating, caught up in an on-again, off-again relationship with a fourth-grade teacher, Tim, whom she'd met at a football game, "of all places" (to Laura, the fervor over football was bizarre) and who she liked quite a bit but was nervous about getting serious with, because she had more education than he did and her mother had told her never to marry a man with less education—an old-fashioned dictum, Laura said, but one she couldn't get out of her head. She had a master's degree in psychology, in addition to her B.A. in English. Her ultimate goal was to be a school therapist, but she thought it was important to try teaching as well. Dean would ask her for advice about Stephanie—to keep her psychology skills fresh, he joked. But he was genuinely relieved when she said she thought that Stephanie's curiosity about her biological father was a good thing, maybe even the beginning of the end of some of the more perplexing aspects of her rebellion.

One day in the cafeteria Laura and Stephanie finally met. Dean and Stephanie usually took separate cars to school and rarely crossed paths during the day, but one morning, Stephanie overslept and stopped by the cafeteria to get the breakfast she had missed at home. When she saw Dean there, standing with Laura in their usual spot by the trophy case, she seemed amused.

"Since when are you on breakfast duty?" she asked.

"Since they started serving decent coffee," he said. "Do you know Ms. Lanning?"

Stephanie shook her head, and Dean found himself introducing Laura in an elaborate way, explaining that she was a long-term sub for Mrs. Abbott, who was on maternity leave. Stephanie excused herself after a few minutes, apparently bored, but Dean thought he caught her admiring Laura's pretty, animated face, or at least noticing it. After she left, Laura expressed surprise at Stephanie's cordial manner, as if she'd expected her to be sullen. That was when Dean began to worry about all he'd revealed to her about his family. Had he betrayed them? He wasn't sure, but after that day, he was cautious, only visiting Laura every few days. Their exchanges became awkward, and Dean couldn't say why, exactly. He weaned himself off her until one day he found an invitation to her farewell party in his mailbox, a xeroxed notice on pale orange paper with *GOOD-BYE LAURA* in a big cursive font and a half-dozen pieces of clip art. Dean gazed at the invitation for a long time, wondering if the notice was some kind of message. And then he looked up and saw that the orange notice was in everyone's mailbox, and he realized that Laura had forgotten about him, just as he should forget about her. He was married. He had two thriving sons and a daughter who was graduating from high school with every honor in the book. He was happy, even if Nicole wasn't.

On the morning of Laura's farewell party he dressed carefully, just in case he decided to go. He shaved slowly, flossed twice, and used mouthwash after brushing his teeth. He trimmed the hairs in his nose. On his lunch break, he filled his car with gas and then, on the way back to school, stopped at the drugstore to buy a farewell card.

Because it was May, there was a display of Mother's Day cards, so he picked out something for Nicole first. The cream-colored cards, with their watercolor flowers and the words *wife* and *mother* in a nearly unreadable calligraphy, looked to Dean like sympathy notes, as if being a mother was some sad, unspeakable thing. The humorous cards weren't any better. The gist of every joke was the same: *Husbands and children are thoughtless, ha ha!* Dean opened and shut a dozen before giving up and returning to the flowery cards. He picked one printed on heavy blue paper, with the words *To My Wife* embossed in gold. Then he grabbed a Snoopy card for Laura and took it to the register. At the last minute, he also bought a small bag of Hershey's Kisses.

The party was in the faculty lounge. Ordinarily it was a drab place, a windowless room in the center of the building, but today it was cheery with bunches of yellow and orange balloons, streamers, and a large flower arrangement in the center of the table. There was a pile of gifts on a small desk near the door, so bright and colorful and obviously thoughtful that Dean couldn't bring himself to add his card and bag of candy. Instead he stuck them in the pocket of his khaki pants, glancing to see if Laura was looking his way. She wasn't; she hadn't even seen him come in. She was talking with a group of young female teachers, women Dean knew only by the subjects they taught. For once she was wearing clothes that showed off her figure, an above-the-knee skirt and a sleeveless red silk blouse. Nicole never wore red; she said it made her skin seem too pink. Pink was the color of health; it was the color of Laura's flushed cheeks. He looked away and let himself be drawn into a conversation with the vice principal, who always approached him at faculty events, usually because one of Dean's players was on the verge of being suspended.

Dean almost left twice, but the second time he headed toward the door, Laura caught his eye and gave him a gaze that said *wait*. So he stood by the door until she came over and then—he didn't know what made him say this, because it wasn't true—he said he had to do some paperwork in his office and that he would be down there if she wanted to stop by when her party was over. And she said she couldn't because there was a dinner after and then everyone was going to a bar and maybe he could meet her there. And he said no, he couldn't, he had to get home. And it was uncomfortable, because there were people around them and it was the first time they'd spoken in weeks, and finally she said okay, she'd stop by his office. And then he left. And sat in his office. He had no urgent paperwork, but his grades were due in a few weeks, so he worked on those. Gym grades were based on participation more than performance, so it was just a matter of counting up days missed, but he could barely concentrate as he scanned his attendance records.

He kept thinking of those gold-embossed words, *To My Wife*. The blue card sat in his desk drawer, lightly poetic and sweet, and yet the words *To My Wife* felt heavy in his heart, sinking him instead of providing an anchor.

When Laura finally appeared in his doorway, she was carrying a piece of cake on a paper plate. It was a corner piece, with thick borders of icing, the kind of piece Bry liked best. She placed it on his desk, among his many championship plaques.

"I don't think I've ever been in here," she said. "It's nice. Every teacher should have an office."

"Maybe at your next job."

"Maybe." She gave him a bland, unreadable smile.

"Here, I forgot to give you this." Dean handed her the card and the candy.

She opened the small package of Hershey's Kisses and ate one right away. Dean couldn't tell whether she was trying to do something rude or she just had a sweet tooth. Either way he liked the gesture; it showed passion.

She read the card, which pictured Snoopy and Woodstock embracing underneath the banner *A Good Friend Is Hard to Find*. Dean had labored over his short note, trying to convey his affection without going over the line. It said, *To Laura, whose conversation I have greatly enjoyed and will miss. Best of luck in all your future endeavors. Yours Truly, Dean Renner.*

"Kind of a mixed message," she said, closing the card.

"Sorry, I'm no good at writing cards."

She waited for him to meet her gaze again. "If you enjoy my conversation so much, why have you been ignoring me for the past month?"

"I didn't mean to." He got up to close his office door. His plan was to return to his desk and finish what would likely be a very painful conversation. But when he turned around, she was right there and just his height in her high heels. He kissed her without even thinking about it.

Her mouth tasted sweet, like the candy she'd just eaten, and her hair smelled like perfume and something else, something familiar—chalk, he realized. She was wearing pantyhose, which both aroused and frustrated him. He was dying to take them off, and after they'd kissed for several minutes, he began to move her toward his desk in order to do so. But she stopped him.

"I don't want to do it this way."

"Neither do I," he said. At least not for their first time. But he could imagine a version of his life where he had sex with her in his office regularly. Where he had a private place to be with her and it wouldn't affect anything else—a fantasy of love contained.

"I mean, I don't want to do it at all," she said. "Not this way. You're married. It's not the kind of person I am. And you're not that kind of person, either."

He stepped away, embarrassed and guilty, sickened by the thought of the cloying Mother's Day card in his desk. *To My Wife*.

"You're a good guy and I'm just . . . I'm being reckless because I'm leaving."

"Where are you going?"

"I don't know." She took a step back, away from him, and smoothed her skirt. "I have a tentative offer from Greenville. A teaching position. They won't know until August, so I don't have to decide now. I'm going on a road trip to California. My college roommate is coming with me. She just finished grad school. She doesn't have any real job prospects, either."

"That sounds great," Dean said. What he wouldn't give to take off and drive cross-country with her. He had never even seen the Pacific.

"Yeah, well. I need to get my head on straight. Tim and I broke up. Again."

"He's an idiot." Tim was the last person Dean wanted to talk about right now.

"It was more like I broke up with him."

"He's still an idiot."

"Maybe." Laura gave her first genuine smile. "I should go."

Dean watched her leave, resisting so many impulses—to run after her, to get her phone number, to sit with her in her car and say ridiculous things. But he stayed in his office, looking out the window that provided a view of the football field and the track. Some of the football players also lettered in track, and Dean remembered that he'd promised them he would attend the semifinal meet. He had future commitments. A job he loved. Family. He had to drop these fantasies of road-tripping with Laura. He was just feeling lonely. Everyone felt lonely from time to time.

On the drive home, he resolved to take the episode seriously, as a warning. And so, for the next month, he doted on his sad, exhausted wife and planned a family vacation to his father's bucolic corner of Pennsylvania. If and when he thought of Laura, he shepherded her memory to the dark corners of his mind, with all the other things that were too dangerous to remember.

After several weeks of good behavior, Dean felt better, and it seemed to him that Nicole felt better, too. Stephanie's graduation day was a triumph for the whole family, and a few days later, when they left for his father's horse farm, Dean had an optimistic feeling about the summer ahead.

A week later, Nicole was dead.

After that, it wasn't hard to stop thinking of Laura.

STEPHANIE LOOKED DOWN at Irene Baker's wrinkled, ringed fingers as they grasped hers, bare and young. The old woman's veins bulged, the blood clearly blue. Mrs. Baker was in her mideighties and was beloved for sending birthday cards to everyone in the congregation. Stephanie had always thought of her in a slightly condescending way, as a cute-granny type, but as she held Mrs. Baker's well-worn hands, she wondered what tragedies had befallen her. Stephanie wondered this about everyone now.

"We've all been praying for you. It just breaks my heart." Mrs. Baker's eyes began to fill, and she shook her head.

Stephanie nodded, not knowing how to reply. This was the exact reason she had been avoiding coming to church.

"There's a very good cobbler," Mrs. Baker said, quickly recovering her composure. "The peaches are exceptional this year."

The peaches are always exceptional, Stephanie thought, sourly, but when she got to the table, she chose the cobbler, taking a big gooey bite. Bits of streusel topping clung to the tines of her fork and she licked them off. She thought this cloudy feeling might be a hangover. Before last night, she'd never really gotten drunk. She took another bite of cobbler, one with a big slice of peach, and all at once she remembered why people felt the need to say, every year, that the peaches were *exceptional*. Because they just were. And they didn't last. You had two, maybe three weeks to eat them. She remembered a time when she and her mother bought peaches on a whim. It was just the two of them, and they were driving home from somewhere when her mother stopped at a roadside stand and bought a bag of peaches, which Stephanie held in her lap in the front seat, the paper bag warm from the sun. "Mmm, I can smell those peaches!" her mother said, as they drove along. And then, all of a sudden, she pulled over to the side of the road. "I have to eat one now! I can't wait!" And so the two of them had sat there, eating peaches in the car with the windows rolled down and the juice dripping between their fingers. And Stephanie remembered her mother saying, "These really are the best peaches in the world. No one can say they've ever had a better peach." It was kind of a silly thing to say, but it had made her life feel big. Her mother could do that; she could isolate a moment and make it stand out.

"You were hungry," her father observed.

"Yeah, I guess." Stephanie was surprised and a little embarrassed to see that the cobbler was already gone. "Where are Robbie and Bry?"

"They probably went outside with the other kids."

"I'll go find them."

"You don't have to."

"I want to." She suspected her father would like to escape, too, but he couldn't go outside and be a part of the kid world, the way she still could.

In the foyer she ran into a clique of girls slightly younger than she was, decked out in their new back-to-school clothes. They were dressed up more than they needed to be. Stephanie paused to reflect on which was the more un-Christian behavior, their vanity or her judgment of their vanity. In the midst of this private debate, Pastor John approached her. She liked him, even though she didn't believe in what he was selling. And she suspected he knew that. But he never made her feel bad. Even this morning, as she stood here hungover, judgmental, with cobbler crumbs on her shirt, she felt her own goodness in his smile.

"It's nice to see you, Stephanie," he said. "I know you're busy getting ready for college. When do you leave?"

"Next Saturday."

"Less than a week," he said. "Are you excited?"

"Yeah. I mean, I think so."

"You know you always have your family here, but I hope you find a new church family at Swarthmore."

"I'll try."

"Just keep it in mind," he said, not taking her white lie personally. He never took offense. That was what made him such a good pastor. She would be religious if it meant being that objective all the time, but in her experience, most religious people were not like Pastor John.

Outside, she looked for her friends in the side yard, but there were just a bunch of middle-school kids sitting at the picnic tables. She waved to Robbie and Bry, who were playing with Bry's rubber-band ball, bouncing it high in the parking lot. She was hoping they would invite her to join them, but they only gave her a nod. She stood near the church's stone wall, feeling like a real prisspot, the kind of girl who took it upon herself to be a playground monitor.

The kids moved from the picnic table to the row of pine trees that bordered the cemetery. Stephanie longed to join them, to sit in the shade on the soft orange carpet of dead pine needles, to smell the sharp piney smell, to hear the wind in the higher branches. Lately she had the sense that growing up meant trading in all the haphazard sensual pleasures of childhood for—what? Sex? She doubted that could make up for the loss. She stepped into a block of shade cast by the church and so narrow at this time of day that she had to lean against the stones to feel its coolness.

All the graves at the front of the cemetery were old, dating back to the nineteenth century, their headstones slanted and engraved with names no one went by anymore, although some of the surnames were still in use. Her mother's maiden name, Bowers, wasn't there, but her first married name, Shank, was on several headstones. Stephanie had changed her last name from Shank to Renner when her father had adopted her—or rather, Stephanie's mother had changed it. Apparently Stephanie had approved, but she couldn't remember. She kept Shank as a second middle name after Geneva, which was her maternal grandmother's first name. Stephanie sometimes thought of how both the Shank and the Renner would drop off when she got married. If she got married. She'd never had a boyfriend.

Her mother had always had boyfriends. She had never really been single. It was as if she had to die to be alone.

Her mother wasn't buried in this cemetery. There wasn't room. And anyway, her grandmother—Geneva—had a little cemetery on her farm. There was also a spot next to her biological father in a completely different cemetery. That had been a debate with her paternal grandparents—*the Shanks*, as everyone in her mother's family referred to them. They pushed for her mother to be buried in the Shank family plot, next to Sam. They talked about how it was "prepurchased," so it shouldn't go to waste. An odd argument, especially since the Shanks were practically rich. Her father joked that it was a "sunk cost." That he was able to joke was simultaneously upsetting and reassuring to Stephanie. In the end, he let Geneva decide, and of course she chose to bury Stephanie's mother on the farm.

The graveside service was awkwardly cramped, with the Shanks off in the long grasses in the corner, probably getting ticks. Stephanie worried about the Shanks. Everyone thought they were so uncaring, but she saw their vulnerability. Offering a gravesite was their clumsy way of being helpful. They didn't mean to be annoying; they were just the kind of people who always seemed liked they were butting in. Stephanie wondered what had really happened between them and her mother after Sam died. She'd heard different versions of the story, but what it came down to—according to her mother—was that the Shanks disapproved of her second marriage. And her mother had been hurt by their judgment. And then the Shanks had moved away and that had somehow frozen the relationship, so that both parties remembered only the resentment, not the attachment that must have preceded it.

For a few years, the Shanks continued to visit on holidays—

Stephanie had the photos, if not the memories—but after Robbie and Bry were born, the Shanks must have felt left out. Or maybe they had no interest in her new brothers. All Stephanie knew was that they stopped visiting, and it was up to her mother to take her for visits. Which she did, at Christmas and Easter. But it was always so stilted and overly formal that as soon as Stephanie was old enough to say no, she would rather not go, she did. And her mother let her get away with that. From age eleven to seventeen, Stephanie didn't see her grandparents. Stephanie felt guilty about that now, but it was a guilt mixed with anger. Because why didn't her grandparents insist? Stephanie's mother said they were workaholics, and that their marriage had gone bad a long time ago. They were unhappy.

When Stephanie finally visited the Shanks again, in the fall of her senior year, she found that her mother was wrong. Her grandparents seemed quite happy together, proud of their growing franchise and eager to show it off. They'd had Stephanie meet them at one of their newest branches in Frederick, a small city about an hour east of Willowboro. They took her on a tour of the store, giving her samples from the deli, the olive bar, the bakery, and the Cheese Cave, the innovation for which the stores were most famous. At the back of the store, adjacent to the parking lot, was an outdoor café with a stone patio and an artificial pond with a fountain that her grandfather referred to as a "water feature." Stephanie ordered a wheat berry salad for lunch, wheat berries being something she had never tried before, and she remembered their gummy, foreign texture in her mouth while her grandparents held forth on Nicole and her various missteps in the wake of Sam's diagnosis. There had been a question of malpractice, because the doctors might have caught the disease earlier. And then, there was the general shabbiness of the hospitals in Hagerstown, the city closest to Willowboro. They had begged Nicole to take him to Johns Hopkins, but she wouldn't because the long drive made her "anxious." And Stephanie just listened, chewing her way through her fibrous salad, thinking they sounded a little manic but at the same time wondering if what they said had any merit. At home, she asked her mother to show her the medical files pertaining to Sam's illness, a request her mother had honored without question, pulling down the ceiling ladder that led to the attic and handing down the dusty boxes. Stephanie couldn't make much sense of the files—it was mostly insurance billing—but she found a snapshot of Sam's leg, postsurgery, and she could see it was a young, muscular leg beneath the angry red stitches, the leg of a boy she might know. And she could see no point in blaming her mother, or even the doctors, for never suspecting that a young, muscled leg could conceal a large, soft, festering tumor.

But her mother felt blamed, and instead of telling Stephanie about Sam, she told Stephanie about the way she had been treated in the aftermath of his death. How the Shanks had basically abandoned her, leaving her alone with her baby, their grandchild! How her parents had been in serious debt, scrambling to save the farm, too preoccupied with their own problems to help her. How Joelle was the only one who seemed to care. But Joelle was in college at the time, and she could only visit on the weekends. During the week, Stephanie's mother was left by herself. That was the first time that she began to feel what she referred to as "the dread." But she told Stephanie that it felt like the dread had always been inside her, like it was waiting for an excuse to get out.

"I know a stronger person would have handled it better," she told Stephanie. "I know I let you down. But I was dying of loneliness. I talked to you—a little baby. I told you everything. You listened, it really seemed as if you were listening."

And as Stephanie's mother spoke, Stephanie felt cast in the role of listener again. For the first time, she was aware of how angry she was to always be put in this position. Here she was, asking for stories about Sam, and what did she get? More stories about her mother. About her mother's pain.

Finally, one night, when her father was out at a Boosters event, Stephanie's mother brought out a small album Stephanie had never seen before, a cheap-looking drugstore album with clear plastic sleeves for pages. It was from a trip, her mother said, a trip that she and Sam had taken to Chincoteague Island when they were in college. It was on this trip that Stephanie's father had proposed. And as Stephanie's mother stared at the photos, she began to cry, saying it was difficult to talk about Sam because she didn't remember him as clearly as she once had. And then she started telling Stephanie a bunch of random, disconnected facts about him. She told her that he had big, fleshy hands. That he wasn't as tall as he seemed. That he loved mustard—he put it on everything—and that on game days he always wore the same blue-and-white-striped tie. That he had a good singing voice and for a while he was in a rock band. That he didn't read very much but he liked books about Civil War history. That he'd considered volunteering for the draft but his parents had objected. And then, after he got sick, he wished he had gone into the draft, because maybe he wouldn't have passed the physical and then he would have known earlier. Either that or he would have died nobly, for his country. Sam had actually thought that would be a better way to die—in a foreign country, away from his family. Being sick hadn't given him any clarity. It hadn't made him a better person. He didn't die in peace or in love. Instead he died angry, not knowing what he wanted to do with his life or what it had meant to him.

Once her mother started talking, it was as if she couldn't stop. Stephanie was quickly overwhelmed. She'd gotten what she'd wanted, but it didn't answer the question that seemed to grow more and more with each passing day, expanding to fill her body as well as her mind, the question of *Who am I? And who will I become?*

The Shanks told her she looked like him, an observation Stephanie wasn't sure how to take. Sam had been attractive in a masculine way, with a jutting chin and a heavy brow. Stephanie had always felt that her features were lacking in delicacy and that her jaw was perhaps a bit too pronounced. She could pass for pretty with plucked eyebrows and mascara to bring out her hazel eyes, but she wasn't like her mother; no one would ever compare her to Tuesday Weld, or any movie star.

And that was okay with Stephanie, for the most part. She felt that people were inordinately fixated on her mother's beauty, especially after her death, as if it was beyond them to imagine how anyone with symmetrical features could be unhappy. As if her mother's death could have been averted by her looking in the mirror. It dawned on Stephanie that the whole culture of women's magazines was premised on this idea, that if you seemed healthy and pretty you just wouldn't die, and now when she saw the glossy covers of magazines and catalogs with their smiling blond models—everyone was always blond!—she wanted to rip them off. And yet listening to Courtney Love and Bikini Kill and Sleater-Kinney and all the riot-grrrl bands she loved didn't make her feel better. Instead she listened to John Denver, because her mother had loved his voice and Stephanie felt guilty for all the times she'd made fun of her taste in music.

Stephanie hated to think of how hard she had been on her mother. Her father had told her that her mother's death was no one's fault, but then what was that thing he had said last night? About her giving her mother the silent treatment? It wasn't true or fair, but her father got like that when he was angry and feeling out of control. She remembered a time last November when her mother was supposed to go to the football awards banquet and she said she couldn't face it. And her father had lost it and said, "What can't you face? You don't have to do anything! You just have to sit there and look pretty!" His dismissal had shocked Stephanie, but what was even more shocking was that her mother had actually gone to the banquet and she had sat there and said nothing and her father had seemed okay with that. After that it was like her father gave up trying to make her mother happy. Stephanie couldn't tell if he'd given up because he was tired or because he was afraid, and she couldn't decide which was worse. And she also couldn't decide whether or not to blame him for escaping into coaching, because hadn't she begun to visit her grandparents, in part, to get away from her mother?

The Shanks turned out to be a lot of fun. The sour ruminations of their first visit were never repeated—it was like they had to get it out of their system—and they devoted her remaining visits to spoiling her. They had season tickets to the Baltimore Opera and they took her once a month, treating her to dinner beforehand. One night they took her to Haussner's, an old-fashioned place with oil paintings stacked up the walls and a coat check and a dessert cart, a kid's idea of what a fancy restaurant should be. And Stephanie let herself be a kid, getting a little thrill out of their dinner of oysters and crab cakes and filet mignon—and for dessert, German chocolate cake! They took her there a second time to celebrate her acceptance to Swarthmore, allowing her one small glass of champagne. It was their idea for her to apply to Swarthmore (and Johns Hopkins, and Haverford, and Carnegie Mellon). They told her not to worry about money, that they would pay if she got in. When Stephanie told her parents, they shrugged, slightly baffled. It didn't occur to them that her academic record was good enough to compete with kids from prep schools. And it didn't occur to them that she would want that. Stephanie herself was unsure, but as she read the Fiske Guide that the Shanks bought for her, she began to imagine herself attending the kind of brick-and-ivy places she'd only seen in movies. And then Mitchell borrowed it and began to share her daydreams. Her life got busy as she wrote her applications and studied for her SATs and then her subject tests (she was one of only three people in the county to take them) and then her AP exams. And when she wasn't doing that, she was either hanging out with Mitchell at his house or hanging out with Mitchell backstage, because he did the lights for the school play. Stephanie liked standing in the wings during rehearsals, watching the same scenes unfold again and again, but never in exactly the same way; it was like getting glimpses into subtly altered worlds.

So much of Stephanie's imaginative life was devoted to the construction of alternate universes. In the weeks after her mother's suicide (without warning, without explanation, without even a note) she kept reimagining the day it happened, different versions of it: a day when she didn't go for a horseback ride; a day when she did, but with her mother instead of her father; a day when the whole family rode together, having a picnic, laughing in the sun; a day when she woke up sick with a stomach bug, so sick that her mother had to take care of her, had to bring her a bowl to vomit in and a cold compress to drape on her forehead when she was through. For some reason this last fantasy was the most compelling; it seemed to be the scenario that might have convinced her mother to stay on earth just a few days longer.

Stephanie breathed deeply to dissolve her gathering tears. She stepped out of the shade of the church and headed toward the sidewalk, where Robbie and Bry were still playing. She called to them to say she was going to get Dad and they barely nodded in her direction. Stephanie remembered how much her mother hated this, how she would point to herself and say "Acknowledge me!" She wondered if Robbie and Bry remembered the last thing their mother said to them. Stephanie couldn't. She had tried so many times, but she could only guess. It must have been something banal and forgettable: *have fun* or *see you later* or *bye now*. It made Stephanie think that her mother's act must have been impulsive, because if she'd been planning it, wouldn't she have said something of significance before Stephanie went on her ride? Wouldn't she at least have said "I love you"? Then again, maybe she had, and Stephanie hadn't even noticed.

Her father was in the lobby, talking to a woman with shiny brown hair and dangling leaf-shaped earrings that Stephanie admired. She looked familiar, and when her father introduced her, he acted like they'd met before. Apparently she was Ms. Lanning, a sub at the high school.

"Are you still subbing?" Stephanie asked, just to be polite.

"Actually, I got a job at the middle school as a guidance counselor."

"That's where my brother Robbie's going to be," Stephanie said. "He's starting sixth grade this year."

"You didn't mention that!" Ms. Lanning said, turning to her father.

"I guess I forgot. I still think of him as being at the elementary school."

"Forgot your own son!" Ms. Lanning laughed. Stephanie was alarmed. Was going to college in the fall really the right thing to do? Aunt Joelle had hinted to her that it might be better if she deferred her acceptance. But her father had already said no, that he didn't want her "backsliding" because of her mother.

A tall, thin man approached. He was young, with a scraggly goatee and wire-rimmed glasses. On his left wrist were a large black digital watch and two faded friendship bracelets, the kind that little kids make at camp. Stephanie knew he had to be Ms. Lanning's boyfriend because he looked like her: a little different, a hint of sophistication. Like he was possibly connected to some nearby urban center—D.C. or Baltimore or even just one of the wealthier suburbs like Chevy Chase or Falls Church. After a minute or two of small talk, he said they had to leave for a picnic and the two of them were off. Her father stared after them for a moment and then mumbled that it was always awkward to see people from work out of context.

"Does she go to this church now?" Stephanie asked.

"She's just here for today, for the baptism. That guy she's dating is the godfather."

"Oh, yeah." Stephanie remembered him, now. He had stood up front while the baby wailed in her white dress, offended and confused by the drops of water on her head. Stephanie's own baptism had yielded the one and only photo of her entire biological family: her mother and her father and both sets of grandparents. It was disconcerting to look at it now, to see the Shanks standing so close to her mother.

Once, driving home after a night at the Baltimore Opera, Mrs. Shank had attempted to apologize for her absence in Stephanie's life.

"I think I resented that your mother could have more children. That she could start over. I know that's petty. I don't expect you to understand."

Stephanie didn't know what to say.

"The irony is that I've always been grateful to your mother for having you," Mrs. Shank said, that same night. "I know she pushed Sam to start a family."

Stephanie wanted to ask, *If you're so grateful, why did it take you fifteen years to get to know me?*

"Are Robbie and Bry still outside?" her father asked. He didn't wait for an answer, leading Stephanie toward the door. But they were intercepted by Ms. Lanning, who had come back to ask Dean about a referral for a good sports doctor. Apparently Tim was having trouble with his knee.

Stephanie left them and went to find Robbie and Bry. When she found the lot empty, she looked immediately toward the road, her heart pounding. But then she heard them calling to her. Their voices came from the pines. They had climbed one of the trees.

"Steffy!" Bry waved from a surprisingly high branch. Robbie was lower down; she could see the white of his button-down shirt.

"Get down before you hurt yourself!" Stephanie wasn't actually worried. Pine trees were easy to climb, with their evenly spaced branches. The only danger was how spindly the branches were near the crown.

"I can see Dad from here! He's talking to some lady!"

"Be careful," Stephanie said, knowing the boys wouldn't listen but feeling the need to pester them anyway. She was only going to be here for a few more days. And then they would be on their own, with no one to warn them of anything.

NICOLE'S YOUNGER SISTER, Joelle, lived in the turn-of-the-century farmhouse where she and Nicole had grown up. It was made from fieldstone. The roof, recently replaced with expensive copper, had been purchased with Joelle's inheritance after her father's death. The copper was beautiful, especially in the late afternoon, when it turned a peachy-gold color. Inside, the house was dingier, with wall-to-wall carpeting and a mish-mash of furniture: the very old, very simple chairs and crates, faded with use; the heavy-looking inherited pieces, made of dark lacquered woods; and the newest purchases, puffy chairs and sofas, chosen for comfort and upholstered in faux leather. There were knickknacks, framed craft projects, and family photos everywhere, arranged in no particular way. It was chaotic but also cozy.

Joelle got to live in the house because she was the one who married a farmer. Dean liked her husband, Ed, a big-gutted, easygoing man whose tendency to bullshit about subjects he knew nothing about had earned him the nickname of Cowpie. Over the years he had amassed a number of novelty T-shirts that featured turds in one form or another. He was wearing one today as he grilled burgers and hot dogs.

"Why on earth would you wear a shirt like that if you're going to be serving people food?" asked Geneva, Dean's mother-in-law.

"Never mind Uncle Ed," Stephanie said. "What is Aunt Joelle wearing?"

Joelle's outfit was perplexing: an oversized white tunic with plastic gems sewn on the collar and down the front, like buttons, and beneath it, purple leggings. It seemed better suited to an elementary-school-aged girl than a short, chesty woman with skinny legs.

"Maybe that's how people dress at her new church," Geneva said. "Bejeweled for Jesus."

"Grandma!" Stephanie chided. But she was smiling.

"I finally caved and went with her to a service. I knew it was going to be bad as soon as I saw the church. Have you seen it? It's prefab. Real shoddy construction. I said, 'Joelle, Jesus was a carpenter!'"

"I bet she loved that," Dean said.

"You can't joke with her anymore—that's the worst thing."

Dean had no idea what he'd done to get his mother-in-law on his side, but it felt good to have at least one person in the family rooting for him. She had an independent streak that he admired, one that he felt the rest of the family failed to recognize. They were all shocked when, after her husband, Paul, died, she decided to renovate one of the old outbuildings at the edge of the pasture and live there. Joelle and Ed insisted she continue to live with them in the farmhouse, and even offered to build out an addition, but Geneva said she could smell Paul's death in the rooms.

"Who's ready for a burger?" Ed called from the grill.

"I'm going to go help Aunt Joelle with the salads," Stephanie said, glaring at Dean before heading into the house.

"What was that about?" Geneva asked.

"She wants me to ask Joelle to help out with her brothers this fall, but I'm not crazy about that idea."

"I don't blame you," Geneva said. "Did you know she's going to homeschool Megan and Jenny this year? She doesn't want Megan going to the high school."

"That's crazy; she won't be able to play sports," Dean said. Megan was the older of Joelle's two daughters. She was a petite girl, and Dean still thought of her as a little kid around Robbie's age. But now she was moving into Stephanie's world.

"Of course sports are the first thing that comes into your head!" Geneva laughed.

"They give you confidence. I always told Stephanie that. She got her confidence from her grades, but that's not available to everyone."

"Most people would see it the other way. They think sports take away confidence."

"Those people are overly competitive. They can't enjoy something they aren't winning."

"Aren't you that way?"

"I'm a coach," Dean said. "I'm supposed to want to win. But I don't say you can't enjoy yourself if you don't. Maybe it's harder to. But you still get the physical benefits."

"I've touched a nerve."

"I'm just tired of my PE classes getting cut. Or I see a girl who looks athletic and it turns out she's a cheerleader. I told Stephanie I'd break both her legs if she became a cheerleader."

"Maybe it's good Megan's not going to high school. She won't risk getting her legs broken by her fanatical uncle."

Dean smiled. "I shouldn't be so hard on cheerleaders. They raise their own money. They can do what they want."

"I shouldn't be so hard on Jo," Geneva said. "All this Holy Roller stuff started after Paul passed on."

Dean took his mother-in-law's hand. It was cool, despite the mugginess of the afternoon—like Nicole's used to be.

"There goes one of my buzzards." Geneva watched a bulky-looking bird take flight from the pasture adjacent to her little house.

"Are you still encouraging them?" Dean asked.

"I left scraps out this morning."

Geneva's vulture fixation had started when she noticed the birds were eating the dry mix that she put out for the barn cats. She began leaving meat scraps for them—gristle and poultry gizzards. After a few months, the vultures got accustomed to her treats and would hang out in her yard, waiting. No one could understand why she fed them, and Joelle thought she was just plain losing it. But Dean trusted she had her reasons.

More guests had begun to arrive, mostly Ed's family and people from Joelle's church. Stephanie emerged from the farmhouse to greet an older couple that Dean didn't immediately recognize from a distance. Their white-gray hair was cut in similarly short styles and they were dressed somewhat formally in khaki and white, as if they were on safari.

"Is that the Shanks?" Dean said. Even though Stephanie had been spending a lot of time with her grandparents, Dean rarely socialized with them. They usually didn't come to Willowboro. Instead, Stephanie drove to Frederick or Baltimore to meet them. They had stores in both cities and lived outside Baltimore.

"I told Joelle not to invite them but she insisted," Geneva said. "I've never understood those people. The way they left Nic high and dry after Sam passed on. I think they blamed her. Like he wouldn't have gotten sick if he'd married someone else."

"That was a long time ago," Dean said. "They probably just needed someone to blame."

"Aren't you forgiving."

"They got Stephanie into a good college." Dean wasn't in the mood to hate the Shanks. He got up out of his chair. "I'm going to see if the boys are in the barn."

"You are avoiding the Shanks," Geneva said, pointing a finger. "The Shanks *and* Joelle."

He was avoiding everyone. He didn't know what to say about his life anymore. He patted his front pocket, where he'd placed the napkin Laura had given him. She'd written down her number and handed it to him at the end of their conversation about physical therapy (for her boyfriend, who seemed perfectly healthy). She said to call her if he ever needed someone to talk to. And then she said she was sorry she hadn't gotten in touch after Nicole died, that she didn't know right away, and then when she did know, she didn't know if she should contact him, because what could she say, she hadn't even known Nicole, and anyway it wasn't as if they'd ever had that kind of friendship, the kind that entailed phone calls, and then she had blushed and said again that she was sorry, really so sorry, and Dean had finally interrupted and said it was okay, because it was; in fact, it was a relief to know that she still thought about him, and even more of a relief to know that she wanted to talk to him.

The gravel driveway that led from the farmhouse to the barn and down to the fields was flecked with sharp bits of hay. Dean picked one up and stuck it behind his ear, knowing it would make the boys laugh. But when he got to the barn, there was no sign of them. He stood in the darkened, cool space, savoring the dusklike feeling. Sunlight filtered in where the door was ajar, sending a stripe of gold across the beams. He became aware of the sadness inside him, an ancient, placeless feeling, and at the same time he felt marvelously alive. It had something to do with the smell of the barn, of the hay and the animals that slept there at night. It reminded him of his childhood and of his father, of the sweet through line connecting him to his past and extending to some unknown point in the future.

Dean heard someone behind him and turned to see Joelle standing in the doorway. Her jeweled tunic was even more out of place in the barn's soft light.

"I'm just trying to find my girls." She began to head back outside.

"Wait, Joelle, I wanted to ask you something."

"If you're wondering about the Shanks, Stephanie's the one who wanted to invite them, not me."

"I don't mind the Shanks." He wanted to say something conciliatory, something to bridge—or at least start to bridge—the divide that separated them. But now that he was face-to-face with his wife's younger sister, he could only think of how old and set in her ways she seemed. There was a hardness to her, a toughness. Maybe that was why Nicole had tried so hard to please her. It was as if Joelle were the older sister and Nicole the vulnerable young one. Their dynamic was such that when they had gone out together, people often assumed that Nicole was the baby of the family. "It's because I have such big boobs," Joelle once said, to Dean's amusement. But over the years, she had wielded an influence that Dean often resented. Nicole always sought her advice first, weighing it against everyone else's as if it were the sensible standard. She'd even tried to believe in Joelle's version of God.

"Steffy says you're looking for a babysitter," Joelle said. "I can watch them if need be."

"Thanks, but we'll be okay."

"You can't ask my mother, you can't put that on her."

"I wasn't planning to."

"What's your plan?"

"For now, the boys can come with me to practices. When school starts, I'll have Monica come over on weeknights when I have to work late."

"Monica graduated."

"I'll find a new Monica."

"That's not going to work."

Dean shrugged. "Maybe it will, maybe it won't."

"*Dean*. I know what your schedule is like in the fall. You're never home. You can't get a babysitter every night. Kids need consistency, they need routine—especially now, with their mother gone."

"You think I don't know that?"

"I'm trying to help. Tell me honestly, do you really think it's the best thing to drag them around with you?"

"Do *you* think it's the best thing to take Megan and Jenny out of school?"

"My decision to homeschool is between me and my pastor. I don't need to defend it to you."

"And I don't need to defend my life to you."

"Why don't you take a season off? You know you could. People would understand."

"I don't *want* to take a season off," Dean said.

"You know, I used to stand up for you. I used to say to Nicole, 'He loves his job, nothing wrong with that.' But now I see that she was right, you're obsessed."

"I *do* love my job," Dean said. He wasn't about to explain that he *needed* to coach right now, that football was all he had left, it was the only place he felt at home. The players were like his sons, except they were better than sons because they listened to him, and he understood them—unlike his own sons, who were becoming more mysterious to him with each passing day.

"I'm not going to let you do this to my nephews," Joelle said. "Nicole wouldn't approve. She'd be up in arms."

"Nicole doesn't have a say anymore!" Dean was angry now.

Joelle crossed her arms. "I can take them after school. Megan's old enough to babysit."

"You don't get it," Dean said. "I don't want you to take them."

"That's funny, because Nic dropped them off all the time last year."

"Leave Nic out of it," Dean said. "This isn't about her."

"I think it is. I think you're still angry with me. But that's no reason to punish Robbie and Bry."

"This has nothing to do with you, Joelle."

"You blame me. I know you do. I never told her not to see a psychiatrist. All I ever said was that she should be careful about taking medications."

"Look, I told you I didn't want to go down this road, and I meant it."

"This is where every conversation is going to end up until you forgive her—and me. Not that I did anything wrong."

"You told her she was depressed because she didn't have faith. You didn't support her."

"You want to talk about support? You know what she told me? She said, 'Jo, I never knew marriage could be so lonesome.' She must have called me practically every night last fall. I don't think you even knew how bad off she was. She's always been sensitive. After Sam died, she was a wreck. She couldn't even dress herself. Who do you think took care of her? Of Stephanie? *I* was the one. Not the Shanks, not Mom and Dad, and certainly not you."

"I didn't even know Nic then."

"That's right, you waltzed in after the dust cleared. You

think you saved her but you have no clue. I've always told her to put her trust in God because that's what I believe in. You're the one who told her she would feel better if she exercised more."

"Exercise does make people feel better. It's scientifically proven. If you take care of your body, your mind will follow."

"Is that what you told Nicky?"

"I told her lots of things. I told her to see a doctor, I told her to get a new job, I told her to make new friends. Maybe they weren't the best ideas. Maybe you're right, maybe I didn't understand how unhappy she was. But I don't think you did, either. Tell *me* honestly, Joelle, did you have any idea she would do this?"

"Of course not! But I'm not married to her." Joelle turned to leave. She was tearing up. "I can't talk about this anymore. I came in here to find my kids."

Dean stayed in the barn after she left. Whenever he talked to Joelle, he had the feeling she was trying to give Nicole's suicide back to him, like it was a mess that only he could clean up. Like it could be cleaned up. He hated the way she made everything seem so straightforward, the way she took words like *marriage* and *forgiveness* and acted as if they were transparent and uncomplicated. He couldn't believe she was actually that smug and simpleminded. She had to be pissed off to be left alone with her widowed, buzzard-loving mother. She had to be in pain, big pain. And she had to be angry about it. She just wasn't that good a person.

He was too riled up to return to the picnic and make small talk. He sat down on the bottom row of a pyramid of hay bales. But then some old instinct took over and he felt the need to climb to the top. The bales were arranged like stairs and as he made his way up he recalled boyhood summers when he was allowed to roam through the stables where his father worked.

Now, when he visited his father, he would think of what she'd done. She must have known that, she must have known and decided she didn't care. Or maybe she thought it would be better than doing it at home. She knew how much he loved their house. Then again, maybe it had nothing to do with that. Maybe she saw the rope swing and thought, *This is my chance.* Maybe she had the swing in mind the whole time they were planning their vacation, maybe that was why she had been so eager when he suggested it. Going to his father's farm was supposed to be a kind of last hurrah for Stephanie, a chance to visit with the horses she had grown up riding. And a chance, too, for Stephanie to return to a sweeter, more girlish phase of her adolescence.

Nicole had waited until he and Stephanie were out on a trail ride together. Robbie and Bry had been swimming with their grandfather. She was supposed to go with them but had begged off. Dean remembered her saying that she needed a nap. He remembered thinking that it was nice that she had time to take a nap. That she should take more naps. He hated his innocent, optimistic thoughts. He wondered how long she had waited. She'd probably assumed he would find her, when he brought in the horses after the ride. It probably never occurred to her that Robbie and Bry would come back early, that Robbie would race ahead in his wet bathing trunks, wanting to swing on the rope she'd knotted—and where did she learn to make a slipknot? More planning that Dean didn't want to think about. He had tried so hard to understand her state of mind in those days leading up to it. She had seemed fine, even better than fine; he had thought she was finally returning to normal. He specifically remembered the relief he felt as he watched her swim across the lily pond, the swimming hole of his teenage years, the first place he ever skinny-dipped, the first place he ever saw a girl naked. She seemed so graceful and whole in her yellow bathing suit. And then she'd performed her old trick of swimming underwater for a full minute or two, emerging unexpectedly at some random point in the pond. When the boys were little, they would stand worriedly at the water's edge, waiting for her to appear. She would burst out of the water, out of breath and exhilarated. A show of athleticism, Dean had always thought, but now he wondered if there wasn't something ominous in her performance.

Dean lay back on the straw bale, looking up at the barn's peaked roof. He was so tired of remembering that week, trying to decide if her good mood was faked or authentic. He felt doubly betrayed as he tried to calculate her motives, wondering if she'd faked her mood in order to leave them with good last memories, or if it was a way of convincing him that she was okay so he wouldn't suspect what she was plotting. And if she had the self-control, the wherewithal, to put on such a good show, then why did she not have it in her to get well? Or was it darker than that? Was she genuinely happy that week because she knew she was at the end of her life? Was the vacation actually *her* last hurrah? He hated to think of her secret thoughts; he felt almost jealous of them, as if she'd been having an affair with death. They'd had sex that week, sex like they hadn't had in months, maybe years, if he was honest. He'd made some crass joke, implying that all she had needed were a few good orgasms. He hadn't really meant it. He was just teasing her, feeling high off her high, happy to see her appetite restored. The memory made him sick now, because he'd felt close to her and maybe it was a lie. And there was shame because if he'd known it was the last time, he wouldn't have been crude for one second. He would have memorized her, he would have told her again and again how much he loved her. Not that professing his love had ever helped. He'd tried that. He'd tried many times.

He heard the barn door swinging on its hinges and sat up. Bryan was walking down the wide center aisle, his small figure half-illuminated by the uneven light. Dean called to him, taking pleasure in his surprised smile. "Come on up!"

Bryan climbed up quickly and sat next to Dean on the bale, leaning back as if they were on a sofa. "Guess what? Robbie fell in the creek. He was trying to catch a crayfish."

"Is he okay?"

"He's totally fine," Bryan said, sounding like Stephanie. "He's wearing one of Uncle Ed's shirts with cow shit on it."

"Don't say the S-word."

"With cow crap on it. You should see it; it's so big that it covers his shorts. It's like he's wearing a dress."

Dean sucked in his breath, thinking that Bryan was going to bring up the cross-dressing incident from the other day. But instead he began to talk about his mother. How she would have enjoyed going to the barbecue and what she would have brought to eat and did Dean remember the time that she made "dirt," the dessert that was layers of chocolate pudding and crumbled Oreos and then she put gummy worms in, too? He chatted so happily, as if Nicole were not dead but just on a trip somewhere, that Dean wondered if he should say something to bring home the reality of the situation, but then Bryan asked if Mommy was watching them from heaven, able to enjoy the barbecue from afar.

"Maybe," Dean said. "I don't know for sure."

Bryan frowned. "That's what Aunt Joelle said, too. She said God might have kept her out because it's cheating to kill yourself."

"I doubt that's what she really meant," Dean said, too shocked to come up with a counterargument. This was Joelle's version of forgiveness?

"So she's definitely in heaven?"

"I don't know. And neither does Joelle."

"So she might not be?"

Dean paused; he didn't believe in heaven, at least not in the sense that Joelle did, and he didn't want to encourage Bryan in beliefs that were anything like Joelle's. At the same time, he didn't want to take away Bryan's fantasy of his mother living somewhere, happily.

"If there's a heaven, I'm sure your mother's in it, waiting for you."

"I just want to know if Mommy's looking down on us," Bry said. Tears began to pool in his brown eyes. "That's what Pastor John says."

"Then that's who you should listen to. He's the expert." Dean didn't know why he couldn't tell his son yes, there was a heaven, and yes, his mother was in it. He knew it was a flaw of his, this inability to give simple comfort. He was better at telling people to buck up, at getting them to push through pain.

"I didn't mean to make you mad at Aunt Joelle." Bryan was such the peacemaker, had always been this way, starting from when he was little and was trying to get his toddler brother to like him, giving him his baby toys and smiling guilelessly when Robbie threw them back at him.

"I'm not mad," Dean said, taking his son's hand and leading him down the bales. "Come on, let's go find your brother."

Outside the barn, the sun seemed unreasonably bright. It was hot and only going to get hotter, one of those days that required a late-afternoon or midnight thunderstorm to crack it open. Dean liked nighttime storms best of all, the way they awakened him for a few minutes, and the way Nicole would move closer to him in the darkness.

Chapter 3

Stephanie's roommate, Theresa, had long, soft brown hair and a frank, pale face—a face that could use some makeup, in Stephanie's opinion. But she seemed like the kind of girl who never wore makeup, on principle. She looked like her parents: tall, sturdy people made nervous by the fact that Stephanie had arrived at school without her family. Theresa's mother offered snacks she'd brought along "for the road," raw almonds and a small bunch of damp green grapes wrapped in a paper towel. When Stephanie declined, Theresa's mother seemed overly concerned, as if Stephanie might be anorexic on top of being neglected. But she cheered up when she found out that Stephanie was from Maryland.

"We're from Columbia!" she said. "It's right near Baltimore."

Stephanie knew of Columbia, but it was so distant from her experience that Theresa might as well have been from California. Likewise, Theresa and her parents were unfamiliar with Willowboro.

"It's close to the Battle of Antietam, if you know your Civil War history," Stephanie said, aware that she sounded like a huge nerd, but not caring because it was obvious that Theresa was going to outnerd her in every area, except perhaps music. Theresa had an extensive CD collection and a really nice stereo, which she had unpacked first, arranging her CDs into a sleek rotating tower.

"Antietam sounds familiar," Theresa's father said politely.

"It was the single bloodiest day in American history," Stephanie said, emphasizing the word *bloodiest*. She had the perverse desire to shock these people, who seemed almost pathologically sensible with their healthy snacks and thick-soled shoes.

"Do you like the Indigo Girls?" Theresa asked Stephanie. She held up their debut CD with an expression that hoped so earnestly for approval that Stephanie felt embarrassed—for herself or Theresa, she wasn't sure. She gave a thumbs-up but then excused herself, leaving her suitcase open and half-unpacked.

The hallway was crowded with parents and younger siblings, the parents either busy or trying to seem busy. Some were beginning to depart, giving long hugs, their expressions frankly sorrowful. One girl sneezed as she was saying good-bye, and when her mother handed her a tissue, she lost it completely. Stephanie was glad her father and brothers had not accompanied her. It would have been awkward with Robbie and Bry getting bored and her father not knowing what to say. She was glad they hadn't come and yet she kept imagining her brothers playing in her dorm room, sitting cross-legged on the bare linoleum floor and flicking a paper football back and forth between them.

Outside, more families were spread across the freshman quad, the grass Crayola green, the border gardens freshly mulched, the tall oaks and elm trees casting generous shadows, perfect for reading and contemplation, as well as for farewell conversation between parents and children. No one noticed Stephanie as she walked by. She felt like a ghost. And in the days that followed, her sense of alienation only deepened. She kept meeting people from Maryland, but they were always from Columbia or Chevy Chase or Silver Spring or some other blandly named place near a Metro stop she didn't know. Her classmates' Maryland was a suburb of D.C.: international, professional, secular, well-to-do. Her Maryland was small-town: rural, blue collar, evangelical, down-at-the-heel. Their Maryland was the Maryland that she and Mitchell fantasized about living in, a Maryland where no one would say *Where's the funeral?* if you dressed all in black. Her Maryland was their place of exile, a place she had longed to get away from. A place she now missed dearly.

She set up her e-mail account and wrote a message to Mitchell with the subject line *Nostalgia's a bitch.* He was the only person she knew with e-mail. When a couple of days passed and he hadn't written back, she thought maybe he hadn't checked his account yet. But that wasn't like Mitchell. He loved anything to do with computers. Maybe he was busy. Maybe he was already happy. Maybe he'd made new friends.

Or maybe he was out by himself, enjoying Boston, reveling in his independence, going to whatever movie he wanted, listening to whatever music he liked. Stephanie didn't know why she couldn't enjoy her freedom. She missed the rigidity of her summer. She hadn't understood how comforting it was to take care of her brothers. She had to keep reminding herself that she had earned the right to be at a school so nice, that she'd sacrificed nights and weekends to get the right grades, to participate in the right extracurricular activities. And yet these were the same things that had pushed her away from her parents, especially her mother.

When classes started, Stephanie threw herself into the selection process, sitting in on two or three lectures a day. But that only made her feel more like a ghost as she sat in one-armed desks in crowded classrooms and took notes on subjects she doubted would end up on her schedule. The only class she knew for sure that she would take was Psych I. It was full of first-year students, and when she went to the used section of the bookstore, she was disappointed to find that secondhand copies of the required textbook had already sold out. At the same time, she was pleased to have an excuse to purchase a new copy. The pages were clean, unmarked by anyone else's highlights and underlining, a stranger's idea of what was important to remember. In the safety of her room, Stephanie turned to the chapter devoted to depression, skimming until one paragraph stopped her, forcing her to read slowly:

> Postmortem examinations indicate that suicide victims have low levels of serotonin throughout the brain. Decreased levels of serotonin are caused by stress and increase stress, which in turn increases aggressive behavior—the "fight or flight" instinct. Suicide can be seen as an aggressive behavior against the self.

It had never occurred to Stephanie that her mother might be characterized as "aggressive." For Stephanie, the emblematic moment of her mother's depression was a cold winter morning when she came down to breakfast to find her mother standing stock-still at the kitchen counter, staring at a lemon on the cutting board, staring at it like it was a Rubik's Cube. When she finally noticed Stephanie watching her, she asked Stephanie if she wouldn't mind quartering the lemon for her, because she needed to drink her black tea with lemon and honey, and it was somehow too difficult to find the right knife and to hold the lemon still and to wield the knife precisely enough to slice it into pieces. What could Stephanie do but cut the lemon? But when Stephanie drove to school, she had to pull over to the side of the road because she couldn't stop crying. She remembered the frost on the windshield that morning. It had given the window a cracked appearance. For the first time she understood that whatever was wrong with her mother was not just "in her head." It was in her body, too.

Stephanie shut her brand-new textbook and impulsively called her father, even though it was early in the evening and the long-distance rates would be expensive.

"Stephanie! How are you, sweetheart?"

"Okay. I was just calling to say hi."

"We're actually heading out. There's a team dinner—pizza night in the gym. You know how that goes; I have thirty pizzas showing up. But tell me how school is. Real quick. Have you picked your major yet?"

"You don't declare your major until your sophomore year."

"Oh, right. I wouldn't know. I majored in football."

"That's not an option here," Stephanie said, her voice going tart. She couldn't help it; her father was being so breezy, it was as if he wasn't even sad she was gone.

"You're going to be the intellectual of the family. Listen, I have to go—"

"Wait, how are Robbie and Bry?"

"Oh, they're good, they're good. Getting more independent, which is good. They got your postcards. I told them to write back."

"It doesn't matter, they're just kids." Stephanie wondered what her father meant by "more independent." He was probably leaving them on their own too much. Dragging them along to every practice. Making them babysit themselves. She knew what it was like to be the football coach's kid. But she'd always had her mother.

She hung up the phone. Never in a million years would she have guessed that college could be lonelier than high school. She couldn't stay in her room any longer; she couldn't risk running into Theresa, who would no doubt invite her to some boring, tame event for whatever boring, tame club she was thinking of joining. Stephanie gathered together her new books. She would go to the library and study. She would just be that person, the same person she was in high school, escaping into academics.

Outside, the sun was setting. It was Friday night, the first official weekend of college, with all the students now on campus, not just the first-years. The dining hall was busy and noisy. Stephanie grabbed a to-go sandwich and an apple and left without saying boo to anyone—as her grandmother Geneva would say.

To Stephanie's surprise, there were other students in the library. She had to wait to use one of the computers to check her e-mail. She sat down on a nearby sofa, one with oversized and faintly prickly cushions. She felt impatient and wondered if she should take her grandparents up on their offer to buy her a computer for her room. But the Shanks were already paying for so much of her education. She felt guilty accepting even more. She was so tired of feeling guilty.

There was another memory of her mother she couldn't get out of her mind: One morning—after the lemon incident—Stephanie had come down to breakfast to find her mother reading the Bible. But when her mother saw her, she put it away, returning it to its spot on the kitchen counter, next to the phone book. And when Stephanie asked her mother why she was reading it, her mother had said, "Oh, it's just something I started doing in the mornings. I thought it would help." And for some reason Stephanie had let the conversation end right there. She had not asked, "Help with what?" Even though Stephanie didn't believe in God, the idea of God slipped into her thoughts. It wasn't divinity she craved so much as an omniscient perspective, something to help her see past the speck of her ego-driven life and even past her family.

She glanced around the library at the quiet tall shelves of books that surrounded her and at the other students sitting at the long wooden tables. She felt exposed, sitting alone with her thoughts of her mother. As if everyone who passed by could see what a foolish, childish person she was.

Another girl was waiting with her on the couch. She was paging through the most recent issue of *Spin* magazine, a paper cup of tea balanced precariously on the cushion next to her. Stephanie recognized her from her brief trip into the cafeteria, in part because the girl had also avoided dining, but mainly because of the girl's clothes. She didn't wear the preppy, boxy, semi-unisex attire that dominated the campus. Instead she was dressed in a flowered minidress, shiny black tights, and purple lug-soled Mary Janes. Her short, bobbed hair was dyed red and adorned with plastic little-girl barrettes in bright neon colors.

"I like your barrettes," Stephanie said in a library voice.

The girl seemed startled, but then she touched her hair. "These? I got them at the drugstore." She gazed at Stephanie, who immediately felt self-conscious in her relatively pedestrian ensemble of black jeans, white button-down shirt, and Chuck Taylors.

"Are you taking Psych I?" the girl asked.

"Yeah." Stephanie was flattered, thinking the girl had recognized her, too, but then she realized that her textbook was visible in her tote bag.

"I haven't decided if I'm going to take it."

"I kind of have to," Stephanie said. "There are a lot of crazy people in my family."

"That's a good reason." The girl laughed and then introduced herself. She was Raquel, or at least she was trying to be Raquel, now that she was away from home. At home she was Kelly.

"I mean, *God*," she said, making a face, "is there a worse name?"

"It's not so bad. There were a lot of Kellys in my school."

"That's just it! There are so many Kellys. You must know how that is, as a Stephanie."

"Yeah, I was always 'Stephanie R.' Or 'Steffy.'"

"Don't tell me that's your nickname!"

"Sometimes, yeah. I have a good middle name: Geneva. It's my grandmother's name."

"I *love* that." Raquel squinted at Stephanie. "Do you want to go out tonight? I got invited to an incredibly stupid party."

"I was going back to my dorm."

"Come on, please come with me. It's with a bunch of football guys. I can't go alone, I'll get raped."

Raquel's way of exaggeration was familiar to Stephanie. It was how Mitchell talked, and it was how Stephanie used to talk with Mitchell. But lately, she hadn't felt like exaggerating. Her emotions always threatened to overwhelm; she didn't feel the need to inflate things anymore.

"Maybe another time," Stephanie said, standing up. "I should go."

Raquel began to apologize in a reflexive, vague, and faintly pathetic way, but Stephanie strode toward the library's front door without replying. She knew she was acting like a weirdo, and also that she was throwing something valuable away. But it felt good. It felt like a repudiation of the person she'd been in high school, a person she no longer liked, a person constructed to repudiate the person her mother was.

A person who had never really existed in the first place.

THE PIZZA BOXES were smashed flat, piled high next to the trash cans. Asaro's had thrown in a few extra pies, but everything still managed to get eaten. Dean added one more grease-stained box to the tower. Out of nowhere that night Robbie had announced he was a vegetarian, picking off his pepperoni one at a time and stacking them at the edge of his paper plate. Tummy Boyer—nicknamed for his appetite—grabbed them off Robbie's plate with a cheerful "You saving those for me?" Dean was pleased to see how well his boys were getting along with his players. It was good for them to be around older boys; it strengthened them—that was what Joelle and Stephanie couldn't understand.

The team had a scrimmage tomorrow, against Greenbrier, an easy opponent, but it was their first time playing without Laird. Today was his last day. Dean nodded to Garrett to get the cake for him—a surprise sent over by the boy's mother. Dean had stopped by Laird's house earlier in the week to say good-bye to his parents, but Laird's father had already left to start his new job. The hallways were crowded with cardboard boxes bearing the name of a moving company. Laird's mother seemed tired, so Dean kept his visit short. But she ran out to Dean's car after Dean and the boys had said good-bye, wanting to know if she could provide a cake for pizza night. She knew of a place that made football-shaped ones.

Garrett brought out the oversized cake on a wheeled ball cart, balancing it on the top two bars.

"Whose birthday?" someone called out.

"That's just for Tummy."

Tummy laughed and smacked his belly. For the time being, he was Laird's replacement.

"Mrs. Kemp sent this over," Dean said. "Laird, come on up here."

Laird came to the front of the room, his head slightly bent in embarrassment. His dark, almost black hair was recently cut, and with his strong neck prominently displayed, he seemed more like an adult than ever before. He stood next to Dean, slouching until Dean put his hand on his back to make him stand straight. Dean felt unreasonably proud of him, as if Laird were an ambassador of Willowboro, going out into the world to represent the town.

"You all know Laird's leaving," Dean said. "And you all know what a loss it's going to be for us. Maybe some of you who are seniors remember when Laird was starting out. He was always athletically gifted. He didn't have to try. But he did. He worked harder than anybody on this team. He *built* this team. And now he has to leave. That's a hard thing to do, gentlemen. So I want a big round of applause for Laird, for everything he's done for us. And let's wish him well in his new endeavors—and be grateful he'll be playing Division II at his new school, so we won't see him staring us down on the field."

The boys whooped and clapped, immediately getting to their feet. The gym echoed with noise. Laird turned red, but he couldn't stop smiling. "I'll be back to see you play!" he yelled. "You guys are going to States!"

The noise got even louder as the boys began to stamp their feet. Dean felt a familiar swell of happiness in his chest. The buzz of youth. It was contagious. He looked for Robbie and Bry—he wanted to see their expressions—but the standing, cheering players blocked his view of them.

LAIRD LEFT THE next morning. That afternoon the team lost the scrimmage against Greenbrier. It was unusually hot, especially in swampy Greenbrier, but still. That was no excuse. Dean brooded on the bus ride home. He couldn't remember the last time they'd lost a scrimmage in preseason. He stayed up late trying to figure out what went wrong. They just weren't strong enough, he decided. More weights, more conditioning—it was that simple.

But the next day it was hot again, and Dean didn't want to trap them in the muggy, padded weight room. Also, he didn't think Robbie and Bry would put up with it. They were sitting in the bleachers now, eating candy and reading the comic books he'd bought for them. Bribery. Lately it was the only thing that worked.

At the far end of the field his players were jogging slowly, cooling down between drills. They looked scrawny from this distance.

"You still thinking about yesterday?" Garrett said.

"I didn't even want them playing yet. They're sloppy. They're going to develop bad habits."

"They're just tired. When school starts, they'll be back on their feet."

"When school starts, they'll be distracted," Dean said.

"Hey, is he allowed to do that?" Garrett pointed toward the chain-link gate at the other end of the field, where Robbie was exiting.

"Crap," Dean said. "Excuse me for a minute."

"You want me to go ahead and run the next drill?"

"Yeah, thanks." Dean pulled down his cap. This wasn't the first time Robbie had run off without permission. Dean had to admit the boys were getting harder to manage without Stephanie. At first, things had been easier. It was a relief to have her gone, to live without the feeling of her watching him, judging him. On a purely logistical level, he no longer had to keep track of her schedule, or deal with her dishes in the sink or her car in the driveway or her stuff on the stairs. He felt a kind of bachelor's freedom. He and the boys went to the Red Byrd three nights in a row and Bryan constructed a sprawling Lego village in Stephanie's room. But the novelty was wearing off, and now the boys were restless. They complained about the double days. Robbie was outright rude, while Bry was his usual sweet, placating self. This morning he'd asked if they could visit Joelle's farm so he could see the animals. But Dean couldn't take them to Joelle's without admitting defeat.

"Hey!" he called to Robbie. "Where do you think you're going?"

"Nowhere!" Robbie called back. He was making his way across the baseball field, which abutted the football field. He stopped when he reached the pitcher's mound, smoothing the dirt with his foot while he waited for Dean to catch up.

"You can't run off whenever you get bored."

"I want to get a Coke from the soda machine."

"There's Coke in the clubhouse."

"It's in a bottle. I like my own Coke in a can. It tastes better."

"Robbie, come on, give me a break."

"Why should I? You said we would go to the mall yesterday after the scrimmage, but we just went straight home and then all we did was watch game tapes."

"I'm sorry," Dean said. "I forgot. I have a lot on my mind. We can go next weekend. There'll be sales for Labor Day."

"No, we can't, you have to go to the parade."

Every year the town threw a parade to showcase the high school band and football team—but mostly the football team. When it was over, the players stopped by all the stores to drop off season schedules.

"We'll go after the parade," Dean said.

"Yeah, right."

"I promise," Dean said. "Okay?"

Robbie allowed Dean to guide him back toward the field, but when they got to the chain-link gate, he stopped abruptly.

"I'm not going in there," he said. "I'm sick of sitting on those hard bleachers."

"Don't be so dramatic, it's not that bad."

"It *is* that bad." Robbie planted his feet. Then he sat down on the worn grass.

Dean glanced back at the field, relieved to see that his players were absorbed in their sprint ladders, too exhausted to pay attention to him. Only Bryan had taken notice and was making his way over to them.

"Pull yourself together," Dean said. "You're going to middle school this year and you need to start acting like it. You want Bryan to see you like this?"

"I don't care what he thinks," Robbie said. "He's such a fucking goody-goody."

Dean was shocked.

"What?" Robbie said.

"Don't *what* me. You are not allowed to use that kind of language with me—or anyone."

"I don't care."

"You don't care? Do you want to go to the mall next weekend or not?"

"*I don't care!*" Robbie said, yelling loudly enough for some of the players to look their way. Without warning, he threw himself on his stomach like a toddler and began to pound the grass with his fists.

"Robbie, get up! You're embarrassing yourself."

"I want Stephanie!" Robbie said, yelling into the grass. "Stephanie was nice to me. She made s'mores in the microwave and promised to call and help me pick what to wear on the first day of school *once I got new clothes.*"

Dean struggled to keep his cool. He knelt down and spoke gently. "I'm sorry we haven't gotten your school clothes yet. And I'm sorry you miss your sister. I miss her, too."

"No, you *don't*." Robbie sat up. Blades of mown grass stuck to his wet cheeks. He pushed his overgrown hair out of his long-lashed eyes. "You don't love us as much as Stephanie does."

By now Bryan had approached. "Daddy loves us," he said. "He's just busy with football."

Robbie sneered. "You're such a tool."

"Don't talk to your brother that way. He's your ally."

"He's your *ally*," Robbie repeated, mocking.

"Fine, you want to sit by yourself, sit by yourself," Dean said. "You can sit here for the rest of practice."

Dean strode back onto the field, his anger fueled by the sense that he deserved none of it. He stood next to Garrett, who was discreetly looking down at his clipboard. The players were setting up cones on the yard lines for yet another conditioning drill.

"My brother and I used to fight all the time when I was that age," Garrett said. "All the time."

"It's me they're pissed at." Dean kept his eyes on the field, but he was too upset to concentrate. His glance flitted to the gate, where Robbie was still sitting on his patch of dirt. Bryan squatted in front of him, cajoling.

"I'm sorry, I have to go talk to them again," Dean said. He walked back across the field toward his sons. He was aware of his players watching him, the sun shining on their white helmets. Behind them, the field goal's yellow bars reached up, ecstatically, to frame the sky. It was a sight that, in any other year, would have filled Dean with a sense of happiness and anticipation. There was nothing he loved more than a hot summer day at the beginning of a new season, the way it stood in contrast to the nights to come: when the black sky would be kept at bay by bright lights, when the field would smell like kicked-up dirt and mud, when it would rain, or the wind would blow cold, and the game would go on anyway; when the crowds behind him would holler and cheer and stamp their feet on the bleachers, their noise the backdrop for what were actually very calm and decisive moments for Dean. He didn't second-guess himself when he was on the field. Because then he was part of something bigger. But today, he felt uncertain and detached. There was something brutal about the sunshine, the way it brought everything into such sharp focus. It reminded him, he realized, of the day Nicole died, how bright and hot the sun had been when he and Stephanie arrived at the edge of the field, and how all the subtlety of the trail ride—the rich, faintly metallic smell of the creek bed and the layered cool shade of trees—fell away, and it was just the barn and the ambulance in the distance, glaring white.

He remembered Robbie's face, too, that dark, dark terror, an animal bewilderment. His first instinct that afternoon had been to cover Robbie's eyes, to pull him close to his own body. He had that instinct now, as he approached his sons. All at once he could see how dirty and tired they were, with sweat-dampened hair and knees scuffed with dust and grass stains. He saw in their expressions a mix of hope and fear.

He knew then that he was going to resign his coaching position.

Part Two

Chapter 4

Before the parade, Dean had gathered his team in the locker room and told them what he would announce at the parade's end. The seniors took it the hardest. Brett Albright, Dean's QB, lagged behind, waiting for Dean as he locked up.

"Coach, I don't mean to be rude, but I'd much rather have you coach than Mr. Schwartz."

"He'll do a good job," Dean said, sternly—but secretly pleased.

"I just always thought you'd be my coach senior year."

"Me too," Dean said. "But I have to do what's best for my family."

Brett nodded, but he didn't make eye contact.

"You don't need me," Dean said. "You can lead this team. You know the game inside and out."

Dean walked with Brett all the way to the parade's starting point on Main Street, talking with him about his plans after graduation. Brett was thinking of junior college, and then maybe a four-year school depending on what he wanted to study. He was sweet and earnest with Dean in a way that Dean knew he probably wasn't with his own parents—in a way that Robbie wasn't with him. When Dean told his sons he was giving up coaching in order to spend more time at home, Robbie's response was to shrug and then retreat to his room to do whatever he did in there. Bryan gave him a big hug and said, "I'm so glad!" And Dean thought, *You're not the one I'm doing it for.*

The Labor Day parade was like a preview for Friday-night football, with the band, the cheerleaders, and the football players all in uniform. The blue-and-white color scheme looked glossy and new beneath the cloudless sky. Everyone was happy to be outside. Dean felt like a killjoy when they reached the parade's end, in Willow Park. There, the Boosters had set up a small wooden stage for speeches from the mayor, the principal, the president of the Boosters Club, and of course, from Dean. Normally Dean introduced the senior players and went over the home game schedule and then led everyone in a fight song, but on that afternoon, he explained that he would be leaving his position as head coach. He didn't give a reason, and it was awkward until Dean introduced Garrett as the new coach. Then everyone had a reason to applaud.

Afterward, Dean drove the boys all the way to Frederick, in the next county, where there would be no chance of running into anyone they knew. He took them shopping in Frederick's busy downtown—not quite a mall, but there were chain stores like the Gap and Foot Locker. Robbie wanted a very specific pair of jeans and made them go to multiple stores.

"How do you know which pair to get?" Dean asked, slightly annoyed but curious, too. He had never been someone who paid much attention to clothing.

"He just sees what other people are wearing," Bryan said.

"It's not that simple," Robbie said, going into the dressing room.

"You should try something on, too," Dean said to Bryan.

"You can get me what's on sale."

"Don't be silly, pick out what you want," Dean said.

"I don't want to waste money."

"Why are you worried about that?"

"Because you just quit your job."

"No, I didn't." Dean knelt down. "I'm still teaching gym."

"But didn't you get paid a lot more for football?"

"Not really."

"Oh." Bryan still seemed confused. But also relieved. "I guess I'll go get some jeans, then. Can we get sneakers, too?"

"Sure."

It occurred to Dean that they hadn't been spending much at all. They hadn't gone on summer vacation, and if they ate out, it was the Red Byrd or subs from Sheetz. Dean felt guilty. When they were finished shopping, he took them to one of the nicer restaurants in the area, a Mexican place that Laura had mentioned to him once, describing it as "surprisingly authentic." He wondered if she'd actually traveled to Mexico, if she could speak Spanish. She seemed like someone who would know another language for no particular reason.

The restaurant was popular, filled with couples sitting at small, colorfully painted tables, but the staff was friendly to kids. Dean got a margarita before dinner and tried to relax and enjoy his sons' company. When the food came, the boys had good appetites and everyone cheered up. The guacamole had a secret ingredient and if you could guess what it was, you got a free dessert. Bryan guessed "mayonnaise" and the waitress laughed, shaking her head, but brought him some churros anyway.

The answering machine was blinking crazily when they finally got home. Dean waited until the boys were in bed to listen to the messages. Joelle and Ed had called, as well as Garrett, the Boosters president, the school principal, a couple of parents, and the local newspaper reporter. He had warned everyone in advance, but they all wanted to commiserate after the fact. Dean called back the reporter, who asked Dean if he was sick. Dean said no, he just needed to spend more time with his family.

"I know that sounds like an excuse, but in my case it's true," Dean said.

"Why'd you wait so long to resign?" the reporter asked.

"I don't have a good answer for that. I guess I forgot how all-consuming football is."

THE IRONY WAS that after resigning, Dean's life got even busier. The boys were in school, which made life easier, but he was back in school, too, with new students to meet and names to memorize. In addition, he had to help the principal find a replacement for Garrett, who couldn't be athletic director anymore, and he also had to pinch-hit as A.D. for a few weeknights until the replacement took over. As he attended to one logistical concern after another, he found himself thinking of Laura, of how much more interesting everything would be if she were still working at the high school.

Dean also had to train Garrett. Although his former assistant was well prepared for his new job, there were certain details and scheduling concerns that Dean had to enumerate, a whole slew of keys, contacts, and equipment to hand over. Dean gave him everything except his office.

Now it was the first football Friday of the season and there was a game-day feeling in the air, with a warm September breeze blowing through Dean's office window. The freshly limed field was like an empty stage in the distance. Dean could make out someone walking along the perimeter, near the clubhouse. Probably Garrett—or possibly the assistant Garrett had recently hired. Dean was planning to attend tonight's game with the boys, but when he mentioned it to Stephanie, she seemed surprised, and a little annoyed, as if she'd expected him to renounce football altogether.

She was coming home for the weekend. He had no idea why. She had assured him that nothing was wrong, that she was coming because Joelle said she should, that the boys missed her. That bothered Dean, but when he called Joelle, she said Stephanie was the one who had contacted her and it wasn't any of her business but she thought Stephanie sounded homesick and didn't Dean want to see her, in any case? Of course he did, but what he really wanted was for her to start her life. He wanted someone in the family to feel free of obligation. He was also grumpy that Stephanie had invited herself over to Joelle's for dinner, and now they all had to go.

"What's five times seven?" Bry asked from the corner of Dean's desk, where he sat doing his homework. The elementary school started and finished an hour earlier than the middle and high schools, so Dean had been letting him hang out in his office during the last period of the day, which happened to be his planning period. It was a convenient arrangement, if not strictly allowed, but Dean knew no one would give him a hard time.

"Is it thirty-seven?" Bryan asked.

"I think that's a prime number."

"Come on, just tell me. I hate sevens."

"Here, it's easier this way." Dean grabbed a handful of paper clips from an unused ashtray on his desk and began to arrange them into seven groups of five.

"I get it, I get it." Bryan began to manipulate the piles himself and Dean wondered if his teacher had shown him this method. She was an older woman who insisted on memorization. Dean found her to be a little harsh, but Bryan seemed to like the strict rules; they satisfied his innate desire to please.

Robbie had not adjusted to the school year as well as his younger brother. Yesterday Dean had gotten a call from the vice principal, who informed Dean that Robbie had been sneaking out—he had actually used the word *sneaking*.

"He's been going out for lunch instead of eating in the cafeteria," the vice principal said, "which, as you know, is not allowed even at the high school level."

"Does he get back in time for class?" Dean asked.

"Yes, but he's not allowed to go out in the first place."

"I was just trying to find out if he's skipping lunch or class. Maybe he hasn't made new friends yet and he doesn't like going to lunch."

"That's exactly it, Mr. Renner. According to his teachers, he's a bit of a loner, and we think it may be because of some of the difficulties he's facing at home."

"Difficulties?" Dean repeated. The vagueness of the word disturbed him. He recalled one of Robbie's former teachers describing Robbie as "sensitive"—a good thing, at the time, or at least Dean had heard it as good. But it was also the word that Nicole's family used to describe her. He was grateful to be on the phone, so the vice principal could not see his shaking hands.

He said yes to the vice principal's recommendation that Robbie start seeing the school counselor a couple of times a week. When he hung up the phone, it occurred to him that Robbie wasn't even being punished for breaking the rules. That he was considered too fragile to punish.

The bell rang, which meant Robbie was getting out of school and would be heading their way soon. Dean didn't know what he would say to him, but he put the worry out of his mind, because he was supposed to meet with the girls' cross-country team. The girls had a race the next day, but no coach. Their coach had taken a new job over the summer and no one had thought to replace her. It was something Garrett should have attended to, as A.D., but Dean felt guilty about it, since he was the one who'd thrown everything into chaos at the last minute. The principal said he had a new coach in mind, but he wouldn't share the name with Dean. Which meant he was scrambling. Probably he'd bribe one of the young teachers with the promise of a better schedule—honor students and electives.

"I have to go talk to some students," Dean said to Bry. "You okay hanging out here for a while?"

"Yeah, okay." Bryan was still moving the paper clips.

Dean headed to the big gym, where he'd told the girls to wait. But it was too big a meeting place. Dean realized his error as soon as he saw the four narrow-shouldered girls sitting on the bottom row of bleachers with their backpacks balanced on their laps. When he gathered the football team here, they would sprawl across several rows of bleachers, shedding coats and backpacks. Dean would always have to wait a few minutes for them to settle down; it was as if they needed the space of the gym to absorb their energy. But the girls seemed dwarfed by the room's expanse. With the exception of one very tall girl with long legs and square, sturdy knees, none of them looked like runners—or even athletes. In addition to the tall one, there was a blond girl whose skinny arms and pudgy middle seemed to come from two different bodies; a serious-seeming redhead with a skim-milk complexion; and finally, a small, wiry girl whose short, bleached hair made her look like a baby chick—not the look she was going for, Dean guessed, with her dark clothes and triply pierced ears. All were dressed casually for the warm day in shorts, T-shirts, and sandals.

"You girls don't have the tradition of dressing up on game day?" Dean asked.

"Why would we dress up for the football game?" asked the tall one with the runner's legs.

"No, I mean for your team. Because you have a race tomorrow."

"No one really cares that we have a meet tomorrow," the pierced girl said.

"How can they care if they don't know?" Dean said.

"Even if they knew . . ." The pierced girl didn't bother finishing her sentence.

Dean scanned the ten names on his roster. A small team.

But you didn't need a lot for cross-country. It only took five to score.

"I guess we should wait until everyone gets here to get started," he said.

"I think this is everyone," said the serious-looking redhead. Her hair was pulled back into a tight French braid that clung to her skull and went straight down her back, as if keeping her posture in check.

"Not according to this." Dean held up his list.

"Let me see," the red-haired girl said. "You must have last year's team. Those girls graduated." She pointed to the first three names. "I don't know about the others."

"Daria's not coming, she quit over the summer," the blond girl said. "And Tamara and Julie didn't like practicing with the boys' team, so they quit, too."

"Who cares, Tamara wasn't any good anyway," said the pierced punk duckling. "And Julie wanted to play soccer, she was just looking for an excuse."

"Tamara wasn't bad," the blond girl said. "She was faster than Jessica—no offense."

The red-haired girl—Jessica, apparently—waved away the remark, but her skim-milk cheeks went blotchy.

Dean asked the girls to introduce themselves and learned that there was one from each grade. The tall girl was actually the youngest. Her name was Aileen and she was a freshman. The punk duckling was the senior. She went by See-See, short for Tennessee, a nickname bestowed upon her because she had been born there, on a commune, her mother having once been a sort-of hippie. (All this was explained to Dean very quickly and so efficiently that he understood she had been giving this spiel for many years.) The other two were Lori and Jessica. Lori, the blonde, was a sophomore. Jessica, the French-braided redhead, was a junior.

"So which of you is the captain?" Dean asked.

They looked at one another and started laughing.

"What's so funny?"

"There are *four* of us," See-See said. "It's not, like, a situation in need of leadership. We all run the same race, the same way. Nobody's calling any plays."

Dean heard the youngest girl, Aileen, whisper, "Wait, is he the football coach?"

"Every situation needs a leader," Dean said. He pointed to See-See. "You're the captain by default, you're the senior."

"Okay." See-See turned to the other girls. "Hey, I'm your captain."

Dean was annoyed by her nonchalance, but he pushed on. "Tell me about your conditioning regimen."

No one said anything.

"From this summer?" he pressed. "What did you do to prepare for the season?"

"You mean how many miles did we run?" Lori asked.

"Yes, exactly. Whatever your coach told you to do."

"She didn't say much," See-See said. "I think she was looking for another job already. She didn't like it here."

"She was from Bethesda," Jessica said, as if this explained everything.

"Did you girls meet up during the summer?"

There was another nervous silence. Dean got the sense they weren't really friends. It was the opposite of the football team, where the players had been together since elementary school.

"So you didn't meet up," he said. "You're allowed to, you know—as long as it's not with a coach."

"I ran on my own," See-See said.

"Me too," Lori said. "I got up to twenty-five miles a week."

"You were supposed to get to forty," See-See said.

"Look who's already captain!"

"No one got to forty," Jessica said.

"*I* did—and so did Aileen."

"Okay, so it's just the four of you tomorrow?" Dean said, interrupting. "There's no chance that the others could be convinced to join us?"

They stopped talking abruptly.

"You're coming with us to the meet?" See-See asked.

Dean had been using the word *us* in the spirit of friendliness, but for the first time, the girls were looking at him with hope. He couldn't remember the last time anyone had looked at him that way.

"Somebody should go with you," he said. "It might as well be me."

Stephanie stood in her aunt's kitchen, stirring fresh mint into a pitcher of iced tea, the way her mother used to do. Aunt Joelle's house had that subtle farm stink, a putrid yet not unpleasant mix of manure, milk, and wet straw. Back at school, her dorm mates were probably getting ready for a night out, drinking shots of vodka or sipping from plastic cups filled almost to the brim with sugary red wine. The last time Stephanie had touched a drink was the night she and Mitchell cut her mother's dress. Her new classmates probably all thought she was uptight, boring, antisocial. Actually, it was more likely that they hadn't noticed her at all. Maybe this was the real reason she'd come home: to be seen again.

She brought the iced tea to the dining room table, which was set nicely, as if for a special guest, with a tablecloth, place-mats, cloth napkins, and a bouquet of Queen Anne's lace and bachelor's buttons. An aluminum-foil-covered casserole of baked pork chops took pride of place in the center of the table, surrounded by smaller dishes of coleslaw, applesauce, potato salad, and Parker House rolls made from scratch. It was rich, heavy food, and Stephanie was hungry for it after three weeks of the salad bar at school. She always ate the quickest thing, not wanting to linger in the cafeteria.

Stephanie counted up the places. "Isn't Grandma coming over?"

"It's her bingo night," Aunt Joelle said. "Don't be offended, she's addicted. I had the new pastor and his wife over last week and she still went. I couldn't believe it."

"Jesus Christ himself could be coming to dinner and she'd pick bingo," Uncle Ed yelled from the living room.

"Ed, don't say that. What's wrong with you? It's time for dinner. Turn off the TV and come sit. Dean, you too."

Stephanie called out into the backyard, where Robbie and Bry and her cousins, Megan and Jenny, were playing on the steep hill that sloped up toward the dairy. Large limestone for-mations jutted out of it, steps and shelves to climb on. As a kid, Stephanie had always designated one rock as "hers" to arrange whatever treasures she'd unearthed: a smooth pebble, a turkey feather, or maybe something from the abandoned railroad tracks nearby—a piece of a rusted metal spike or old, cloudy glass.

"I swear you got taller since I left," Stephanie said to Jenny, who gave her a bored eye roll, like she expected something more original from someone who wasn't quite an adult yet. But Stephanie was genuinely shocked by the speed of her cousin's growth spurt, which was giving her body no time to adjust as it suddenly lengthened. Her older sister, Megan, had entered adolescence more gracefully, easing into her adult body like a woman slipping into an expensive silk gown. Then again, Megan was going to be beautiful, and Jenny was not. It hadn't become apparent until recently, when everything that had made Megan's face a bit severe, as a child, came into focus to reveal a young woman with serene, widely spaced blue eyes. She had a small, elegantly shaped head, and she wore her dark hair pulled away from her face in what Stephanie's mother used to call a "half ponytail," but that seemed too casual a description for Megan's shining hair.

Stephanie kept staring at Megan throughout the meal; she tried to be discreet but it was as if her gaze had gotten caught on her cousin's face. She was halfway through her dinner before she figured out what kept pulling her back: Megan's eyes were like her mother's. The same color, the same intensity.

"So Dean," Uncle Ed said. "Let me ask you something, now that you're a running coach—"

"I'm not the coach. I'm just going to a meet tomorrow."

"And dragging us along with you," Stephanie said. It bugged her that her father had volunteered for a coaching gig on the weekend she was visiting. She couldn't help thinking he'd done it on purpose.

"You don't have to go," her father said. "What was your question, Ed?"

Uncle Ed jumped on his cue, eager to dissolve the tension. Probably that was his role in this estrogen-rich household. "Since you're a running coach, tell me: Do you really need to pay a lot for running shoes? Because Megan wants these air ponies—"

"Air *Pegasus*," Megan said.

"I'm sorry, but there's no way a pair of shoes is worth sixty dollars," Aunt Joelle said. "What's wrong with your regular sneakers?"

Stephanie's father turned to Megan. "I didn't know you were a runner."

Aunt Joelle stood up and began to clear the table. "There's dessert."

Stephanie noticed that her father was still looking at Megan. She wondered if he was picking up on the eye thing.

"How many miles are you running?" he asked.

Megan shrugged. "I run for an hour in the morning, before Mom starts school."

"And you do that every day?"

"She's worn out two pairs of Keds," Uncle Ed said. "That's why I'm wondering about these pony shoes."

Aunt Joelle returned from the kitchen with a plate of brownies. "You're paying for the brand when you buy those shoes. You might as well tape a fifty-dollar bill to the bottom of your foot."

"Megan, you should run for our team." Stephanie's father was excited, leaning forward. "You could even run in tomorrow's meet. We actually need another runner. There's only four girls. You have to have five to score."

"I would love that," Megan said.

"You can't," Aunt Joelle said. "You're not a student at the school."

"That doesn't matter," Dean said. "I've had a couple football players who were homeschooled."

"I don't think it's a good idea," Aunt Joelle said. The dessert plates clinked against each other as she passed them out.

"But, Mom, I would learn good things. I would learn teamwork. And endurance."

"You want to learn endurance? Jesus, wandering in the desert for forty days, being tempted by the devil. That's endurance."

Stephanie had to stifle a laugh. She didn't know how her father kept a straight face. He was still so fixated on Megan.

"Joelle, with all due respect, I think this could be an opportunity—"

"Dean, if you want to respect me, drop the subject."

Stephanie watched her father absorb this reprimand. Behind him, a framed cross-stitch above the sideboard said TRY A LITTLE KINDNESS. Stephanie had stared at that thing for years before she realized it was an acrostic that spelled TALK.

Uncle Ed reached for a brownie. "These look great, Jo. Come on, everybody, eat up. We have to get going soon."

"Yummy!" Bryan said, with an especially adorable smile. He had a way of turning up the cute when things were tense.

In the car on the way to the game, her father was still annoyed. "Joelle really pisses me off. Here she's got this daughter with God-given talent and she denies her. For what reason? It makes no sense."

"I guess she doesn't want Megan involved with anything at the high school."

"I don't get that. Maybe it's not the best school academically, but it's not the worst. Anyway, she doesn't care about academics."

"Maybe she doesn't want Megan to be too into clothes or being popular or whatever. Maybe she's against materialism. You heard her going off on those shoes."

"She's controlling and narrow-minded. That's what happens if you stay in one place your whole life."

Her father wasn't exactly a world traveler, but Stephanie could see that he wasn't in the mood to be tested. She had never heard this kind of bitterness from him. They were driving through town, past houses whose porches were level with the sidewalk, past the drive-through Tastee Freez in need of renovation, past the gas station that sold Swisher Sweets, past Mike's Video Time (where she and Mitchell had once seen the home ec teacher going through the beaded curtain into the adult section), past the fire station, the bank, the Catholic church, the liquor store, the stoplight, past the town cemetery where her father, but not her mother, was buried. Night was falling quickly, darkening everything that was familiar to her.

DEAN COULDN'T REMEMBER the last time he'd watched a game from the bleachers. They were playing against Beech Creek High, a small school that was traditionally an easy win. Beech Creek had never been known for its athletic program; it was considered an "artsy" school, with a year-round theater program and several choirs. Dean had a theory: Methodists founded Beech Creek, and Methodists liked to sing. Willowboro, on the other hand, was founded by Brethrens—a pacifist, agrarian people. Kids who grew up on farms were doing chores from the time they could walk; they naturally became strong and athletic.

"How does it feel to be a fan? Takes the pressure off, right?" Ed handed Dean a fountain soda.

The band marched in, and then everyone stood for the national anthem. Dean eyed his players. They still felt like *his* players, especially Brett Albright, who had not seemed like anyone's idea of a football player when he started in ninth grade. Now he was QB! Dean had seen that he was not truly scrawny, just underweight. He had an eye for late bloomers, probably because he had been one. Those years of waiting for your body to catch up to your mind were difficult, but ultimately beneficial. You learned to be patient with your body, to let your mind pick up the slack. Maybe you also learned to be patient with your mind, to trust that your body would pull through. That was what he had been trying to explain to Joelle about Nicole, the life philosophy she had mocked. He glanced in her direction; her eyes were shut and she had a little smile on her face as she listened to the music. For a moment, he could see the sweet, sincere girl she must have been once, the girl Nicole admired.

Ed nudged Dean to take the lid off his Coke and poured some Jack Daniel's into the cup. The first sip reminded Dean of college, and of beach vacations on the Eastern Shore. The second sip was just sweet on sweet.

Willowboro lost the coin toss, and Beech Creek chose to receive. As the players took their positions, Dean noticed a new player on the field. He couldn't recognize him from a distance.

"You see that kid? Devlin?" Ed pointed to the very player

Dean was eyeing. "He's from the baseball team. Apparently he joined this week! They were desperate because Laird up and left without any warning."

"You shouldn't put someone with no experience in the defensive unit," Dean said. He couldn't believe Garrett had gone behind his back. He'd clearly made an effort to hide his new recruit. Or maybe he hadn't; maybe Dean hadn't noticed a new name on the roster. It bothered him that some part of his mind had actually let his job go.

"Here we go!" Ed said, as Willowboro kicked off. It was a good strong kick that angled left, moving the action toward Willowboro's fans. Everyone cheered, but Dean was too worried about the baseball recruit to enjoy the pure drama of the scene. Beech Creek was quickly pushed out of bounds. In the next play, Willowboro intercepted a pass and gained possession. The offensive unit came out, to Dean's relief—until he realized that Brett Albright was not lined up at QB. Instead Garrett had him at tight end, and Jimmy Smoot was QB. This made no sense; Smoot had good hands, yes, but he wasn't the brightest.

"Don't run," Dean said under his breath. Theirs should be a passing strategy. But Smoot ran. The others rushed downfield, slamming into the players headed toward Smoot. It was a mess, but it was working. Smoot had already covered enough ground to get a first down. He didn't make it much farther, though; after a few seconds, a Beech Creek player tackled him from behind.

"Not bad," Ed said. "Not bad at all."

"He should have passed," Dean said.

Ed shrugged, and Dean realized he sounded sour. He told

himself to sit quietly through the next few plays. But he couldn't understand why his team had been rearranged. Maybe Garrett was having trouble managing the players and this was his way of showing them who was boss. Or maybe he'd always thought Dean was doing everything wrong. He winced as he watched the baseball player, Devlin, trot back out onto the field to try his hand at offensive tackle.

"They could have scored by now," Dean said, "if they would throw the ball."

"Take it easy, Coach." Ed tipped a little more booze into Dean's soda.

"I'm going for a hot dog." He couldn't sit here any longer and pretend to be happy getting wasted and nostalgic.

He slid past Robbie and Bry and the girls, who were paying more attention to the band and the cheerleaders than the game. He caught sight of Stephanie as he made his way down the bleachers. She was sitting with some girls he recognized as former cheerleaders. Not her usual crowd by a long shot, but then, her usual crowd was at college. As she should be. He felt disoriented as he stepped off the bleachers and onto the worn grass at the edge of the field. A group of teenage girls brushed past him, not recognizing him, and almost knocking his Coke out of his hand. The band was playing "Go, Fight, Win!" noisily and slightly off tempo. Suddenly the crowd cheered crazily, and he heard the shuffle of the scoreboard numbers flipping into place. Willowboro had finally scored a touchdown.

He got in line for the concession stand. The wait was longer than he expected, and he could barely see the field, but that was fine with him.

The woman who had come to stand behind him in line tapped him on the shoulder. He turned to find Laura.

"I thought it was you!" she said. "Everyone looks a little different in their civilian clothes."

She was wearing a blue baseball cap and a blue zip-up sweat-shirt, both emblazoned with Willowboro's eagle mascot. Her long hair was in a ponytail, pulled through the back of her cap.

"Looks like you made a run on the school store," Dean said.

"I guess I'm just excited to have a permanent job—one that actually makes use of my degree." She smiled nervously, which made him feel better; he was nervous, too. "Tim's home sick," she added. "Apparently he always gets the flu at the beginning of the school year. All those little-kid germs."

Dean wondered if she lived with Tim now, but he couldn't figure out a way to ask.

"He actually mentioned you before I left," Laura said. "He says you're not coaching anymore?"

"It's better for my kids if I take a season off. I'm a single parent now." Dean couldn't keep the bitterness out of his voice.

Laura nodded without saying anything, and Dean knew he'd made things weird.

"Sorry, this game is making me antsy. The guy who took over for me, he's changing everything up . . ." He stopped him-self, realizing that Laura didn't care what happened in football games. And that was kind of a relief.

"What are you sorry for?" she said. "I'd be bummed if I had to give up the thing I loved best in the world. Anyone would."

"Yeah, well." Dean felt embarrassed; he still had the napkin she'd given him at church. It sat on top of his bedroom dresser, next to his dish of loose change. He glanced at it every night when he emptied his pockets.

"Who's next?" called the teenage girl working at the concessions booth. "Oh, hi, Coach!"

Dean insisted on buying Laura's pretzel along with his hot dog and then the girl wouldn't let Dean pay, saying his money was no good. He put five dollars in the tip jar that went straight to the Boosters.

"I should hang around with you more often," Laura said. "Free snacks!"

"You want to watch the game over there?" Dean pointed to an empty spot at the fence.

"I actually have a friend waiting for me in the bleachers."

"I should get back to my kids anyway." He felt like he'd pushed things too far, but he'd thought she seemed flirtatious. Or at least bored.

"Right," Laura said. "I should tell you, uh, I actually talked with Robbie today. He was sent to my office."

"Oh," Dean said. For a couple of treacherous seconds it was all he could think to say. "I guess that makes sense. You're the counselor now."

"I'm sorry, I should have said something right away. He's a great kid, really great." Laura's voice had changed, gotten cool and smoothed out, like she'd flipped on the professional switch. "I'm really looking forward to working with him."

Amid Dean's confusion and embarrassment, a sense of loss was emerging. He wouldn't be able to talk with her in the same way anymore, not if Robbie was confiding in her.

"You know, I pack his lunch," Dean said. "I pack him the

same thing I pack for myself. I don't know why he's been going to Asaro's."

"You don't have to explain anything."

"The vice principal says it's because he doesn't have friends, but he has friends. He's a popular kid. Good-looking. I'm trying not to make too much of it, but between you and me, I think it's odd—"

She interrupted him with that professional voice. "Dean, I shouldn't be talking with you about Robbie. I mean, not informally."

"Of course," Dean said. But he was confused. What about the way she'd touched his arm in the church parking lot, what about giving him her number?

"I'm sorry, I don't mean to be rude," Laura said. "They don't tell you about this scenario in graduate school."

He wondered what the scenario was in her mind.

The crowd was very loud again, chanting over the cheerleaders and the band. Dean turned to see Smoot barreling down the field. The boy dodged his attackers elegantly, as if he had some foreknowledge of their trajectories. Dean remembered being his age, the exquisite feeling of gaining control of his body, of his mind, of the two forces being braided together in perfect accord.

"Come on!" Dean said, heading toward the empty spot at the fence. "Go, Smoot, go! Bring it home!"

Dean gave himself over to the excitement, clapping and yelling, allowing himself to believe that his claps and yells were bringing the boy closer to the end zone. In the stands, everyone was on their feet, chanting "*GO EAGLES!*" Smoot slowed, ever so slightly, a few yards from the end zone, and a member of the Beech Creek team slammed into him, coming at him from an angle. Dean was exhilarated by the heavy, animal sound of their bodies smashing together beneath the clanking layers of equipment. He remembered getting the wind knocked out of him. The dizzying, disconcerting pain of it.

"God," Laura said. "It's like they have a death wish."

STEPHANIE SCANNED FACES in the darkened basement room, searching for someone who seemed weird. She had a philosophy—one that she sensed was basically adolescent but that she was not yet ready to discard—that there were two types of people in the world, the weirds and the normals, the normals being those who traveled serenely through life, unhindered by extremes of thought or feeling, and the weirds being those deemed "sensitive," who felt lots of different emotions about lots of different things. All through high school, Stephanie had assumed that she was in the weird category of people (had assumed that anyone who was even *aware* of there being two categories must automatically be in it), and that her parents were in the normal category. And with this assumption had come the idea that it was somehow better to be in the weird category, that to be normal was to be timid in some essential way, to not live fully.

Now Stephanie thought she had gotten it wrong. Certainly, she had been wrong about her mother. It was possible she'd been wrong about her father, too, though if her mother was in the weird category, it made sense to her that she would be attracted to someone normal, someone who could distract you from life's big questions.

That was how Stephanie had felt about Julie Ashbaugh, a girl she barely knew: she was distracting. She had graduated with Stephanie, and when she saw Stephanie at the game, she greeted her as if they'd been very friendly in school, even though the only class they'd ever had together was chorus. They gossiped about the handful of friends they had in common and then they'd watched the game, which turned into a close one and ended up a victory, the perfect game for fans. Even Stephanie got into it and cheered herself hoarse.

Julie was a student at the junior college, and after the game, she and Stephanie went to a party with other junior college students, where they drank coconut rum and smoked menthol cigarettes, a combination that reminded Stephanie of fluoride treatments at the dentist. Julie deemed the party lame and so they decided to cruise the dual, except they didn't do it ironically, as Stephanie and Mitchell would have. They just drove around and around, listening to the radio—country, of course—and looking for something to do, as if a new restaurant or movie theater might magically appear along the strip, or, more likely, a place that had initially seemed boring would begin to seem interesting after true boredom set in. As the ride went on, Stephanie began to feel claustrophobic in Julie's car, a Mazda Miata that smelled strongly of synthetic banana, emanating from a yellow pine tree that swung merrily from the rearview mirror. Everything that was dull about Julie could be summed up by this particular aesthetic decision, Stephanie thought. And it was in thinking of Mitchell, and what bitchy thing Mitchell might say about this tropical pine tree car freshener, that Stephanie heard herself say aloud that she missed high school.

Which was how they had ended up at a high school football party.

"Steph, you have to catch up!" Julie said, pointing to her beer bottle, still three-quarters full.

The low-ceilinged room was crowded and hot. Green Day, the one rock band that seemed to cross all clique lines, played loudly from small speakers perched on top of a mostly empty bookshelf. Some of the football players started dancing—not actual dancing, more like jumping around—celebrating their win.

Stephanie reluctantly took a sip of her drink. She didn't get beer. She remembered an article she'd read about alcohol use before Prohibition, how people used to drink beer all day, even for breakfast. It was milder then, apparently. She told Julie, just to say something, but Julie barely listened.

"You read a lot of articles." Julie looked around the room restlessly. "I thought I would know more people here."

"Me too," Stephanie said, even though her friends had all graduated. "I'm going to get a soda," she said. "You want my beer?"

"Yeah, okay," Julie said. She held out her empty bottle. "Throw this away?"

The party was in the basement rec room of the big suburban house of Brett Albright, her old crush. He'd given her a wave when she came in, but she clearly didn't mean anything in particular to him. He had a girlfriend, anyway, a sophomore girl who wore his chunky class ring on a gold chain that hung between her breasts. Brett's parents were home and his father, a jowlier version of Brett, occasionally came downstairs to replenish the refreshments. He seemed to know about the beer stash but not about the liquor that was being surreptitiously added to sodas. His presence made Stephanie feel especially pathetic. She poured herself a Coke from a freshly stocked two-liter bottle and ate an Oreo.

Someone tapped her on the shoulder and said her full name. She turned to find Laird Kemp looming over her. He was one of those football players who actually intimidated her, with his five o'clock shadow and oversized feet and hands. At the same time, he had a calm face, with sleepy eyes set beneath hopelessly undergroomed eyebrows.

"I thought you graduated," he said.

"I thought you moved."

"I did. I'm visiting."

"Me too."

"Why?" Laird asked. "Does your dad need help or something?"

"Why would my dad need help?"

"I don't know. Sorry. I'm just confused . . . with your dad quitting and all." He held out a flask, helplessly. "Want some?"

She accepted his generous pour without even asking what it was. Rum, she decided. She had never really considered Laird before. He didn't seem quite at home in his big square body. He wasn't graceful like Brett. But she liked being near him, she liked his broad forearms with their thick black hair, she liked his shoulders, and she liked his sleepy yet curious gaze. Around his neck was a silver chain with something on it—but it was hidden beneath his T-shirt.

"You a Pearl Jam fan?" he asked, catching her gaze on his T-shirt.

"Yeah, kind of. I mean, I wouldn't say I'm a huge fan. I don't have their albums or anything. But I like their music. When it comes on the radio, I don't change the station." Stephanie took a sip of her drink to stop her nervous chatter. *You're in college*, she told herself sternly. *A very good college.*

"No one at my new school likes Pearl Jam," Laird said. "I mean, no one on the football team."

"Is that why you're back here—to find a Pearl Jam fan?" Stephanie said, lamely. She felt like she'd made an old-person joke.

"I'm back here because I miss it," he said. "I'm fucking homesick. I hate my new school. I love these guys."

"Why are you talking to me, then?"

"I don't know," he said. "I guess I thought it would be more fun to hang out with them. But I wasn't in the game. It's not the same. And everybody keeps asking me why I'm back and what my new team is like and it's like I don't have any good answer."

"I'm getting the same thing."

"Why *are* you back?" Laird asked. "I thought college was great."

"It is," Stephanie said. "I just don't know anyone there."

Laird nodded. "My new school sucks. Everyone is snobby. They say I have a hick accent. The coach isn't half as good as your dad."

"Maybe you just don't know him that well."

"No," Laird said. "You can tell. He's a yeller. Your dad isn't like that. I can't believe he's not coaching anymore. I didn't find out until tonight. I was like—what? All the guys are so bummed."

Stephanie shrugged. "You guys won tonight without him."

"That's Beech Creek," Laird said, dismissively. He fixed his gaze on her, suddenly seeming less sleepy. "Do you even *know* how good a coach your dad is? He has a football mind."

"Isn't that an oxymoron?"

"You don't get it, your dad can work with any team, it doesn't matter how good they are. He'll come up with plays to match the players. If he'd been coaching Beech Creek tonight, they would have beaten us. That's a fact."

"A verifiable fact."

"Basically, yeah." Laird grinned at his hyperbole. Behind him, his teammates were bellowing the lyrics to a Garth Brooks song. "I don't miss that," he said.

"What's on your necklace?" Stephanie asked.

"It's my number." He pulled on the silver chain to reveal a silver *12*.

Stephanie reached out to touch the charm. It was warm from his body. "So it's a football thing. Everything's a football thing for you guys."

"Not everything," Laird said. He took a step closer to her.

Stephanie kept hold of the number for another moment before letting it go. "Did you drive here?"

"Yeah, why?" He grinned.

"Because maybe we could drive somewhere else."

AFTER THE GAME, Joelle volunteered to let the boys sleep over so that Dean and Ed could go out. Ed took Dean to Coach's, a new sports bar that was owned by one of his friends. "Thought you'd get a kick out of it," Ed said when Dean commented on the blinking neon sign, shaped like a football. Inside, it was busy, with the Orioles game playing on all the TVs. The staff wore baseball caps and team jerseys, and the walls were lined with salvaged trophies and old sports posters. The overall effect was cluttered and casual, as if you were in someone's disorganized basement—wholesome and easygoing. Not the effect, maybe, that Ed's buddy was going for, but more appealing than the seedy places along the dual highway.

Ed got the first round and a basket of salted peanuts, which he began to shell methodically, amassing a pile of nuts before devouring them in one quick handful. They watched the baseball game for a while, Dean marveling, as always, at how relaxed baseball players seemed as they stood at the plate, waiting for a ball to be hurled at them at ninety-plus miles per hour. They reminded him of cows, the way they chewed their cud and calmly regarded the cars whizzing by. Maybe that was why Ed liked the game so much.

In between innings there was a commercial for Nike shoes, featuring a long-legged girl running through the woods. Ed started talking about "air ponies" again, unable to get the name right even when it was right in front of him. He said he was thinking of buying Megan a pair anyway.

"She's such a good kid," he said. "And she never asks for anything."

"They'd be better for her feet," Dean said. "You ready for another round?"

"Yeah—and some more of these?" Ed held up an empty peanut basket.

Waiting at the bar, Dean glanced around the room. The crowd skewed younger than he'd expected, everyone around Garrett's age, in their late twenties to early thirties. He checked for his assistant coach and was relieved not to find him. He'd congratulated Garrett after the game, shaking his hand on the field, but he didn't go to the locker room to see the players, afraid he would be called upon to say something about the game—a victory despite Garrett's rearrangements.

A woman was waving to him from a table in the back. Laura, he realized. He waved back with a tentativeness that made her laugh and say something to her companion, a dark-haired woman Dean vaguely recognized.

"I'll be right back," Dean said to Ed, dropping off their round. "I just need to say hello to someone."

"Sure." Ed's eyes were fixed on the game as he started in on the new peanut basket.

"I thought you'd never see us," Laura said as he approached her corner table. "We were waving for, like, ten minutes—this is my friend Abby. She teaches music at the middle school."

"Your son Robbie is in one of my classes," Abby said. "Chorus."

"You probably hear his voice more than I do, then," Dean said.

Abby looked at him like he was pretty much the asshole she'd expected, but Laura smiled.

"Sit down with us," she said.

"I would, but I'm here with my brother-in-law."

"Invite him over, too."

"I don't want to spoil your ladies' night."

"You're not spoiling anything! Come on, one beer."

Dean allowed himself a grin after he turned away from them to check in with Ed. He assumed Ed would decline, but Ed was more than happy to meet two young women. He followed Dean to their table and immediately engaged them in conversation, asking what subjects they taught and what they thought of the new principal.

Upon learning that Laura was not a teacher but a therapist, he grilled her about homeschooling.

"I need to know the long-term effects," he said, pushing his empty beer glass toward the center of the table as if to clear away all distractions. "For girls," he clarified. "Two girls."

"That's hard to say," Laura said. "It depends on a lot of different factors."

"Let's say, one year of homeschooling, for religious reasons—what does that do?"

"Um, I guess that could be fine. In a lot of cultures, it's traditional for children to devote some time to religious studies."

"So it doesn't mess them up for life?"

"It takes a lot to mess up a kid for life," Laura said, with a quick glance in Dean's direction. "They're pretty resilient. That's why I like working with them."

Ed nodded sagely, as if he had suspected as much, and then began to ask Abby about her life, one question after another, like he was shelling his peanuts. It amused Dean to see this side of Ed, who rarely initiated conversation at family gatherings, maybe because he knew everything already. Or maybe it was easier to let Joelle take charge.

Laura turned to Dean. "That was awkward at the game. I'm so sorry. I got nervous. There's no reason we can't still be friends."

"You were just trying to do right by Robbie," Dean said.

The mood between them relaxed, but then neither of them knew what to say next, so they let themselves be drawn into Ed's conversation. He was telling Abby about his latest side venture, a cardboard-shredding operation he had set up using an old wood chipper. According to Ed, there was a market for shredded cardboard among alpaca farmers. Dean couldn't tell if this was actually true or one of the many lines of bullshit that had earned Ed his Cowpie nickname.

"There's a ton of people raising alpacas on the Eastern Shore," Ed said. "A whole sheep and wool community. You should see their hairdos; everyone has white-and-gray dread-locks, like they're trying to be sheep. You know how people say dog owners start to look like their dogs?"

"Does that mean dairy farmers look like cows?" Dean asked.

"What do you think, could I pass for a bull?" Ed flared his nostrils and made horns above his head with his fingers.

"Maybe if you got a ring through your nose," Laura said.

Ed's laugh, a deep bellow, made everyone else laugh, too.

They drank quickly, amid increasingly vulgar jokes about farming life, but when Laura made a move to get the next round, Ed insisted that he had to go.

"Sorry," Ed said. "I have to be up early to milk the ladies."

"Yeah, I should get going, too," Dean said. But he was disappointed.

"I could give you a ride if you want to stay," Laura said.

Dean declined, but Ed interrupted, saying he could drive Dean's car back. "Just have Laura drop you at our place."

"That works for me," Laura said.

"It's settled, then," Ed said, with a wink that didn't even try to approach subtle. "I'm going, you're staying."

Abby left, too, to Dean's surprise.

"She never stays out late," Laura said. "I can't seem to find a drinking buddy around here. Not that I'm a huge drinker. But sometimes you need to let loose."

"Sure," Dean said. "Especially with all the delinquent kids you have to deal with."

"Oh, let's forget about that!"

"Wait, did you think I was talking about Robbie?"

Laura smiled at him, fondly, like they were old friends. "How did you end up here, anyway? I mean, in Willowboro?"

"I got a job, and then I fell in love with someone who lived here."

"But why did you take *this* job? You could have worked anywhere."

"Not really. Willowboro was the only place small enough to give me a head coaching position at twenty-five—or wait, twenty-six. I was twenty-six when I moved here. Before Willowboro I was on staff at a Div I school in Virginia."

"But you didn't like that?"

"I did, but I wasn't going to wait ten years to get promoted. I wanted my own team. They basically let me start from scratch here. There was a football program in place, but it was still pretty new. Not what it is today."

"So the football team is your baby."

"I wouldn't put it that way. I have actual kids. The boys on the team, they're not my sons."

Laura smiled. "Okay, let me ask you this: Was there any point when you thought twice about staying here?"

"Not really," Dean said. "I guess you think I should have, though."

"No, of course not! It's just that Tim and I have been talking about, well, marriage. And where we'd like to live if we get married. A lot of his family is here. They would think I was crazy if I moved him away, especially if it was to no place in particular. I mean, if it wasn't to be closer to my family. Which it wouldn't be."

"You don't get along with your family?" Dean asked. He realized he knew very little about her upbringing.

"We get along fine, but we're not close. We're not like Tim's family. They see each other all the time, and all the little cousins play together. Not that we're planning on kids yet. But he does want a big family."

"That's good, right?" Dean said.

"Yeah. It's just . . . a lot." Laura picked at the label on her beer bottle. "I think Tim thought that as soon as I got offered a full-time job, I'd be ready to talk about the future. And that was definitely a factor. But it's not the only thing I'm thinking of."

"What else are you thinking of?"

"Oh, stupid things. Superficial things. I guess I never thought of myself as the kind of person who would settle down in a small town. You should have seen my boyfriend before Tim. We were going to travel the world together."

"You mean the goat farmer who brought you to this god-forsaken place?"

"Yeah, him. He was a very alternative guy, lots of tattoos, lots of, um, political views. Tim isn't like that. With him, *I'm* the wild one."

"He sounds like a good guy." Dean wondered where he landed on Laura's spectrum.

"Yeah, he is." Laura stood up. "I never got us that drink, did I? Last round, okay?"

Her jeans rested loosely on her hips, and when she walked, her T-shirt rode up, revealing the smallest glimpse of her waist above her thick belt. Dean thought of the one time he'd held her, but then pushed the thought out of his mind, willing himself not to be attracted to her. He tried to think of her as a daughter; he imagined himself describing her to someone that way: *She's like a daughter to me.* But that only made him think of Stephanie, who had left the game without saying good-bye. He wished she would go to college, stay there, let herself be spirited away to adulthood on a raft of books and high-flown ideas.

Laura returned to the table with two glasses of whiskey. "I decided I was tired of beer."

Dean took a sip of the amber liquid, savoring its warmth. He thought of his sons, sleeping cozily at Joelle's, probably tucked into the twin beds in the guest bedroom, the one with the shaggy carpeting that smelled vaguely of breakfast foods (it was right above the kitchen). He and Nicole used to sleep there, on Christmas Eve, when the farmhouse was still occupied by Nicole's parents and they all lived by the fiction that Santa Claus made just the one stop. Dean wondered how well the boys remembered those days and whether they missed them. He was a bad father to leave them alone without warning, thrusting them onto their Jesus-freak aunt. He was shirking his responsibilities, he was a shirker, he was behaving just as Joelle said he would. Joelle had never trusted him, not really. When he and Nicole announced their engagement, Joelle made him promise never to move her away. And Dean had promised, because he was in love, and what did he care where he lived, as long as he could coach his own team and be near this beautiful, melancholy woman and her eager, chatty toddler. His life came into focus after he met them.

"I did worry about living here," he said. "Now that I think about it. Not because I didn't like it here. But I thought maybe, one day, after I got some experience, I'd want to coach a bigger team, at a bigger school. A place with more money. More talent."

"What changed?" Laura asked.

"I don't know. I became a father. Life got busy. I stopped thinking about what else might be out there. Or maybe it's that people started to accept me."

"How long did that take?"

"Longer than I thought it should. People around here are friendly, but they're not as friendly as they think they are."

Laura nodded. "Most of them have never had to start over. They don't know."

Dean remembered a secret wish to start over with Nicole. To move to a place where people would assume he was Nicole's only love and that Stephanie was his biological daughter. There were times when he almost had Nicole convinced, when she and Joelle had one of their minifeuds or when her father, Paul, was being especially rigid. But then she would worry about leaving her mother alone, or about taking Stephanie from her grandparents. And Dean would see that these were excuses, that she was too scared to go someplace new. He might have coaxed her, but his own fears intervened. The last thing he wanted was to get stuck someplace where they knew no one and she was pregnant and resentful and borderline depressed. He didn't think their marriage was strong enough for that. Or maybe he wasn't strong enough for it. Same difference.

"Maybe I'm having a midlife crisis," Laura said. "I'm getting it out of the way early."

"You would know if you were having a midlife crisis," Dean said. "Trust me."

"Oh, Dean," she said. "I'm so sorry. Here I am, talking about my stupid life and you have real problems."

"I like talking about your stupid life," Dean said. "You know that."

THE BARTENDER KNEW Laird, and they bought drinks without any trouble. They sat in the back where no one would notice them, a corner booth that afforded a glimpse of everyone in the bar. Stephanie had never really seen Willowboro's nightlife and on some level she assumed there was none, that everyone did their socializing at football games or church. She associated bars like this—wood-paneled and sports-themed—with movies and TV shows, and so its very banality struck her as exotic. She felt almost glamorous sitting with this good-looking boy, a boy who was trying to impress her by bringing her to a place he considered adult. They drank rum and Cokes, and Stephanie felt the booze hitting her in a floaty, festive way.

"I knew we would see some teachers from school," Laird said. He nodded toward a woman standing at the bar. She wore a cap-sleeved tee and jeans with a beat-up old belt that Stephanie admired. Her hair was in a low ponytail from which wispy strands had escaped, framing her face. She looked familiar but Stephanie couldn't quite recognize her in the dim light. Stephanie wondered how you got to be like her: young but grown-up. She wished she could leap over the next ten years and just be an adult with a job and a boyfriend and a vintage belt.

"Is she new?" Stephanie asked. "I don't remember her."

"That's because you're not a guy," Laird said.

"You think she's sexy?" Stephanie was surprised; she thought this woman's appeal was too subtle for teenage boys.

"Definitely," Laird said. "Especially for a teacher. She talks like us and she has this leather jacket she wears."

"Oh my God, you totally know all about her."

Laird shrugged, unembarrassed. "I would see her in the halls. I wonder if she has a boyfriend. She wasn't married."

They both watched as she carried two drinks across the crowded room. A man was waiting for her at one of the small square tables against the wall, a graying older type, but Stephanie barely glanced at him; she was more interested in this woman. She tried to picture her walking down the hallways at school, wanting to remember how she knew her.

"Uh-oh," Laird said. "We better get going."

"Why?" Stephanie said, unnerved by Laird's tone.

He looked confused. "Isn't that your dad?"

Stephanie looked back at the woman, now sitting at the table with the older man. Her first split-second thought was that Laird was mistaken, that her father was not as old as the man she'd glimpsed, but all at once she realized he was right. Her heart began to pound, as if her blood was actually pulsing with this new information. And she had gathered so much more information than she realized: In those objective seconds, before she recognized her father, she had seen a portrait of two people who were more than acquaintances or even friends. They had the kind of physical attraction that you could see across a room, like someone had drawn a circle around them, bringing them together.

"We have to go," Stephanie said. But she didn't make a move to leave. She couldn't stop staring at the woman. She recognized her now; she was the lady from church, and before that, the lady in the cafeteria. Stephanie had never given any special thought to her, but it was as if some part of her mind had detected something amiss and held on to the memory of her.

"Come on." Laird guided Stephanie out the back door. Outside it was unexpectedly chilly, as if autumn had arrived while they were inside. Stephanie shivered in her thin cardigan and jean skirt, and Laird put his arm around her as they walked to his car. When he pulled away to get his keys, she wouldn't let him and instead put his other arm around her. He laughed and said, "Okay," even though she hadn't said anything, and he kissed her softly, their lips barely touching because his head was bent awkwardly. Stephanie leaned back against his car, and they began to kiss in earnest. He was calm at first, deliberate, but as their kisses deepened, his breathing got heavier and he took a step away from her. "What?" she said, feeling her cheeks redden. Her whole body felt like it was blushing. All she could think was *more*. Nearby they heard someone getting out of their car, the doors slamming shut, laughter.

"I was just thinking—we could go to my old house. No one bought it. I still have the key."

DEAN THOUGHT IT would be exciting to be in Laura's car, this small, intimate space, but instead he felt cramped. He was disappointed to learn that she was messy, to see the empty soda can in her cup holder and the backseat cluttered with papers and binders. She was a good driver, but she drove fast, especially considering how much she'd had to drink. The familiar countryside spooled past, everyone's house lights out, everyone's lawn full of dark, innocent shapes: hedges, lawn ornaments, picnic tables. Sheetz loomed in the distance, an alien, neon-lit structure. If Dean were alone, he would stop and get something to eat. A slushie, a sub, a chocolate-frosted doughnut. Anything to extend the night. That was the problem with staying up this late. Something happened after midnight; he lost his strength, the tiny bit of willpower he needed to get through those chasm minutes alone in bed before he fell asleep.

Laura almost missed the turnoff that led to Ed and Joelle's farm, swerving at the last minute. The farm's long driveway, which snaked behind the town, parallel to Main Street, was a mixture of gravel and dirt, deeply rutted by tractor wheels. Laura struggled to fit her little car's wheels into the ruts and they bounced uncomfortably. "Sorry, sorry."

"I hope you can find your way home," Dean joked. But he was actually a little bit worried.

"This is good, it's sobering me up."

She had her high beams on, and to Dean's relief she turned them down as they approached the farmhouse and barn. Still, her headlights caught the night-shining eyes of some little animal—probably a cat—and she lurched to a stop. "I don't want to hit a skunk," she said. "I did that my first week here. Oh my God, it was disgusting. I had to take it to a mechanic to get the smell out."

"You can pull in over there," Dean said, pointing toward the barn.

Laura came to a surprisingly smooth and quiet stop, shutting the lights and engine off. The music cut out abruptly and all at once it seemed very dark inside the car.

"So here we are." Laura kept her hands on the steering wheel, her bare arms looking slender and pale in the darkness. She turned toward him. "I shouldn't have bombarded you with all my issues. I've ruined any chance of helping you. Or Robbie."

"You haven't, I promise," Dean said. He wanted so badly to touch her. But her mention of Robbie was a jolt to his conscience. He slid his hand into the door handle, cracking the passenger door. Cool air rushed in.

"I guess I'll see you around," she said.

"Yeah, soon." Dean's leg was out the door now; it was as if his body was coaxing him out of the car, away from the fantasies his mind was spinning.

Dean watched as she drove slowly down the lane, the brake lights flashing every few seconds. After a few moments, the landscape was dark again. Dean walked over to his car. Ed had left his keys on the seat. The last thing he wanted was to drive home. In the distance, he could hear Laura's car making its way down the driveway; but it was odd, it sounded as if she was getting closer. His heart began to beat more quickly as he saw headlights swinging toward him. They cut two silver paths down the lane, illuminating swaths of gravel and leaves. But it wasn't Laura's car; the headlights were too square, too wide apart. It was Geneva, Dean realized, in her shitty old Ford sedan. He couldn't help smiling, even though he was disappointed.

Geneva came to a stop and leaned out the driver's-side window. Her gray hair was slicked back, held in place by a puffy cloth headband, and she wore bright earrings. "Get in," she said. "Come have a nightcap with me."

"I've already had a lot."

"Come on, I want someone to celebrate with. I won fifty bucks tonight!"

He got into her car, which smelled like her lilac perfume. Geneva had stopped the car in second and it stalled when she pressed the gas. "Whoops!" She shifted back to first and gunned it. The road became less defined the farther they went. By the time they reached the end of the lane, it wasn't much more than a cow path. Geneva pulled to a stop beneath a sycamore tree. "Here we are."

Dean breathed in the damp, sweet, faintly rotten smell of the pasture that was Geneva's front yard. At night, in the dark, it seemed especially expansive, a lake that kept the entire farm at bay. He could see why she preferred to live down here instead of in the farmhouse up by the main road.

"You stay on the porch," Geneva instructed. "I'll bring out our drinks. I think I have some of Paul's old liquor."

Dean sat down in the rocker his father-in-law used to inhabit, up on the farmhouse porch. It creaked as he leaned back. He looked up at the night sky, watching as the half-moon slid out from behind the clouds, casting its cobweb light across the field. Dean didn't know how Nicole could stand to leave the world behind.

Geneva emerged from the house with two neat whiskeys.

"So guess how I'm going to spend my winnings?" she said, settling into her chair.

"Filet mignon for the buzzards?"

"Ha, no, I'm buying lingerie! Joelle leaves her Victoria's

Secret catalogs in my mailbox now; she doesn't want the girls seeing them. I told her, it's Ed you have to worry about. Which she did not appreciate. I told you, she has no sense of humor anymore."

"Did she ever?"

"You'd have to have one to marry someone like Ed."

"He's not so bad," Dean said, thinking of how Ed had left him alone at the bar with Laura.

"He came down here the other day with this hangdog expression. He says, 'Geneva, I have to talk to you about those buzzards. It's against the natural order of things for you to feed them. They're supposed to eat dead things, not cat food.' I said, 'I know, that's why I've started feeding them roadkill.' He gives me this look like he doesn't know what to think, so I go on, I say, 'What do you think I do in the mornings when I take my car out?' And he turns pale and says, 'Geneva, please tell me you're not picking up dead animals.' I said, 'I wear gloves, don't worry.' And he gets all concerned. And then I start laughing and he's so nervous he has to wait a minute, to be sure I'm kidding. Oh, you should have seen his face!"

"You shouldn't pull his chain like that. Or Joelle's. They're going to think you're losing it."

"They already do!" Geneva's bright earrings bobbed as she laughed. "I have to admit, I like having those buzzards around. I don't know why; maybe it's because they're not afraid of death."

"I can see that."

"Can you?" Geneva said. "I wonder about you, Dean. You're so self-contained. The way I see it, when something bad happens to you, you either button up and batten down, or you go a little crazy. Obviously, I chose the crazy route. But you? I'm not so sure."

"I'm battening, I guess."

"I couldn't do that," Geneva said. "I don't have the self-control."

"I don't know that I do, either."

"Oh, please. I've never met anyone more disciplined."

"That's the problem. I need something to be disciplined about. Something to do. I can't go to another football game and sit in the stands and eat hot dogs. And I can't go to work every day, come home, and be with my kids. I can't. I'm not built that way. I have to have some sort of goal, some sort of fight. Sometimes I wonder if that's why Nic, if that's why she— if she didn't have a sense of purpose. And maybe that's my fault, maybe I should have given it to her."

"Dean, you could have given her the world. I can't make sense of it, Jo can't make sense of it, and if Paul were alive, he wouldn't be able to, either." She paused. "Actually, maybe he would. He had his dark days. Nicole always took after him. Joelle takes after me. Not that it's that simple. Paul was happy when he was old. He turned a corner after he had grand-children. Life has many phases. That's what I would say to Nicky if I could talk to her now."

Dean looked toward the southern end of the pasture, trying to see if he could make out the little cemetery just beyond it.

"Have you gone to Nic's grave?" he asked.

"I go every Sunday."

"I haven't gone back yet."

"Well, she's not there."

"I know," Dean said. He returned his gaze to the sky. "She used to say I'd be happier without her."

"She didn't mean that," Geneva said. "But don't be afraid to prove her right."

LAIRD'S HOUSE WAS furnished sparsely with rental furniture, some of it blatantly fake, like a large gray plastic television without any wires connecting it to the wall, while other items were uncanny, like a mantel of gold picture frames, all with the display photos still inside, so that the family in absentia seemed to consist of multiple wives and a dozen children. In the kitchen, a variety of cereal boxes were lined up in the cupboard, *Seinfeld* style. When they first arrived, Stephanie and Laird toured the downstairs, commenting, letting their eyes adjust to the dim light. There were no shades or curtains on the windows, and light from the waxing moon filled the rooms.

"There are even beds upstairs," Laird said, leading her up the carpeted staircase. In his other hand was a plastic bag with two tall boys and a bag of pretzels. They'd stopped at the Sheetz on their way over.

"Why do they bring all this furniture in?"

"My dad says it helps the house sell," Laird said. "That's what the Realtor told him. It's bad that they didn't sell it before we moved. But my dad had to start his new job. And they didn't want me to start the school year here and then move."

"But you would have wanted to," Stephanie said.

"I don't know anymore." Laird reached ahead to feel where the wall was. It was darker in the upstairs hallways because there weren't as many windows. "We should have gotten a flashlight, I guess—here, come with me." He stopped feeling for the wall and took her hand.

They turned into the master bedroom. A queen-size four-poster bed loomed in front of them. There were windows on either side, and the moonlight gave the quilted comforter a blue tint. Laird pulled back the quilt. There weren't any sheets.

They both looked at the bare mattress. Some of the intensity of their kiss had burned off during their car ride, but it was still there, beneath their conversation.

"Let's go to my room," Laird said. "This is too much my parents' room."

They both laughed when they saw what had become of Laird's room: there was a crib, a child's dresser, and an airplane mobile hanging from the ceiling.

"This is actually mine," Laird said, standing next to the little dresser, which reached his waist. "I keep one sock in each drawer."

They had better luck in what Laird referred to as the guest room. There was a platform bed there, a desk, and two chairs. Laird pushed the chairs together and moved them in front of the window so they could sit and drink their beers. It was light beer, and it had a thin flavor that Stephanie didn't mind. She let it warm her as she looked out at Laird's backyard, an unadorned lawn bordered by a split-rail fence. Beyond the fence was an overgrown field where orange construction flags seemed to indicate future development. But there were flags like that all over Willowboro. Most of the time, they were just wishful thinking.

"It's weird to be here," Laird said.

"I feel like we're ghosts."

Laird laughed. "You're so morbid! You and that guy you always hung around with—Catrell."

"You mean Mitchell?" Stephanie felt a twinge of longing. He still hadn't written back to her e-mail.

"Yeah, Mitch, that's him. You guys were like the Addams family. We'd always be, like, 'Where's the funeral?'"

"Yeah, I *know*," Stephanie said. "I was there."

"Sorry, we were just kidding." He touched the ends of her hair. "Is this your natural color?"

Stephanie shook her head. "It's blond—kind of."

"Why did you change it?"

"I don't know. To be different, I guess." To Stephanie's surprise, she felt tears coming on. It was as if Laird was exposing all her various costumes. He was more sure of himself than she was, she realized; he had a better sense of who he was. Where had he gotten it, she wondered—from his parents? From the football team? From her father? It seemed unfair that this boy should have been given—and guilelessly accepted—the very thing she wanted most in the world.

"Hey, don't get down," Laird said. "You know we only said stuff because we thought you were cute."

Before Stephanie could think of anything to reply, he took her beer out of her hand and placed it on the windowsill. Then he began to kiss her. Soon they were undressing. Stephanie's jean skirt was a hand-me-down from her mother, and as Laird pulled it down, Stephanie had a disconcerting thought: her mother might have had sex wearing this skirt. She wanted to stop everything, to tell Laird that this was all new to her, that she'd never even seen a boy naked before, but at the same time there was the voice in her saying *more, more.*

They paused to move to the bed. The cheap bedspread was scratchy on her back and she felt self-conscious about her body, but then Laird apologized for being "so hairy" and she relaxed. They figured things out. They had time, she realized, to figure things out. The silvery moonlight was forgiving, Laird was forgiving—the scratchy fake bedspread was not forgiving. They pushed it aside. Laird's hands were shaking when he went to get a condom from his wallet, and Stephanie wondered if it was his first time, too. Having sex hurt and then it didn't. She wondered if it would always be like this, a stinging feeling followed by warmth and sensation. It reminded her of swimming in cold water, that mixture of unpleasant and exhilarating.

"Oh, I am so sore and this feels so good," Laird said, his words murmuring together.

He meant he was sore from practicing. Or maybe he was sore every day, with his muscles always tearing and repairing themselves. Maybe he was happy because his life revolved around his body. Stephanie wanted some of that happiness for herself and pulled him closer, leaning into him.

Chapter 5

The boys' cross-country coach had the healthy yet grizzled look of a long-distance athlete, a body and face chiseled by extreme exercise and a lot of time spent alone. His name was Erik Philips and Dean had never talked to him at length, although he had always been impressed by his athleticism. His long legs were muscular, especially his skinny calves, which had been recently shaved for a cycling trip. He had a kind of pent-up energy about him, as if he might break into a sprint, and he spoke with intensity, a vein on his forehead bulging as he discussed the finer points of cross-country racing strategy.

"It seems easy now, right, nice and flat?" Philips pointed to the soccer field, a pristine expanse that the runners had been instructed to circle twice. "But when you get in the woods, it's uphill for a mile. One of those sneaky, slow-burning hills that doesn't seem like a hill until you're five minutes in and your legs are dying and you say to yourself, 'Why am I so friggin' slow?'"

They were doing the course walk, a prerace ritual that Philips took seriously. Dean had hoped to convince him to take over the girls' team officially, but the first thing he said to

Dean was that he was so relieved he didn't have to coach girls anymore. He didn't know what to do with them; he worried about injuring them accidentally. "Girls have loose ligaments," he told Dean. "It has to do with their hormones. And then their periods get synced up, that's another thing you have to keep track of."

Philips was a true runner, a man who liked to start his day with "a six-mile jog." On the weekends he biked, planning all-day road trips along the Potomac River where he could ride on the flat, shaded C&O Canal trail. Dean didn't even have to ask to know that he didn't have a family.

"I gotta catch up with my men," Philips said. "There's a turn coming up that I want them to take note of. Tell the girls: it's good to catch people before a turn."

He jogged ahead, disappearing as he passed a herd of Middletown runners. They seemed like royalty in their white-and-gold uniforms. Dean's girls were trailing behind them in faded blue singlets. Dean noticed that Jessica had dropped back and was now walking a few yards behind Aileen and Lori. (See-See, who knew the course well, had stayed behind.) He approached Jessica cautiously; there was something stern and quiet about her, with her delicate body and her neat French braid going straight down her back.

"So what do you think of the course?" he asked her.

"Oh, I love it. I love trail runs. And I think this one is one of the prettiest. But it's slow. No one's going to get a PR."

"What's a fast time?" Dean asked. "What does a first-place runner usually get?"

"It depends on the course." Jessica pointed to a runner

ahead of them, a girl from Middletown. "See that girl over there? The one with the high ponytail?"

"The short one?"

"That's Adrienne Fellows. She's going to win the race. She wins every race."

"Does that mean Middletown wins every meet?"

"Usually," Jessica said. "But not always. They have a lot of runners, but none as good as Adrienne."

Jessica then began to explain the intricacies of cross-country scoring, which she likened to the scoring of card games. You could win a game of gin rummy even if you never won a hand, simply by playing smart and never getting stuck with a high card. Same with cross-country meets. Even if none of your runners cracked the top five, you could still win if your top five runners managed to beat the fourth and fifth runners of other teams.

Clearspring's coach, who was leading the course walk, interrupted them. "We're going to make a sharp U-turn up ahead," he said, yelling to be heard. "Then you'll be going downhill for about a half mile, back toward the school."

"This is my favorite part," Jessica said.

"Seems like it would be everyone's."

Jessica shook her head. "Some people hate going downhill. They get so afraid of falling that they slow down. And then they fall anyway."

Dean had a vision of Nicole and Stephanie running down the hill behind the farmhouse—before it was Joelle's house, when Nicole's parents still lived there. It was summer, and Stephanie was little, maybe four years old, with squat legs and arms that motored to keep up with her mother. Nicole was trying to run slowly, so as not to get too far ahead of Stephanie, but at some point she gave up and let gravity take hold. The joy in her body was obvious as she leaped across the last few yards of grass. Dean remembered feeling as if there was something eternal in that joy. As if it was some salient quality that would never leave his wife.

LAIRD'S HOUSE WAS filled with morning light; it shone unimpeded through the bare windows. Stephanie woke up in a mellow, observant daze, faintly hungover and hungry. Laird's broad back faced her, an amazing situation. She tickled the back of his neck. Then a flicker of urgent feeling prodded her to remember something about the morning.

"Shit!" she said, sitting up. "The meet."

Laird rolled onto his back, rubbing his sleepy eyes with his big hands.

Stephanie was already getting dressed, changing out of Laird's Pearl Jam T-shirt and pulling on her skirt. She felt self-conscious changing in front of him, but when she turned away from him, she was facing the unadorned window. And there were houses nearby! Where had they come from? Last night, she and Laird had lived in their own moonlit world. She picked up their empty beer cans and tied them up in the plastic bag. She put the chairs back and rubbed the wall-to-wall carpeting with her foot, trying to erase the indentations the chairs' legs had made. Everything seemed so sordid, the rental furniture dingy. She remembered her father at the bar, sitting at some flimsy table, with that *Laura* across from him. How long had he been seeing her? Had her mother known?

She thought of her mother trying to cut the lemon in the morning light.

"What meet?" Laird asked.

"It's nothing, I have to go. We have to fix the quilt. What if the Realtor comes?"

"I can drive you," Laird said, pulling on his boxers.

"I have to go to Clearspring. That's, like, an hour away."

"You think I have someplace better to be?"

She felt a wave of affection for him, this boy standing in the guest room of his old house.

They stopped at Sheetz for doughnuts and coffee drinks from the cappuccino machine. The sugary brew cut through the fog of her hangover, as did Laird's music, a worn-out mix-tape of hard-edged rock bands like Korn and Nine Inch Nails, bands that would normally be too aggressive for her. But that was what she wanted to hear now, as she stewed over her father's transgressions. Outside, the overcast sky was giving way to sunshine, and by the time they reached Clearspring, the place was an illustration of its name, seeming to exist in its own cloudless atmosphere.

Laird wanted to come to the meet, but Stephanie didn't want her father seeing her with him.

"I'm sorry," she said. She gave him a frugal peck on the cheek and then impulsively kissed his neck.

"No, you're right," he said. "I just don't want to go home."

The starting gun went off as Laird was driving away. The noise came from the soccer fields, where a horizontal line of runners was quickly becoming vertical as they headed toward the perimeter of the field. Stephanie stood at the edge of the school's parking lot, uncertain of where to go. In the race, one girl was already pulling ahead of the others, her gold uniform like a little light for the others to follow. Stephanie had actually run cross-country her freshman year of high school, but only for half a season. She dropped out when she realized that the satisfaction she felt at the end of a race didn't begin to make up for the pain she felt during it. And she couldn't really relate to the girls on the team, who were true athletes beneath their nerdy, skinny veneer. They actually cared whether they won or lost, whereas Stephanie had just been looking for a sport that she didn't hate. That was when she was still trying to want what her parents wanted for her, the simple things they thought would make her happy: health, popularity, routine. A wholesome ideal that would only work for someone who was already whole, who didn't have big parts of her life missing. It had taken all of high school for Stephanie to stop pretending as if pieces of her past weren't missing: her father, her grandparents, her mother's happiness. Now, as she gazed at the long line of girls running around the empty field, it occurred to her that identifying the missing pieces was not enough, that she was also going to have to complete the picture of herself without them.

Stephanie made her way through the crowds of spectators. Everyone here had probably had granola and apples for breakfast, and they had probably eaten it after going for a sunrise jog. The running crowd was *very* wholesome, and their early-morning vigor made Stephanie feel guilty all over again. They were all wearing cuffed shorts—better to show off and stretch their muscular legs. Fleece vests abounded. Stephanie felt dirty and absurd in last night's clothes, her silly grandma cardigan and denim skirt. She took off her rhinestone earrings and shoved them in her handbag. She thought of her mother, how she was always dressed to the right degree of formality. It was a tendency that Stephanie used to see as conformist and demure, but now she wondered if her mother wasn't just trying to fit in, if she dressed carefully as a way to pass as a happy, well-adjusted person.

The runners disappeared into the woods one by one, and a large crowd of people moved toward a flag in the middle of a scrimmage field. Stephanie followed them, her cheap cloth shoes getting soaked with dew. They were Chinese laundry slippers with flimsy rubber soles, like limp Mary Janes. Stephanie ironically referred to them as her "signature shoe," buying three or four pairs at a time at the hippie shops in Shepherdstown, the college town just over the Potomac in West Virginia. She'd actually applied to Shepherd College and been offered a full scholarship. She could have gone there without the Shanks paying for anything. Maybe she should have.

The flag in the distance turned out to be the two-mile marker. Stephanie heard her father before she saw him; he was calling out splits to a pack of girls emerging from the woods. Then she heard her brothers' smaller voices.

"Go See-See, go See-See, go See-See, go!"

Stephanie knew See-See, although she didn't recognize her at first, because her hair was now short, bleached, and spiked. Last year it had been dark blond with long daydreamy bangs. See-See had been in Stephanie's creative writing class, and Stephanie associated her with one of her short stories, a story about a girl who survives a terrible car crash. The girl is left with an ugly scar across her stomach, a scar the girl hates, but over time, the appearance of the scar changes from a straight line to a gentle U shape—a smile. The story was called "The Smiling Scar."

"Steffy!" Bryan called. He ran over to her and hugged her hard, pressing his face into her body, so unself-conscious. Stephanie leaned down to complete the hug, rubbing his back and kissing his forehead. He smelled like fresh air and cinnamon toast.

"Where were you last night?" Robbie asked, hanging back.

"None of your business," she said lightly.

"Dad is PO'd."

"Yeah, he seems pretty broken up."

Their father was standing too close to the freshly mown course. He kept checking his watch and then looking at the course—the watch, the course, the watch, the course. A girl in blue was approaching, and he crouched and yelled forcefully, "Come on, Aileen. Get up there with See-See!"

"She's good," Stephanie said, watching her glide by on daddy longlegs.

"Our team sucks," Robbie said.

Their father turned around. "Stephanie! You're here!"

He ran over to her and pushed a clipboard into her hands. "I'm going to call out the splits and you write them down. Aileen got fourteen twenty-one, and See-See had thirteen thirty, which is good, very good. If she keeps up that pace, she's going to break twenty-two."

Two blue runners were approaching and her father began to holler. "*Go Blue!*"

Bry began to run alongside them, his short legs pumping. "Go blue! Go blue! Go blue!"

"He looks so dumb," Robbie said.

"He's cute," Stephanie said, remembering happier times in their family, when they were a big group of five and Bryan's role was always the little clown.

"Here comes Lori," her father said. "She's going to be six-teen something."

Lori was a feminine girl whose pink skin, yellow hair, and rounded limbs made her look like a stuffed doll. She glanced at Stephanie's father when she ran by, giving a quick smile to acknowledge that she'd heard her time. A few minutes behind, a second doll-like girl appeared, but this one was a porcelain doll, with pale, blue-veined skin and dark red hair pulled back into a tight braid. As she ran by—at a heartbreakingly slow pace—Stephanie recognized her as Jessica Markham, the smartest girl in school. She was famous for completing all the math courses by the end of her sophomore year and was sup-posed to graduate early.

"Steffy, come on." Bryan pointed toward their father, who was jogging toward the gym and the finish line, delineated by two rows of fluorescent flags.

What started out as a jog soon turned into an out-and-out run. Stephanie cursed her shoes and then eventually pulled them off to sprint barefoot in the grass. Her hangover, briefly in hiding, reemerged, and by the time she reached the finish line, her legs and head throbbed with pain. Nearby, an over-sized digital clock ticked off the seconds. A skinny man ran up to her father.

"You missed it. Adrienne Fellows broke the course record," he said. "That girl's talent is wasted in Div III."

"Have any colleges shown interest?" her father asked.

"She's probably going Ivy. I heard she's smart," the man said. "But those schools have crap running programs."

"Not everyone wants to devote their life to sports," Stephanie said.

The man turned toward her with an expression that made her realize how foolish she must seem in her wilted party clothes. *I'm smart, too,* she wanted to say. But all he could see was a girl with a hangover, a girl who didn't take care of herself. Maybe he even knew she'd just had sex.

Stephanie's father began to yell at the top of his lungs, startling her. "Come on, See-See! Come on, girl, you can do it!"

See-See heard him and began to kick harder, her stride becoming shorter and faster instead of lengthening, like a taller girl's would. There was a girl in a green uniform in front of her, from Clearspring, who was also trying to kick, but whose face was strained with exhaustion. The knobby-kneed man began to cheer along with her father and See-See's arms pumped, reaching forward as she passed the Clearspring runner. Her jaw was clenched in a tight, perverse grin. *The Smiling Scar,* Stephanie thought.

"She's a real competitor," the man said. "Here comes another one."

It was Aileen. She was obviously tired, but there was a lightness in her stride that hinted at hidden reserves of strength. When she finished, she stopped cold and then began to jump up and down on her kindling legs, nearly prancing. Stephanie felt oddly jealous as she watched her father guide Aileen and See-See out of the chute to congratulate them. Their faces were red with exertion. "There's Lori!" Aileen cried. "Lori, Lori, Lori!" she chanted.

Lori staggered down the chute on her stuffed-doll's limbs, her body seeming to move forward only by means of some rote memory of movement, not out of any real desire to do so. Runners from other teams breezed by and she didn't seem to notice or care.

The clock read 26:50 when she finally crossed the line. Jessica finished thirty seconds later, looking even more worn-out than Lori. They were dead tired. Stephanie thought it should be the other way around; the top finishers should be the most wrung out, the most pathetic. Instead, the top finishers were now jogging in the soccer field in random patterns, occasionally kicking out their legs or pinwheeling their arms, as if their bodies were giant toys.

"Hey, do you mind keeping an eye on the boys?" her father said. "I'm going to take the girls on a cooldown."

"Sure, whatever," Stephanie said. He was barely making eye contact with her, a sure sign he was angry. But he had no right to judge her; she knew how he'd spent his night.

Spotted Mountain rose up beyond the playing fields. It wasn't a particularly tall mountain, was perhaps not even technically a mountain, but it was known locally for its spectacular views. It was said that from the top you could see north all the way to Pennsylvania and south to West Virginia. Whenever people from school asked Stephanie where she was from, she had taken to borrowing her father's phrase, "the skinny arm of Maryland"; that way people got the proximity to both states.

Halfway up Spotted Mountain was the Outdoor School, a

sleepover camp that every kid in the county attended for a week during sixth grade. Stephanie remembered her week there so clearly; it was her first time away from home, away from her mother. She had been so excited to go, relieved to get out of a house dominated by two little boys, but her mother had been very emotional about their separation, making her promise to write every day. Stephanie had dutifully sent a postcard each morning before breakfast, but she didn't read the letters her mother sent. She always meant to, but at the end of every day she was so tired from hiking and bird-watching and orienteering and cooking outdoors that she never opened them. Stephanie wondered now what had happened to those letters. Her mother must have found them when she unpacked her bags.

Her father returned, slightly winded, his forehead shining with sweat. He seemed happy.

"It's a world away from football, huh?"

"You said it, I didn't."

Her father smiled, an old smile, like the ones he used to share with her when she was a little girl. For a moment, she forgot she was angry with him.

The bus took them back to Willowboro High from Clearspring. Dean waited around at the school to make sure everyone got a ride home. See-See was the last to get picked up. Her mother drove a tan Toyota Tercel, an ugly termite of a car, but she acted as if she were driving a Ferrari, speeding into the lot and coming to a dramatic stop in front of the school. She waved to Dean but didn't bother to roll down her window.

"Great race," Dean said to See-See as he sent her off. She smiled so hugely at this casual compliment that he felt protective toward her. On the bus ride home he'd overheard her talking to the other girls about her mother's latest boyfriend, a salesman who always wore striped shirts with white collars. The shirts seemed to be a black mark against him, but Dean had no idea why. He felt sorry for the salesman boyfriend— and for See-See. If he ever dated again, he would keep it a secret from his kids.

"I'm hungry," Bryan whined. "Can we get lunch at Asaro's?"

"Let's go somewhere else."

"But I want pizza."

"I could go for Asaro's," Stephanie said.

Dean glanced at Robbie, who surprised him by raising his eyebrows and shrugging in an adolescent way, as if to say, *What's the big deal?*

"All right, pizza it is. Give me a minute, I have to get something inside." Dean tossed the car keys to Stephanie. "You can go ahead to the car, I'll meet you."

The empty parking lot sparkled in the midday sun, radiating heat. Dean felt a kind of satisfaction at how much had been packed into one morning. And at the same time, there was dread at the thought of the long, empty afternoon ahead. Was this how Nicole felt, on bad days? He still wasn't used to weekends without her. And now Stephanie was back. He needed to get into a new rhythm with the boys, and she had jolted things out of sync. He'd been embarrassed to introduce her to the cross-country girls in her soggy shoes and wrinkled clothes. He had no idea where'd she slept. He didn't even want to deal with the possibility of sex. But the girls didn't seem to notice or care about her unkempt appearance, or maybe they expected her to dress that way, maybe that was her reputation: disheveled but smart. Dean didn't have a clear picture of how Stephanie was perceived by her peers. She was one of those kids who moved in and out of lots of different groups of people. A good thing, he'd always thought. Or maybe it meant she was lost.

The gym was cool and dark, a sanctuary as always. His office, in contrast, was stale and hot. He opened a window to let in some fresh air and saw the football team gathering on the field for their postgame practice. His chest tightened with longing. They were just starting their day and had a long, sunny afternoon ahead. There was nothing better than working out after a victory.

He'd told the girls he'd run their practices for the next week, until their coach arrived, but he was already beginning to regret that promise. He had nothing to say to four mediocre girl runners. Still, he had admired the way See-See had finished her race with gritted teeth, a race that didn't matter, a race neither she nor her team could win. He wasn't sure if he'd be able to do the same.

His whole life, he had always been on a winning team.

He began to search through his PE files, hoping to find something about running stowed away. It had been a long time since he'd bothered with lesson plans, so he was pleased to discover a list of several track-and-field workouts, as well as some xeroxed articles about stretching and the training habits of elite runners. There were also maps of the school's cross-country course and nearby trails. He grabbed everything, stuffing it all into a manila folder.

When he came back outside, Stephanie had pulled the car around to the front of the building. He thought she would move to the passenger side as soon as he approached, but she stayed put in the driver's seat.

"We're not going to Asaro's," she said, leaning out the rolled-down window. "Robbie told me everything. How he's been going there for lunch, how he got in trouble, how he's seeing a *psychiatrist*."

"*Bry* told her," Robbie said.

"I didn't mean anything by it!" Bryan said. "I was just making conversation."

"Robbie's been talking to the school counselor, it's not a big deal." Dean couldn't understand how the mood in the car had changed so quickly.

"Dad, he *ran away*," Stephanie said. "That's a serious cry for help."

"Stop talking about me!" Robbie covered his ears. Then, upon second thought, he opened the side door and took off running across the empty lot.

"Robbie!" Bry called. He began to scoot across the backseat to follow him, but Dean blocked him.

"You stay put," he said, pointing a finger at Bry.

"Don't yell at him, it's not his fault!" Stephanie unbuckled her seat belt. "I'll go get Robbie."

"You'll stay right here." Dean barely looked at her, instead keeping his eye on Robbie, who was now heading toward the greenhouse at the far end of the school.

"I should talk to him. I know how he's feeling. I've been thinking of seeing a therapist."

"Well, that's just great." Dean couldn't keep the sarcasm out of his voice.

"You're against my seeing a therapist?"

"Of course not! I'd rather have you do that than come home and wallow in your misery, going God knows where at night."

"You're the one who should be explaining where *you* were last night."

"I'm not going to apologize for going to a football game."

"That's not what I'm talking about. I saw you." She glanced at Bry in the backseat. "I was at that bar. That's all I'm going to say."

"Get out of the car," Dean said.

Stephanie shut the door behind her.

"What were you doing in a bar?"

"What were *you* doing? Who was that? Were you seeing her before Mom died?"

"No," he said. "Not that it's any of your business. She's my friend."

"She looked like more than just a friend."

"I didn't do anything wrong, Stephanie. You were drinking underage. You could have been arrested."

"I've seen you with her before."

"Believe what you want," Dean said. "I'm going to go get your brother."

Dean made his way across the asphalt toward Robbie. But he could only think of Stephanie. He never would have talked to his father the way she had just talked to him. Even after his mother left, Dean had not been so sullen—although he had certainly blamed his father for not being able to keep his mother around. Once, when his father was hospitalized for a broken leg and high on painkillers, he told Dean that his mother had cheated throughout their marriage, that she was notorious. Dean remembered that word—*notorious*—

because it was the name of one of the horses his father trained. Dean didn't want to be like his father, tight-lipped with secrets that slipped out under chemical influence. But how could anybody be expected to talk to their kids about suicide?

He found Robbie all the way at the other end of the parking lot. He was sitting in the overgrown grass near the greenhouse that was adjacent to the school's woodshop. Behind him were the clouded shapes of tables, plants, and trees. He looked up at Dean. "Sorry," he said.

"You don't have to be sorry." Dean sat down next to him. The ground was still a little bit wet from the morning's dew.

"You're really not mad?"

Dean shook his head.

"Stephanie seems mad."

"She's mad at me," Dean said, "not you."

"Why isn't she at school?"

"What's going on with you?" Dean searched his son's face for some clue of what motivated him. He still had a babyish profile, round cheeks and soft, wispy hair.

"Nothing much." Robbie plucked one of the taller grasses and began to tie it into a knot.

"There's a lot of new kids, right? Have you made new friends?" Dean said. The middle school was large, bringing together the graduating classes of four littler elementary schools.

"Not really," Robbie said. "Everybody sticks with the people they already know."

"What about joining an intramural team? You could try out for soccer," Dean said. Soccer was the only sport Robbie had ever mentioned.

"Actually, I tried out for *The Wizard of Oz*. They had auditions in my chorus class because they need a bunch of kids to be munchkins."

"Wait, you tried out for the high school play?" Dean said.

"Yeah, and I got the part!" Robbie couldn't help grinning as he spoke. "I'm going to be a munchkin—and a flying monkey and a poppy flower. And I'm singing in the chorus."

"Okay," Dean said. The parts sounded silly to him, more suited to Bryan, but Robbie was obviously proud.

"What's the matter?" Robbie said. "You don't want me to be in the play?"

"It's not that."

"You think I should play a sport."

"I think you should be with people your own age," Dean said.

"They don't do a play in middle school," Robbie said. "And I like older kids. I don't like kids my age."

"You might if you got to know them."

Robbie shrugged. "I don't want to play soccer. I'm not good at it. No one's good at it. It's boring to do something that no one's good at. And everyone's bad at everything in middle school. I'd rather be around older kids who know how to do things. What's wrong with that?"

"Nothing," Dean said. He worried that Robbie's longing for older kids had to do with Stephanie's absence, and that his desire to playact, to live in fantasy, had to do with Nicole's death.

"The rehearsals are pretty much every day after school," Robbie said. "So I'll be out of your way."

"You're not in my way."

"The stage is so big," Robbie said. "My friend Mark was in *The King and I* in fourth grade. He was Anna's son. Do you remember that? He stood on the side stage, and they made it look like a boat."

Dean had no memory of this performance. He'd accompanied his children through the world, and yet sometimes it seemed to him as if he had no way of knowing what really mattered to them.

He stood up and brushed the grass off his shorts. "Come on, let's go home—okay?"

Back at the car, they found Stephanie and Bry listening to the radio with the windows down. Stephanie was flipping through the folder of running stuff he had taken from his office.

"You left this on the roof of the car," she said, handing it to him.

"Thanks." He stuffed it under his seat.

"I'm going back to school as soon as we get home."

"Sounds good to me," Dean said, starting the car.

He exited campus the back way, behind the middle school, so he wouldn't have to go past the football field. He didn't want to see the team practicing. And he couldn't bear to observe local etiquette, honking his horn as he drove past. They would recognize his car and wonder where their old coach was going. Or maybe they wouldn't wonder. Maybe they would just wave, and get back to their training.

Chapter 6

The next morning Dean awakened early from a disturbing dream. He and Laura were on his bed, which was strewn with Nicole's clothes. She undressed, revealing breasts that were like Nic's. "You're too young," Dean said. He meant she was too young for breasts like that, breasts that had borne the weight of three pregnancies, but she thought he was trying to push her away. She began to cry and then she became Nicole, who put her hands on his face and said, "Didn't you want her all along?"

It was Sunday, a day for sleeping in, but when Dean closed his eyes, his just-shed dream netted him again, Nicole's soft voice in his ear. He flung it away, swung his feet to the floor, and pushed back the curtain on the window. The sun was rising, its pale light beginning to fade the stars.

He checked on the boys. They both slept on their stomachs. Bryan still had a lovey, a stuffed giraffe whose long neck got into odd positions at night. This morning the giraffe was pushed off to the side, lying facedown near the edge of the mattress. Nicole used to say it was keeping watch for monsters.

Stephanie's room was empty, untouched. Her bed was still

neatly made with the sheets Dean had washed before her arrival. She'd never even slept on them.

He'd called her dorm room yesterday night, but she wouldn't talk to him. Her roommate, a meek-sounding girl who addressed him as Mr. Renner, picked up. There was a muffled pause after Dean asked for Stephanie and then the same soft voice said she was sorry, Stephanie wasn't around after all. Dean didn't push back against the lie. Now that she'd seen him in the bar, she had a reason for her anger, a point to focus on. Dean hated to think of the stories she was concocting.

When it came to Laura, he wasn't even sure what the real story was anymore.

It was too early to wake up the boys, so he decided to go for a jog. He had to get in better shape if he was going to keep attending races. Outside the air was cool and soft. In the dim light, everyone's backyard gardens were abundantly and deeply green, with their tall rows of corn and sunflowers, and their bean plants and tomatoes climbing chicken-wire cages. Small piles of freshly pulled still-green weeds lay around the perimeter of each garden, evidence of industrious Saturdays. Dean felt virtuous just looking at them.

His heart was beating hard to match his foot strikes. He was going fast, maybe. Or maybe he was tired. He decided to run all the way to Iron Bridge, or rather, the ugly cement thing that had replaced it. Dean's thighs burned as he made his way up the hill that preceded the bridge. His thoughts burned away, too. When he reached the top, he was breathing with a ragged intensity that reminded him of being young. Holding on to that glimmer, he ran hard down the hill, toward the creek, letting gravity lengthen his stride. The pain increased, and by the time he reached the bridge he had to stop. He looked down at the water flowing past and then checked his pulse, timing how long it took for his breath to return to normal. He recalled the agony of running when he first started training in the summers, as a teenager. The sharp stitches at the side of his waist. The weight of his lungs. He used to smoke then, taking a dizzy hit of nicotine after workouts. Then he would douse his face and hair with the garden hose, the water warm at first and then icily cold. In the nearby fields, his father would hose down the horses until their short-haired bodies gleamed like metal. Looking back on that time, it was like his life was one physical sensation after another, with time stretching to contain them all in one unbroken chain. And yet he was impatient to break free, to move away, to become a man, whatever that meant.

He hurried home, worried that the boys would wake up and find him gone.

But they were still asleep when he got back. He stretched on the living room carpet, listening to the radio, some nuts-and-bolts news analysis, a weekend roundup. They played a clip of President Clinton speaking at a campaign rally, hoarsely and vaguely, asking voters to consider the historical consequences of various presidencies: "Think how different this country would be if Abraham Lincoln had not been president when the states said, 'Well, hey, we formed this country; we've got a right to get out.' And then to face the next question: 'Well, if we're going to stay together, don't we have to quit lying about who we are?'" The words hit Dean's conscience like stealthy arrows. His marriage—it was built on . . . what? Not lies, exactly. But not the truth, either. One of the commentators was saying that peace and prosperity were the president's greatest assets. Dean liked Clinton but he didn't trust him completely; he reminded Dean of the silver-haired big spenders who came to the track with their girlfriends, the ones who gambled as a way to show off how much they could afford to lose.

After a hot shower, Dean felt almost normal. The boys woke up and he fixed a big breakfast of pancakes and bacon and fruit. Although he had been planning to take them to church, he decided at the last moment to take them to the Antietam Battlefield, which was closer than church, and for Dean, more sacred.

The park was busy with tourists, as well as the runners and cyclists who took advantage of the empty, paved roads that snaked through the quiet battlefield. Dean made the boys read aloud a few of the plaques. He realized it was close to the day of the actual battle. The bright sky, the clear light, the slight hint of autumn on the breeze—all of it was just as it might have been on the morning of what turned out to be the single bloodiest day in American history. Twenty-three thousand men dead in one day. God knew how many horses. Dean couldn't get his mind around the number. It was a Union win on paper, but there were historians who had devoted their lives to the study of what actually occurred. How it affected the history of the war. The history of the country. Shortly after the battle, President Lincoln had issued the Emancipation Proclamation. It was as if he had to acknowledge what the war was really about.

Driving home, Dean felt calmed. Battlefields gave him perspective. It was their peacefulness that awed him. As if the ground itself had absorbed the violence and confusion of war and made it disappear.

Dean spent the afternoon cleaning. The house needed it, but he was also feeling guilty. About Stephanie. About Laura. About Nicole. He made the boys do the bathrooms before they could play outside, as if they needed to do penance, too.

He cooked dinner again—pork chops with baked apples, one of the few dishes he'd learned from his mother. The boys wanted to watch *The Wizard of Oz* to celebrate Robbie's part and Dean let them, even though it was a long movie for a school night. After the scary parts were over and Dorothy was safely on her way down the yellow brick road, Dean excused himself to call Stephanie. No answer. He tried again later, during the poppy field scene, but he got the roommate again. He left a message, giving up for the day. If she didn't want to talk to him, so be it. She would come around. Still, he felt addled and uncertain.

After he put the boys to bed, he craved bourbon, but instead he pulled out the file of notes and articles about running that he'd gathered from his office. He wanted to plan some real practices for the week. An hour slipped by as he worked on a training strategy and then it was midnight and he was exhausted. For the first time in weeks he went to bed without the aid of booze or late-night television.

"You know what's great about cross-country?" Dean asked the girls. It was Monday afternoon. They didn't seem quite as forlorn or lacking in athleticism as they had on the first day he met them. And now he had an actual pep talk prepared, the kind he used to give his players. He'd never delivered one to such a small crowd and in such a low voice.

"In cross-country, your past record doesn't matter. You get a clean slate for every race." He paused to let this sink in. "You understand what that means? That means the only race that really matters is States. That's the big dance, right? You get to States, you've got yourself a race."

"But you have to qualify for States," See-See said.

"*Yes!*" Dean pointed at her, like she'd won a prize. "So the race *before* States matters, too. Okay. But that's not for another six weeks. Do you know how many practices we have before that?"

Jessica raised her hand. "Are you counting Fridays?"

"Fridays count," Dean said. "From here on out, every day counts. Every day is practice. You know how many miles you can run in six weeks? Over a hundred. Easily. In fact, we'll probably hit a hundred and fifty. And for those of you who choose to run on weekends, you'll get up to two hundred. But mileage isn't even what matters most. What matters most is speed. Pacing. Having a kick. I guarantee, if you have a kick in your pocket, you're going to take down competitors. So let's get out there and run fast."

They looked bewildered but obediently jogged to the track, where Dean led them through an interval workout of six timed half miles with thirty-second rest periods in between. By the end of the third half mile, they began to complain.

"I can't run fast anymore," Aileen said. "I'm too tired."

"Good," Dean told her. "I need to know how fast you can run when you're tired."

The following afternoon they joined the boys' team on

the nearby C&O Canal, where Philips liked to bike. They ran as a big group on the flat, shaded towpath, with See-See and Aileen eventually breaking off to run with the slower boys. The miles slipped by without anyone noticing. When they arrived at the canal, the sun sparkled lazily on the Potomac, and when they ended, an hour and a half later, it was a fall evening, the sun low and golden in the sky and the air smelling faintly of campfires.

Dean was in a good mood that night, and when he picked up the phone and it was Laura's voice on the other end, he felt even better. She said she'd been thinking about him. He said he'd been thinking of her, too. But before he could go on, she interrupted and said that she thought they should keep things professional. And then she told him that Robbie had gotten into trouble again at school. With the aid of a forged note, he had lied to his English teacher and told her that he was needed at the high school for a special choral rehearsal. And then he had walked over to the high school and hung out backstage with the woodshop kids who were helping to design the sets. When his lie was discovered (by the woodshop teacher) and he was returned to the middle school, he had been sent to Laura to confess.

"His teachers want to pull him from the play, but I've discouraged that course of action," Laura said.

"Good. He's excited about it," Dean said, surprised to find himself defending the play.

"I'm glad you understand that."

"He's my son," Dean said, testily. He was annoyed by her "professional" tone. A few nights ago they'd shared drinks, confidences, near-kisses.

In the same careful voice, she proposed a meeting, and Dean lost all patience and just said what he had to say to get through the conversation and off the phone. Laura was confusing him. His dream of her, of her turning into Nicole, of Nicole's hands on his face, of Laura's breath on his neck, had stayed with him.

Upstairs, he found Robbie and Bryan in Stephanie's room, watching MTV on her little black-and-white TV, the 1970s model that had once been Dean's. The TV downstairs was much bigger, but he could see why the boys preferred to hang out in Stephanie's cozy room, sitting cross-legged on her double bed with its bank of pillows and, above, a moody collage of CD covers and flowers cut from seed catalogs—mostly blue and violet flowers, no pink roses for Stephanie.

"Hi, Daddy," Bryan said. "Will you tell Robbie to put on *Jeopardy!*? He promised I could pick a show at seven thirty."

"Why don't you go downstairs and watch it," Dean said. "I have to talk to your brother anyway."

"Is this about today?" Robbie said. "Because I want Bry here if you're going to yell at me."

"Nobody's yelling at you."

"What did you do?" Bryan asked, his bright little face at once eager and nervous.

"Nothing. My teachers just freaked out when I went over to the high school to help out with stuff for the play."

"That's not the whole story," Dean said. "Now will you please go downstairs, Bryan?"

"It *is* the whole story," Robbie said. "Everyone treats me like I'm psycho."

"Do you want to get pulled from the play?" Dean said. "Because you could just as easily come with me after school and go to cross-country practice, like Bryan does."

"That would be so fun!" Bryan said.

"Oh my God, why are you always *such* a dork?" Robbie said.

Bryan frowned suddenly and tearfully, like he used to do when he was a baby, and Dean had to get him out of the room fast, taking him downstairs and setting him up in front of the TV with a bowl of pretzels. When he came back upstairs to Stephanie's room, Robbie had turned off the TV and was lying on Stephanie's bed, staring up at the ceiling.

"You need to be nicer to your brother," Dean said.

"I'm sorry, but he's, like, always around," Robbie said. "I have no privacy. At school all the teachers spy on me."

"You created that situation."

"I don't see what the big deal is. I should be able to go places. I'm not some little kid."

Dean hated that Robbie saw himself that way, as no longer childlike. He remembered feeling the same way when he was Robbie's age, after his mother left his father. It had given him comfort to think that he was more grown-up than others, and that he was somehow well suited to the difficult circumstances he found himself in. But as an adult he saw what a delusion it was. And he thought there was something pathetic about a deluded child. Delusions were for adults to cling to; children were supposed to be innocent scientists, peeling back the layers of the world.

"Look, I know you're responsible, but other people don't," Dean said. "Your teachers don't want you having special privileges."

"And you don't, either."

"Actually, I vouched for you. And so did Ms. Lanning."

"You told them I should do the play?"

"Yes, I did. I want you to be happy, and I want you to do the things that make you happy. So don't mess that up, all right?"

"All right."

Dean headed back downstairs and watched the rest of *Jeopardy!* with Bryan, grateful for his company but also horribly lonely. He had mixed feelings about Robbie going to the high school every day for the play. On the one hand, it wasn't that big a deal; on the other, it was further evidence that Robbie wasn't going to grow up to be someone he could easily relate to. He'd always imagined his children would be his comfort, his companions.

It stormed that night, and the next day it rained on and off all afternoon, the beginning of bad weather. Dean drove the girls to the junior college, where there was an indoor track. Something about being indoors—the novelty, the cooped-up feeling, the sound of the rain on the skylights—helped the girls to run faster. At one point the rain was very heavy, and the muffled sound of the wind seemed to drive the girls. They had energy to burn at the end of practice and wanted to try the hurdles that were set up in the far lane. But Dean said no, they might get injured. That was when he realized he believed in them.

On Thursday, his niece showed up at practice. It was a sunny day, crisp, like the weather was trying to make up for the previous day's tantrum. Dean stood at the gym door, waiting for the girls to arrive. He could see the football team jogging in the distance, doing their warm-up laps around the field. This weekend he was supposed to attend a Boosters' fund-raiser at

Garrett's house. He'd asked Joelle to babysit as a way of forcing himself to go.

"Uncle Dean?"

He turned to see Megan standing tentatively near the gym bleachers, a pair of new sneakers on her feet. They were bright white with a teal swoosh and a kind of peekaboo window to showcase the air bubble within the thick soles. They looked like small appliances on her feet.

"Aileen said to meet her here for practice," she said. "She goes to my church? She says you need runners?"

"Does your mom know you're here?"

"My dad dropped me off." Megan glanced down at her new shoes. "He got me these."

"I don't want to get in the middle of something."

Just then the other girls showed up, entering the gym together, not one at a time like they had the week before. When Aileen saw Megan, she sprinted ahead, waving. "You came!"

Megan looked to Dean, expectantly.

"Promise me you'll tell your mother?"

"As soon as I get home!" Megan said. "Thank you, Uncle Dean!"

Dean had planned a fartlek workout, a training method he'd gotten from one of his old xeroxed articles. It was a long, untimed run, during which the girls would take turns setting the pace—fast or slow depending on how they felt. It was a team-building workout, and so it was slightly awkward to have his niece randomly in the mix, especially since she didn't know her way around the high school campus. When it was her turn to lead, she made unpredictable turns, forcing the other girls to stay close to her. Her foot strikes were fast and even with her new shoes flashing white, teal, white, teal, back and forth, back and forth. It took Dean a moment to think of who she reminded him of: Adrienne Fellows, the championship runner. They had the same small, efficient build.

When the workout was over, the other girls asked Megan the question that Dean wanted to know: Could she come to the race on Saturday?

THAT NIGHT JOELLE called Dean. He assumed it was to chew him out for letting Megan attend practice, but instead she wanted to know if she could take the boys to church on Sunday morning. Since she was planning to babysit them anyway, they could stay overnight. It would be easier, she argued.

"Okay," Dean said. If he gave a little on this, maybe she would give a little on Megan.

"Really? Oh, Dean, I'm so happy. I think they'll like it. We have this new minister. He's very young, very inspiring. You know, I think you might even like it, too."

"I don't know about that," Dean said. *Give Joelle an inch . . .*

"How's Stephanie?"

"I haven't heard from her since she visited."

"Oh. Well, maybe that's good. She's probably busy at school. It's good she's getting on with her life."

Joelle had said pretty much the opposite thing before Stephanie left, but Dean chose not to mention it. Instead he told her that Megan had shown up for practice. And that she was gifted. And that she wanted to run on Saturday.

"She told me she was with Aileen this afternoon," Joelle said.

"Aileen's on the team," Dean said. There was no point in mentioning that Ed had dropped her off. She would figure that out on her own.

"I can't believe she would lie to me."

"Kids lie. They just do. But as far as lies go—"

"This one is not going any further! She can't run, I'm sorry. I don't expect you to understand, but I've seen what happens with other families. One of the kids gets really into a sport and then all of a sudden they aren't showing up at church on Sundays and they're missing prayer groups during the week, and that isn't what I want for my family."

"But this is just running," Dean said. "And she's doing it anyway. The meets are on Saturdays—"

"Dean, stay out of this. All right?" Her voice was sharp.

"All right."

He got off the phone. He had the urge to call Stephanie to complain. She was the only person in his life who would understand. But he'd been trying her room every day, and he always got the meek roommate. It was getting embarrassing.

The next day, one of his students reminded him of Stephanie. He noticed her during the timed mile run, which he was required to administer every year, for the President's Fitness Challenge. He liked to do it early in the semester because it helped him to learn names. The girl had Stephanie's long legs and broad shoulders, but it was her attitude more than her physique that reminded him of his daughter. The way she held her large head high, her chin jutting forward, ever so slightly, in subtle defiance. She didn't like the fitness test and when he called out to her that if she kept her fast pace, she would be in the 99th percentile, she gave him a look like *What do I care?*

But she didn't slow down. In fact, she went faster. That was like Stephanie, too.

A group of boys who had finished their mile began to cheer for her. "Go, Missy!" She scowled, and all at once Dean remembered meeting her at Sheetz, before school started, when he was still the football coach. Smoot's sister. Of course she was fast!

"Did I make your ninety-ninth percentile?" she asked Dean, a few seconds after sprinting over the line.

"Easily," he said. "You should go out for cross-country."

"Yeah, right." She raked her hair into a fresh ponytail.

"I'm serious," he said. "Come to the small gym after school. I'm meeting with the team. It's not a practice; we're just going over some stuff for tomorrow's race. You can meet the other girls and see what you think."

Missy regarded him through smudged eyeliner. He felt certain she was going to turn him down.

"All right," she said. "I have to wait for my brother anyway."

"Great, we'll see you then." He felt like a salesman for how hard he had to work to hide his excitement.

That afternoon, Dean told the girls about Missy, and when she didn't show up, his disappointment hit hard and he felt foolish for saying anything. The girls seemed let down, too. They had dressed up for their meet the next day and looked older in their skirts and dress pants, their loafers and modest heels. Their proximity to adulthood stilled him. He could imagine them with jobs, marriages, children. He got the same feeling, sometimes, when the football players gathered on game days, clean-cut in suits and ties. And with this feeling, he always noticed, came a strong sense of responsibility.

SATURDAY'S MEET WAS in Left Creek, West Virginia. Dean had to wake up early to meet the girls. The boys were late getting up and had a breakfast of graham crackers in the car. Outside the fog was heavy, floating above the pastures and soybean fields along Iron Bridge Road. The cows were like ghosts, visible if you looked for them.

When they arrived at the school, the parking lot was empty. A girl was sitting on the curb and she stood up to greet them, waving. It was See-See; Dean recognized her bleached hair first, and then her muscular, ever-so-slightly bowed legs. She was wearing a faded blue baseball cap that did not quite match the blue of her uniform.

"You took all your earrings out," Bryan observed. He knew the girls well now, from going to practices.

"You can't race in them." She tugged on her naked earlobe. "Hey, Robbie. Long time no see! How's the play?"

"How'd you know I'm in the play?"

"I'm friends with the Cowardly Lion."

"You know Seth?" Robbie seemed to wake up for the first time that morning. "He's really funny."

See-See smiled. "He likes to think so, at least."

The bus appeared, emerging from the fog like some big yellow dinosaur. Two other cars were hidden behind it, and they pulled up to the school to deliver members of the boys' team. A third car joined the line and then drove around the bus to pull right up to the curb, where Dean stood. It was Bill Smoot, Jimmy and Melissa's father. He leaned out the window.

"Coach! I had no idea you've been trying to recruit my girl. I told her, if Dean Renner wants you on his team, you say yes! Go on, Missy." He nudged his sleepy daughter, who sat in the front seat with a gray duffel bag on her lap. She barely glanced at Dean as she got out of the car.

"She's a good runner, always has been. It never occurred to me to sign her up for cross-country. Can you get scholarships for that?"

"Sometimes, sure," Dean said. He couldn't keep back his grin, even though Missy had clearly been dragged here against her will.

"All right then," Mr. Smoot said. "You have a good race, honey! Call me when you get back."

"I'll get a ride," Missy said. She shut the door and didn't bother to return her father's wave as he drove off.

"How'd you know to meet here?" Dean asked.

Missy nodded toward See-See. "She told my brother. He told my dad." She shrugged. "I don't have the right shoes."

She wore black low-top Chuck Taylors. She had drawn enormous eyes on the sneakers' signature white toe boxes, so that her feet appeared to be staring up at her.

"Those are fine for now," Dean said. "I'll get you a uniform."

Chapter 7

Stephanie really had been planning to see a therapist. The school provided free counseling and there were signs in all the first-year dorms encouraging students to take advantage of it. But when she'd returned to school on Saturday, arriving ten minutes too late for dinner in the cafeteria, she had run into Raquel, who had also arrived too late for dinner. So she and Raquel had gone out for pizza. Pizza turned into drinks and then they had wandered into three different parties, all held in the basements of dormitories. The dimly lit, anonymously furnished rooms, so similar to Laird's house, gave her life a sense of eerie continuity. The next day her hangover felt familiar and borderline luxurious as she and Raquel sat in the dining hall and drank burnt coffee and picked at stacks of syrup-drenched pancakes.

On Sunday night she and Raquel stayed up until three, talking about all the students and professors they had met so far and what they thought of each of them. Stephanie apologized for giving such a bad first impression, and Raquel was forgiving in a way that let Stephanie know that her initial refusal had actually charmed her. And then on Monday morning, Stephanie overslept and missed her therapy appointment.

And then she had just plain skipped her rescheduled session, which prompted the therapist—Jill was her name—to call and deliver a minilecture about the importance of keeping appointments, not only for her sake—Stephanie's sake—but also for the sake of other students who might wish to take up Jill's valuable time if Stephanie was going to throw it away. Stephanie apologized and then, too embarrassed to reschedule, and also rattled by her father's obvious disapproval, lied and told Jill she'd found help elsewhere. "I get enough lectures from my father," Stephanie said later to Raquel, who agreed with her that Jill sounded like a bitch, and that anyone practicing therapy at a liberal arts college instead of having her own private office was probably not that great anyway. "She's probably used to way easier problems than what you would give her," Raquel said. "Like, people with time management issues or alcoholics in training or whatever."

Stephanie had told Raquel most everything about her life, including her mother's death, which fascinated Raquel in a way that made Stephanie feel slightly uncomfortable. Raquel seemed to be in the midst of her own suicide project of sorts, eating as little as possible and smoking unhealthy amounts of clove cigarettes (she called them "dessert"). She hoarded food in particular ways, carrying small paper cups of cereal to her dorm room and filling the pockets of her jean jacket with tiny single-serving containers of cream, which she would divvy up, ceremoniously, into cups of black coffee and Earl Grey tea. She never seemed to sleep. Whenever Stephanie wanted to talk, she was game for a drive to the all-night Dunkin' Donuts, where she would torture a French cruller, tearing it into delicate pieces and perhaps letting a few flakes of sugar melt on her tongue. Stephanie knew there was something off about her new friend, but she recognized her as the kind of girlfriend she had wished for in high school, the rebellious, egotistical bad girl, the girl with impeccable taste, the girl who was a little bit spoiled, a little bit reckless, a little bit selfish. The girl who let you be her mirror.

Their friendship was immediately intense. They stayed up late every night, talking, listening to Tori Amos and Ani DiFranco, smoking, and sometimes even studying for one of their two shared classes, Psych I and Evolutionary Biology. Without planning it, Stephanie began to spend most of her nights on the futon sofa in the common area of Raquel's dorm room. The only break they took from each other was before dinner, when Raquel liked to work out at the campus gym. She always asked Stephanie to join her, but Stephanie's rebellion against jock culture was too strong. Instead she used the time to study in the library, reading for her other two classes, a survey of medieval history and a Great Books course that all first-year students were required to take. The Great Books course was easy for her, mainly because her high school's academic deficiencies had not impeded her study of literature, which she could supplement on her own. History was another matter. She had not, to her surprise, been given a textbook. Instead she had been assigned to read parts of nine different nonfiction books. They were difficult books, almost scientific in their presentation of historical facts. She was accustomed to a mode of history that was more theatrical. Her understanding of the Civil War was almost entirely gleaned from the reenactments at the Antietam Battlefield, where people came from all over the country to dress up as Union and Confederate soldiers and pretend to die in battle. It was such an odd hobby, Stephanie thought. Imagine going back in time and telling soldiers that in the future, people would relive their deaths every year.

Stephanie was still homesick, but she'd learned to bury the feeling, piling new experiences on top of it. And something funny was happening to the passage of time. It had to do with how much she was drinking, how alcohol made the nights race by and the mornings disappear. During the summer, her days had passed slowly, like she was stuck in the molasses of childhood. But even though her days were slow, the summer itself had gone by quickly. It seemed like one day she was sitting in the front pew, listening to Pastor John deliver her mother's eulogy, and then a few days later it was summer's end and she was back in church, watching her father talk to a strange-yet-familiar woman with dangly earrings.

College was the opposite. Although her days went quickly, it was hard to believe that only a week had passed since she'd stood in her high school's parking lot, watching her father walk away from her.

Stephanie was back in her dorm room, now, getting clothes for the next few days. She hadn't been to her room since Thursday, and she had timed her return to avoid her roommate, Theresa, whom she didn't exactly dislike, but who had an annoying habit of presenting Stephanie with all her phone messages as soon as Stephanie entered the room, as if she, Theresa, were Stephanie's secretary and Stephanie was the beleaguered and neglectful boss. Stephanie had no idea how this power dynamic had developed, since, in her opinion, *she* was the subordinate, the one who felt like she had to sneak into her own room.

Stephanie quickly dropped some dirty clothes in the hamper and packed some clean ones into her backpack. She gazed at her closet, uncertain of what else to take. She and Raquel were heading into Philadelphia tonight, to a club Raquel knew about. Stephanie had no idea what to wear to a club. Something black, she guessed. Something short.

She heard the door open and there was Theresa, carrying her dinner in a fogged-up take-out container.

"Oh, hi," Theresa said. "You have, like, ten messages from your dad."

"Thanks, I saw them."

"Are you ever going to call him back?"

"Maybe."

Theresa sat down at her desk and opened her container after putting her napkin on her lap. She was going to sit there and eat tofu stir-fry in front of her computer, like college was a desk job.

The phone rang. Theresa gave her a look.

"I'm not here," Stephanie said.

"I'm not getting it."

They both stared at the phone, a beige clamshell touch-tone that Theresa had brought from home. It was exactly like the phone mounted on the wall in Stephanie's kitchen, the phone that she and her mother would sometimes let ring on lonely school nights when her father was out. Stephanie picked up the receiver and then dropped it back down in its cradle, shutting it right up. She wasn't trying to be aggressive, but she succeeded in shocking Theresa, who acted as if Stephanie had killed something living.

"That might have been for me!"

"They'll call back if it's important."

"I don't understand what I did to offend you," Theresa said. "You're never here."

"It's easier to stay over at Raquel's," Stephanie said. "You don't want me waking you up in the middle of the night, do you?"

"I'm just confused because you said on your housing forms that you weren't a partyer," Theresa said. "I mean, that's why we got put together—"

The phone interrupted them. Theresa grabbed it so quickly it was almost slapstick.

"Hello . . . ? No, she's not here. Okay—who? Robbie?"

"I'll take it!"

"Oh, she just walked in the door—" Theresa managed to say. As if Robbie cared.

"What is it?" Stephanie said. "Why are you calling? Did something happen?"

"No . . ." Robbie's voice was tentative. "Steffy, what's wrong?"

"Nothing! Is Dad there? Did he put you up to it?"

"I'm at Aunt Joelle's. I told her I needed to call you and she said okay."

"Where is Dad? Did he go out?" Stephanie imagined her father sitting in a candlelit restaurant with that woman from the bar—that *Laura*.

"He went to a Boosters party at Mr. Schwartz's," Robbie said.

"He's still doing football stuff?"

"Just this," Robbie said. "It seemed like he didn't want to go, but he had to because Mr. Schwartz has been so nice. He brought us Redskins T-shirts the other day. But I would never wear them because we learned in school that it's rude to say redskins. None of the drama kids wear sports stuff, anyway. I like hanging out with high school kids better than middle-school kids. I think I'm mature for my age."

"You *are*," Stephanie said, settling into the call. She asked about Bryan, who, Robbie reported, was downstairs playing Sorry with Megan and Jenny. That meant Robbie was upstairs on the extension in their grandparents' old room, probably lying on their old bed, with its faded paisley comforter.

"Bry is turning into a Jesus freak," Robbie said. "We have to go to church with Aunt Joelle tomorrow and he's so excited—"

"*Have* to?"

"Because Dad's staying out late at the party, so it's easier."

"You don't have to go to church." Stephanie glanced at her roommate, who was eating her dinner and pretending to read her e-mail, not getting the hint that maybe she should step out of the room for a few minutes. "Don't worry about Bry. It's just a phase."

"Yeah, but now he wants to hang out with Aunt Joelle and do church things. And then Dad is with the cross-country girls every day, and on the weekends we have to go to races. I never get to do anything I want."

"What about the play?"

"I *love* the play. But I don't have any friends. They all think I'm strange because I have to go see the guidance counselor. I have to miss class."

"Is it during a class you don't like, at least?"

"It rotates."

"Well, it's good to see a counselor. I told you I saw a counselor." Stephanie caught Theresa looking at her, like she knew it was a lie. Well, she probably did know; she probably had to field calls from the health center, too.

"I have to go," Robbie said. "Aunt Joelle is calling me."

He hung up before she could set a time to call again.

"Was that your brother?" Theresa asked.

"No, my eleven-year-old boyfriend," Stephanie said. Bitchy. For no reason. Something about Theresa's vulnerable desire to please reminded her of her mother. She turned her attention back to her closet and found the black dress with yellow sun-flowers, the one that used to be her mother's, the one she had altered to make her own. She quickly changed into it, pairing it with black tights, her jean jacket, and black lace-up boots that Mitchell had outgrown after just two months.

Raquel was waiting for her downstairs in the lobby, by the phone booths. She wore a 1960s-style wiggle dress, made of some awful/fabulous synthetic fabric. Stephanie had never known anyone with so many cool vintage clothes.

Raquel ran her fingers through her burgundy Manic Panic hair. "Come on, let's get out of here already."

GARRETT LIVED IN one of the brand-new condos plopped down in a cornfield near the school. Their architecture mim-icked the design of the clapboard row houses in town, and they looked odd in the middle of the empty field, the awkward first guests at a party.

The cul-de-sac street was lined with cars, parked and double-parked, almost all of them trucks and SUVs—big, shiny vehicles for the big, shiny-faced ex–football players who drove them. Dean checked his reflection in the rearview, procrastinating. He'd tried to make an effort, shaving and putting on a sports coat, but he was in a sour mood. The morning's meet had gone badly. Missy had stopped running halfway through the race. Just stopped and started walking. He worried she was hurt and ran across the field to help her. But nothing was wrong. She was tired, she said. Her feet hurt, her legs hurt, and even her lungs hurt. Dean told her it was supposed to hurt, that if it didn't hurt she was doing it wrong. She wasn't even breathing very hard.

"Doesn't it drive you crazy that these other runners are passing you?" he prodded her. "You had a good lead."

"I know I'm faster than them, I don't have to prove anything."

"But you do have to prove it. That's what a race is." Dean didn't know how to motivate someone who didn't care about being beaten. "You want to tell your parents you quit your first race?"

"They're not even here," Missy said. "They went to watch my brother practice."

"Finish the race. Then you never have to run another one in your life."

For whatever reason this got her moving, and she ended up coming in third for the team, ahead of Jessica and Lori. But he didn't compliment her. Instead he told her she had run the race poorly, and that he would rather see her run the race correctly for a slower time. Then he made her go on a two-mile cooldown, no stopping allowed. When she returned, she said she was quitting. He told her she had already quit, during the race, and that she couldn't do it again. It was the kind of antilogic she couldn't argue against. Instead, she said nothing, not even good-bye when her father picked her up. Her rudeness stung more than Dean liked to admit. He had to remind himself that he'd dealt with worse.

A bunch of blue and white balloons danced above Garrett's mailbox. Garrett greeted him at the door, opening it before Dean had a chance to knock.

"Coach! I'm so glad you came. What's this? Miller? Classic, just classic."

Garrett's condo was very warm inside. It smelled like potpourri and onion dip, with a hint of Mr. Clean. The furniture was a mix of new, matching items and a smattering of painted wooden "country kitchen" decorations that had to have come from his girlfriend.

"There's plenty to eat," Garrett said, guiding him toward the kitchen. "Connie made everything."

"I didn't know you two moved in together."

"Not yet. Connie's too traditional. But I made sure she liked this place before I bought it. It's going to be part of a new subdivision, with a pool and tennis courts and a playground. They're calling it Fox Knoll. I'm going to put your beer in the fridge, okay?"

Dean headed to the spread of food on Garrett's kitchen island. There were bowls of chips, dips, salsas, pickles, a platter of deviled eggs and crudité, and a make-your-own-sandwich station with honey ham and cheddar cheese. Garrett followed him, filling him in on the team's news, as well as his plan for the season. Dean half listened. He couldn't tell if Garrett wanted his approval or if he was talking to him out of a sense of duty. Other people at the party were smiling in his direction, waving, and patting him on the shoulder as they passed. Dean knew almost everyone in attendance. He felt out of place.

"Oh, there's my friend Tim," Garrett said, nodding toward someone behind Dean. "He's here with his girlfriend—actually, his fiancée now! They just got engaged. I can never remember her name."

"Laura," Dean said. Even before he turned to look, he knew it had to be her. She was so pretty, wearing a soft-looking light-blue sweater and jeans. Her hair was down in loose curls. He had to turn around before she saw him. Engaged. She'd gone and done it. He must have been her moment of doubt, her last night out.

"That sounds right," Garrett said. "I'll be right back. I'm going to say hello."

Dean looked for someone to talk with. He was rescued by See-See's mother, of all people. She walked right up to him, pointing a manicured finger toward his chest, like he was her target.

"I have to thank you," she said. "My daughter has never been happier. And that's saying something, because she is one angsty little thing."

"I'm not sure we're talking about the same See-See," Dean said. "She's a real leader on the team."

"Well, kids always show their mothers their worst." She extended her hand. "I'm Karen, Karen Coulter—different last name from See-See, but I'm working on getting it changed back to my maiden name. Which will still be different from

See's, but so be it. Her dad isn't so bad, really. He even said he might make it to one of the meets."

"That'd be nice," Dean said, slightly overwhelmed by her sudden confidences. He'd only ever seen Karen Coulter in profile, when she dropped See-See off. Up close, she had a girlish prettiness, with her sparkly makeup and pink complexion, her cheeks flushed from the white wine she was drinking.

"It would actually be a miracle if he came! He hasn't been around much. And my second husband was no picnic. That's been hard on See. But now, with you coaching the team, it's like she has that father figure she's been needing."

"I've only been coaching a couple weeks," Dean said.

"According to her, it's made a world of difference. She's even starting to think you guys are going to win a meet."

"Don't get your hopes up," Dean said, and then he felt guilty. He would never say that about the football team. He was embarrassed, he realized. He had the sense that other people were beginning to eavesdrop on their conversation and he worried it would be misunderstood, that people would think—what? That he was no longer interested in coaching football? That he was overcompensating with this nothing girls' team? He wasn't used to this kind of vague, amorphous shame, and he didn't know what to do with the feeling.

"Oh, I don't care if we win or lose," Karen said. "I'm not the sports type at all. I just date athletic guys. I'm here with James Price, who apparently you used to coach? He's right over there."

A bulky, round-faced man came over, smiling widely like a child when he recognized his old coach. Dean returned the smile but could barely find little Jimmy Price, the lithe, energetic running back he'd coached for just two years before he'd graduated and gone to college—Towson, if Dean remembered correctly. He'd been a part of Dean's first team. He had to be in his early thirties now, but his conservative clothing, combined with his weight gain, made him look older—though maybe still too young for Karen.

The next few minutes were spent catching up on the past decade of Jimmy/James's postcollegiate life. He'd gone into sales, his product was X-ray film, and his territory had been in New England, a region he liked at first but over time grew weary of. The long winters, the Yankee reticence. Now he was back home and getting settled. He was apparently settled enough to know not to ask after Nicole, Dean noticed. Then again, maybe he didn't even remember her.

Somewhere in Jimmy/James's reminiscences, Dean started to feel depressed. He had become the thing he never wanted to be: a fixture. He was a person that people came back to, a person people referred to in order to assure themselves that some things never changed. And it wasn't as if he ever got to decide that he wanted to be that person. Nicole had consigned him to it, first by being beautiful and kind, and then by being needy and vulnerable, and then by taking her life and leaving him with his sawed-off one—no, not sawed-off, that suggested a clean break, and his life didn't feel cleanly broken. It felt as if something had been ripped out of him, leaving him exposed. People felt sorry for his kids, and he felt sorry for them, too—of course he did—but sometimes Dean thought it was worse for him, in the long run, because Robbie and Bry were already on a trajectory away from their mother. Their lives were separate from her in some fundamental way, while his was intertwined with hers in a way that was impossible to put behind him. She was always going to be with him, his ghost that no one else could see.

Dean excused himself from the conversation with the pretext of getting more beer. He got one of his Millers, but instead of stepping back into the party's fray, where he would no doubt be called upon to recount some "classic" story, he headed to what he thought was a back porch. It turned out to be a short, steep flight of stairs leading to Garrett's backyard.

Dean walked down to the lawn, a small, neat kingdom of freshly mown grass that stopped abruptly at what Dean assumed was Garrett's property line. Beyond it was an open, barren field, its furrows illuminated by the waxing moon. One day it would be filled to the gills with swimming pools and playing fields and another conga line of condos. It made Dean feel a little sick. What was the point of living in the country, of getting pigeonholed and bored and old, if it wasn't at least going to be beautiful?

He heard someone on the landing and immediately ducked beneath the condo, which was raised up about six feet, on beams, to accommodate the small hill that the condos had been built upon—the "knoll" of Fox Knoll, Dean supposed. He felt ridiculous, like a kid sneaking a beer under the bleachers, and tried to come up with an excuse for his antisocial behavior. He used to invent excuses for Nicole. She would always want to leave too soon. Often he took the fall, especially at family events.

"Dean, is that you?"

It was Laura. He felt such relief. She hurried down the stairs when he answered.

"I saw you escaping. Is everything okay?"

"I needed some air." He gazed at her, trying to see her differently now that she was engaged. But he still felt she was his, somehow. That he knew her better. "I never expected to see you here."

"Tim's a Booster now, apparently." She shrugged. "I didn't know *you* would be here."

"Of course I'm here."

"This may come as a surprise to you, but football, sports—that's not the first thing that comes to mind when I think of you."

"What do you think of?"

"I don't know." She started to turn away, embarrassed, and he reached for her arm, awkwardly grabbing her, at the elbow. She took a tentative step toward him and he made up the difference, kind of leaning into an embrace without even trying to kiss her, which he could tell surprised her, but he wanted the warm weight of her body more than anything.

"Sorry," he said, releasing her. "I heard you're getting married."

She stepped back, as if chastened. "I was going to tell you. He asked me on Thursday. It was my birthday. Everyone says it's the best present."

"You don't sound too sure."

"Well, I do feel like he kind of co-opted my birthday. The day was supposed to be about me and now it's about us." She made a face. "That sounds so petty."

"It sounds like you're looking for an excuse."

"To do what?"

Dean took a step toward her to kiss her lightly on her lips, which were dry. She licked them quickly, and he put down his beer, which spilled immediately on the uneven ground. The smell of beer wafted up, mixing with the smells of new construction—wet cement, Sheetrock, sawdust. Dean was aware of the house just a few inches above their heads, the party above them.

"Let's go to my car." Dean felt high, buzzy, excited by his transgression. He felt as young as he had felt old, minutes before.

"I can't," she said. But she wrapped her arms around him and held him more tightly. He slid a hand beneath her sweater and touched her bare back. She shivered. "I have to get back to Tim."

"No, you don't. Go make your excuse and meet me at my car." He didn't know where this recklessness was coming from, unless it was Nicole's ghost.

"We actually drove separately," she said thoughtfully. "Because I thought I would get bored and want to leave early."

"You're bored," Dean said, taking her hand. He kissed the inside of her wrist. "You want to leave early."

Chapter 8

The next two weeks were all about Laura. How to see her. When to call her. They met in the clubhouse, near the football field, and behind the concession stand. Once they unrolled a tumbling mat in the equipment room near the girls' locker room. Dean felt as if he was discovering the high school his students knew, a place full of secret sexual corners. He and Laura even happened upon a young couple once, a girl and a boy Dean recognized from freshman gym. Their lips were so red and swollen that it was as if they'd spent the entire class period kissing. Maybe they had. Dean thought he and Laura would, if they could. But they didn't have as much time.

One morning Laura met him in the parking lot with coffee and doughnuts. "Remember our old breakfasts?" she asked. "I liked you from the start." He couldn't say he felt the same without sounding like a cheater. He felt like he was cheating now. He wasn't convinced that Nicole didn't know. Somehow she was watching him. And yet that sense that he was getting away with something, the idea that being with Laura was some kind of cosmic betrayal, made their sex all the more satisfying. This, he knew, was the particular pleasure of adultery, enjoyed by many before him. For some reason, he'd thought he'd be immune to it.

Laura was cheating, too. She removed her engagement ring when she arrived at the middle school, putting it in her desk drawer. She told Dean she didn't want to see it on her finger. She hadn't broken up with Tim. It was complicated, she said. The complicated part, Dean guessed, was that she wasn't ready to throw over the promise of marriage for him. Once, when Dean embraced her outside the clubhouse, still vaguely in view of the school, she pushed him away, saying, "I could lose my job!" But he thought there was something gleeful at the edge of her voice. Like some part of her wished to blow apart her life, to detonate all her uncertainties about Tim, about marriage, about small towns. You didn't have to be a raging romantic to believe that love—or sex—could obliterate doubt. It could, for a time. Dean knew that from experience, from falling in love with Nicole for the first time—and for the second and third times, for all the times throughout their marriage that she was lost, and then returned to him.

He wasn't falling in love with Laura. Or at least, he didn't have romantic feelings about her; he didn't walk around imagining a future with her and the boys, the four of them living together as a family. His emotions weren't blurring his thoughts. His senses were sharper; he noticed more details: the subtle changes in Bryan's and Robbie's vocabularies, the variances in the strides of the cross-country girls, the moods of his students. The weather was changing, and the newly cold air seemed a piece of the sharpening, his alertness. Food tasted better. Laura looked more beautiful, the color high in her cheeks after they'd been together. And rosy from the cold, too.

Sometimes she stopped by practice, ostensibly to talk about Robbie. That was the excuse if anyone ever asked. But no one ever asked. And they never discussed Robbie. There was too much guilt there, on both sides, and it wasn't the kind of guilt that made things more exciting.

Worries about Stephanie faded. He let them fade. He stopped calling her. But he was reminded of her every morning during his second-period gym class, when he saw Missy. For a week, she refused to come to practice because she was so offended by the way he'd scolded her at the meet. But he didn't apologize. Instead he made her run during her gym period. The fact that she obeyed let him know he had a chance.

He was optimistic because of Laura. He was passionate because of Laura. It started to rub off on the girls during practice. They ran harder. On race day, Missy showed up. Dean wouldn't let her run because she had missed practice. She stood with him on the sidelines and watched as See-See and Aileen got personal records. Dean could feel her impatience.

The next week Missy came to every practice. Dean worked on pacing. He was trying to teach the girls what a 6:30 pace felt like, versus 7:00 versus 8:00 versus a slow-jogging 9:00. The only way to learn was to run the different paces. They went to the track and did quarters, one fast, one slow, one very fast, one very slow, one kind of fast, one kind of slow. He tried to get them to think in numbers, something abstract to distract them from the pain. It was hard to get them to go really fast because they were scared. He told them they had to feel the pain so they would know how fast they were running. How fast they could go. And so they would know how quickly pain could fade. He told them running was managing pain. He wasn't sure this was true. He felt it was true of grieving. He thought you had to get close to the bone sometimes. And then you had to back off. He worried that Laura was a kind of drug for him. That he was using her to dull his sadness. He would remind himself that he knew her before, that there was real feeling involved. That it wasn't just sex and sensation. Other times he felt defiant—so what if it was just sex, just sensation. He wasn't married. He was alone. Nicole was dead; he could do what he wanted.

MEGAN STOOD IN the doorway of Dean's office. Her shoes were bright, toothpaste white, as if she'd scrubbed them that morning. Her hair was up in a tight, high ponytail, the hairstyle pulling at her temples, making her entreating gaze even more intense.

"What are you doing here?" Dean asked. It was barely eight on a Saturday morning.

"I want to race," she said. "I'm dying to try."

"Megan, I can't let you run, you're not on the team."

"It's okay; I've been doing the practices," she said. "Aileen has been telling me them. I do them the day after you give them. But I didn't run yesterday because I wanted to be fresh today. And Aileen's mom made us pasta last night so I'm all carbo-loaded."

"Does your mother know you're here?"

Megan shook her head. "I stayed overnight at Aileen's."

"I have to call her." Dean picked up his office phone. Outside, in the parking lot, the bus was waiting for him. Today's meet was a big invitational in Langford, a large school in the next county over.

"Please don't," Megan said. "She's going to say no. But it's not fair for her to decide."

"She's your mother; it doesn't matter what's fair."

"I just think if Aunt Nic was alive, Mom wouldn't be like this. It's not your fault you can't convince her."

It startled him to hear his niece invoke the alternative world where Nic was alive, a world he thought only he inhabited. He looked into Megan's blue eyes, and it hit him that she looked like Nicole, she had the same intensity of expression. He had wanted, so many times, to see this kind of ambition in his wife's eyes, this desire to compete, to be a part of the world. He couldn't say no to it. Joelle would have to understand.

The girls received Megan easily—so easily that Dean wondered if they'd known about her secret training all along. They had good energy on the starting line. Dean warned them not to sprint too much at the beginning, to remember their pacing workouts. He told them that if they started to feel nervous to remember that this race was practice for the largest races, later on. In truth, the Langford Invitational was one of the biggest races of the year, with runners of a caliber they would not encounter in many other meets, including States.

The gun went off with a cloud of smoke, and Bryan, who was standing next to Dean, clapped his hands and yelled "*GO EAGLES!*" at the top of his lungs. Robbie was waiting at the finish with Philips. Dean looked for his runners, but it was too difficult with blue being one of the most popular school colors. The gold-and-white uniforms of the Middletown runners stood out, and Dean remembered that Adrienne Fellows would be in this race. He wondered how she would do with some real competition.

The course began in an open field and then looped around eight serene tennis courts, bordered by gardens and chain-link fences that managed to look majestic rather than punitive. Public schools like Langford bugged Dean, even though he'd gone to a high school that was just as nice. But he'd felt like he had to earn his place there by being a good athlete, while other kids—kids who stabled horses in his father's barn—felt entitled to a beautiful education.

"Daddy, look, it's Megan!" Bryan pointed toward the courts, where the perimeter trail had forced the runners into a narrow line. But there was a blue-shirted figure running outside the line of racers, like a car driving in the breakdown lane, and she was steadily passing other girls, picking them off one by one. The girl—Dean couldn't quite believe it was Megan—was heading toward an open space near the front of the long, stretched-out pack.

"She's going to be first!" Bryan said.

"No, Adrienne's got the lead." Dean looked beyond the courts to the next part of the trail, a footpath bordered by pine trees, where Adrienne's gold-shirted figure was pulling ahead.

"Come on," he said to Bryan. They had stopped jogging toward the mile marker to gawk at the race. "We have to get Megan's split."

There was a crowd of parents and coaches at the first mile marker, which was at the top of a slight hill near the high school's gym. They began to cheer when Adrienne's head appeared, cresting the hill. Everyone seemed to have affection for her, regardless of school affiliation. Behind Adrienne was a small pack of three runners, each from a different school. They all clocked in with sub-six miles. A good fifteen seconds passed, and then Megan appeared, her gaze on the ground a few feet ahead of her.

"Holy crap, she's beating See-See!" Bryan said.

"She's going out too fast," Dean said. He hadn't even thought to warn her about the adrenaline rush at the beginning of a race. He ran ahead to an open space just beyond the mile marker, where he could talk to her. She saw him then and gave a little smile.

"You're looking good," he said, calling to her as she ran toward him. "It's okay to slow down here if you need to, okay? You need to finish strong, that's the main thing."

He started to run alongside her, but she was concentrating so deeply that he wasn't even sure she'd heard a thing he'd said. "Finish strong!" he said again, before falling back. He turned and saw that See-See and Missy were coming his way. He checked his watch: 6:02. He had three runners in the top fifteen, which was as good as any of the big schools. There was no way it would last and he didn't have the depth to back them up, scoring-wise, but it was so far beyond what he had imagined that he felt a little manic. He wanted to sprint ahead to the second mile marker to see if Megan would hold on to fifth place, but Robbie and Philips were already there. And anyway, he wasn't in good enough shape. There was no way to do that and also make the finish line.

The mile clock hit seven minutes, and then Lori and Aileen appeared, running together, with Lori pulling ahead slightly, buoyed by the crowd's cheering. With just a few weeks of practice, soft blond Lori had become more muscular and, it seemed to Dean, more confident.

"Good steady start!" he called to them. "Good steady start! Now it's time to kick it into a higher gear, you've only got two miles left. That's eight laps on the track. You do that every day in practice, eight laps, two miles, fifteen minutes, that's it, fifteen minutes and it's all over."

"You sound like an auctioneer," Bryan said.

"It's called patter," Dean said. "C'mon, let's get to the finish line."

"No! We have to wait for Jessica."

Jessica passed the first mile marker at eight minutes, twenty seconds, her French braid still stiffly in place. She managed a nod when she saw Bryan, but her face was flushed with exertion, as if she'd just run a sub-six. As soon as she was out of sight, Dean ran toward the finish, which was on the track, inside the football stadium. Willowboro's football team played Langford every year, and at night, when the white lights shone down on the stadium, with the surrounding unpopulated darkness, it seemed majestic and important, a minor city. Today, in the midday sun, the tall lights and tall silver bleachers were still impressive, but now Dean was paying attention to the red rubberized track and the long finishing chute that was lined with fluorescent pink and yellow flags. The runners would enter the track at the far end, opposite the scoreboard, and then they would run almost a full lap before they crossed the finish line. A crowd had gathered in the bleachers, and a couple of reporters and photographers were waiting near the finish.

The crowd began clapping and whistling when Adrienne

entered the small stadium, her white-and-gold uniform shiny in the sun, her stride quick but not lengthening, her shoulders relaxed, her chin lifted, her body a model of efficiency and form. When she passed Dean, he was surprised by how fast she was going, how labored her breath was.

Adrienne had a clear, unshakable lead, with the next group of three runners coming into the stadium about thirty yards behind her. They had their own miniature competition for second place, each runner trying to get the inside lane, a negotiation so interesting that Dean did not notice Megan's arrival. She had held fifth and was gaining on the minipack.

"Dean, you didn't tell me she was this fast!"

It was Philips, his lean face clean-shaven. He was slightly out of breath, having run from the two-mile mark. Robbie was at his side, dazed but happy. "Go, Megan!" he screamed. "Reel them in!"

She heard him; there was some micromovement on her face that Dean felt only he could see. He watched as she began to make up the distance between herself and the runners ahead, shortening the space as if she were manipulating time. It was as if she were doing it with her eyes, with Nicole's faraway gaze.

Adrienne had crossed the finish line, and the crowd was now following Megan's trajectory with greater excitement. Dean noticed one of the reporters directing the photographer to get a picture of Megan.

When Megan finally passed the minipack, there was real agony on her face, but she still had ten yards to go. Dean started to scream her name, and the people around him picked up the chant. Robbie and Bryan jumped up and down like younger versions of themselves. Megan's arms turned sinewy as she crossed the line, reaching past an imaginary ribbon.

She stopped almost immediately and bent over like she was going to throw up or gag. The other runners, the ones she had beat, came rushing across the line in third, fourth, and fifth. They kept jogging, as directed, but Megan wouldn't move. Dean ran over to her, ducking beneath plastic tape to get to her.

"Megan! You broke twenty on your first race!"

"My heart." She pressed her hand to the middle of her chest. She meant her lungs. "I'm going to die."

"Keep running," he said. "Real slow. I'll go with you."

She started to jog, barely picking up her feet, her eyes on the ground. When she got to the end of the chute, she sped up just enough to sit down in a grassy spot, free of foot traffic.

"You have to keep moving," Dean said. "You have to cool down."

"Okay," she said, lying down on her back. She stretched her arms above her head and smiled at the sky.

LATER THAT DAY, Dean tried to describe the moment to Laura. They were lying on her futon, looking up at her slanted ceiling. Late-afternoon light glowed on the pale yellow sheets and the walls, which Laura had painted sage green.

"She's going to remember today for the rest of her life. No matter what happens to her, she's always going to remember today. How she felt. How that grass felt, how blue the sky was. It makes me proud."

"Why does it make *you* proud?" Laura teased. "All you did was cheer her on."

"It just makes me happy to see a kid like that. Someone who's got everything going for her."

"Don't you feel that way about Stephanie, too?"

"No . . . I mean, I'm proud of her. Of course I'm proud. I love her. But it's more complicated. I can't appreciate her the same way. There's guilt, because of her mother."

"Do you blame yourself?"

Dean rolled over onto his side to face her. "I don't know, Doctor."

"Sorry," Laura said. "I'm not trying to analyze you."

"I know." Dean tucked her hair behind her ear, admiring her long neck. He traced her collarbone with his finger, and then down past her clavicle, between her breasts. He wished he could stay all afternoon, all night.

"I wish you could stay," Laura said.

"I could," Dean said. "The boys are with Joelle again to-night."

"You know I can't," Laura said. Tim was a subject they really couldn't discuss. Dean didn't know why he was pushing. He didn't want to force a breakup. He just wanted comfort. And little pockets of time. That's what it felt like in her pale green room. Like he had found a place to go for a little while, where the past and the future didn't press down on him.

"So what did Joelle say about Megan running?" Laura said. Dean could tell she was trying to get past the awkwardness, that she didn't want to discuss Tim, either.

"She was waiting in the parking lot when we got back. But Ed was there, too. When he saw the medal, he couldn't be-lieve it. He said the only reason he was angry was because he hadn't gotten to see the race. What could Joelle say after that?

Bryan actually smoothed things over by asking if he could go to church with them the next day." Dean sat up and searched for his underwear at the foot of the bed. "I should probably get going, right?"

"Maybe . . . I don't know. Stay for a cup of coffee?" Laura pulled on her robe, a plaid flannel that matched her faded slippers.

Dean finished dressing and followed her down the cramped stairway that led to her small living room. She lived in an old stone house that had been divided into three apartments. Her slice of the pie was a narrow two floors, the downstairs a living room and misshapen kitchen and the upstairs a low-ceilinged bedroom that was likely once a maid's quarters.

Laura described her decorating style as "recovering graduate student." There were stacks of books and magazines on the floor, a pilled sofa draped with scarves, a large trunk that doubled as a coffee table, and two precarious CD towers, looking like miniature skyscrapers amid a city of low book buildings. Dean examined her books while she made coffee. He didn't recognize any of the authors, except for a romance novelist Nicole sometimes read.

"You know, she lives around here?" Dean said, holding up a paperback. "She's very nice. You'd never know she's a millionaire."

"Oh God, I can't believe you saw that!" Laura laughed. "I got that at the airport."

"Looks like you go to the airport a lot."

"Stop it! Everyone has their guilty pleasures."

"What's the guilt?" Dean skimmed the summary on the back.

"You want to borrow it?"

"Maybe I will." Dean stuck it in the back pocket of his jeans.

Laura smiled. "I bet you read two books a year—and neither of them is a novel."

"Maybe two and a half." Dean held up a thick paperback called *Abnormal Psychology.* "Is this part of your self-help collection?"

"Ha, right. I should have sold all my textbooks when I had the chance." Laura came over to him, bringing a mug of milky coffee. "I keep thinking I'm going to use them again."

Dean skimmed the titles. Many referred to depressive disorders. It occurred to him that Laura probably understood Nicole's psychological makeup much better than he ever could.

"Are you thinking of your wife?" Laura sat down next to him.

"Yeah."

"Is that okay for me to ask?"

"It's fine," Dean said. "I just don't know what to say about it. I try to understand it. People say it's a sickness of the mind, but I lived with her and she wasn't crazy."

"Sometimes I think suicide is a way of controlling death. There's a logic to it."

"That's some logic."

"I always try to look for the germ of reason. I don't believe in crazy."

"Is that what you tell Robbie?"

"You know I can't talk about that." She adjusted her robe, covering her neck with the shawl collar. "He doesn't really ask about those things, anyway. He's trying to figure out how to live without a mother."

"Sorry, I shouldn't have said that," Dean said. He was shaken by her simple summary of his son's predicament.

"It's my fault. I shouldn't be talking to you at all, let alone about Robbie, let alone doing any of this . . ."

"Hey, don't beat yourself up," Dean said. "This started before things got complicated."

"Did it?" She raised her eyebrows. "You know, I already broke up with Tim once for you. Last spring, before you stopped talking to me."

"I never stopped—"

"You did. It was after Stephanie saw us together. You got scared. And you know, I didn't blame you. I understood. I think you sensed that I had broken up with Tim because of you. Because I had feelings for you."

"I didn't know that."

"On some level you did. That's what I mean when I say people aren't crazy. They do things for some kind of reason even if they don't understand it."

"Did you think I was going to leave my wife for you?"

"Just the opposite. I thought you backed off because you realized how I felt and you were trying to protect your marriage."

"And now what do you think?"

"I don't know," she said. "I never expected this. And I don't want to analyze it, I just want to live it. I realize that makes me a hypocrite. But therapists are always the most fucked-up people."

She was getting upset, and he saw how precarious their situation was. They couldn't talk about the things that really mattered to them without untangling the past.

"God, I have to have dinner with Tim's family tonight." Laura stood up, twisting her hair into a knot at the nape of her neck. "I need to take a shower."

He stood up with her, slipping his arm inside her robe and around her bare waist. Her skin felt soft and cool. Outside, the sun was low in the sky, the shadows long.

Chapter 9

A tray came meandering down the conveyor belt with a message—HI GABE!—spelled in Froot Loops, the cereal glued into place by a small pond of syrup.

"I think this is for you." Stephanie pushed the tray toward her fellow dishwasher, Gabriel Hahn. She was on dumping duty, while Gabe had the relatively cleaner job of loading the dishes into plastic crates before sending them on their way toward the industrial dishwasher. They had agreed to switch off every other morning.

Gabe came over to admire his friend's handiwork. "Must be Evan, he's the only one I know who'd be up this early."

"Do you get a better choice of shifts after a couple semesters?" Stephanie asked.

"Yeah, sure." Gabe expertly rinsed the syrup-sticky tray, the Froot Loops message briefly spelling I BE before being washed away into the drain. "But I love breakfast. Nobody eats breakfast. Dinner is hell, it's carnage. If anyone asks you to take their dinner shift, you tell them no. That's my advice to you, young grasshopper."

"Okay, got it." Stephanie turned her attention to the half-finished bowl of cream of wheat coming her way. There was no way she was going to continue working in the dish room as a junior, like Gabe. She'd already put in applications everywhere else: the admissions office, the faculty day care, the library, the museum, and even the gym. But she'd been told that, with the exception of day care, these positions were usually given to upperclassmen. First-years had to start in the cafeteria.

"How about some music?" Gabe said, switching on the portable radio that was perched on the dish room's one windowsill. He tuned it to the college's station, explaining that his friend deejayed the morning show. Gabe had a lot of friends. He had an exuberant, babyish appeal, with blond curls that seemed to be constantly springing from his head; round, flushed cheeks; and large, light eyes made even more innocent by blond eyelashes. Combined with his angelic name, it was almost too much.

"I love this song!" Gabe said, turning the music up. Björk's "Hyperballad" blasted through the dish room, competing with the sound of industrial-weight china and silverware clanking together.

Stephanie had only just been introduced to Björk—by Raquel, of course. She told Stephanie that "Hyperballad" was about the sacrifices made for love, but Stephanie felt certain it was a song about suicidal depression. Drunkenly, she had argued that everyone had a sliver of suicide in their hearts, that it was the other side of the self-deceiving behaviors humans had evolved in order to deal with the crushing weight of consciousness. Knowledge of death was the apple Eve bit into from the Tree of Knowledge. Stephanie was getting everything she was learning mixed up in her mind, her classes were blending together in a way that was exhilarating and also muddying.

She knew she wasn't thinking clearly, that everything kept bending back to her mother, to the past, her fears, her loneliness. She was learning how alcohol could lift her up, but also how it could throw her back onto herself. The mornings were the worst. She had hoped this cafeteria job would help her get through them, the way the Red Byrd had helped her over the summer. But the dish room was too chaotic, and the reek of bleach got to her, as did the ugly lumpiness of the leftover uneaten foods, the sickening smell of it. The waste.

"Oh shit!" She dropped a plate. It broke neatly into four pieces.

"Don't worry about it," Gabe said. He picked up the pieces and tossed them into the trash can so quickly it was like it didn't happen. "I did that all the time my first few weeks. They're slippery."

Stephanie nodded, grateful and also a little embarrassed by his kindness. Maybe it was just work-study camaraderie. As far as Stephanie could tell, only a small percentage of the student body had to work; everyone else spent their savings or had allowances from their parents. Stephanie had plenty of cash from her summer of waitressing, but if the past couple of weeks were any indication of her spending habits, she was going to go through it well before the end of the semester. She and Raquel bought things every day, usually just food and coffee and occasionally booze, but there had also been another weekend jaunt to Philadelphia, where they had dropped quite a bit of cash in a used-CD store, a Goodwill, and a makeup boutique that carried beautifully iridescent eye shadows. Not to mention the cost of lunch and train tickets. It was clear to Stephanie that Raquel thought nothing of their expenditures, which bothered Stephanie only because she wished Raquel could share in her own sense of financial abandon. Stephanie's favorite euphemism for drunk was *wasted* because that was how she felt and how she wanted to feel. Like she was wasting something good.

The trays were coming intermittently. It was just the slow eaters now, the students who lingered over coffees with reading assignments. A big group of trays came all at once, which meant the cafeteria had been cleared out, finally.

"We can start stacking," Gabe said. Stephanie followed him to the other side of the dishwashing apparatus where there were metal shelves for storing the clean dishes, trays, and silverware. Some of the dishes were almost too hot to touch and she passed them off to Gabe as quickly as she could, getting into a rhythm. What was it about physical labor that she found so satisfying? Was this how her father felt about athletics? Maybe she should drop out of school and be a waitress. Or she could work outdoors. Somebody was going to have to run her uncle's farm one day. Her little cousin Jenny would probably take it over; she took after her father. Stephanie hated how her thoughts kept returning to Willowboro and to her family.

Downstairs, in the basement, she and Gabe took off their rubber gloves, put their aprons in a bin for the laundry, and punched out. When they finally got outside, it was surprisingly warm and students were lounging on the quad, sitting on their jackets, heads bent over books or in discussion.

"Look at this postcard for the liberal arts!" Gabe crowed.

"It's a beautiful day," Stephanie said, repulsed by her own banality. But as she looked at the scene in front of her, all she could think was that she deserved none of it.

"Hey, do you want to get a cup of coffee?" Gabe asked. His blond curls shone in the sun.

"I have to shower before my class," Stephanie said.

"Oh yeah, what class?"

He was making conversation, she realized. He liked her company. Why? He was a cherub floating on his good fortune, while she was a backward-looking rain cloud.

"I have to go," she said, turning away from him. She gave a little wave without really making eye contact, as if that was enough.

Back at her dorm, she stood for a long time under the hot shower, washing off the cafeteria smells. The bathrooms were mercifully quiet and empty. It was one of those off times, still too early for the late risers but too late for those who had morning classes. Stephanie let herself cry a little. God, she was miserable. She missed her mother—it was that simple—but her longing was mixed up with an anger so powerful that she couldn't really touch it without hurting herself. She had no idea what she was supposed to do to save herself. She didn't have God; she felt lost to her father. She could devote herself to her education, but her idea of becoming a doctor did not seem big enough, or maybe specific enough, to carry her to a different place. Lots of people here wanted to become a doctor; it was an ambition so ordinary that many of her classmates—Raquel included—viewed their undergraduate years as a kind of respite before medical school. It was a kind of entitlement Stephanie wasn't familiar with, but which she recognized, because she had also envisioned her college years as a kind of respite—from her mother. And now she needed her mother more than anyone else. She didn't care if her mother was depressed, she didn't care what her mother said or did, she just wanted her mother's body in the world.

Stephanie had the urge to take a nap when she got back to her room, but Theresa's neatly made bed seemed to goad her to action. She couldn't skip another class. And anyway, she liked going to Psych I. Raquel would be waiting for her, saving her a seat. She would write notes to Stephanie in her notebook and slide her sticks of gum. Afterward they would get lunch or maybe they would fill paper cups with cereal and go to the library to nibble granola and sip tea. Stephanie tried to dress in an outfit that Raquel would approve of: a plaid shirt, clashing plaid skirt, black tights, and Mitchell's hand-me-down boots. She still hadn't heard a word from him. At this point his lack of communication felt deliberate, a message in and of itself. He was saying that she had to learn how to be herself without his friendship.

She was drying her hair when she heard her phone's high ring over the dryer's blurry roar. Her instinct was not to answer it, even though her father hadn't called in almost two weeks. Or maybe Theresa had stopped giving her messages. She and her roommate had reached a wary understanding: in exchange for minding her own business, Theresa got to have the room to herself most of the time.

The phone kept ringing, so finally she switched off the dryer and picked up. A small voice answered.

"Steffy? It's Robbie."

"Oh my God, Robbie!" Stephanie hadn't heard from him since the weekend he'd called from Aunt Joelle's. That was the night she and Raquel had gone dancing, a night Stephanie could really only remember in flashes, as if the whole evening had been edited with severe jump cuts. Blackout drunk, Raquel said. Stephanie knew she wouldn't have gone that far if her brother hadn't called, if his high voice hadn't reminded her of everything she missed and had lost.

"Guess where I'm calling from? A pay phone! I snuck out of gym class. I said I was sick and they sent me to the nurse's office. But then I just walked out the door."

"Robbie, you can't do that, you're going to get in trouble."

"They won't notice. I have lunch right after gym. I'll get back in time."

"You could get suspended."

"It's only middle school," he said. "No one cares what you do in middle school. It's just where they hold you until you're ready for high school."

There was some truth to this, so Stephanie let it go. She didn't want to antagonize him. "So aside from sneaking out of school, what's new?"

"Um, I'm going to Outdoor School at the end of the month."

"You are? Already? That's cool. October is a good time to go. Our class had to go in the winter, it was so cold. All the animals were hibernating. We had to study taxidermy animals instead."

"Gross, like the dead stuffed animals?"

"Yeah, exactly. But the end of the month will be good. The leaves will be falling. You'll have fun. How's Bry?"

"He's completely a Jesus freak now," Robbie said. "We went to church with Aunt Joelle again last weekend and he went down front and witnessed."

"What does that mean?"

"It's like when you hear God talking to you and you start

crying. They give you a chance to do it at every service. Like, after the sermon and the money basket and all the prayers for everyone, the minister asks if anyone wants to take Jesus into their heart. And last time this lady raised her hand and everyone made a big fuss over her, so Bryan raised his hand this time and the minister asked him to come down to the front. And then in front of everybody the minister asked Bryan if he wanted to take Jesus into his heart and he said yes and then the whole church clapped and then the minister said this prayer and put Jesus in his heart. And ever since then he's been bugging me and Dad to put Jesus in our hearts because otherwise he doesn't get to be with us in heaven."

"What does Dad say?"

"He ignores it."

Stephanie heard cars in the background of Robbie's call. "Are you at the pay phone by the Tastee Freez?"

"No, the one near the post office."

"I didn't know there was one there."

"It's kind of hidden. I saw it when I was walking by and then I thought, 'Let me call Stephanie.'"

"So it's not like Dad doesn't let you call me or anything?"

"No, I just don't want Bryan hearing me complaining because he'll make me feel bad. I like church fine, but I don't understand Aunt Joelle's. I think it's cheesy."

"Why do you keep going?"

"I don't know, we just do. Dad doesn't go. He stays home."

Listening to him, Stephanie got a glimpse of her own childhood, the way things just happened to her and she just accepted them because what choice did she have? Maybe going on walkabouts was Robbie's way of getting some freedom.

"Hey, Steffy, a voice said I have to put in more quarters but I don't have any. So good-bye!"

"Wait, Robbie! Go back to school, okay? Robbie? I love you!"

The line was dead. Stephanie wondered how much he'd heard. A sense of his vulnerability overwhelmed her. Where would he go next? To Willow Park? The cemetery? Back to Asaro's, where their mother used to take them? She had an urge to tell someone his whereabouts and wondered if she should try to call her father at school. But at the same time she took a kind of angry satisfaction in knowing something he didn't.

LAURA'S SMALL, WINDOWLESS office was barely unpacked, the decor echoing her apartment, with stacks of books and files piled on the floor, waiting to be shelved. "I keep meaning to come in some weekend and straighten things up," she said airily as she let Dean in. Dean understood her small-talk excuses were a show put on for her receptionist, a woman who also worked for the principal and vice principal. Their offices were nearby, but more prominently located, with interior windows overlooking the main corridor.

He began to kiss her as soon as she shut the door, feeling protected by the painted cinder-block walls.

"Dean!" Laura pushed him gently away. "We can't."

"Why not?" He stroked her arm, bare below a silk shell. A blazer was draped over a chair nearby. He liked how formally she dressed for work.

"Because we have to talk about Robbie."

"Oh, right," he said, uncertainly, stepping back. He had

thought that Robbie was just an excuse to meet midday on a Friday—a meeting they needed because they probably wouldn't get to see each other over the weekend.

"I thought I had made it clear . . ." Laura trailed off. "On the phone?"

"Yeah, you did," Dean said, recalling a certain sternness when she had called the day before to schedule their meeting. But sometimes she was stern as a way of being flirtatious.

Laura sat down at her desk, pausing to put on her blazer. She gestured for Dean to take a seat in one of the two vinyl chairs across from her. He felt ridiculous in his gym teacher clothes, his shorts and warm-up jacket. He should have changed into khakis, at least.

"I know this isn't ideal, me talking to you about this stuff, but it's what we're dealing with, so I'm just going to tell you and I want you to respond to me as a parent, if you can. What I mean is, don't worry about hurting my feelings or anything like that. We're talking about Robbie now."

"Okay," Dean said. "Did he get into trouble?"

"No, not really," Laura said. "But he did leave school yesterday—again."

"What? Why wasn't I notified?"

"Because he wasn't caught. He told me yesterday afternoon, which is when we usually meet—"

"Where did he go? What did he do?"

"He walked around town. Then he came back at the end of his lunch period. No one was the wiser. I think on some level he wanted to get caught, though. He was eager to tell me, and he wanted to know if he would be in trouble."

"He should be. He has to stop doing this."

"That's what I wanted to talk to you about. I'm not sure it's the best idea to report him. I think the punishment would be too harsh. At the very least, he would be put in long-term detention, which would keep him from doing the play. And he probably wouldn't be allowed to go on field trips, not to mention his Outdoor School stay, which is coming up soon."

"Oh yeah, I keep forgetting about that."

"I wanted to talk to you about that, too. Robbie told me that he brought home a list of things he needs for the trip and he's worried that you aren't going to get those items for him."

"Of course I'm going to get them," Dean said. "It's basic camping stuff, a lot of it we already have. He doesn't even go until the end of the month."

"I think Robbie just wants a little more fanfare around it. You know, he wants the two of you to spend an afternoon getting these things together from around the house or going to the camping store or whatever you need to do. He wants attention."

"He wants attention? That's your great psychological advice?" Dean was trying to be lightly sarcastic, the way Laura sometimes was, but the words landed too hard.

"I know it sounds trite. But I also know the lines of communication are, you know, not what they were, now that Stephanie is away at school. I'm sure she used to fill you in on stuff like this. And obviously with your wife . . ." She looked up from her notes. "Is any of this making any sense?"

"Not really." It bothered Dean that she hadn't finished her sentence about Nicole. Wasn't it her job, as a counselor, to state plainly what others shied away from? But what really bothered him was that she was evaluating him as a father, and this evaluation had not been shared with him; it was a secret sketch drawn with knowledge gleaned from his son and who knew what psychological theories.

"I'm sorry," Laura said. "I shouldn't presume any of this stuff."

"I know I should talk with him more. It's just a lot, Laura. I have a long day at work and then I get home and there's the boys and I have to get them fed and into bed. And there's errands and things to do around the house. I don't even want to get into it because it's not worth complaining about. It's my life and I accept it. The point is I'm not their mother, and I'm not going to turn Outdoor School shopping into a big production."

"You sound angry," Laura said.

"You sound like a therapist."

She raised her eyebrows without saying anything, and he knew he'd proved her point, whatever it was.

"Sorry," he said. "I'm just tired of being told that I'm angry."

"Who else tells you that?"

"Who do you think? Stephanie, Joelle, Nicole—" It was an odd slip, one he wouldn't have made in front of anyone else. "In my mind, Nicole," he corrected.

"And why is she angry with you?"

"I don't know, because I didn't do anything wrong. I'm not saying our marriage was perfect, but it wasn't something to kill yourself over."

Genuine alarm flashed in Laura's eyes, her youth betraying her. "We don't have to talk about this if you don't want to."

"You're the one who brought it up." It was such a charade, her talking to him like she knew nothing of his life. He tried to think of what she might know, what insights she might have uncovered from their cafeteria conversations, way back when. Had he complained about Nicole to her? He didn't think he had; that was what a good husband he had been—he hadn't even allowed himself that small betrayal. He should have made a move on Laura when he had the chance. She wasn't above sleeping with a married man.

"I know this is difficult," Laura said. He could see she was right on the edge of tears, as if she could read his thoughts.

"Just admit to me that you're not objective. That you can't be."

"I never said I was."

Dean stood up. "If you're going to be Robbie's counselor, we obviously can't be doing what we're doing."

"I know, I know." Laura wiped away tears. "I'm sorry I'm crying. This is ridiculous, this is not supposed to go this way, we're supposed to talk about Robbie."

Her naïveté shocked Dean even as he knew it was the very thing that had drawn him to her in the first place.

"I'm going to go." He stood up. "Let's take the weekend, okay?"

"Take the weekend and what?"

"Just be by ourselves. To think things over. I have to take care of my boys. And the girls have a race."

She nodded without saying anything. Dean left her office carefully, barely opening the door. He gave the reception- ist a big smile—not that it mattered, she was hardly paying attention—and he jogged back to the high school, letting the conversation, and the feelings it had provoked, fall away. He felt fine when he got back to his office, full of resolve to be a better father, a better teacher, a better coach. The feeling was ratified when the front office called to say he'd received a UPS package from Tri-State Sports. It was the new cross-country uniforms he'd ordered after the first meet, before he'd even realized he would be coaching the girls for the rest of the season. He opened up the large box as soon as he could, eager to see the clean new uniforms inside. It felt like a delivery from the most optimistic part of himself.

There was a short practice scheduled that afternoon, and at the end of it, Dean had Bryan hand out the brand-new shorts and singlets to both the girls' and boys' teams. Everyone was pleased with their new outfits, the blues so much deeper than the faded colors of their old uniforms.

Only Megan seemed uncertain about the change. She'd been coming to practice since her big win, and at first Dean thought it was a superstitious thing, that she wanted to wear the same jersey for every race. But it turned out she was worried about the length of the shorts, which were a few inches higher than the old ones.

"You can wear biking shorts underneath," See-See suggested. "Or tights when it gets cold."

"I won't have time to get them before tomorrow," Megan said. "Can't I just wear the old shorts?"

"We'll figure something out," Dean said. He could see this was a Joelle issue, probably something to do with their new church.

Megan came over to him after he dismissed everyone. She apologized for being so picky.

"Don't worry, I'll get you some bike shorts tonight," Dean said. "I was going to take the boys to the mall anyway."

"We're going to the mall?" Bryan said. "We haven't been there since before Mommy died!"

Megan answered Bryan casually. "What did you get the last time you went?"

"Bathing suits. But we got a winter coat on sale, too. Do you remember, Dad? It was for me, for this year. I wonder where Mommy put it."

"I don't know, buddy, we can look for it tonight. C'mon, we have to go pick up Robbie. We'll see you tomorrow, Megan. Get a good night's sleep."

They found Robbie sitting outside in the chilly air with the theater kids, as well as See-See, who was catching up with her friends. They were all dressed in layers of dark colors, a style Dean associated with Stephanie. It had been almost a month since he'd spoken to her, and he was starting to worry again, but he told himself not to, that he'd been exactly the same when he was her age. Especially those first weeks of college.

"You smell like cigarettes," Bryan said when he and Robbie got into the backseat. Sometimes they sat together in the back, giving the car a feeling of expectation, as if they were saving the passenger seat for Nicole.

"Cory and Seth smoke," Robbie said. "Seth is like my stage dad."

"He's a bad dad," Bryan said. "Bad dad! Bad dad! Bad dad! Bad dad! Bad dad!"

"Will you knock it off?" Dean said.

"Say it!" Bryan demanded. "It's like a tongue twister."

Robbie began to chant: "Bad dad bad dad bad dad bada bada bada bada bada batta batta batta batta sa-*wing*!"

"That's from Ferris Bueller!" Bryan said. "Can we watch it tonight, Daddy? With popcorn? Please?"

"After we go to the mall."

"We're going to the *mall*?" Robbie leaned forward between the seats.

Dean hadn't been avoiding shopping, exactly, but the Pleasant Valley Mall had to be one of the most ironically named places in the world. It was built on a wetland, and its low-lying buildings, planted in a field of asphalt, always looked as if they were sinking. It was Nicole who had first identified the specific nature of their ugliness, the way they resembled the nearby prison. At some point the bleakness got to be too much, and they stopped going. Instead, if they needed to do a big shop, they drove an hour and a half to a large mall in one of the D.C. suburbs.

Luckily, Robbie and Bry were far less particular, and only associated the PVM (as it was referred to by the locals) with fun and new clothes.

They went to Dick's Sporting Goods first. Both the boys needed new winter boots. They got their feet measured and to Dean's surprise, Robbie had gone up a size. Dean winced to think of him walking around in ill-fitting shoes and bought him two pairs of sneakers, one practical and the other a pair of blue Chuck Taylors that Robbie found fashionable. Passing the Nike display, Dean saw Megan's "air ponies." Nearby were thin-soled racing flats in fluorescent colors. Dean had noticed that Adrienne Fellows had a bright yellow pair that she always wore. He wished he had the girls' shoe sizes; he would buy them new shoes to go with their new uniforms. Remembering Megan's request for something to wear beneath her shorts, he asked a salesgirl for help. She sold him a pair of dark blue aerobics shorts made of thick spandex.

They had dinner at a popular chain restaurant of the boys' choosing. The restaurant was lively, and the boys loved the novelty of eating at a place they'd seen advertised on television. The waitress doted on them, giving them plastic souvenir cups and extra french fries. Dean was glad to see them so happy, but, personally, he felt lost and uncomfortable in the world. He often felt this way on Friday nights—there was always the knowledge that the white lights were shining down on Garrett, not him—but tonight his regret went deeper. He felt as if he'd gotten marooned in the wrong life, as if his real life, not just his career, was going on somewhere else. It was a feeling of loss so diffuse he didn't know how to pin it down.

After dinner he and the boys shopped some more. In a camping store, a display of polar fleece jackets caught Dean's eye and he tried on a dark blue one with white piping. It was what the other running coaches wore. He decided to get one for himself and asked Robbie and Bry if they wanted them, too.

"Are we going to get one for Steffy?"

"Sure, why not?" Dean said. "Pick a color you think she'd like."

Bry chose a lavender jacket, but Robbie said it was too pretty, that Stephanie would want black. They compromised and got dark purple.

Their last stop was JCPenney, for the very practical purchase of underwear, something the boys had not thought to tell him they needed but that Dean was sure was lacking. He sent the boys to the boys' section to pick out the ones they wanted while he retreated to the men's department to replenish his own stores. The perfume and cosmetics department lay between these two worlds and as Dean passed by the mirrored displays he caught a scent of whatever flowery essence Laura wore. The thought of her, of her warm skin, caught him. He was pulled back to her small, windowless office, to her tears, to the anger she'd provoked. He had to apologize. He couldn't let things end—not yet. Because when he said good-bye to her, he would have to say good-bye to Nicole, too. Somehow the two of them were connected in his mind.

Chapter 10

Hawk's Peak was the smallest school in the district, nestled in the westernmost corner of the county, high in the foothills of the Appalachians. It was so small that the middle and high schools were combined in one building. Even more telling was the fact that it didn't have a football team. Dean had never seen the campus, and when the bus began to ascend the bumpy corridor of a road that led to it, he joked with the girls that they should have done altitude training. He was actually somewhat concerned. Megan was the only one who had run regularly on trails and hills, on her family's farm.

See-See and Jessica had run the course before, so they stayed back to set up the tarp that Dean had brought to stow everyone's stuff. Lori had run it before, too, but she wanted to accompany the ones who hadn't. She pointed out certain tree roots and rocks and muddy spots, as if Megan couldn't see them herself. She was being protective, Dean realized, because Megan was so talented. All the girls deferred to her now, even See-See. Megan bore it lightly, in part because she didn't go to school with the others, so she didn't have a sense of her accomplishments beyond what happened on the day of the race. The other part was that Megan had that athlete's way of shutting out the world. Dean saw it in all his best players; they could make their mind a field of nothing. It didn't require a huge amount of intelligence, yet a lot of intelligent people couldn't do it. Dean still recalled the bliss of it, when he was younger and deep into his training. He couldn't remember what it felt like, though.

Missy and Lori walked slightly ahead of him. The two had become friends, an odd pair, physically, with Lori's rounded, soft limbs in direct contrast to Missy's broad, blunt shoulders. But they were both strong, able to lift more than the other girls on the team. They'd started as weight room partners and now were pacing partners, although Dean expected Missy to pull ahead of Lori soon. She'd turned in a respectable 24:14 for her first race, finishing second to last for the team, but well ahead of Jessica, which had brought up their team score considerably. Still, Missy had run the race badly, going way too fast in the first mile and then getting crushed during the second and third miles, when dozens of runners passed her. Dean worried about her on this course, with its shrouded second mile. These woods were made for giving up. They were hilly, with difficult footing. You lost your sense of distance when you were inside them. Dean kept looking for landmarks to mark their progress, but every stand of dark-trunked trees was the same, and every craggy root was the same craggy root they'd stepped over two minutes before. When they finally emerged onto a large, weather-beaten field, Dean felt a visceral sense of relief. The final leg of the course took the runners on a long, sloping downhill, leading back to the school.

Dean returned to the tarp to find Jessica and See-See playing cards with Robbie, Bry, and Jenny. Joelle and Ed stood nearby drinking coffee with some of the other parents, including Karen Coulter.

Joelle tried to get Megan to eat some peanuts and raisins that she'd brought along in a plastic baggie, but Megan refused. "Not right before the race!"

"You're not running for another hour," Joelle protested. "You need fuel."

"See-See's the same way," Karen Coulter said, patting her daughter's spiked hair. "She hardly eats breakfast."

"Megan ate breakfast," Joelle said definitively, like she didn't want to have anything in common with See-See's mother.

"So, Dean, does our team stand a chance of winning?" Ed asked.

"Hard to predict," Dean replied. He had to get the girls away from this nonsense. He called for a warm-up, even though it was too early, and took the girls to a grassy clearing that he had noticed when they got off the bus. It was too small to be called a field, but large enough to give them a feeling of privacy and distance. Dean guided them through a series of stretches without saying much. Above, the clouds were moving across the sky, pushed by winds they could hear in the dry leaves just barely clinging to the trees. Time seemed to slow down. Dean thought of how strange it was that he was standing on this particular spot on the planet. It was a feeling akin to the malaise he'd encountered the night before in the mall. But this time there was no anger. Instead he felt a kind of disoriented wonder. Six months ago he never could have conceived of this moment.

"We should get back soon," See-See said, pointing toward

the starting line, where other teams had begun to gather in warm-up gear.

"You lead the way," Dean said. He'd meant to give them some pointers for the race before they left, but it didn't seem as necessary.

The starting line stretched out across a puddled, bowl-shaped field. Dean told the girls to be careful of the mud, a warning they received with scorn.

"I'm serious," Dean said. "It's October. One month until the big dance. You can't afford to twist your ankle now. So play it safe!"

See-See saluted him and then led the girls away to form a huddle.

The boys' team was heading off for their warm-up. Philips gave Dean a wave and promised to cheer the girls on at the end of the race. As he ran off, Dean realized he'd been counting on him to take the second-mile splits. He quickly recruited Karen for the job, handing her a clipboard and draping a stopwatch over her neck.

"Sorry you'll miss the start," he said.

"No problem." She pulled her dirty-blond hair into a pony-tail. "I'm glad I wore sneakers!"

With Joelle, Bryan, and Robbie in tow, Dean headed to the first mile marker. A small group of coaches were waiting there. Dean positioned himself just beyond the marker so that he could run alongside the girls if he felt like it. Before he even had time to organize himself, Bryan started jumping up and down and calling Megan's name. Dean looked up to see her small figure clad in bright blue, an echo of the sky above.

"Is that really her?" Joelle said.

"Daddy! She's in first!" Bryan was still jumping.

Dean's stopwatch said 5:45. Way, way too fast a start. She was excited because her parents were here, maybe.

"You're too fast!" Dean yelled. "You need to stick with See-See and slow down in the woods. It's okay if you lose first. This isn't the big dance. You need to run smart, run smart! Don't trip in those woods!"

She nodded, giving him a quick darting glance. She seemed rattled, happy, high, a little out of control. Her leg turnover was so quick that Dean felt like he could see the adrenaline animating her muscles.

The other girls passed by in order with their partners: See-See and Aileen, Lori and Missy, and finally, Jessica. The field of spectators fell silent as the runners entered the woods.

"I can't believe she was first," Joelle said. She seemed shaken. "I knew she was fast, but I didn't realize . . ."

"Come on, we have to get to the third mile," Dean said. He wanted to jog but settled for a brisk walk. Almost as soon as they made it to the marker, Megan popped out of the woods, still holding first. The clock ticked past nineteen. She was going to break her personal record *and* win the race. This was only the second race she had ever run. Dean wondered if Joelle and Ed understood how talented their daughter was. He wondered if *he* understood. She needed a real coach, someone who actually knew about running.

"Here." He thrust the clipboard and stopwatch toward Robbie. "Finish taking the splits."

"Thanks for asking," Robbie muttered.

Dean ran diagonally across the field toward the finishing chute, where other parents and coaches were already waiting at the line. They began to cheer as Megan came into view. Dean heard someone behind him yelling and turned to see Karen Coulter looking flushed, exhilarated, and about ten years younger. "Holy shit! Is that little Megan in the lead?"

He just barely saw her cross the line. The next runner was at least ten yards behind. Megan slowed to a jog this time, not stopping abruptly like she'd done before. She was red-faced, clearly exhausted, but she waved when she saw Dean.

"What was my time?"

"Nineteen thirty-two."

She frowned. "I wanted to break nineteen."

"You will," Dean promised.

Ed and Jenny had seen Megan win and were making their way over to her with dumbfounded glee. Dean ducked out of the scene and returned to the line where Aileen and See-See—they had stuck together until the end—were racing to the finish. Aileen edged See-See out by one stride. Dean thought there was a chance for a halfway decent team score, but then a big group of runners—none of them blue—came across the line and he knew a win was mathematically impossible.

Missy, Lori, and Jessica were so far back that they had no clue of Megan's win. Telling them was like giving them a present. They ran over to Megan, who was now being interviewed by a reporter. The reporter wanted to talk to Dean but he said not until he'd taken the girls for their cooldown jog. Then he led the girls away, back to the clearing where they'd stretched before the race.

"I JUST DON'T want to get into a pattern of drinking all the time," Raquel said. "It's so cliché. And I'm so sick of going to dumb jock parties on Saturday. It's their one night to have fun and they all binge."

They were sitting together in the cafeteria, Stephanie with her apron on because she was taking a break from the dish room. Gabe had told her to go get a cup of coffee because she seemed so tired. Stephanie couldn't understand how Raquel could look glamorous after so many late nights in a row. It was as if all the things that made other people seem undone—messy hair, a drawn face, the residue of last night's makeup—instead conspired to make Raquel utterly chic.

"We could go to the movies," Stephanie said.

"You always want to go to the movies."

"It's just what Mitchell and I would always do when we were bored," Stephanie said, missing her old friend.

"We should go visit him—he's at Harvard, right? We could go to a Harvard party! Seriously, we could get a bus from Philadelphia. Or you could drive! I always forget you have a car."

"He's at MIT."

"Oh, right." Raquel seemed genuinely unhappy, plagued by her fantasies of the parties just out of reach. It had to do with growing up near a city, Stephanie thought. When you grew up in a small place, you just accepted that there were more exciting things going on pretty much everywhere else in the world.

"We could go into Philadelphia," Stephanie offered, even though she really wasn't in the same restless mood.

"I'm bored of Philadelphia," Raquel said, drawing out the word *bored* into two self-consciously bratty syllables.

"Gabe invited me to something." Stephanie reached into her apron pocket, where Gabe had tucked a xeroxed invitation.

"It's at the Arts House—a First Saturday party? They have them every month."

Raquel examined the hand-drawn flyer, which pictured a crescent moon smiling down on a group of dancing stick figures reminiscent of Keith Haring or maybe Matisse. A Grateful Dead bear was thrown in for good measure. Stephanie expected Raquel to reject this idea, since it had pot written all over it and Raquel was surprisingly contemptuous of potheads, but instead she rewarded Stephanie with an earnest smile, the kind she reserved for her most closely cherished pop songs.

"Stephanie! These are supposed to be the best parties!"

"I didn't know." Stephanie couldn't help feeling pleased. It was a rare treat to surprise Raquel.

"Seriously, I have heard so many stories about these parties. The crazy things people do. You know what we should do?" Raquel lowered her voice. "I have some E. My ex gave it to me. We were going to take it together, but we never did."

"He didn't want it back?" Stephanie said. It was all she could think to reply. This was only the second time she'd ever heard of ecstasy; the first time was from Mitchell, of all people. He'd said it was the one drug he was curious to try.

"I've been saving it. For the right time. And I think it could help you. You know, to be happy."

"I am happy!" Stephanie said. "I mean, I'm happy enough."

"All I'm saying is that we're in college, we should be having fun, trying things. It's ridiculous to feel like we're in a rut already. And I mean, let's face it: We drink too much. It's not good for our health."

"And ecstasy is?"

"Well, it's not bad for you. No one does anything stupid on

it. The worst reaction I've ever seen is that some people want to talk a lot. But most people just dance, and, like, touch soft fabric, and feel amazing."

"I don't know, maybe," Stephanie said. She wished she could consult with Mitchell. He would be honest about the risks. She felt as if she had run out of honest people in her life.

"You don't have to decide now. We can see how we feel tonight." Raquel stood up to bus her tray. "I'm going to the library—to our usual spot. Want to meet me there?"

"Yeah, okay. Here, I can take your tray."

In the dish room, Stephanie dumped Raquel's half-eaten scrambled eggs and told Gabe to take a break. Without him to help her, she had to work fast. The radio was turned up loud, Radiohead's "The Bends" blasting. Stephanie remembered playing the song loud in her car on her way home from school and hollering the chorus. She had thought of herself as miserable, bored, constrained, isolated, uncertain, but looking back on the memory, she saw a joyful girl. She remembered the fresh air blowing through the rolled-down windows, her skin warm from the sun, the exhilaration of driving fast on the rolling, empty hills, the roads her own private roller coaster, the music her own private anthem, propelling her to something unknown but likely very good. Happiness.

She sprayed hot water into a bowl of half-eaten oatmeal. With a gloved hand, she placed it onto the dish rack, along with two nearly empty mugs, and then sent the rack on its way down the conveyor belt toward the Hobart. She'd worked so efficiently that she had a couple of minutes of downtime before the next tray came down the pike. As she stood there in the steamy, bleach-scented air, she thought of how nice it would be to just take a pill and feel happy again. If it was truly possible, she wanted to try it.

DINNER AT JOELLE's again. Dean sat on the front porch steps with a postprandial beer, watching the sky begin to grow dark. He could hear Robbie's and Bry's high voices mixing with Megan's and Jenny's inside the house. They sounded happy. The boys wanted to stay overnight again, and he couldn't think of why they shouldn't. Nicole would be shocked by how laid-back he was being; they used to fight about how often to come here, the gist of their argument that she wanted to visit more often than he did. But there was another layer, the sense of obligation that she couldn't admit to feeling. The sense of guilt she clung to, as if her life was disappointing to her family. Dean couldn't understand it, didn't want to try anymore. He wanted to hold on to the morning, the joy of seeing Megan crossing the finish line, exhausted and exhilarated. At dinner she'd looked like a different girl, with her hair down and her bangs curled, wearing jeans and a turtleneck sweater. An ordinary girl.

The front door creaked open, and he turned to find Joelle. She had a beer in hand, a rare sight.

"Can I join you?"

"Of course." Dean moved over even though there was plenty of room. "Beautiful night."

"It sure is. Nice and clear. I might take the kids stargazing down at Mom's. She has the best view."

"Thanks for letting them stay over tonight," Dean said. "They always have fun."

"Oh, it's my pleasure! It's a nice way for me to see the boys every week. And I'm glad we're getting along."

"Me too, Jo."

"No, really. I'm not just saying it. I've been thinking about this a lot, praying on it. I have to admit, I was mad when Megan went to your practice. And then Ed took your side. I felt like I was trying to maintain a commitment to Christ, and my whole family was against it. I said to God, 'Why did you put me in this position? Why did you give Megan this talent for running?' And then I realized it was so that she would go to you, and so our families would come back together. Doesn't that make perfect sense?"

"It's a nice story."

"It's more than nice! I mean, look at Bryan—he's getting so close to God's light. I see it in his little face and it makes me so happy that he's found that comfort. Have you noticed a difference in him?"

"Sure, maybe," Dean said. It was unbelievable to him that Joelle could not see how self-serving her theories were. What kind of petty god gave a shit if Dean and his sister-in-law were getting along? He recalled a book about Christianity that Stephanie had received as a present upon her confirmation, a book geared toward teenagers and their particular theological concerns. It was called *If God Loves Me, Why Can't I Get My Locker Open?* How he and Stephanie had laughed at that title! It became a joke, whenever they encountered something trivial and annoying. *If God loves me, why can't I open this CD case? If God loves me, why are we out of Rice Chex?* God, he missed his daughter. He even missed her silences.

"I worry about Robbie," Joelle said. "He seems anxious."

"He's dealing with some tough stuff."

"Is he still seeing the school counselor?"

"Yeah, he is." Thoughts of Laura came rushing in and Dean stood up. Joelle probably thought he was embarrassed about Robbie. Fine, let her think that. He couldn't sit here, talking about his kids while secretly wondering what Laura was doing now, if she was with Tim, if she was alone, if she was thinking about him.

He and Joelle went inside, where they found the kids playing Sorry. Ed was watching the Orioles in the playoffs and he invited Dean to stay, but Dean begged off, saying he'd watch from home, where he could fall asleep in front of the TV.

His car was frigid, his steering wheel cold to the touch. He felt like driving somewhere far away, but when he started the engine, he saw he was low on gas. He headed toward Sheetz, and on the way he saw the neon light of Coach's. At the last minute he pulled into the crowded parking lot.

The bar was full of Orioles fans and for ten, maybe fifteen minutes, Dean felt content to be part of the group, staring up at the green field glowing on-screen. But the game was a slow one, with no one getting any hits. His beer started to taste warm, and then he spotted See-See's mother in the crowd. She caught his glance and came over to say hello, surprising him with a warm hug and a kiss on the cheek. Her perfume was like honeysuckle, and she was wearing an Orioles baseball jersey, the cut of the shirt somehow flattering to her breasts. She looked cute, but his attraction to her was complicated by the fact that, in the bar's dim light, he could see her resemblance to See-See. She started talking about the race, saying how much fun it had been, how it was a great way to start the weekend, how from now on, she was going to go to all the meets, no matter how much See-See protested.

"Where's See-See now?"

"What, you think I bring her to the bar with me?" Karen laughed. "She's at a friend's house, that's all I know. I don't ask too many questions at her age."

"My daughter's in college, but for all she tells me she could be on the moon."

"At least she made it to college. See won't let me see her applications, she won't even say if she's going to apply. I'm hoping this running thing will motivate her, like maybe she could run on a team?"

"I could talk to her, if you want."

"Oh, *could* you?" Karen leaned closer, her honeysuckle perfume filling the space between them. "That would be so great. I think she would listen to you."

"I don't know much about college running, but I could make some calls."

"You don't even have to do that. If you could just get her to take the idea of college seriously, that would be such a big help. I haven't set the best example. I never finished my degree."

"That doesn't matter," Dean said. "She's a good kid."

"I'm so glad you see that. Some people get the wrong idea about her, with her hair and earrings and her clothes. I tell people, that's how kids are dressing these days, it doesn't mean anything. But it wasn't like this when we were young. I mean, I wanted to be pretty, you know? And the music I listened to was pretty, too. It had its darkness, of course. But it was *melodic*. I don't understand the music she listens to, I don't understand her jokes, I don't understand why she's always sarcastic. And I don't understand how I'm suddenly out of the loop. I mean, we were cool when we were young, weren't we?"

"I don't think I was. I was just a jock."

"Oh, you were a popular guy, I can tell. Maybe you were a little serious. But girls like that."

Her flirting disarmed him. Was this his life now? Going to bars and chatting up the mothers of kids he taught? She was wrong; he hadn't been that popular. When he looked back on his high school years, all he could remember was football practice followed by evenings alone with his father. His dream then was to be a part of a big family. He loved being on a team. Anytime anyone extended an invitation, he took it.

"Let me get the next round." See-See's mother pointed to his half-drunk beer. "Same thing?"

"I actually have to go," he said. "My boys . . . they're at their aunt's."

"Oh, okay! Well, next time!" She seemed unfazed. She was used to being single, used to living outside of family lines. He didn't want to learn to be like her; he had a dread of that life.

He stepped in a puddle in the parking lot, and the odor of wet leaves came wafting up, mixing with the cigarette smoke he could now smell on his jacket. When he got into his car, he had the strange feeling that Nicole had recently been in it. He turned the radio up as he headed toward Sheetz, as if trying to scare off the ghost. But it wasn't a ghost, exactly. It was the memory of her physical presence, a kind of phantom-limb sensation. He couldn't shake it, even when he arrived at the gas station and the inside of the car was filled with the bright lights above the pumps.

The kid behind the register was unknown to him. Dean bought gum, a box of condoms, and a scratch-off lotto ticket. *Play when you're feeling unlucky*, Geneva once told him. Outside, at the pay phone, he called Laura. He didn't expect her to pick up, because she spent her weekends with Tim. That was her life. This was his. He listened to the rings, counting them. He thought about going to church the next day. He wanted to be around people who were trying to be good, even if they were hypocrites. Three rings. Four rings. Laura's answering machine picked up. He shouldn't leave a message, Tim might overhear. The machine beeped and he said "Hello?" like he wasn't sure he had the right number. And then Laura's voice.

"Dean? Wait—let me stop the machine." There was a shuffling sound. "Oh my God, I'm so glad you called."

"What's the matter?"

"I broke up with Tim. Last night. I didn't tell him about us."

"What happened?"

"Don't worry, it doesn't have to do with you. I mean, it does. But I needed to do it anyway."

"I'm not worried," Dean said. Instead he felt a gut-level relief that she was no longer sleeping with anyone else. He hadn't realized how much it was bothering him. It was like he could love her now, if he wanted to.

"Are you alone?" she said. "Can I come over?"

"I'm already out," he said. "I'll come to you."

STEPHANIE SAT ON a worn-out futon couch in the basement of the Arts House, waiting for the ecstasy to kick in. She was nervous but optimistic. Gabe had convinced her of the drug's goodness. He had done it several times, and he described it as a "big warm hug." Gabe seemed like someone for whom nothing bad could ever happen and so, by some transitive property, the things he recommended could not be bad for others. He had already checked in on her twice, refreshing her vodka and orange juice.

The drug had already begun to work on Raquel, who was sitting next to her, rubbing the futon's striped canvas upholstery. She didn't seem much different, except for the fact that she was now enjoying the band, which she had previously deemed "sloppy." Stephanie was slowly noticing that Raquel, for all her wildness, was actually quite intolerant of things that seemed messy or unplanned.

"Do you feel it yet?" Raquel asked. "Do you want to dance?"

"Not yet," Stephanie said. And then she felt something, a delicious relaxation spreading throughout her body, like the feeling of dozing off, those precious milliseconds when her anxieties slipped out of view, just before sleep overtook her body and mind. Except sleep didn't arrive. Instead she stayed in the velvety slipping phase, the little party worries—about her clothes, about the music, about the time—skittering away. It was a contentment that reminded her of something specific, a memory that she couldn't quite grab hold of. Certain smells came to her. Warm smells of grass, hay, dust; cool smells of water, plant life, and mud. She remembered riding a horse, the trees above her, a cool tunnel of shade. She remembered the sun on her arms. The bone-deep relief of being finished with high school. Of moving away from her mother. Slowly, the day came into sharper focus, with names and dates: June, Juniper, the muddy creek . . .

And then, like a stubborn hook finally catching the latch, the rest of the memory fell into place.

Stephanie turned to Raquel. "This is a terrible drug. How do we stop it?"

"What do you mean? You're feeling it? How do you feel?"

Stephanie shook her head. "I can't. You have to stop it. How do we stop it?"

"It's supposed to feel good. It doesn't feel good?"

"You're repeating yourself," Stephanie said. A horrible clarity was coming over her, mixed with overbearing anxiety, anxiety whose cause was at first obscured but then became plain. There was something, she realized now, that she had worked hard to avoid, but now that the drug had rapidly cleared all the stupid shit that had distracted her up to this point, that thing had come forward, it had center stage, it had the microphone, it was asking her, what did Robbie see? And it kept asking her and asking her, what did Robbie see, what did Robbie see, *what did Robbie see?* And she was forced to imagine that thing that Robbie must have seen: her mother's neck in a noose, her mother's body stretching toward the floor, her mother possibly struggling at the last minute, possibly changing her mind, as so many suicide victims—she had read—were known to do. And what the funeral home had done to fix her mother's neck and face was a kind of dark sorcery she didn't want to think about. And what poor Robbie had witnessed, she didn't want to think about, and why he had gone to the barn in the first place, she didn't want to think about, and how close he had gotten, she didn't want to think about, and if he had looked at her face, she didn't want to think about.

"Please, please, you have to stop this drug." Stephanie took Raquel's hands, as if to keep her on the sofa. "You must know a way. What if I throw up?"

"You can't, it's in your blood," Raquel said. "Come on, let's dance, you'll feel better."

"You don't understand. It's not affecting me in the right way. I'm having a bad reaction. Maybe I'm overdosing. Maybe I'm getting brain damage. Have you ever heard of anyone having this reaction?"

Raquel shook her head. Her expression reminded Stephanie of a babysitter she'd once had, who'd watched the boys when Robbie was potty-training and didn't know what to do when Robbie couldn't make it to the bathroom. She almost began to tell Raquel about this babysitter, but the clear part of her mind told her to stay focused on the task at hand, which was to get the drug out of her system.

"I think I need to go to a doctor," Stephanie said. "Or I need to talk to a psychiatrist. Do you know any psychiatrists?"

"Stephanie, chill out, you're not supposed to be this anxious."

"I *know*. That's why something is obviously wrong, I'm having the wrong reaction. I feel like I'm falling inside, like I'm losing my mind. Why did you think this would be a good idea? Why did you think this would be fun? This is the worst night of my life. It's worse than the night my mother died."

Raquel stood up. "I'm getting Gabe. He'll calm you down, okay? He has a good vibe."

"Did you just say *vibe*? You never say things like *vibe*. You're nervous, I can tell you're nervous. Just be honest with me, am I going to die of this? Oh my God, what a stupid way to die."

"Stay there!" Raquel commanded. "I'm getting Gabe."

Stephanie obeyed. She stared at the dancers in front of her, who shook their bodies happily, ironically, self-consciously, and occasionally gracefully, oblivious to her agony. The music, a hazy melody with an unsteady beat (they *were* a sloppy band), could not distract her. Her thoughts were so loud, so unquiet, so insistent. She sipped her drink, and it tasted like her life ten minutes ago, a faraway place that she'd lost forever, a place where she was in control of her mood, where her fears didn't have a death grip on her thoughts.

She had to get out of this basement. She was so tired of parties in basements.

She found the back stairs, and it bothered her that they were carpeted. They felt soggy, somehow. Upstairs was the ballroom, or what passed for a ballroom in a reclaimed fraternity house. The large room was shoddily grand with scuffed parquet floors, high ceilings, tall windows, a large defunct fireplace, and a bar. Stephanie felt a breeze coming through one of the windows. The music was now a vague hum beneath her. She settled down a little. She watched the people at the bar, lining up to receive red plastic cups of beer and cheap liquor. She remembered Mitchell saying that alcohol is a *known poison*. Why hadn't her mother taken poison? Why not pills? Wasn't that the nicer way? The feminine way? The way that could be perceived as an accident?

Gabe and Raquel had followed her upstairs. They looked like cartoons of themselves, Gabe with his sproingy blond curls and Raquel with her big eyes exaggerated into place by heavy eyeliner.

"Hey, Stephanie, what's going on?" Gabe rubbed her arms and shoulders. "Calm down, girl."

"Why did she have to do it that way? It was like she wanted everyone to know. But *I knew.* I knew!" Stephanie pointed to herself.

"Knew what?" Gabe asked.

"I knew how bad she was feeling and I didn't do anything!" Stephanie felt like crying but she couldn't.

"You didn't do anything wrong," Gabe said.

"You don't even know what I'm talking about."

"I know, but I know you didn't do anything wrong."

"Of course you didn't, you're a good person," Raquel said.

"Good people can do bad things!" Stephanie was struck by Gabe's sweetness and Raquel's callowness. They weren't going to be able to help her tonight. She felt no resentment toward either of them. She couldn't; it would be like resenting Robbie and Bryan for not writing back to her postcards.

The sadness was coming back, overwhelming her. It was thinking about her brothers that did it. She thought of Bryan, praying to some made-up father in the sky. And then she thought of Robbie wandering around town, going from pay phone to pay phone, calling her when who he really wanted to call was their mother. This drug was too much, it brought on too much, and that was why people like Gabe and Raquel liked it, because they loved this feeling of too much, because they didn't know what too much was really like. She had to get away from them. She had to get away from these too-much people.

She took off running, exiting the ballroom through one of the floor-to-ceiling windows and jumping out onto the front lawn. Some people heading into the party cheered on her apparently high spirits and she thought of the cross-country meet she had gone to after waking up in Laird Kemp's empty house. She had been wearing the same cloth Mary Jane shoes. She could feel the evening dew seeping through to her bare feet the same way it had that morning. Thinking of Laird brought a glimmer of happier feelings. Not sexual feelings, though. The drug made her detached from that part of herself, which was strange because she thought ecstasy meant wanting to touch soft objects and dance and stare into other people's eyes and be romantic. She didn't want to touch anything. That was why running was good; your feet barely touched the ground when you ran, you got to be airborne.

She remembered her mother showing her how horses ran. The leaps they took. All four legs off the ground.

Her mother had died with her feet off the ground. Not airborne. Not floating. Hanging. *Suspended by the neck.* That was the proper definition. Stephanie had caught Robbie looking it up. She knew he knew anyway. That he had just wanted to put words on what he'd seen.

She was running downhill. Down a winding sidewalk broken up by steps. When the steps came in twos and threes, she leaped them, not wanting to slow down. She didn't care if she fell. If she fell, then people would see that she was hurt.

Her mother had wanted people to see that she was hurt.

Her mother had done an amazing thing: she had taken invisible, inarticulate, unnamable suffering and made it visible.

Suicide as transubstantiation.

The plastic soles of Stephanie's flimsy shoes slapped the paving stones as she followed the sidewalk toward her dormitory. She felt like she was going fast, she felt like she was outrunning something and at the same time tunneling deeper. A memory bloomed: Confirmation class. Twelve years old. Asking Pastor John if you had to take Communion literally, like the Catholics did. The answer was no, it was a metaphor.

What else is a metaphor?

Nothing, Pastor John said.

But Stephanie knew he was lying.

She had gotten confirmed anyway, for her mother's sake. Her mother who thought you had to do it. As if God would kick you out of heaven if your papers weren't in order.

Heaven was obviously a metaphor.

As was the Resurrection.

Probably the divine birth, too.

But what about the Crucifixion?

That was supposed to be real. That was a kind of bodily suffering you were supposed to imagine. You were supposed to think of that pain, all that pain, and behave better. It didn't make sense. Jesus could have done more good by staying alive. Maybe he had gotten tired. Maybe he had said, *Enough, God! Just let me die!* Maybe he wanted to inflict his misery onto the world. Maybe Jesus was just another fucked-up suicide case.

Stephanie had reached the freshman quad. Her lungs burned, and the bottoms of her feet felt almost bruised. Her dorm was on the north end of the quad. She looked up at the tall building with its gray stone exterior.

She hurried to the front door, punching in her key code mindlessly, the numbers already more of a physical memory than a mental one. She ran up the back stairs and found her room empty and unlocked.

The overhead lights were dimmed, but Theresa's lamps were on. Her computer monitor glowed in the corner, the screen white with the blank space of a just-started document. "Man on the Moon" played softly from Theresa's stereo, the dreamy lyrics so familiar to Stephanie it was like pulling on an old sweater. She sat down on the rug in the middle of the floor and began to cry.

"Stephanie?" Theresa stood in the doorway. She was wearing plaid flannel pajama bottoms and a thermal top with little roses on it. Her long hair was wet from the shower. "Where's Raquel?"

"She gave me ecstasy," Stephanie said. "I'm having a bad time. I think I need to see a doctor, maybe I'm allergic? I don't know."

"How many did you take? Is it a pill? I thought it was a rave drug?" Theresa looked disoriented. "I can call my parents."

"No. Don't call your parents. What can your parents do? I need to see someone in person."

"Okay, okay, calm down. We could go to the health center?"

"No, I need a hospital where they can check my blood."

"A hospital? You mean, like, the ER?"

"Yes! Let's go there!" The thought of a waiting room, the thought of an orderly with a clipboard, of uncomfortable vinyl seating, of beige linoleum, of old magazines with wrinkled, torn covers, of benign watercolors cheaply framed, of all the banalities and conventions of hospital care, which existed to disguise death and disease, comforted her deeply.

Stephanie got her keys from her desk drawer and handed them to Theresa. "I have a car, you can drive it. Just drive me to the hospital, please, just do it."

"What about your parents?" Theresa said. "I know you don't get along with your dad, but maybe we could call your mother?"

"My mother's dead," Stephanie said. "She killed herself in June."

DEAN AND LAURA sat on Laura's sofa eating Ritz crackers with peanut butter and drinking Jack Daniel's. He thought he'd never eaten anything better—the salty peanut butter mixed with the faintly sweet crackers mixed with the sweetish liquor. His appetite was good, his body relaxed from a long hour upstairs in Laura's pale green room.

"I'm sorry I don't have anything better to eat," Laura said. "I usually go shopping on Saturday, but I didn't want to run into anyone from Tim's family. I almost drove to Frederick to go to that fancy grocery store—Shank's? Have you been there?"

"Yeah," he said, smiling, realizing he didn't have to explain his connection to Shank's—to *the Shanks*—if he didn't want to, that everything with Laura could be reframed.

"I wish I would have gone," Laura said. "There's nothing for breakfast here."

"We can go out," Dean said. "We can go to the Red Byrd."

"Won't people see us?"

"So what if they do?"

She studied his face. "What are you saying?"

"I don't want to sneak around anymore. I've been sneaking around, hiding things for years. I'm tired of it. What do we have to hide? There's no reason we can't be together."

"What about Robbie?"

"We can figure it out. This can't be the first time something like this has happened."

"No, I guess not," Laura said. There was something measured about her expression, as if she was trying to hide her enthusiasm. He wanted to tell her not to worry, that there was nothing she could say that could frighten him. She could start talking about having kids and he'd start listing names. He was just happy to be with someone who could accept his love—of life, of the future.

"You know I love you," he said, kissing the inside of her wrist. He kept his lips there for an extra beat, wanting to feel her pulse.

THE HOSPITAL STAFF was treating Stephanie like she was another idiot kid, but that was fine with Stephanie; she wanted to be something that simple. She sat on an examining table in a very small room. She was alone; Theresa had gone to get snacks, and the nurses had pretty much stopped checking on her. It had taken hours to get to this examining table; college kids high on illicit drugs were not a priority in a busy city hospital.

She was hooked to an IV, an apparatus she had at first rejected, but the first nurse told her to relax, that it was water, and that it would make her feel better while she waited for the doctor. She didn't feel better. She didn't feel worse, though. The drug's power was possibly waning. She had figured out that she wasn't drowning. It was more like she was on a raft in dangerous currents and if she didn't hold on, she would go under. But she thought she could hold on. And it was easier in the hospital, surrounded by officious uniformed people who had seen every variety of agony.

Theresa returned with a bag of M&Ms, a bag of potato chips, and a Diet Coke.

"Sweet or salty?" she asked.

"I'm not hungry yet."

Theresa sat down on a plastic chair next to the examining

table. She opened her Diet Coke and the pop-and-fizz sound it made was briefly pleasing to Stephanie. For a split second she got a glimpse of what ecstasy would be like if she were a happier person, deep down.

"You feeling any different?" Theresa asked.

"A little," Stephanie said.

"Well, it has to wear off soon, right?" Theresa's long hair had dried completely but was uncombed, with flyaways and random curly pieces. She looked exhausted.

"I'm sorry I ruined your night," Stephanie said.

"You didn't ruin anything. I was just writing some boring paper. This is way more interesting." Theresa smiled tentatively. "You know I'm kidding, right?"

"I know you are," Stephanie said. "You're so nice. I've been . . . not nice."

"It's okay. I didn't realize what was going on with you."

"I didn't, either."

"I wish I'd known," Theresa said. "I feel bad."

"Why do *you* feel bad?"

"Because I thought you were mean. I was really judgmental. I thought your dad seemed nice. It never occurred to me that there was another side to things. I feel like I should have guessed."

"I'm the one who should feel bad," Stephanie said.

"Look at us: two girls competing over who should feel worse about herself."

"We're a triumph of feminism."

Theresa held up her Diet Coke ironically.

Stephanie smiled. She felt like she might start crying again. "Thank you," she said. "I really mean that."

"It's no big deal," Theresa said. She took a sip of her soda. "I hope you don't mind, but I called your dad. I wasn't going to tell you except that I ended up leaving a message. I called a bunch of times. I thought maybe he was screening."

"What did you say?"

"Just to call you at school. That's it."

Stephanie's thoughts began to ramp up again. Her father always answered the phone. She felt her mind reaching for reason, clinging to the raft. "How did you even know his number?"

"I've written it down enough times. Sorry, I felt like I should call him, in case something happened."

"It's okay," Stephanie said. "I just don't want to involve him if I don't have to."

There was a knock at the door and a doctor came in. Theresa excused herself for the examination. The doctor was young, with a goatee and a sort of unformed look about his mouth, as if he'd heard an off-color joke and couldn't decide whether or not it was okay to laugh. He worked quickly, chatting as he checked her vitals. He explained he was a resident and that it was a busy night. He asked her what she'd taken and how she was feeling, giving no indication of his opinion of her behavior. His breath smelled like coffee and licorice gum. When he was finished examining her, he put his clipboard down and took a step back.

"Okay, here's the deal. You have a slight temperature, but that's normal with this drug. Your blood pressure is good. Physically, you're fine. But you did a really dumb thing."

"I know."

"Do you? Because this is not a soft drug. Don't let anyone

tell you differently. First of all, I don't know where you got it, but unless you made it yourself, you really have no idea what's actually in it. I am not exaggerating when I say you could have poisoned yourself to death. Second, even if you assume it's pure MDMA, you basically flooded your brain with serotonin and dopamine. You know what those are, right? They're the feel-good chemicals, okay? But they're supposed to be regulated. Your brain keeps them in check—behind doors, let's say. But MDMA, it comes in and it beats down those doors and rips them off the hinges. So now your brain has to repair all those doorways."

"I already feel bad."

"Well, you're going to feel worse." He detached her IV. "You're going to be down, really down, depressed. There's nothing you can do; it's the hangover of this drug. So be aware."

"Okay," Stephanie said, holding back tears. She felt like the doctor thought she deserved to be depressed. "What do I do now?"

"There's no treatment; you have to wait for the drug to wear off. I can't keep you overnight unless I send you up to Psych, and I don't think you want that. It's not the right place for a girl like you."

She wanted to ask him what he meant by "a girl like you." Did he think she was spoiled? Sheltered? Suicidal? She wasn't any of those things, but why would he give her the benefit of the doubt? She had the urge to see the Shanks, wanting the comfort of being around people who thought she was smart and sensible. But if she called them to pick her up here, would they still think that?

"You should wait until morning to go home," the resident

said. "It's almost three, so you don't have that long to wait. You can go to the cafeteria or wait in the lobby. I'm sure this won't be your first all-nighter."

"Okay, thanks," Stephanie said. Shame rippled through her, the resident's unspoken assumptions filling up the room. She stayed seated on the metal examining table for a few minutes after he left, trying to gauge the progress of the drug. But now it was hard to separate the intensity of the high from the intensity of the situation. All she knew was that she couldn't calm herself in any of the usual ways.

Theresa was dozing on a sofa in the waiting area. Stephanie didn't wake her. Instead she went to the pay phone and called her father. He didn't pick up. She hung up right before the machine answered and dialed two more times, repeating the pattern. Still no answer. She wanted to believe that he was sleeping so deeply he couldn't hear the phone, but she couldn't convince herself of that.

She called the Shanks next. She didn't know the number by heart and had to check her wallet, where she kept the pink sticky note with their number and address. Her mother had given it to her last fall, back when Stephanie first expressed an interest in seeing them. The sight of her mother's handwriting, so round and buoyant and girlish, filled Stephanie with remorse. She thought of what the doctor had said, about the depression coming her way. She tried to project herself to a place beyond the drug's hangover, but it was like her mind could only go downhill.

JOELLE WANTED DEAN to stay for lunch after church, but he was eager to take the boys home, to spend the afternoon doing

Sunday things, the chores and errands that would help prepare them for the week ahead. For the first time since the beginning of the year, he was looking forward to his job. He didn't even mind that Garrett was coming over to "pick his brain" in advance of "A Night with the Coach," the Q&A that the Boosters hosted every year, midseason.

He drove fast down the bumpy farm lane and into town, where he stopped at the market for lunch meat, bread, and potato salad. The boys waited in the car, and when he came back, they were arguing over the radio. Robbie had tuned it to the Top Forty countdown, but Bryan wanted to listen to a tape of Christian music that Joelle had given him. On the radio, a girl with a warbly voice seemed to split the difference with a secular song about souls being saved.

"Who's that in our driveway?" Bryan asked as they approached their house. There was a maroon-colored sedan parked there.

"I don't know," Dean said. His first thought was Laura, but it wasn't her car.

"Maybe it's someone from church dropping off food," Robbie said.

"Maybe," Dean said. But no one had left food for some time. It had stopped when the school year began.

He pulled into his driveway next to the strange car, feeling spooked and unseated, his good mood slipping away.

Dean's driveway was adjacent to the side porch, separated by a tall, gated wooden fence, upon which a sweet vining flower grew.

"Hello?" Dean called out as he approached the gate. When

he opened it, he saw the Shanks sitting on the steps of his porch. They stood up, brushing off their clothes. As always, they were dressed a notch too formally for the occasion, Mrs. Shank wearing a white oxford-cloth shirt and navy pants, and Mr. Shank in gray chinos, a collared shirt, and a pullover sweater.

"It's Stephanie's grandparents!" Bryan said. Always friendly, he ran to them and gave them each a hug. "Is Stephanie here?"

"No, my dear, she's busy at school," Mrs. Shank said. But she gave Dean a look that let him know that something was wrong.

"Robbie, why don't you go inside and make a sandwich for yourself and your brother," Dean said, handing him the groceries.

"Are you staying for lunch?" Bryan asked, not getting it.

"Come on, Bry," Robbie said. "Leave them alone. They have to talk about something."

"What?" Bryan asked as Robbie pushed him toward the door. "What is it, Daddy?"

"It's grown-up stuff, sweetheart," Mrs. Shank said. "It would bore you; it's about tuition."

"Oh, money," Bryan said, with a put-on knowingness that Dean had never seen before. He felt a wheel of panic spinning in his chest; he felt as if he did not know his children at all.

"Dean, I'm sorry to descend on you like this," Mrs. Shank said as soon as the boys were out of earshot. "We just felt it was the right thing to do."

"What happened?" Dean asked. "Is Stephanie in trouble?"

"She's fine, but she reached out to us last night—actually, in the morning—and we thought we should tell you in person." Mrs. Shank glanced at her husband. "Maybe you should tell him. I'll go help the boys with lunch."

"You don't need to do that," Dean said. But she was already heading inside.

"Should we sit down, then?" Mr. Shank nodded to the two rocking chairs on Dean's porch. It was maybe the sixth sentence Mr. Shank had ever spoken directly to Dean.

"Let's take a walk," Dean said, trying to get some control over the situation. He couldn't be out-and-out rude to a man his father's age.

Mr. Shank followed Dean to the backyard. They ended up standing at the edge of Dean's property, where his overgrown lawn bordered on a weedy meadow.

"Any idea who owns this field?" Mr. Shank asked.

"It's part of the Baker farm."

"You should try to buy it. It doesn't seem like they're doing much with it. And you don't want them to sell it to a developer. You'll have people looking right into your backyard."

Dean couldn't deal with small talk. "Mr. Shank, with all due respect—"

"Call me Walter. We've known each other long enough."

"Walter, what's going on? I know you didn't come all this way for no reason."

"We came because we're worried," Mr. Shank said. "Stephanie called us early this morning after a night of partying. She was under the influence of a drug, something I've never heard of, but apparently it's a kind of pharmaceutical. Something that induces intense moods. She was extremely distraught when she called us. She had checked herself into the ER because she was so scared."

"Stephanie was in the hospital?" Dean felt sick.

"She claims she called you, but that you didn't answer. Do you remember getting any calls last night? Did you have messages on your answering machine?"

"I don't know, I haven't checked yet." Dean was uncertain of how much to leave unsaid. "I wasn't home last night."

"Oh, I see. That explains things." Mr. Shank gave Dean a look that was surprisingly sympathetic. "I learned a long time ago not to judge people for their private lives. But I've never seen Stephanie behave this way. Granted, I don't know her all that well. And I regret that. But I know her well enough to say that she's not herself."

"I can't believe she would use drugs," Dean said. "It doesn't sound like her at all."

"Grief makes people do strange things." Mr. Shank kept his eyes on the meadow.

"That's not an excuse. I'm sorry you had to pick her up."

"Sometimes there are things that parents can't do."

"I could have gone to get her. I would have if I'd known—"

Mr. Shank turned to him. "What I mean is, Vivian and I would be happy to help out more with Stephanie."

"You're already helping plenty."

"I don't mean financially. I mean that we would like to take a more active role in her development as an adult. It's a difficult transition for anyone. And I think she might be more likely to listen to us. It may help that we have some distance from recent events."

Dean nodded, unable to speak. Shame and anger mixed within him, directed mostly toward himself but also toward the Shanks, whose arrogance—or maybe it was cluelessness— was getting to him. He felt as if Walter was telling him to step aside. That they would take over now, with Stephanie. That they could do a better job. Because they weren't mixed up with the messiness of Nicole's death. This, he saw now, was why everyone in Nicole's family disliked the Shanks. Their strategy for getting through life was to stay as clean as possible. To always be blameless and rational.

"We thought we might visit more," Walter said. "And if it's all right with you, maybe she could come to our house for Thanksgiving and even for—"

"It's up to her," Dean said, cutting him off. "If that's what she wants, what can I say?"

"I know it's a hard time," Walter said. "Sam did the same thing to us when he started college. He came back, though. Stephanie will, too."

"Thanks," Dean said. He still felt condescended to, but he was reminded that he was talking to a man whose son hadn't even made it out of his twenties. Maybe he wanted another chance to be a parent.

The two men walked back to the house, where they found the boys eating sandwiches on the side porch. Mrs. Shank had made herself a cup of tea. Dean invited her and Walter to stay for lunch, but she declined. He would have been shocked if they'd accepted.

As soon as the Shanks left, Dean called Stephanie, but there was no answer, not even the roommate. He checked his answering machine. The number of messages was high, but the first three were blank. Finally, a girl's soft voice implored Dean to call Stephanie at school. The meek roommate. After her message there was another blank message. Dean thought he heard a sigh before the click, a slight exhalation from his drugged-up daughter. If she was the one who called.

The last message was from Laura. *Hey, I'm just calling to say I miss you already. And that I love you. Call me tonight, okay?*

Dean's cheeks burned. He went into the kitchen and got some paper napkins.

"Boys, wrap up your sandwiches, we're going to see your sister. You can finish them in the car."

"But we just got home!" Robbie said. "I have homework. I have a project due tomorrow."

"I'll write a note to your teacher. Come on, it's a family emergency."

"Is Stephanie okay?" Bryan asked.

"She's fine, she's just doing stupid things. She needs a come-to-Jesus talk. So to speak."

"I'm going to pray for her," Bryan said. "I'm going to pray for God's wisdom to visit her."

"Oh my God, excuse me while I barf," Robbie said.

"Don't be rude to your brother," Dean said. "He's your ally."

They were getting onto the turnpike when it occurred to Dean that he didn't know how to get to Stephanie's college, only that it was near Philadelphia. He made Robbie get the Pennsylvania map out of the glove compartment and figure out the route. Then he stopped at a gas station to double-check it and realized it was faster to go through Maryland. He filled up the tank and bought the boys snacks. He didn't want to stop again if he didn't have to. For himself, he got a large coffee. He was tired and a little bit hungover beneath it all.

Bryan fell asleep in the backseat as soon as they got on the highway, the hum of the road putting him out the way it used to do when he was a baby. Robbie tuned the radio to the same alternative rock station that Stephanie listened to and that Dean tolerated reluctantly. Actually, after four years, he was getting used to it, even beginning to appreciate some of it. He could hear the melodies now, beneath the feedback. He listened closely to the lyrics of each song, as if they could provide a window into his daughter's character. He kept thinking back to when they were close, when she was nine, ten, eleven. Even twelve and thirteen were good years. She used to tag along with him for every errand, every little trip into town. She loved to go with him to the printer's to pick up programs for the game; she said she liked the smell of ink. She went with him so often to Tri-State Sports that the owner had a special windbreaker made for her, with her name embroidered on the pocket. She had been wearing it the night Bryan was born. Dean remembered her pulling the hood over her head and dozing off in the waiting area. When she was finally allowed to see Bryan, she said he looked like Robbie when he was born. A simple thing to say, but in that moment, Dean realized how many memories he shared with her. There were things in the world that only the two of them had seen.

Dean's vision blurred a little, the road ahead a shaky line. He'd let his girl down, he'd let her get lost. He glanced at Robbie to see if he was looking at him, but he was staring out the passenger-side window. In the backseat, Bryan's expression seemed utterly transparent, even in sleep. Bryan was always hoping for good things. Even in dreamland he was hoping.

STEPHANIE WALKED BACK to her dorm in a daze after seeing a movie. The photogenic old oaks that guarded her campus cast long, pleasing shadows. It was magic hour, a term she'd only recently learned, and the mellow early-evening light was the perfect balm for her wrung-out senses. She was happy she'd gone out alone, that she didn't have to talk to anyone about the matinee she'd just seen, a lush, intense romance about a man who falls in love with another man's wife in the desert. The man's wife, an Englishwoman, had had her mother's golden glow.

On the lawn in front of her dormitory, two boys were playing Frisbee—actual boys, not college boys. They looked to be the same ages as her brothers. As Stephanie got closer, she realized they *were* her brothers. She ran to them, calling their names, a rush of excitement coming over her and then fading rapidly as she registered that her father must be nearby. She had asked her grandparents not to tell him.

Bryan got to her first, throwing his arms around her neck. He was sweaty from running around outside, his hair damp and smelling sweetly floral, like he'd been using a girl's shampoo. Maybe hers, something she'd left behind.

"What are you doing here?"

"I don't know," Bryan said. "It was something you did."

"Yeah, what happened?" Robbie asked. He gave her a brief hug, barely touching her. "Dad won't tell us."

"He said it was stupid," Bryan said.

"I'm fine," Stephanie said reflexively. So she was stupid.

That was the official summary. "Dad's exaggerating. You know how he is. Where is he, anyway?"

"He's on the phone inside. He's calling your room."

It was strange to see her father on a campus phone in the foyer, leaning against the cinder-block wall like a student. Something about the sight embarrassed her. He looked vulnerable and out of place. When he saw her, he ran to her, embracing her with a force that surprised her. Sometimes she forgot he was an athlete. That he was stronger than most people. It felt good to have him holding her so tightly, but at the same time, she felt a vast, dark sky of confusion opening up within her—the sky that the drug had shown her; and which she didn't think she would ever be able to forget.

"Honey, I'm so glad you're okay. I was worried when you didn't answer the phone."

"I was at the movies."

"The movies?"

"What's wrong with going to the movies?"

"Nothing, it's just not what I expected." Her father glanced at Robbie and Bry. "Is there a lounge where they can watch TV or something?"

Stephanie led them to a common area on the first floor, where there was a TV, sofas, and a couple of shelves filled with cast-off books, magazines, and games. Two boys Stephanie vaguely knew were watching *Labyrinth*. They smiled as Robbie and Bryan settled onto the sofa next to them, as if it were perfectly normal for small children to join them. There was something so nonchalant about some of her classmates. Stephanie still wasn't used to it.

She brought her father to an adjacent room, a small, wood-paneled library with built-in shelves, a relic from earlier in the building's history. She watched as he took in all the genteel details: the fireplace with its long mantelpiece, the old-fashioned standing pencil sharpeners, the thick windowpanes, the heavy curtains drawn back with wide sashes, and the small, gilt-framed oil painting of the pinkish and well-fed man who lent her dormitory its name. She saw how pretentious it must seem to her father, how ridiculous she must seem for wanting to be here.

"Dad, I'm sorry," she said. "I know why you're here, okay? You don't need to yell at me."

"I didn't come here to yell at you. I came to check on you. I got a visit this morning from your grandparents."

"They came to the *house*?"

"They were worried. I'm worried, too."

"I'm sorry. I told them not to bother you."

"They didn't bother me. I'm grateful to them. As you should be. I don't think I need to remind you, they're paying your tuition."

"I'm on a partial scholarship."

"Even more reason not to mess it up."

"You *did* come here to yell at me. I get it, okay? I'm a stupid person."

"That's not what I'm saying." Her father glanced around the library, as if looking for a prop. "This is a really nice school. I don't want you to do anything to jeopardize your future here."

"I'm not. I'm really not. No one knows what I did, okay? No one would care anyway."

"I don't care who knows. I care about your health, I care about your brain, I care about what you're doing to yourself."

"If you care so much, where were you last night when I called?"

"That's not relevant."

"You say you want to be there for me, but you're never there when I need you. Where were you? What were you doing? Were you out with that woman?"

"You know what, Stephanie? It's none of your business."

"Then it's none of your business what I was doing last night."

"It is when the Shanks show up on my doorstep to tell me that they picked you up from the hospital."

"I *said* I was sorry."

"I don't care how sorry you are. You're being reckless. You're not acting like yourself."

"You don't even know who I am!" Stephanie said, hearing the cliché even as she said it. But it seemed so true. It seemed like no one in her family had bothered to find out who she was, where she had come from, and now both her parents were dead and she was never going to know.

"You're my daughter. I've known you since you were a little girl."

She saw he was getting choked up, and she felt sad, too, but not crying sad. Empty sad. It was as if her soul—or her cache of dopamine receptors, whatever—was a barren creek bed. What had once been flowing was dried up. She wondered if this was how her mother had felt. She wondered if she had wanted to find out how her mother had felt. If that's why she'd done the drug in the first place. There was no way she could ever explain that to her father. He was too levelheaded a person. He would never understand.

"You're not my real father," she said, calmly. "We don't actually have anything in common."

"That's not how I see it," he said. "But if that's how you really feel, I don't know what else I can say to you."

He paused, and when Stephanie didn't refute him, he told her to go say good-bye to her brothers, that he would catch up in a minute.

Chapter 11

The girls were still high off Megan's win on Monday afternoon. They were waiting for her on the sidewalk when Ed dropped her off, cheering and clapping, like a miniature fan club. Dean watched from inside the school. Saturday's meet felt like a distant memory. He was tired from driving to and from Stephanie's school, tired from arguing, tired from loneliness. He wanted to tell Laura, to be comforted, but he hadn't called her yet. He was too embarrassed. Laura didn't really know that much about his daughter. He didn't want illegal drug use to be among her first impressions—especially since Laura probably knew more about the drug than he did.

"All right, girls," Dean said, calling them inside. They arranged themselves on the bottom row of bleachers. "You had a good race this weekend, every single one of you. There were three PRs, and as a team, we got the lowest score we've ever had."

"Thanks to Megan," See-See said.

"Thanks to all of you," Dean said. "We race as a team and we practice as a team. And now it's less than a month until Regionals. For some of you, Regionals is the end of the season.

For others, it's the gateway to States. But we're all going to practice like we're all going to States, because you never know. We've already caused a stir—did everyone see the article yesterday? We were 'underdog Willowboro.' "

Jessica had a funny, knowing half smile, and Dean guessed she'd read the article in full, including the part where the reporter pointed out that "former football coach" Dean Renner was in the unusual position of coaching a team with "long odds." Dean had read that line and felt himself marginalized: already a *former* something. And at the same time, there was freedom in coaching a team that no one followed or cared about. He wasn't trying to impress a crowd of fans or justify a big budget. No one was looking over his shoulder saying he should have done *x* or *y*, no one was calling in to a radio show to say that See-See slowed down too much in the second mile, and why wasn't Coach Renner taking splits on the third mile? There was a purity to the sport that pleased him; the athletes who won races were the ones in the best physical and mental shape, period.

He sent the girls off on a two-mile warm-up run and told them to meet him and Bryan behind the middle school, where there was a wide, flat playing field that the band sometimes used for its practices. Dean planned to use it for a speed workout of ten 100-meter sprints. He wanted the girls to develop a kick. Philips had told him it was the key to getting more points.

Dean measured the distance on the field, and Bryan set up orange cones to mark the start and finish. He leaped over the cones while he waited for the girls to finish their warm-up. "Daddy, look, I'm hurdling!" he said.

"You're not hurdling," Dean said. "You're jumping. Like a little frog."

"I'm a jumping frog, I jump, jump, jump for joy!"

Dean smiled uneasily. Lately, Bryan seemed almost maniacally happy, as if trying to make up for Robbie's and Stephanie's melancholy.

The girls arrived on the field and Dean started the workout. He told them to run the first hundred as fast as they could and then to run the next four at three-quarters speed. The shorter distance rearranged them; Missy came in first, followed by Aileen, Megan, See-See, Lori, and Jessica. Now he knew who could really sprint. They were starting to show the strain after they finished the first five. All except Jessica. She still seemed relatively energetic. Dean realized she was holding back. He pulled her aside.

"You're not pushing yourself," he said. "Why?"

"It hurts to go fast," she said. "I feel like I'm not good at it."

"You're not a natural sprinter," he conceded. "But it hurts for everyone, even the people who are really good. Ask Missy—Missy, are you in pain?"

"Hell, yeah!" She covered her mouth with a glance toward Bryan. "Oops, I'm sorry."

"He's heard worse," Dean said. "In fact, let's get a hell yeah from all of you. I've said it before and I'll say it again. It doesn't matter how fast you can run. What matters is how fast you can run when you're tired. So let me ask, are you tired?"

"Hell, yeah!" they yelled back.

"Are you ready to run five more?"

"Hell, yeah!"

"Are you ready to run fast?"

"Hell, yeah!"

They lined up and waited for Dean's signal. Dean felt their happy anticipation as his own. He raised his stopwatch, yelled "*Go!*" and watched them race across the fading green field. Life could be so easy.

He had them alternate between half speed and three-quarter speed. Jessica improved. So did Lori. For the last hundred he told them to go all out. Only Megan hit a time faster than her first splits.

Dean sent the girls on a cooldown run and then headed to his office with Bry. Robbie was usually waiting for them there, doing homework, but today Dean's office was empty.

"I guess he's still at rehearsal," Dean said.

"Can we go watch?" Bryan asked.

Dean shrugged. "I don't see why not."

Dean used his master set of keys to take a shortcut through the locked-up school. Outside the chorus room he saw a couple of kids sitting in the hallway, artsy kids with headphones and homework.

"You looking for Robbie?" one asked. He hooked his thumb toward the auditorium. "The dance rehearsal is going long."

"Thanks," Dean said.

He let himself and Bryan into the theater through the side door. Raucous, stormy-sounding music was blaring, so loud that no one noticed Dean enter. He and Bryan sat down in the old creaky seats with itchy upholstery, seats that Dean associated with faculty meetings. He thought fleetingly of Laura and then watched the stage, where a group of children were dancing in violent circles, kicking their legs and arms. It took him a moment to locate Robbie in his dance attire. He was wearing black sweatpants and a black T-shirt that accentuated the whiteness of his arms. He was moving with a fluidity that Dean had never seen before. The expression on his face was calm, focused, and sincere. Dean was surprised by how proud he felt. Was it his imagination or was his son more graceful than the others?

The music was shut off abruptly.

"You guys can't just flail about!" the teacher said. "Think of how monkeys move. They swing from place to place. They're going somewhere. They're playful but deliberate. The only one of you who is following the choreography is Robbie. I want you all to stop and watch him. Is that okay, Robbie?"

Robbie nodded with the same calm expression.

Dean felt as if he were snooping. As a coach, he knew there were interactions between students and their teachers that were somehow too intimate for parents, those times when children revealed their potential, the ambitions they couldn't share with their parents because to do so would expose their intention to separate. Dean wondered if he and Stephanie were close—had been close—because he was more like a teacher than a father, if she had felt she could reveal her true nature to him in a way that she couldn't with her mother. Now she had taken that sliver of distance and turned it into a weapon.

Onstage, Robbie's dancing was expressive but controlled; his movements were angry and urgent like the music, but there was a hint of joy, too. Dean could tell that Robbie knew he was good. That was all Dean really wanted for him—to be good at something and know it. He wouldn't have chosen dancing, of course, but he was glad that it was something physical. Maybe it was the dumb jock in him, but he felt that the physical world was more reliably rewarding than the intellectual one.

If Dean had come into the auditorium alone, he would have left without letting Robbie know what he'd seen, but he had Bryan with him and Bryan wouldn't understand that impulse. Instead, he clapped at the end of Robbie's impromptu solo. The spell was immediately broken. Robbie blushed in displeasure and all the elegance disappeared from his body at once, his limbs going slack. He returned to his usual "whatever" posture. But Robbie's teacher was happy to see Dean.

"Coach Renner! Thanks for dropping by." She smiled as if she knew him already, and Dean struggled to remember her name as they shook hands.

"Abby," she said. She lowered her voice. "We met once before. At Coach's? You were with your brother-in-law?"

"Oh right, of course." Dean felt awkward. One of Laura's friends. She probably knew more about his personal life than he did.

"I'm so glad you got to see Robbie dance."

"Me too," Dean said. "Sorry to interrupt. We'll wait outside so you can finish up."

"Oh, it's fine. Robbie, you can actually go home now, if you'd like. You've got it down."

"I can stay," Robbie said. "I don't mind."

"It's fine, don't worry. Go home with your dad."

Robbie reluctantly left the stage and grabbed his backpack and school clothes from the first row of theater seats.

"You can go change," Dean said. "We're not in a hurry."

"Let's just go."

Outside it was already dark. Robbie hurried ahead to the car, clearly embarrassed. Dean apologized for intruding and Robbie mumbled "It's okay" and then unzipped his backpack and started to reorganize its contents.

"I'm glad I got to see you rehearse," Dean said. "You're really good."

Robbie shrugged. "It's only dancing."

"You know what they say—the most grueling sports are football and ballet."

"That wasn't ballet. And I know you'd pick football if you could choose—or basketball, or soccer. Anything with a ball."

"That's not true."

"Dad."

"All right, there's some truth to it. But that's only because I'm a terrible dancer."

At last, Robbie smiled, a little. "You've still got Bry," he said. "I mean, to play football."

"Did you hear that, Bry?" Dean said. "It's all on you."

"Put me in, Coach!" Bryan said, eager to make them all laugh. And they did.

At home, Dean made a quick dinner of chicken drumsticks with mashed potatoes and green beans. Laura called when Dean was loading the dishwasher.

"I can't really talk now," he said. "The boys . . ."

"Oh, are they right nearby?"

"Yeah. I'll call you back later, okay?"

"Okay."

But he didn't call later. Instead he read about racing strategy after he put the boys to bed. He stayed up to watch Letterman, mindlessly, like he used to do over the summer. The guest was an actress he'd never heard of. He dozed off during her interview and woke up, an hour later, to a commercial for a CD collection of hits from the 1960s. Song titles scrolled down the screen, lyrics from his childhood. He felt disoriented as he made his way upstairs to bed, stopping as always to check on Robbie and Bry. The room seemed thick with their breathing. *Two lives*, he thought vaguely. That night he dreamed of his mother. He had dinner with her at the Red Byrd diner and she was very charming, asking him questions about the football team. He kept trying to tell her about the cross-country girls, but she was dismissive. "You never got to know me," she said. In the midst of the dream, Dean became lucid and, realizing he was in a dream, tried to interpret it. He had the idea of calling Laura but he couldn't, he was in a dream. Then it was morning, and he was waking up. He could call Laura, if he wanted, but when he picked up the phone, the receiver felt too heavy in his hand.

That day at practice, Dean took the girls to the Antietam Battlefield for a fartlek workout. It was one of the first truly chilly days of the season, with a cold wind that seemed to warn of winter. On the wide-open battlefield, whipped-up clouds slid across the sky.

Dean warmed up with the girls, leading the first mile at a relaxed pace. He'd brought Bryan's bike so that Bryan could keep up. It felt good to run on the battlefield's smooth, paved roads and to breathe the cold autumn air. The leaves were beginning to change on some of the trees, spots of red and gold at the edges, and the grasses were yellowing. It gave the park the bleak sepia tones it had in photographs of the war.

After about ten minutes, Dean dropped back and told Missy

to take the lead—and to run fast. She bolted ahead, and the other girls rushed to follow. Dean's own lungs burned as he kept the pace. He thought she would tire after a few minutes, but she kept it up for almost a mile. Then See-See took over and slowed things down for a while. They came to a steep hill, and Bryan lost momentum on his bicycle and had to stop and walk. Dean dropped back to help him, watching as the girls crested the hill and then disappeared from view.

"Come on, Bry, let's cut across and meet them at the other side of the loop."

As he ran across the transverse road, Dean kept glancing to his right, watching for the girls in the distance. He couldn't see them and worried they might have taken a wrong turn. Ahead, Bryan made lazy loops on his bicycle. "Daddy!" he said. "I see them!"

Dean sprinted ahead. There they were, running toward them, Jessica in the lead. He felt a sense of relief that he knew was out of proportion, but he didn't care. He let the feeling wash over him as he ran.

On Thursday, the last hard workout of the week before race day, it was overcast and gray. The football team had reserved the weight room, so Dean used his planning period at the end of the day to set up a simple circuit-training workout in the small gym. He was in the midst of pulling out the tumbling mats from the equipment room when he saw Laura heading toward his office.

"Hey!" he called to her.

"Hi!" She waved back, but in a cautious way that made Dean feel guilty. He hadn't talked to her since their brief conversation on Monday night. Instead he'd left an apologetic message with her secretary, calling at a time when he knew she wouldn't be available.

"You're a hard man to get a hold of," she said. "I was coming to the high school anyway, so I thought I'd see if you were here."

"I'm glad you did." He gave her a quick kiss on the cheek and led her into his office. "Bryan's around, just so you know."

"I know," she said. "He goes to practice with you, right?"

"Sometimes Robbie, too. But not today, he has rehearsal. He's actually really good, I saw him dancing the other day, not that I know the first thing about dancing. But still, he's got something!" Dean could hear how fake and jovial he sounded. He could see on Laura's face that she heard it, too.

"What's going on with you?" Laura said.

"I'm sorry, I've been busy."

"If you're busy, that's fine," she said. "I'm busy, too. But you don't have to avoid me."

"It doesn't have to do with you."

"Dean, I've been through this before with you. Where you fade out. I can't do it again."

"I'm not fading out. It's Stephanie. She got into trouble over the weekend and I've been trying to deal with it."

"What kind of trouble?"

"I shouldn't get into it," Dean said. "For her sake."

"Okay, but I want to be there for you, if I can."

"You can't," Dean said, more sharply than he'd intended.

"I don't even get to try?" Laura took a step back toward the doorway, and he remembered kissing her when he was still married.

"I'm sorry," he said. "It's just more serious than you think. She was in the hospital."

"She was in the hospital?" Laura said. "Was it a suicide attempt?"

"No, of course not! She would never do that." Dean felt jolted; he couldn't believe this possibility hadn't occurred to him.

"I'm sorry," Laura said. "I don't know why I assumed that."

"You don't know why?"

"I mean, it was insensitive." She looked at him uncertainly. "You're never sarcastic. I don't like it."

"I need to get my head together, I'm about to run a practice." He took his clipboard from his desk, the one Stephanie had decorated with a Sharpie years ago, without asking him. He'd been annoyed then, but now he liked seeing his name in little-girl lettering.

"So that's it? That's the end of our conversation?"

As she spoke, the bell rang for dismissal, as if to answer her question. But they couldn't even joke about it.

"The girls are waiting for me," Dean said.

"You can't just blow me off," Laura said. "I can't be here for you when you need me and spend the rest of my time wondering what's going on in your head."

"Sometimes you overthink things."

"That's better than what you do. I'm starting to see why your wife felt like she was shut out."

"Who told you that?"

"*You* told me that. You told me everything about your life and now I'm just supposed to be the girlfriend you keep on the side?"

"Nobody told you to break up with your fiancé. If you needed me to be your excuse to change your life, that's fine."

"I didn't need an excuse. You're projecting things onto me."

"I don't have time to be analyzed, Laura. I've got three kids. I have to think about them."

"You know I can't argue with that." Her eyes were filled with tears. "I think that's why you're saying it."

"I'm sorry—"

"No, let me go. I'm going."

He followed her into the hallway, but he couldn't say anything more because Megan was waiting outside his office. She was sitting on a bench near the small gym, at a respectable distance, which made Dean think she must have overheard something.

"Hey, Megan. What's going on? Did you talk to your dad about getting racing flats?"

"Not yet. My mom just wanted me to ask if you still need us to babysit tomorrow night."

"Oh, yeah." Dean had forgotten that he was supposed to go to an away game. Garrett had asked him to come along, a couple of weeks ago—not to coach, but to ride in the van with the Boosters, as a "special guest." In the back of his mind, he'd thought of asking Laura to meet him there.

"So you'll drop them off tomorrow?" Megan said.

Dean paused. He really didn't want to go. This was his chance to cancel. He nodded and said he'd drop them off at five.

ON TUESDAY, STEPHANIE took her Psych I midterm and failed it. She had never failed a test before, and when she got it back, on Thursday, the letter was written so neatly and precisely that it didn't immediately register as a bad thing. In her mind's eye, an F would be written with a thick red pen; it would be angry-looking. This F was a small notation at the top right-hand corner of her blue book. She flipped through the pages, skimming the corrections in the margins of her error-ridden essays. She barely remembered writing them.

Next to her, the margins of Raquel's exam were punctuated with checkmarks and stars. She had done well, somehow. Her mind wasn't caught in the same fog.

"How'd you do?" Raquel whispered.

Stephanie shrugged. "Not great."

"I pulled this B-plus out of my ass," Raquel said. "I don't like cramming, I never want to do that again."

"Yeah, I know what you mean." Stephanie shoved her booklet into her backpack. Something had shifted in her relationship with Raquel. Without discussing it, they'd stopped eating meals together and now only met to study in the library, where they couldn't talk much. It was as if Stephanie had swum out to a place that Raquel didn't want to go. Or maybe it was simpler. Maybe Stephanie had admired Raquel and now she didn't and without that admiration, the coziness between them was gone.

The professor started to go through the exam, question by question. Stephanie couldn't take it. She excused herself to use the bathroom, but once she was in the hallway, she knew she was going to leave the building. Outside, the day was overcast, the sky a dull white sheet in need of washing. She went to the library to check her e-mail. There, sitting in her inbox, was a message with the subject line *Re: Nostalgia's a bitch*. She opened it hungrily.

Steph, I am so sorry I didn't answer this sooner. I kept putting it off because I wanted to say the right thing. Anyway, I'm sure you're feeling much better about school now. The first weeks were hard for me, too. I think I had this ideal in my head. I thought none of the guys here would be like the guys we knew in high school because they were smart, but it turns out that being smart does not prevent you from being a boring asshole. Also, it has to be said, there are a lot of nerds here. And the drinking is out of hand. Apparently it gets worse in the winter. I don't know how that is even possible. All that being said, I am pretty fucking happy. My roommate is really funny and he's getting me into improv comedy. We've been going to shows in town. And my classes are amazing. For the first time in my life I am struggling to keep up and it's a weirdly good feeling. I already know I want to go to grad school, maybe even get a PhD. It feels possible. There is such a huge distance between my life here and my life at home. I don't know if you feel that way, too, but it makes me feel lonely sometimes. This is going to sound so sentimental but I was thinking of you the other day, wondering what kind of person you are going to grow up to be (and at the same time wondering what kind of person I am going to be) and imagining us as friends ten years from now. It was all very vague but I just had a strong sense of how happy we would be, and that maybe the hardest thing—leaving Willowboro—is behind us. It was a big leap for me. Maybe not as much of one for you, because you always knew you were going to have a different kind of life from your parents. One more thing,

Steph, I had a dream about your mother: She was walking in a field behind my house. I stopped her and asked if she needed directions. She said, "Oh no, I just wanted to let your father know that I'm dead." I said, "Because my dad's a pastor?" But she didn't answer and that was the end. I don't know what the dream means, probably my own Freudian shit, but when I woke up it was like I had seen your mother. I remembered so many things about her—the smell of her hair and her smile and the way she had of pausing, very slightly, before she answered a question. And I thought, if I can miss her this way, then Stephanie must really really miss her. So I am so sorry, Stephanie, I am just so sorry. I don't know what else I can say except that. And I miss you. And I hope we will always be friends.

Love, Mitchell

Stephanie read the e-mail twice. Then a third time. She inhaled deeply through her nose every time she reached the end, needing to keep back her tears. Relief, sadness, and a sense of deep, deep longing. She closed her e-mail without answering Mitchell's message and left the library. Outside, she let out a brief, involuntary moan. Then she felt better. Not good, not normal, but better. Something had been cleared away. She felt she would never forget this day in her life, the cold air on her face, the gray sky, the worn grass, the red brick, the bare trees, and the voices of her classmates in the distance. She walked back to her room, and as she made her way down the paved pathways, she listened, with childlike concentration, to the sound of her own footsteps.

THE NEXT MORNING Stephanie woke up early, had a quick breakfast of raisin toast, and headed toward the other end of the campus, to the history building, where her academic adviser had his office. Every first-year student was assigned an adviser, a professor randomly selected and, more often than not, ill-suited to his advisees. In Stephanie's case, this was Professor Haupt, a short, good-humored man whose glasses were almost always pushed to the top of his forehead, balancing uncertainly, waiting to be called into service.

Stephanie knocked softly on his door, nervous because she was visiting right at the beginning of office hours. When no one answered, she turned to leave, only to see him coming down the hallway carrying a cup of coffee and a large muffin on a paper napkin. He seemed so contented that she didn't want to disturb him. She began to write her name on the sign-up sheet outside his door, as if this had been the original purpose of her visit, but when he saw her, he called to her.

"Sarah! How can I help you?"

"It's Stephanie," she said.

"Oh, right. Beg pardon. I got the *S* right, at least."

He invited her into his office and she sat down in a wooden chair across from his desk, which was noticeably messier than on her previous visit, at the beginning of the school year. There were stacks of file folders, fat with student papers, as well as piles of books, all of them about Lincoln or the Civil War.

"I'm reviewing a new Lincoln biography, and it's taking over my life," Professor Haupt said, clearing a space for his breakfast. "I'm also writing a book *about* Lincoln, fool that I am. If you go into academia, do yourself a favor and stay away from the great men. They're already covered in other people's fingerprints, so the best you can do is to write about the fingerprints—or over the fingerprints. Remind me, what are you thinking of majoring in?"

"I haven't decided yet," Stephanie said. "I came because I need to use my freshman drop—for Psych I."

"Are you sure?" Professor Haupt asked. He pushed his glasses down and began to search for her file. "As I recall, that's not the most challenging course on your schedule."

The freshman drop was a kind of safety net for first-year students, allowing them to stop taking a class midsemester, no questions asked, and with no adverse effects on their GPA. Students often invoked its magical powers in conversation when they were feeling nervous about an upcoming test or paper, but Stephanie had not yet heard of anyone actually using it. She wondered if she had misunderstood and suddenly worried that she would be penalized for using it on a gut course.

"I just failed the midterm," she said.

"You can make it up on the final and with the labs." He had found her file and was flipping through it. "At the very least you could wait a few weeks and see how you feel."

"I don't want to study psychology," she said. "It's not what I want to learn right now."

Professor Haupt's face registered surprise, and she knew she sounded stubborn, like she was issuing a pronouncement to the world: *I refuse to learn psychology*. The truth was, she didn't want to waste her psychology professor's time. Or her own. She had other things to learn.

"Fair enough." He handed her an add/drop form and continued to look through her file while she filled it out. "I didn't realize you were from Willowboro," he said. "That's a very small town."

"It's not that small," she said, feeling defensive. He probably thought she was on the slow side. Admitted for geographic diversity.

"Don't get me wrong, I love Willowboro." Professor Haupt pushed his glasses back up to his forehead.

"You've been there?" Stephanie said.

"Many times. I wrote a book about the Battle of Antietam."

"The single bloodiest day in American history."

"That's right! My book was actually about the hospitals that sprang up nearby, the way people turned their houses and barns into makeshift infirmaries. You probably already know this, having grown up in the area, but Lincoln visited several of these residences. But there are no official records of it. All we know of his visits is from the letters that soldiers wrote home. Apparently, he gave speeches at each one—incredibly beautiful speeches. One man wrote to his daughter that every soldier was moved to take out his handkerchief."

"That's interesting," Stephanie said neutrally. She was a little bit suspicious of anyone who fetishized the Civil War. It was always men and boys who knew the battles intimately, memorized the gains and losses and the weather patterns and the terrain. She got the feeling they saw these old, prenuclear wars as a kind of lost sport—a pure, brutal game that could only exist in a simpler time.

Professor Haupt pushed his glasses back down to sign Stephanie's add/drop form. "I would give anything to hear those speeches. History is such a heartbreaking field. Don't become a historian."

"I won't," Stephanie said. "Thank you."

Classes were letting out when she left the history building. Stephanie headed toward the campus center to get her mail. She was waiting in line at the packages window when she saw Raquel checking her mailbox. Her maroon hair was in a stubby ponytail, and her natural color showed at the roots like a dark halo. She must have felt someone staring at her because she looked up and Stephanie had to wave.

"You disappeared!" Raquel said.

Stephanie just nodded.

"You waiting on a care package?"

"Yeah. Probably another Bible from my aunt." Stephanie still felt compelled to be sarcastic in Raquel's presence.

"Isn't it totally bizarre that we're studying serotonin right now?" Raquel leaned in to whisper, "I mean, considering?"

"That's karma for you." Stephanie had no idea what she meant. She was just trying to get this conversation over with. She realized she'd been fooling herself: She and Raquel were no longer friends. They were acquaintances, and in a few months, they'd be even less than that. At graduation, Raquel would go back to using her real name, Kelly. Her hair would be a deep, good-girl brown, her clothes would be ironed, new, preprofessional, and she'd have a one-way ticket to graduate school. That was her future, if she wanted to take it, and she would, because it was never really going to be any other way. She was like Theresa, except she wasn't as kind.

The boy working at the package window called to Stephanie, and she used it as an excuse to say good-bye to Raquel, who seemed equally relieved to go.

"You have two," the boy said, glancing at her slip. He ex-

cused himself and then returned with a large box from her
aunt and a small white FedEx package from her father. It had
been mailed two-day express, a lavish expense. Guilt sickened
Stephanie. It felt like a poison she had to spit out.

Back in her room, Stephanie opened her aunt's package
first. The box was full of food: pretzels, Hershey bars, dry-
roasted peanuts, raisins, jars of peanut butter and Marshmallow
Fluff, gummy bears, gum, mints, and a shoebox of homemade
chocolate chip cookies. At the bottom of the package was a
folded-up newspaper article and a Garfield card containing a
ten-dollar bill and a coupon for Herbal Essences. How did she
know Stephanie's favorite shampoo? Families were so strange.
The trivial things you knew, the big things you didn't. The
two getting confused, one masquerading as the other. Her
aunt had written a short note:

Dear Stephanie,

*Hope you're having fun at school! We're fine here but
we miss you. You've probably heard from your dad how
well Megan is doing. She's a runner now on his team.
Her picture was in the Sunday paper. I put a clipping in
the box.*

*Love,
Aunt Joelle*

Stephanie unfolded the newsprint and there was Megan
running, the camera catching her midstride, head-on, so that
she appeared to be floating above the ground. Her expression
was pained, making her seem older. Behind her was a huge

expanse of sky bordered by pine trees. Where were they? It looked like Colorado. Stephanie skimmed the article, which covered several cross-country races across the county. Megan's surprise win was mentioned in the first paragraph. The reporter noted that she was coached by "Willowboro's former football coach." That bugged Stephanie. It was like her father was getting credit for Megan's talent.

She opened her father's box, expecting something practical like her mail from home. Instead she found a fleece jacket. She unfolded it, baffled by the gesture. It was the kind of present her mother would have sent her, because her mother always wanted her to wear the thing that everyone around her was wearing. And she would have been right about this jacket because everyone had them. It was kind of a joke between her and Raquel. They called them Muppet pelts.

Stephanie pulled it on. It was cozy, she had to admit. She got why people wore them. She checked her reflection in the full-length mirror that hung from the bedroom door. She had lost weight and her clothes fit her loosely, her boring clothes: faded brown corduroys, a black turtleneck, black Chuck Taylors. The purple fleece was a dose of richness; it would be called *aubergine* or maybe just *plum* in a catalog. She recalled a line of dialogue from the matinee she'd gone to on Sunday: "a *plum* plum." The movie had stayed with her longer than she'd expected. Much of it took place in an abandoned farmhouse that reminded Stephanie of an old, falling-down stone house that she used to play in as a kid. It was in the woods, on the other side of the creek. You had to cross over at the shallow part, where Robbie and Bry liked to build dams. Maybe it was one of Professor Haupt's Lincoln houses. As a little girl, Stephanie dreamed of buying the house when she grew up—buying it and fixing it up. She was obsessed with fixing things up. When she drove through town with her mother, she would try to imagine how everything would look if the buildings were remodeled and made to appear new again—still with their old façades, but with fresh clapboard and shingles and doors. It bothered her that things got old and fell apart. It wasn't until she was older that she learned to see the beauty in decay and even gloom. Grunge had schooled her in that sensibility. Or maybe it was her way of learning to live with her mother.

Stephanie got her books together to go to the library. She was tired and depressed, but she had to catch up on her reading for her medieval studies class. She thought of Professor Haupt telling her not to study history. He was one of those people who told you not to do the things they clearly enjoyed, some kind of defensive irony. Or maybe it was the luxury of those who paid nothing for their happiness. She was never going to be like that. She was never going to pretend like she wasn't feeling something.

THE AWAY GAME was in Plattstown, a half hour's drive. Dean dropped the boys at Joelle's before dinner and headed toward the highway, a route that took him by Coach's. He pulled into the bar's parking lot knowing that he was never going to make it to the game. It was an out-of-body feeling. He knew he should go for the sake of his players, but they were playing fine without him. They weren't going to be a championship team, like last year's, but Dean doubted that he could have brought them to that level anyway. They were too young. Key players had graduated. Last year's team had been special; there was an intensity to that group, a brotherly dynamic that let competition, love, and aggression mix together. He wondered if girls could have that, too, if he could build the cross-country team the same way he'd built the football program.

He didn't notice Karen Coulter coming into the bar. She sat down next to him, ordered an Amstel Light, and then nudged him with her elbow.

"Looks like you're having some deep thoughts," she teased.

"Hey, you." He was flirtatious without exactly meaning to be. There was something relaxing about her presence; she was the kind of person who made you feel more casual about life. "Ready for tomorrow?" he asked.

"I'm not the one running. Thanks for talking to See, by the way. She's applying to University of Maryland. She said she might get in free because her grades are pretty high. Is that true?"

"Yeah, it's to keep the smart kids in state. To prevent brain drain."

"Do a lot of kids take it?"

Dean shrugged. "Most of my football players didn't qualify."

Karen smiled and sipped her beer. "I would love for her to stay in state. It's crazy, she barely talks to me these days. Sometimes I think she's trying to prepare me for next year, when she's gone."

"Stephanie kind of did the same thing." Dean didn't know why he was bringing up his daughter. He didn't really want to talk about her. It was too painful.

"How's she doing, by the way?"

"She's good . . ." he began, vaguely. He was going to give

a quick gloss. But then, to his surprise, he told Karen every-thing.

"It's not as bad as you think," Karen said. "She's going through a rough time. I mean, who wouldn't be? Considering what she's dealing with."

"I know. It just kills me that I can't do anything."

"What do you think your wife would do? If she were alive?"

"I don't know," Dean said, a little taken aback by the question. "This wouldn't be happening if she were alive."

"You don't know that."

Dean tried to imagine the scenario. Right away he saw Nic sitting on the front porch with her tea, pushing the lemon back and forth with a spoon, not saying a word while he stood there waiting. They would argue, eventually, the same argument they always had about the way she withdrew, and how this was his fault, because he didn't understand what she was going through. But how could he understand if she didn't explain?

"You've done what you can do," Karen said. "She's not in danger. Now you have to wait."

"Thanks," Dean said. He felt a little ridiculous. "Let me buy you a beer. Where's your friend James, by the way?"

"He dumped me!" Karen said it with a certain amount of relish. "I was too old for him, I guess."

"If you're old, I'm old."

"I have news for you: you're middle-aged. Unless you're planning to live past ninety."

"Maybe I am," Dean said. Life already seemed long. One day, his marriage to Nicole would be just one part of his life, not the whole of it.

They talked for a while longer. Karen worked at a company that manufactured aboveground pools as well as lawn ornaments, but her own yard was unadorned. She preferred gardening. She talked a little about her divorce, and a little about her dating life. She kept things light, but Dean could see that it was a learned lightness. He admired her way of being in the world; she protected herself without being guarded. He had the sense that she would come home with him, if he wanted. And he did want it. He needed to sleep with another woman in his own house. It was an obstacle he hadn't yet acknowledged to himself.

When it came time to order another round, he told her that he couldn't drink any more and still drive. She said she felt the same way.

"But I'd like to keep talking," he said. "Do you want to have a beer at my place? I have a nice porch."

She laughed and said, "I like porches."

Chapter 12

The next morning, Dean drove to Joelle's house to pick up his kids and Megan for the meet. But when he arrived, only his boys were ready to go. Megan was still in bed. She was sick.

"I am so sorry, Dean, but she's running a fever," Joelle said. "Whatever it is, I want to nip it in the bud."

"Uncle Dean?" Megan called down from upstairs. "I think I could run if you really needed me. Maybe I could sleep a little more now and run later—"

"You can't run in the cold! Are you crazy?" Joelle yelled upstairs. She turned to Dean, irritated, as if he'd infected her daughter with athletic ambition.

"I don't want her to run if she's sick," Dean said. And he didn't. But it was as if something had been taken from him when his back was turned. In an irrational way, he felt he was being punished for his dalliance with See-See's mother.

Karen and See-See were waiting at the school when Dean arrived. Karen was dressed in a zip-up sweatshirt and jeans. She had brought a cup of coffee for Dean, but nothing in her demeanor gave away their new intimacy. Beside her, See-See looked sleepy and childlike without her usual heavy eyeliner and jewelry. Her bleached hair was growing in naturally now, the same sandy blond as her mother's. Dean had been nervous about seeing them, but now he felt nothing but relief. He told them about Megan, and they both frowned in the same way.

"We still have enough to score," See-See said.

The meet was at St. Luke's Academy, a small private school near the Pennsylvania-Maryland border. It reminded Dean a little of Stephanie's school, with its winding sidewalks and brick buildings. She hadn't called to say she'd gotten the jacket. FedEx said it had been delivered. So he had to assume she'd gotten it and decided not to respond.

All the girls' parents attended. They stood in a small crowd near the tarp, drinking hot cider and commenting on the beautiful weather and the changing leaves. Dean had sent the girls off on a warm-up run with Robbie and Bry tagging along. Meanwhile, he busied himself with the racing bibs.

Karen came over to him. "Would you like me to take splits again? I can stand at the second mile."

"If you don't mind," Dean said, catching her eye, trying to read her mood. She'd been so discreet up to this point, barely even smiling at him.

"I really don't," she said, taking a stopwatch from his box. "I'm feeling pretty single right now, with all these married couples."

She said it confidentially, as if he in particular would understand, and it threw him off balance.

"Even with me here?" He meant that he was single, too, but as soon as the words were out of his mouth, he realized they could be taken another way.

"Especially with you here." She held up her stopwatch. "I better get to my post."

The girls came back from their warm-up and stripped down to their uniforms to pin on their bibs. Dean gave them a racing strategy as they jogged toward the starting line. Missy would lead on the first mile, then See-See and Aileen would run as a twosome for the reminder of the race.

"What happens to me?" Missy asked.

"Hopefully you'll keep running," Dean said, lightly sarcastic. He turned to Lori and Jessica. "You two are my snipers. You stay together for the first mile. Don't go out too fast. Stay in the back of the pack. Relax, enjoy the scenery. Okay? But when you hit mile two, I want you to start picking people off. You'll flank them on either side, and then you'll pass them at the same time. You know how demoralizing that is?"

They had reached the starting line. The other teams were gathered there, many from private schools they'd never raced against before, large teams that were two, three, and four times the size of theirs. One team with green-and-white uniforms formed a ring, the girls holding hands and laughing, the ring getting larger and larger as they stretched their arms to their full length. The girls kicked their long legs into the center. They all seemed to be long-limbed, with long ponytails. They were like horses.

Aileen said what they were all thinking: "I wish Megan was here."

"You've run without her before. You can do it again." Dean gathered them together into a huddle. "Treat this like a practice, okay?"

The girls nodded without saying anything.

"Can I get a hell yeah?" Dean asked, now desperate to loosen them up. Other teams were beginning to chant and yell their pep-talk slogans. They were surrounded by jittery energy. Over by a tree, a girl was holding her side, throwing up. Dean recognized her as Adrienne Fellows, one of the top competitors.

"Look!" Dean said, pointing. "She's nervous, too, okay? Harness those nerves and get out there and run hard. It's a beautiful day. You're a strong team. You've got everything going for you."

He had to leave them at the line so he could get to the first mile in time. St. Luke's was basically an out-and-back, and the first mile was at the end of a long dirt road. Dean heard the starting gun go off while he was still jogging toward it. He was barely in place with the other coaches when he saw Missy coming down the lane. On either side of her were Aileen and See-See. They were in the top twenty, better than he'd expected. He called out their splits and they quickly glanced at him, barely turning their heads. He could hear them breathing, the soft thuds of their feet hitting the ground.

Jessica and Lori came by two and a half minutes later. They were several yards behind a big group of runners. "Go get them!" Dean pointed. They looked ahead warily and then Lori accelerated. Of all the runners, she had improved the most. He watched as she passed one girl and then another. Jessica lagged behind. They rounded a curve and disappeared behind a stand of pine trees.

That was it. His runners were gone, off to finish the race on their own. He began to jog toward the finish, cutting diagonally across an open field. He was struck by the silence. He recalled going to horse races with his father, the way the horses seemed so far away when they were on the backstretch. His father stopped going to races after his mother left. Dean never asked him why. He was too busy being angry with his parents for splitting up. A few years after their divorce was finalized, he'd had a choice of moving to Ohio with his mother and starting over in another high school. Or he could stay in Pennsylvania with his father. He chose to stay because he'd made varsity as a sophomore. He hadn't wanted to prove himself all over again at a new school. It was such kid reasoning. Sometimes Dean wondered how much that one decision had set the course of his life.

The draft ended a year before he turned eighteen. He wondered about that, too. During her junior year, Stephanie had visited the Vietnam Veterans Memorial on a field trip to D.C. Before she left she asked Dean for names to search for. She said her teachers had told her to ask. *How morbid*, Nicole said. But Dean was moved when Stephanie brought home a piece of paper with the name of one of his old teammates—a rubbing showed the etched letters. Dean remembered his friend's big hands, how they held the ball so casually. At the end of every practice he would take off his socks and cleats and lie on his back with his legs up in the air; he'd heard this was the best way to recover after a hard workout. Sometimes Dean would lie next to him, the two of them looking up their outstretched legs, their bare feet foregrounded against the sky's expanse, their bodies relaxing into the grass. *It doesn't get any better than this*, his friend would say. He was named Bruce, after his father, but everyone called him Dash because he was so fast.

Robbie was waiting for Dean near the finish line. "Dad, Bry is hot but he says he's cold. I think he has a fever."

"Where is he?"

"He's lying down on the tarp."

Dean hurried back to the warm-up area, leaving the race behind. He heard Adrienne's finish, the crowd yelping with delight. Bryan was lying on his side on the tarp with Dean's fleece jacket wrapped around his narrow shoulders. His blond hair was damp, and his cheeks were flushed. Dean realized he'd shown signs of sickness earlier, when he'd dozed off on the bus. He must have caught whatever Megan had.

"Daddy, I'm okay. The sun is giving me vitamins," Bryan said.

In the distance, Dean could hear the girls finishing their race. See-See and Karen were the first ones back. See-See had gotten a PR and her face was still blotchy with exertion. She seemed disappointed to find Dean at the tarp instead of at the finish, but when she saw Bryan, she softened.

"You have to get him home," Karen said.

"We rode the bus," Dean said. "We're stuck until the end of the boys' race."

"Take my car," Karen said. "I can get a ride. Or I'll take the bus back with the kids."

"We can stay; he's not going to get any worse."

"I insist—as a mother," Karen said. She pushed the keys into Dean's hand.

Both boys fell asleep on the car ride home. Flu was going to sweep through his house; Dean could see it coming. He felt stranded. It was being in a different car and driving unfamiliar roads. It was having to accept favors from a woman he barely knew. It was realizing he was truly alone in the care of his sons. His heart began to beat crazily, and he had to pull over to the side of the road to steady himself. Cars sped by; nobody stopped to see if he was okay. Eventually, he pulled back onto the highway.

THERESA'S PARENTS, STEVEN and Candace, were physicists. They worked in a lab at Johns Hopkins where they studied laser technology. Stephanie could tell by their vague description that this was a significant generalization of what they actually studied, and she pressed them for more details. Theresa interrupted. "They make weapons," she said. "It's a government lab."

"That's an exaggeration," Candace said, pointing a long, manicured fingernail. She had touches of femininity, but you had to look for them. "There are military applications for some of what we do, yes, but we're hardly making weapons."

"Whatever you say, Mom."

Stephanie couldn't get a read on Theresa's sarcasm, whether it was politically motivated or if she thought there was something square about working for the government. Stephanie was slightly dazzled by Theresa's parents; they were easily the smartest people she'd ever met. Maybe Mitchell would be like them.

"What does your father do?" Steven asked Stephanie.

"He's a football coach."

"I'm afraid I don't know much about football," he said.

"For me, football is too much stop and start," said Candace. "And I don't like the tackling."

"My dad doesn't let people hit during practice," Stephanie said. "Only games. And only certain kinds of hits."

"Still, I would be wary of letting Andrew play," Candace said.

"No danger of that," Theresa said. "Andrew's arms are like twigs."

Andrew was Theresa's older brother. He was in the sciences, too, studying epidemiology, a word Stephanie didn't know, but she was too embarrassed to ask for a definition.

"Andrew's a runner," said Steven. "Just a fun runner, like me."

Stephanie nodded. She could say that her father was a running coach, too, that he actually wasn't coaching football anymore, but it seemed like too much to explain. She had the sense that Theresa's parents knew about her mother, that Theresa had briefed them. She'd probably also told them not to bring it up. That made things easier, in a way, but at the same time Stephanie wanted them to acknowledge that she was missing something important.

Her depression hangover was starting to lift. It was fall break, a mysterious interlude that did not correspond with any holidays. Stephanie's plan had been to spend the long weekend studying and picking up extra cafeteria shifts, but when Theresa extended an invitation, she felt such relief that she realized she was desperate to leave campus.

It felt luxurious to be in a house, to have so much domestic space to move about in. Everything about Theresa's house was soft and personal, from the gently curving road that delivered them to Theresa's driveway, to the carefully pruned shrubberies that concealed their house from the road, to the wall-to-wall carpeting and blond wood furniture. Theresa's parents explained that Columbia was a planned community, and that all the roads and property lines had been mapped out in advance. There were no houses on the main road; everyone lived on a small side street, each house arranged at the perfect distance from its neighbor, uninterrupted by random expanses of field, broken-down barns, or hastily constructed prefab homes. The overall effect was one of extraordinary calm; it also felt opaque. Stephanie had no way of reading the landscape; she couldn't see in it a history of the town's rising and falling fortunes. She couldn't tell what anyone did for a living or for fun. It was disconcerting and yet she liked it. It gave her a feeling of privacy, which she badly needed—not only to grieve, but to figure out who she was in the wake of her grieving. She was becoming someone, or maybe she was figuring out who she had always been.

Her father always said that people revealed their character on the playing field, and she had always thought it was such an old-fashioned belief—both the idea of character and the idea of sports as some kind of crucible. But now she thought she had taken him too seriously. All he was saying was that if an athlete was determined or lazy or bold, you saw it in his actions when he was challenged physically. And here she was, being challenged physically—she saw her depression as something physical—and she knew, deep down, that it wasn't going to break her. She wasn't like her mother. There was relief and sadness in this realization, the two feelings mixed together in a way that was so different from her high school years, when she would feel one emotion so strongly it was like an engine in her chest. Was this adulthood, she wondered, or was it grief? Was grieving how one became an adult?

After dinner, she and Theresa hung out in Theresa's room, where Theresa showed Stephanie photos of her high school boyfriend, Jason. He was tall and pale, with a long dark ponytail. He wore wire-rimmed glasses that made his eyes look smaller.

"He went to Brown," Theresa said. "He broke up with me the first week of school. I think he was planning to do it all along. He wanted to keep having sex up until the last minute, I guess."

"Maybe he was scared of being lonely," Stephanie said.

"I hope all the Brown girls ignore him."

"There's probably only a certain percentage of girls who like a guy with a ponytail, so already he has pretty low odds."

Theresa laughed. "I know! That stupid ponytail! I really hated it. I tried to tell myself it was cool. He could trick you into thinking things were cool that weren't. He was kind of a snob, I guess. I still miss him, though. I really miss him a lot. Isn't that the stupidest thing?"

"It's not stupid," Stephanie said. "I'm sorry I didn't know about it when it happened."

"Honestly, I probably wouldn't have told you anyway. I was too embarrassed. I think he's already going out with someone else. I called him last week. I swore I heard a girl's voice in the background. Something in the way he was talking to me, too; it was like he didn't actually need to talk to me anymore."

"I'm pretty sure my dad's dating someone. I even think they may have been dating before my mother died."

"Oh my God, that's awful. Is that why you're so mad at him?"

"Sort of. It's hard to explain." The easy thing to say was that she blamed her father for her mother's death—except that wasn't an easy thing to say. And she didn't blame him. But she wanted to. She wanted to blame someone and she couldn't. But what would it mean to blame someone? Would it be a way to absolve herself? And why couldn't she just blame her mother? Was it that she didn't really believe it was her mother's fault? Or was it that it would hurt too much, there would be too much blame, it would be all-encompassing? Her mother's life choices had determined Stephanie's life; her mother's choices were her father and her brothers and the landscape she'd grown up in. She didn't want to take any of that back.

"The weirdest thing," Stephanie said, "is I want to talk to my mother about it."

Theresa nodded. "I can see that."

"What did your mom say about Jason breaking up with you?"

Theresa shrugged. "She wasn't very sympathetic. She doesn't want me having boyfriends right now. She says I need to concentrate on school. She says 'wait until graduate school' because that's when she met my dad. But that's not good advice. I mean, why would I meet my husband in graduate school just because she did?"

"Do you think you want to get married?"

"Yeah, eventually. Do you?"

"I think so," Stephanie said, although she remembered telling her mother she didn't, just to be contrary. She had always felt pressure from her mother to have a boyfriend; it had started in middle school when her mother would arrive early to pick her up from school dances to see if she was dancing with anyone. And Stephanie would feel as if there was something wrong with her because she felt nothing in particular when she slow-danced with boys from her school, and she found it hard to believe that other girls did, because the boys in middle school were just slightly taller versions of the noisy and hyperactive boys she'd known in elementary school. These other girls were pretending, they were acting out a love they'd seen on television and in the movies. But when Stephanie had shared this theory with her mother, her mother looked at her with such sadness that Stephanie felt guilty. And then her mother told her she was wrong, that it was possible to fall in love at age twelve or thirteen and that it was a very special kind of love, an easy kind of love, and that the only reason she pushed Stephanie to attend dances was that she wished for Stephanie to have it, because she'd had it, and it had meant the world to her. And Stephanie had felt guilty, because she knew then that her mother was speaking about her father, her real father, a man she had supposedly met but did not remember or miss.

Sometimes Stephanie was even secretly grateful that he had died, because she couldn't imagine a father better than the one she'd grown up with.

She couldn't believe she'd told her father that he wasn't real to her. It was so far from what she actually believed. In the moment it had seemed simpler to cut herself off from him, to say to herself that both her parents were dead.

Theresa wanted to discuss boys from school, a topic that naturally dissolved into a more general discussion of sex. They told each other about their first times, and Theresa was shocked that Stephanie's was so recent and that she had told no one. Beneath her romantic attachment to Jason, Theresa had a kind of analytical attitude toward sex, and she gave Stephanie advice for the future, for how to make it feel better.

They started to get sleepy and eventually gave in and went to bed. Stephanie was given Andrew's room, a boyish blue space that reminded Stephanie of her brothers' room. As she drifted off, she wondered if Robbie had taken over her room yet, or if he was still too scared to sleep alone.

Chapter 13

The days disappeared in a haze of flu, with Robbie catching it just as Bryan was recovering. Dean was making a batch of cherry Jell-O when he realized that he was coming down with it, too. He had a sore feeling at the back of his throat that wouldn't go away. That night he woke up with aching limbs and a violent urge to use the bathroom. He took a shower in the middle of the night, as if he could wash off the illness, and shivered under the hot water. By then he'd already missed two days of work to take care of the boys. He ended up taking the rest of the week off. It was unsettling to be alone in the house during the day. He tried to distract himself with TV, but the commercials depressed him. They seemed pitched toward some unhappy population, a host of minor Jobs in need of credit consolidation, mortgage refinance, diets, vitamins, antidepressants, and kitchen knives. Dean had to stop watching. Instead he sat on his porch wrapped in blankets and listened to the portable radio. Karen dropped by one afternoon and found him dozing there. She brought sick-person food: soup, saltines, and ginger ale.

"Why are you being so nice to me?" Dean asked her, his tongue loosened by fever.

"Because you're nice to my kid," Karen said. "The other coach, she was fine, but she didn't care as much."

"I'm missing a week of practice," Dean said. "I'm hardly coach of the year."

"Don't worry, See is under the weather, too, and I heard that Aileen missed a few days of school."

"I guess I don't need to do a taper, after all."

"What?"

"It's when you ease up the mileage for a week or so. But we got the flu instead."

"This is what I'm talking about," Karen said. "You're turning sickness into strategy!"

"Thanks for the soup. When I feel better, I'll take you for a three-course dinner at the Red Byrd."

"Sounds classy," she said, smiling. But then she paused, as if considering whether or not to say the next thing she was thinking. Dean liked her mix of openness and reserve, the mild unpredictability of it and the way it fell away completely when she was having sex.

"You know, you don't have to ask me out," she said. "I don't like to jump into things. I don't need the drama."

"Who's jumping into things?"

"You are," she said. "I know where you're at. I've been there. If we're really going to date, I'd rather wait."

"Fair enough," Dean said. He quickly changed the subject. He didn't like that his careening emotions were so transparent to women. After Karen left, he dozed off, thinking of Laura. He wondered if she knew he was sick.

With more than half the team downed by the flu, Dean decided to forfeit Saturday's meet and spent the morning on the sofa with the boys, watching cartoons and eating toaster waffles. By then, he was starting to feel better. He could smell the sickness in his house: it was finally a thing apart from him. He did four loads of laundry, washing all the sheets and towels, and then he scrubbed down the bathrooms and kitchen. On Sunday he made a big spaghetti dinner with garlic bread and a salad, and served ice cream for dessert. He and the boys ate ravenously, thinned by their week of illness, and went to bed early. Monday morning, it was as if he were returning from a long, strange vacation.

Adding to the strangeness was the fact that it was Homecoming Week and the school had been transformed. Every hallway was garlanded with streamers and blue and white balloons, and the doors were adorned with posters announcing the week's events: the rally, the game, and the dance. Photos of the homecoming queen nominees were hanging in the cafeteria, and all week long there was a special menu of "pep" foods—basically, all the junky items that were sold à la carte at football games, plus cupcakes with blue frosting. Dean viewed the hoopla from a distance. He recalled Stephanie's complaints, her idea that the football team got too much attention and adulation, and that it was all out of proportion to the actual accomplishments of football players. Dean had always argued that the institution of cheerleading was to blame, but he could see now that the entire school was in cahoots with them. His girls seemed somewhat cowed when he met them for practice in the big gym, lined up beneath a football banner that read WINNING IS A HARD HABIT TO BREAK.

"Let's get off campus today," he said. "Now that we're all back in good health, we should do some hill work."

They drove in two cars, his and See-See's. Dean wasn't completely sure where he would take them and told See-See to stick with him. His backup plan was to go to the battlefield, but as they turned onto the highway, he had an inspiration and changed course.

The Pleasant Valley Country Club was in the southwestern part of the county, a hilly wooded region close to West Virginia. It was a somewhat wild area, a place where well-to-do families bought large plots of land on the hillsides. They would cut down two or three acres of trees to create sloping yards with sunset views. Down low, on the road, there were shabby trailers and ranches surrounded by chain-link fences, usually to contain a bored, barking dog. Many of the people who lived in this area worked at the prison just over the border, and Dean remembered Nicole remarking that they had seemed to re-create their working conditions at home.

The club was situated in such a beautiful spot that it had become a place for tourists to visit in the midst of vacations to Civil War landmarks—a break from history to play a round. The course's rolling hills were landscaped with swaying locust trees, pine copses, low limestone walls, and a narrow feeder stream that eventually emptied into the Potomac. In the midst of so much natural beauty, the putting greens did not seem quite so artificial, and even the turquoise-blue pool seemed semipastoral.

The pool had been emptied for the year, and its lounge chairs were pushed up against the fence, stacked and pillowless. It looked exactly as it had the last time Dean saw it, sometime last April, when he had picked Nicole up from work because her car was in the shop. Nicole didn't play much golf and neither did he, which was why they never came here on the weekends and why the club still struck him as unfamiliar. He had always felt that management was not the best place for Nicole, that it stressed her unnecessarily, but she had been good at it, and the money had been good, and she had taken so many years off to be with the boys that it was the easiest thing to return to. She took pride in the club, having been there back in the early days, a part of its transformation from a random, out-of-the-way golf course to what tourist maps now referred to as a "family recreation retreat." Dean could barely remember its prior incarnation; all he could really recall was seeing Nicole at the front desk and wanting to know her, wanting to make her smile, wondering about her thoughts and the world she came from.

As soon as Dean saw the expression on the manager's face, he realized there was something awkward about his coming here. And he further realized that it was within the manager's rights—in fact, probably his responsibility—to deny a group of random girls access to the grounds. But the manager—whether out of pity or a desire to avoid conflict—said it would be fine.

So the girls did their workout, with Bryan running to the tops of the hills and calling to them when they got tired. And as the girls ran up and down, up and down, their bodies disappearing and reappearing as they crested and descended, crested and descended, Dean found himself thinking of Nicole. How she was down when he met her and how he brought her up. How she was down after Robbie's birth and how he brought her up. How they had not planned on Bryan, but there he was, beckoning to a bunch of teenage girls from the top of a hill, and how could he not have existed? Nicole hadn't wanted to have Bryan. It was the first major fight in their marriage. Dean remembered thinking that he was lucky that it took them so long to have a big fight. That was his way of comforting himself. Because he was frankly shocked by the idea of abortion within marriage. "I think God would forgive me," she said. As if that were the issue. He'd promised her that she wouldn't regret having another baby, and she had cried and said, "I know, I know, I know." After Bryan was born, she begged him to forgive her for even thinking of terminating. And he had. In fact, he rarely, if ever, thought about it. He wasn't even sure that she had meant it; she was the kind of person who said extreme things when she got overwhelmed.

Their last big argument: June 26, 1995. Their thirteenth wedding anniversary. They'd made plans to go out. They'd been getting along. Not great, but getting along. Dean thought the summer would help them. He'd decided not to coach football camp, his usual occupation for the month of July. Stephanie had a full-time job. So it would just be him and the boys and Nicole most nights. Less fighting that way, without Stephanie around.

Their anniversary fell on a Monday and the plan was for Dean to pick Nicole up from work. She would bring clothes so that she could change out of her uniform at work, like she used to do when they were dating. It would be romantic, nostalgic, sexy. She would surprise him, he would surprise her. But when he got there, she was still in her uniform. She'd forgotten her dress. And when they drove back home, anticlimactically, so she could change, she said she really didn't feel like going out after all, and would it be okay to just have dinner with the kids? And he had pulled over to the side of the road and said no, it would really not be okay, that it was their anniversary, and that she wasn't even trying, she wasn't even pretending to try, and if she wasn't going to try, then he wasn't going to, and when they got home, he sat on the porch and drank whiskey while she took forever to get ready, so that when she finally came down in her dress, he was too drunk to drive anywhere, and she was too angry to drive him. For thirty, maybe forty silent minutes they sat on the porch in their dress-up clothes, waiting there as if they'd both been stood up by the same ass-hole jock. Finally Dean gave in, his drunkenness lifting like a heavy fog, and he made them sandwiches. And then, while the kids were still awake, watching a movie downstairs, they had sex upstairs, quietly, furtively, the only way of communicating to move each other's hands and bodies into place. And when it was over, Dean felt close to his wife again, and grateful that they could still be close, that they had this relatively easy fix at their disposal. But he also wondered if it was enough for him.

The next day the director of the football camp had called to say that one of the coaches had dropped out at the last minute. Dean accepted the job with relief. The summer became about logistics as he and Nicole balanced their schedules that re-volved around other people's leisure activities. They had one, maybe two dates. On one of them, they went to a movie that was supposed to be romantic, about a farmer's wife who falls in love with a visiting photographer when her husband and children are out of town. Dean remembered thinking that he would never be drawn in by the attentions of a kind stranger, that he wasn't susceptible to having an affair. He remembered feeling vaguely superior to all the moviegoers swooning in their seats. That fall, he met Laura.

AT THE END of their workout, after the girls stretched on the playground, Jessica asked Dean if he would mind dropping her off at home, because she lived close by. The other girls had already squeezed into See-See's car anyway.

"Sure," Dean said. "I had no idea you lived around here."

Jessica shrugged. "My parents finished the house last year."

Her house was at the end of a long, winding dirt road that was the driveway of either someone very poor or someone well-to-do. Jessica's family obviously fell into the latter category. Built on a slope, the front part of the house was raised up on tall sturdy posts, with a wraparound front porch overlooking the valley. Its architecture was modern, all angles and windows. Jessica's mother came out onto the porch to greet them.

"Hey, honey!" Mrs. Markham called. "I was just about to leave to pick you up." She waved to Dean. "Come on up, let me get you an iced tea."

Dean and Bryan followed Jessica through the garage and up a set of narrow stairs, which led to the kitchen, a large marble-and-stainless-steel affair that opened onto the living room.

"Would you prefer hot tea?" asked Jessica's mother. She was a redhead, like Jessica, but the color was softened by strands of gray, and her hair was cut in layers to frame her face. "I can make some, it's no trouble."

"Iced tea would hit the spot, thank you."

Mrs. Markham prepared four glasses of iced tea, dropping a slice of lemon in each. It was unsweetened and slightly bitter. Dean worried that Bryan would complain, but he said nothing. He seemed awed by the large living room with its vaulted ceilings and high windows. There were oversized pots and vases everywhere, and after a few minutes of small talk, Dean learned that Mrs. Markham was a potter. Her studio was below, next to the garage. Behind the house there was a kiln. Jessica's father worked for the Department of Labor and commuted into Washington three days a week.

"What made you decide to live all the way out here?" Dean asked.

"It's just so beautiful. And it didn't hurt that there's a golf course right down the street. I love that you practiced there. Jess, did you tell Coach Renner about all the times we left you there last summer?" Mrs. Markham smiled at Dean. "It took us forever to build the house, and we kept dropping her off at the pool while we argued with contractors. Poor thing had to do all her summer reading in the clubhouse."

"It wasn't so bad," Jessica said. She was blushing.

"No, there was that sweet woman who worked there. I can't remember her name. But she started doing all the same reading as Jessica and then they would discuss it. You two had your own little book club. It was so nice."

Jessica's expression was pained, and all at once Dean understood that the sweet woman was Nicole. But it was clear that Mrs. Markham had no idea. Dean was glad she had no idea; he needed privacy to absorb this new glimpse of Nicole. He couldn't really imagine it; he didn't remember her as a reader, it was just something she did before bed. More than anything, he was embarrassed by the idea of his wife striking up a friendship with a sixteen-year-old girl. It wasn't something a happy, busy adult would do.

"Whatever happened to her?" asked Mrs. Markham. "I don't think I've seen her there for a couple months."

"I don't know," Jessica said. She glanced at Dean apologetically—a look that gave a glimpse of the adult she would become.

NIGHT FELL QUICKLY as they drove back to the school, and Dean sped along the hilly roads, trying to return in time to pick up Robbie from his play practice. He kept trying to attach some meaning to Jessica's connection to Nicole. If Jessica's family hadn't moved there . . . If Nicole hadn't worked nearby . . . If he hadn't started coaching cross-country . . . If, if, if . . . Then what? Then nothing. His wife would still be dead; he would still be lonely; Jessica would still be the same sensitive girl, gifted in all areas except the ones that could make her a great athlete.

When Dean pulled into the school, he found Robbie sitting outside with a bunch of the theater kids. Robbie was wearing some other kid's hat, a kind of newsboy cap. His jean jacket was draped over his shoulders like a cape. He looked grown-up, confident, expressive—like the boy Dean had seen, briefly, onstage. Dean felt a profound sense of disconnect. He called to Robbie and watched as he removed the borrowed cap and wriggled his arms back into his jacket.

ON THURSDAY, THE girls had a dual meet, at home, which Megan won easily. The team won, too. It was their first win and it was an easy one, even a predictable one, but it wasn't a win they could have pulled off at the beginning of the year. They were no longer the worst team in the county. The race ended on the track, and the football team stopped their practice to watch the finish. They whooped and hollered for Megan, who seemed slightly alarmed by the attention and only ran faster.

"I see you found yourself a ringer," Garrett joked.

"Yeah, I guess you could say that," Dean said, willing himself not to say something snide about the poached baseball player. "You ready for homecoming?"

"Don't worry, we'll win. I won't spoil the dance. Are you going to be there?"

"Yeah, I'm chaperoning."

"Me too—with Connie. I'll look for you."

With only two teams competing, the race was over quickly, and both teams headed to the gym to stretch. After the opposing team left, Dean gave the all-clear and the girls let loose, doing cartwheels on the basketball court. Above them, blue and white balloons were hanging from the rafters, already tied into place for tomorrow's pep rally. Dean watched See-See execute a series of round-offs, throwing her arms back, Mary Lou Retton style, after each one. With her hair growing out, and with her small sturdy body, she actually resembled the gymnast a little bit. She'd done well in the race, coming in third overall and second for the team. Dean was glad she'd gotten the win. He felt, in a way, that the team wouldn't exist without her, because she was the one who'd kept after Aileen and Lori over the summer—Jessica, too.

"Hey, See," he called to her. "Come here a minute."

See-See eyed him and came over, reluctantly.

"Girls, I want you to give a round of applause for your captain, See-See Coulter—"

"See-See *Meyers*," she corrected.

"Oh, right, I'm sorry," Dean said. "This girl is the one who led you to victory. She's the one who kept this team together when you didn't have a coach. And she's the one you should thank next year when you start placing at the big meets."

The girls clapped and whistled, but See-See shrugged it off. Dean sensed she was embarrassed, maybe even a little sad, so he called for a *hell yeah* as a way of keeping things light.

"You have tomorrow off," Dean said. "And as you know, there's no meet this weekend in advance of Regionals. But you need to run on Saturday and Sunday. So take it easy tomorrow night, okay? Don't stay out too late."

"We won't!" they promised.

And Dean knew that, unlike the football players, they wouldn't.

THE NEXT AFTERNOON one of the cheerleaders delivered a boutonniere for Dean to wear to the dance. It was a white carnation dipped in blue dye and tied with a blue ribbon that said *Go Eagles* in cursive script.

The phone rang and it was Laura. Her tone was cold and businesslike, but he couldn't help feeling soft toward her. He tried to tell her that he'd just been thinking of her, but she cut him off.

"I'm calling about Robbie," she said. "That's all I'm going to discuss. I'm sure you can appreciate that."

"Laura, I was sick last week—the boys, too. I was completely underwater—"

"I'm serious. I only want to talk about Robbie. He said

some things that I find concerning, especially since he's heading to the Outdoor School next week. Honestly, I'm not sure if he should go."

"Why not?" There was something strange about her tone; it contained an emotion he couldn't place.

"He's very angry with you. He told me that you've forgotten about his mother and that you're dating another woman."

"That's not true." Dean realized what he'd heard in her voice: jealousy.

"You don't have to lie to protect my feelings. Robbie told me who it is and it seems pretty likely. I mean, I get it, Karen Coulter is pretty, she's nice, she's convenient."

"I'm not dating her. We've spent some time together, that's it. How did Robbie even find out?"

"Because you live in a small town, Dean. Because your son hangs out with high school kids every day after school—high school kids who are friends with See-See. She probably told someone who told someone who told Robbie. I shouldn't have to explain this to you."

"How did See-See know?"

"Her mother probably told her! Or she figured it out. She's seventeen years old, she's not an idiot."

"You're right." Dean was remembering the way See-See had backed away from his praise after the dual meet. Now that he thought about it, she had been a little bit distant all week.

"Whatever," Laura said, sounding young. "The point is, Robbie's upset and you need to address it. Preferably before he leaves. I know you don't think it's a big deal for him to be away from home for a week, but for a kid who's been through what he's been through, it's going to be very dramatic to be without his family. So you need to reassure him. Talk about your wife with him. Be open about what's going on with Karen."

"Should I also *be open* about what's going on with you?"

"Do what you want."

She hung up without saying good-bye. Dean called back but she didn't pick up, forcing him to leave a message with her secretary. He felt like he'd been kicked. What was he supposed to say to Robbie about Nicole? *Your mother didn't have the decency to off herself with pills. Your mother was a coward. Your mother was a secretive person. Your mother was impulsive, she was always impulsive, she married me on impulse, she had you on impulse, she killed herself on impulse. If she could change her mind, she would. I'm sure of it.*

Except Dean wasn't sure of it.

The bell rang for last period, the nasal sound jolting him. It was time for the pep rally. He went out to the gym's main entrance to meet Bryan, who would be on his way over from the elementary school. The students were coming down the hallway in a flood, the majority of them wearing something blue or white. Dean had a strong feeling of déjà vu, not exactly like he'd lived this scene before, more like he was stuck in an endless loop of high school. He remembered a burned-out teacher telling him, *They get younger and younger the older you get.*

"Daddy!" Bryan called to him. "I didn't know there was a party today!"

Dean led him toward the gym, where students were already filling up the bleachers. The cross-country girls, Dean noticed, were sitting together.

THE HOMECOMING DANCE was held in the cafeteria, where Dean and Laura had first met, and whether out of habit or accident, Laura was standing near the window where they used to chat. He was surprised to see her, since she worked at the middle school now, but she was standing with one of the younger female teachers at the high school, so maybe she had come out of friendship, to lend moral support. Both women were dressed in old-fashioned 1950s-style party dresses. Dean suspected they were wearing them ironically, but they looked pretty. Dean wanted to talk to her, but she stuck to her friend in a way that made him feel as if she was doing it on purpose, as a way of avoiding him. As an experiment, he moved toward her side of the room to see if she moved in the opposite direction. She did. All around him, students were engaging in similarly covert maneuvers.

He checked the boys' bathroom for smokers and imbibers and, finding none, sought refuge in the faculty bathroom. There was someone else in one of the stalls, but he thought nothing of it until he was at the sink washing his hands. When he shut off the water, he heard a groan. His instinct was to leave immediately, not wanting to encounter a colleague in the wake of a gastrointestinal emergency, but there was another sound and all at once he knew there were two voices, two people.

"This is Coach Renner," he said loudly. "I'm going to stand outside this bathroom for thirty seconds. If you do not exit within that time frame, I'm getting the vice principal."

The couple left quickly, a boy and a girl. Dean knew them both from gym classes. He didn't realize they were together and wouldn't have pegged either of them as the type to sneak off for public sex. The faculty bathroom! Was that a known place? He had to tell someone, it was too funny. The obvious choice was Laura, but he couldn't bring it up with her, it would seem like a come-on. It was a come-on, maybe. He missed her. He wished they had met in a different way. That he hadn't known her when he was married. There was too much guilt attached to her. And yet it was that guilty feeling he craved.

The cafeteria was getting warm as more and more kids arrived. The girls were dressed sweetly or provocatively; there seemed to be nothing in between. Dean saw the cheerleader who had given him the boutonniere; she was in a short, sequined dress and her hair was in a French twist. She was overdone and looked about thirty-five. Her date was Larry Moats, a JV player. He looked like a used-car salesman in his shiny suit and conservative tie. Dean imagined them ten years down the road, married and fat with small children and money problems. His cynical thoughts disturbed him; they felt rank and sour.

The music changed to a saccharine ballad and couples began to slow-dance. Dean checked across the room for Laura but she was gone. After a moment, he found her. She was talking with the high school guidance counselor. She looked completely engaged, interested in whatever her colleague-in-psychology was saying. Dean wondered if she was happy, and if she'd gotten back together with Tim. Had she begged his forgiveness? Maybe she didn't even have to beg. Maybe Tim had been in his own kind of trouble; maybe he'd asked for her to come back. Maybe this whole time, Laura's mind was on Tim, and Tim's mind was on Laura, and years from now, the story would be about how tumultuous things had been at the beginning. Dean would be the lonely widower Laura had befriended because she was a softie.

Dean began to walk the perimeter of the room, trying to be a good chaperone. At the edge of the dance floor he noticed See-See, dancing with a very tall boy Dean remembered vaguely from freshman PE a couple of years before. Travis something. He was not very athletic, as Dean recalled. He had to bend slightly to dance with See-See, who seemed especially petite in her off-the-shoulder party dress. Dean had never seen her in a dress before. She seemed so vulnerable, with her bare shoulders and back and her arms reaching up to embrace this long-stemmed boy. Dean had to leave. He went outside, to the parking lot, a zone that chaperones were theoretically supposed to police, but he didn't bother walking the aisles of vehicles. Instead he went to his own car and drove home.

LATE THAT NIGHT, Dean was awakened by the sound of heavy rains and winds. Tree branches slapped against his windows. The next morning, his backyard was transformed. All the branches were bare and the yard was covered with leaves. He and the boys spent the weekend raking them into piles and stuffing them into bags. They spread some over their garden beds, and the rest they drove over to Joelle's for mulching.

"We missed you at church," Joelle said to Bryan and Robbie. "What are you up to this afternoon?"

"We have to help Robbie pack," Bryan said. "He's going to Outdoor School."

"You got a cold week," Joelle said. "Megan got lucky, she went in May."

"Dad got me some new boots," Robbie said. "I'll be fine."

"We'll send you a care package," Joelle said.

"He's only gone for a week," Dean said.

"He could still use some treats—Thursday is Halloween! I'll mail it tomorrow, that way you'll get it in time."

Robbie shrugged, but Dean could see he was pleased. He remembered Laura's worries about Outdoor School and wondered if she was right to be concerned. He'd been trying all weekend to get a few minutes alone with Robbie to talk with him about See-See's mother, or at least to approach the subject indirectly. But Bryan kept interrupting, or else Dean would begin the conversation in too banal a way and Robbie's attention would drift and he would ask to be excused.

On Monday morning, with everything carefully packed, Dean had the idea to put Bryan on the bus and drive Robbie to school by himself. They would talk in the car. With the familiar road ahead it would be easy to assure his son that they were still a family, and that he thought often of his mother. That none of the rumors he'd heard were true.

But when they got into the car, Robbie turned on the radio and started to sing along. Then, when Dean brought up the subject of play practice, thinking this would be an easy way to segue into a discussion of any overheard gossip, Robbie began to talk about the play, about how they were in tech rehearsals for the week, and how, when he got back, it would be time for dress rehearsals. He was excited to see himself in all the various costumes: munchkin, poppy flower, flying monkey. He talked so animatedly that Dean couldn't bring himself to interrupt him. It even crossed Dean's mind that Laura might be wrong about Robbie, and that perhaps *she* was the one who was angry with him and offended by rumors.

When they arrived at school, Dean kissed him good-bye on both cheeks (Robbie allowed this!), and then he watched as he boarded the charter bus hired for the occasion. There were dozens of parents on the curb, some of them crying. Dean thought of Nicole's sadness at the beginning of every school year when the kids would be returned to their schoolyard kingdoms. Then he drove over to the high school to begin his day.

Part Three

Chapter 14

Robbie checked his compass, which hung from a lanyard around his neck. All week long, he'd been learning about orienteering. He'd learned about tribes in South America where kids didn't have words for left and right. Instead they learned north, south, east, and west. During that lesson, Robbie raised his hand to ask how people knew their left hand from their right hand and everyone laughed and the teacher thought he was being a smart aleck. But he honestly wanted to know what they said. He was fascinated by the idea that certain words could exist in one language but not in another. He was fascinated by lots of things, but he was constantly being told that he was "off topic" or that he "had tone." No one had ever told him these things in elementary school. But now, in middle school, he was getting a reputation for being mouthy and difficult. It had started with his teachers, and now it was drifting down to his friends. He felt strongly that nothing within him had changed. The only thing that was different was that his mother had killed herself. But he wasn't allowed to talk about that; he wasn't even allowed to repeat things his mother used to say, because when he did, people thought he was an even bigger weirdo. It was like he was supposed to pretend that he'd never had a mother at all. Even his father went along with this new reality.

It had been nice to be away from home for a week. Robbie could admit that, here, in the quiet, bare woods. The fallen, dried leaves made shushing sounds as he walked. They faded more and more each day, from red and gold to auburn and yellow to brown and brown. Above, the sky was overcast, matching the pale gray bark of the trees. *Monochrome* was a word that Robbie had recently learned, and which he liked. He made up his own word from it: *moonchrome*. This was the color that moonlight gave to trees and leaves and grass and houses.

He and his mother used to make up words: *iceslip, ponins, delicatessies, lemonstone, snarfle*. His mother told him he had been slow to talk, but once he'd started talking, it was in fluent sentences. She used to call him Robbie-robin-red-breast. He had no idea why, it was just something she said.

He and his mother had their own language, and now he was the only remaining speaker.

Robbie could no longer hear the voices of other kids nearby. He had deliberately gone in the opposite direction of where he knew he should go, leaving his buddy group behind. They were supposed to find their way back to the school by themselves. It was the final orienteering challenge before they went home tomorrow. But Robbie didn't want to go home.

His original plan had been to sneak off the bus going home. As long as his name got checked off during attendance, he would be in the clear. He was pretty sure he could get past the bus monitor; he could say that he had to use the bathroom and never come back. His friends wouldn't notice—or care—that he was gone.

But then the teacher announced there would be an orienteering test on Thursday afternoon, and he realized that was the better time to go. He was disappointed to miss the Halloween campfire, but maybe they wouldn't have one, anyway, because of what had happened at last night's campfire. The school director was pissed with them because they had laughed when he tried to teach them "Blowin' in the Wind." They had laughed because the questions were like something from a kid's book—*How many seas must a white dove sail?*—and because the face the director made while he was singing was so hilarious, like he was constipated. And they had laughed because they wanted to laugh, because they were making s'mores and the moon was out and for a whole week they didn't have to go to school. But the director wanted the campfire to be more like school.

He chided them: "This is protest music! I guess you're not mature enough for this." Robbie wanted to raise his hand and say, *I am, I love music, I know about Bob Dylan*. But instead he had turned to his best friend, Kyle, and said, "I liked that song," a sentiment Kyle had then conveyed to everyone sitting nearby, and everybody cracked up as if he'd confessed to liking Barney the purple dinosaur.

And then the school director thought it was Robbie's fault that everyone was laughing at him, that Robbie had been the one to say something sarcastic. And Robbie hadn't even bothered to defend himself, because he knew there was no point.

His legs were getting tired. He sat down on a rock and

gazed up at the trees. The branches at the top were so spindly, they tapered sharply, like pencil tips. He imagined the trees writing letters on the air—to whom? This was the kind of question he would share with his mother, to amuse her, to make her smile. He knew the kinds of questions she liked best, the ones that would get her talking. She would ask him for a word for tree letters. *Leaflets*, maybe—except that was a real word. Maybe *Leaflins*. Or should he start from tree? *Treescrolls*. A girl at school was named Sylvia, and she said her name meant "woods." It was from Latin, she said. He liked talking to Sylvia; she had a round, calm face, and when she walked through the hallways, it was like she was floating gently down a river and everyone else was hiking uphill. But she was only in school in the mornings, because she was studying ballet. She left every day at lunch to go to a studio in Frederick. She had to get special permission from the school board. Robbie wished he had some special reason to leave early. He'd seen her going a few times, climbing into a car with her duffel bag over her shoulder. Her mother picked her up.

Once, Ms. Lanning had asked him what he liked about sneaking out of school. He said, "Sneaking out of school." And she had laughed.

He didn't tell her about the way his mind could drift in the direction of fear, the sense he would get of a storm coming, darkening all his thoughts. He would get a cold panicky feeling in his bones and he would have to escape. He would concentrate on planning his escape if he couldn't leave right away. Once he got out, he would instantly feel better.

The only time he didn't worry about that feeling coming on was during play practice, when he stood under the lights or in the wings looking onto the stage, that flat empty space that every afternoon became full of life, a little pocket world within itself.

His favorite person—after Sylvia—was Seth. Seth played the Cowardly Lion and everyone liked him. He had shoulder-length hair that he wore in a ponytail and he played the guitar. There was always a group of people around him between scenes, and he would let Robbie listen in on his conversations. Afterward, he would explain anything Robbie didn't understand. Robbie kept the new words filed away for future use: *weed, hottie, forty, douchebag, blow job, Deadhead, shrooms*. There were bands to learn, too. Seth made him a mix for Outdoor School called *Happy Camper Tunes*. Robbie listened to a few songs every night before he fell asleep, sneaking his Walkman into his bunk. Then he switched tapes and listened to *Les Mis*. He had to hear "Castle on a Cloud" before he fell asleep. He loved the sweet way the little girl sang it.

The first time Robbie saw Bryan standing on the altar at church, chin tipped up, tears streaming, he thought Bryan was an actor, too. Someone who needed a stage. He told Seth about it, one day after school, and then Seth told him his theory of religion, how it was a made-up world for people to pretend in, and how if you were going to live in an imaginary world, you might as well pick one that didn't make you feel guilty all the time. Seth was going to be an actor when he finished school. If he didn't get into his first-choice college, he was going to cut his hair and move to California. He liked to say that when something annoying happened: *Fuck it, I'll just cut my hair and move to California!* Sometimes Robbie said it, too. It always made Seth laugh.

Robbie wanted to be an actor, too. His plan was to call Seth when he graduated. Seth would be famous by then and would help him get his start. It wouldn't matter that he and Seth were six years apart, because when you grew up, you were allowed to hang out with people who were older than you and it wasn't strange.

Robbie's hands were getting cold, even with his gloves on. He put them in his pockets and retrieved one of the two Snickers bars he had secreted there. Aunt Joelle had sent them to him, along with some raisins, gum, and a word find from some lame Christian kids' magazine. He didn't even do word finds anymore. He had moved on to cryptograms. Still, he was grateful for the package. His dad hadn't even sent him a letter.

He bit into the candy bar, trying to savor each layer. It was close to four thirty. His classmates had probably already made it back to the school. He wondered how long until they began to search for him.

THE GIRL DRESSED as Glinda—her name was Lacey, Stephanie was pretty sure—had an illegal pet bunny who everyone agreed could serve as Toto. Stephanie coaxed the large, sleepy black rabbit into the small wicker basket she had found at Goodwill.

"He's a very chill bunny, don't worry," Lacey said. She adjusted the puffed sleeves of her straight-from-the-eighties Laura Ashley gown. "I think I need more glitter."

"You all need more glitter!" someone yelled from the hall-way. Stephanie invited her inside to join the preparty. She was uncostumed, save for a pencil-thin mustache, drawn with eye-liner. "I'm John Waters," she said. "From Baltimore?"

"I'm from Baltimore—sort of!" Theresa called from the

corner, where she was applying her Tin Man makeup. Her ensemble was a cleverly constructed mix of tinfoil and spray-painted cardboard. Nearby, Gabe was the Cowardly Lion, his golden curls perfectly playing the part.

"Come on, everyone, let's get a photo," Stephanie said. "We have to take one to show my little brother."

John Waters took the photo, taking turns with everyone's cameras. Stephanie enjoyed the moment self-consciously. It was like she had to keep checking in with herself to see if she was actually having fun. She was, she was. And if she wasn't happy—she wasn't quite—she felt the possibility of happiness shimmering at the edges of her life. She felt pretty and feminine in her blue dress. On her feet were her red cloth Mary Janes, decorated with red sequins. They were the reason she got to be Dorothy—that and her dark hair. She'd dyed it again, for the night, a deep, semipermanent brown.

People started coming into their room, helping themselves to red Jell-O shots quivering in Dixie cups. It was Halloween and there were parties all over campus, culminating in a dance at the campus center. Stephanie and her roommates were hoping to win best group costume. The prize was a month's supply of cookies from Sugar Rush, a local bakery. The wholesomeness of the prize pleased Stephanie. It was the kind of thing Raquel would never want to win. She had run into her old friend earlier in the day, at the library. When she asked Raquel what costume she was planning, Raquel said she wasn't going to bother, that costumes were for people who needed an excuse to dress up. Stephanie walked away from the conversation thinking that Raquel really had no sense of fun.

She and Gabe had invented drinks for each of the charac-

ters. The "Cowardly Lion" was ginger ale and whiskey; the
"Tin Man" was any kind of canned beer; the "Scarecrow" was
Boone's Farm; the "Glinda" was champagne; and the "Dorothy" a.k.a. "There's No Place Like Home" was a red Jell-O
shot.

Stephanie stuck to the "Tin Man," hoping her natural aver-
sion to beer would help her to follow her grandmother's advice
about drinking: one drink per hour and no more than three
drinks in one night.

"Stephanie!" Theresa called to her. "You have a phone call!"

Stephanie hadn't even heard any ringing, that was how
noisy their room was getting. "Who is it?"

"I don't know. A kid."

Stephanie's first thought was that it was Robbie. She'd gotten
an unremarkable letter from him that morning, postmarked
from the Outdoor School. Maybe he was getting lonely. She
remembered calling her mother from the Outdoor School pay
phone. You had to sign up for it and then you only had five
minutes to talk. Some kids would start crying as soon as they
heard their mother's voice. But most kids were like Stephanie,
calling only because their mothers had insisted on it.

"Stephanie? It's Megan."

"Megan?"

Before Stephanie could say anything else, Megan started
talking. "Your dad told me to call you. We were at practice,
and one of Robbie's teachers came running over from the
middle school to say that Robbie is missing. And then Uncle
Dean said I should call you from his office. He's driving to the
Outdoor School right now with Bryan. He didn't want to wait.
He said he'll call you when he gets to the Outdoor School."

"Wait, what do you mean Robbie is missing?"

"I don't know much," Megan said. "The lady from the middle school said he got lost on some hike? Or something? I don't know. But now it's dark, and they're getting worried about him being all alone out there."

The rabbit started moving in Stephanie's basket, reacting to the way her body was shaking. She had to put the basket down and as she did, the rabbit hopped out.

"Hey, watch out!" Lacey hurried over to her, her Glinda skirts swishing. "You can't let him jump out, he'll run off—hey, what's the matter?"

"My brother's missing," Stephanie said. She began to cry, and everyone turned toward her. Just when life was getting better, she was plunged back into loss.

THE MOON ILLUMINATED the bare branches and the pale undersides of newly fallen leaves. The soft blue light made the woods less frightening, but also more cinematic, adding to Dean's sense that what was happening was not really happening. A half mile away, Robbie's classmates were gathered around a campfire, toasting marshmallows and telling ghost stories; Dean could smell the smoke on the breeze. They all knew about Robbie; they all knew and had been instructed not to worry, their teachers accomplices in this fiction, handing out chocolate bars and graham crackers. Why weren't they all out here with flashlights, an army of children to find his son?

"Goddamn," Dean said, running his hand over his face. He kept walking through spiderwebs. The feeling of the sticky threads on his nose and mouth was like being lightly suffocated.

"I can take the lead," said Ian, the Outdoor School's director. "I'm fine," Dean said. He was furious. He didn't want to walk behind this bearded, high-strung hippie who spent his days in the woods teaching children how to use compasses and bows and arrows, as if preparing them for the apocalypse. Ian had a whiff of paranoia about him. He'd told Dean at least four times that they'd used this orienteering test for years, that it was age-appropriate and well supervised, and that no one had ever gotten lost, at least not for this length of time. Dean wanted to tell him to relax, he wasn't going to sue the school, but at the same time he was annoyed that this man he'd just met was basically asking to be let off the hook. As if that was what mattered. Who cared how any of this had happened? He wanted his son back.

They'd been walking for almost two hours, starting from the school and retracing Robbie's steps as best they could. Ian showed Dean where the test began, at a large limestone rock that was nicknamed "Pirate Rock" for its shiplike shape. It was one of dozens of boulders scattered throughout the woods, the remnants of some long-departed glacier. Dean used them as landmarks, something to keep him going; he would trick himself into believing that Robbie might be curled up behind one and he would stride toward it eagerly, some part of him actually expecting to find his son. He felt prone to delusions, his body pumped up on stress hormones. He tried to be rational, tried to talk himself down: *You're high on adrenaline and cortisol; take it easy, Dean, take it easy.*

He was disturbed to notice that there was an edge of giddiness to all these feelings. He felt just as he had the week after Nicole's death, when there was so much to do, immediately, and he was cast in the role of leader. His strongest memory of that time was not of the funeral, or of the burial, or of all the visitors who came by the house, but of eating alone, late at night, filling a plate with cold fried chicken and macaroni and cheese and coleslaw and soft rolls, his appetite so huge it was as if he were back in college, recovering from a hard practice, his body ruling him, demanding attention, his mind placid. Nicole's absence wasn't yet real to him, although it had been during the hours immediately following her death, when he had been allowed to view her body. He'd braced himself for something grotesque—her face bloated, her tongue hanging, her neck broken—but instead her eyes were shut and she looked placid, her skin pale and faintly gray, as if she'd been lightly erased. She was wearing a sleeveless button-down shirt, the collar partially obscuring the rope burn that crept up past her ears. Dean pulled the collar away from her neck to see the full extent of the damage. Something in him had to know. As he gazed at the dark red bruising, he had an out-of-sync thought: *Somebody strangled her.* For the briefest of moments, he had a fantasy of revenge. He was going to get whoever had done this awful thing to his wife. But then he realized he was looking at the murderer.

"She didn't suffer," the coroner said, watching him. "She would have lost consciousness immediately."

Dean had straightened Nicole's shirt, embarrassed.

"Make sure your kids know she didn't suffer," the coroner said. "Especially your son, the one who saw her. He's probably going to have some questions."

"Okay," Dean promised. But as soon as he got back outside, some survival gene kicked in and sent a message to his body to disregard those strange, protracted minutes with a complete stranger and his wife's dead body, to keep them separate from his daily mind.

"There's the fire road." Ian pointed ahead, where a break in the trees was barely visible. "There's a good chance Robbie hit this same spot. The question is, would he have walked on the road or gone back into the woods?"

"I don't know," Dean said. And he really didn't. Of his three children, Robbie was the one he knew the least.

"If you take this road north, it dead-ends, but obviously it hits the main drive if you go in the other direction. Hard to believe he could have walked on the main drive undetected."

Not that hard to believe, Dean thought. How and when the school lost track of Robbie was unclear to Dean and, it seemed, also to the teacher who had been supervising him at that time. She had not been able to stop crying when Dean questioned her. Dean's conversation with Kyle, Robbie's orienteering partner, had not gone much better. Dean knew Kyle well—the boy had stayed overnight several times, although it occurred to Dean that it had been a long time since Robbie had hosted a sleepover or been invited to one. When he spoke to Kyle, he sensed that something had been lost in the boys' friendship, something that neither Kyle nor Robbie was even aware of. All Kyle would say was that Robbie had been walking slowly, and that he had gotten tired of waiting for him.

"You're supposed to stay with your buddy," Dean said. "That's what the buddy system is."

"He didn't stay with me!" Kyle said, his freckled face going red. And then Ian had intervened, with soft words for Kyle, and even softer words for Dean, assuring him that the children knew and understood the concept of the buddy system. This was before the police had been called, when Ian probably thought the whole thing was going to blow over, that Robbie would show up for dinner, like a dog. But then he didn't. And then after dinner, another boy—one Dean didn't know— volunteered that he had seen Robbie removing money and candy and a flashlight from his bunk drawer right before they gathered for orienteering class. This corroborated something Bryan had said, which was that Robbie had emptied his shoe-box bank when he was packing.

So he had planned it. Dean remembered Robbie's insistence on a new flashlight, extra batteries, new gloves, new boots. He didn't know his son could live with that level of deception.

They had reached the fire road, and without the trees overhead it seemed almost bright. Dean remembered Nicole telling the boys that the moon was a nightlight for the animals.

"I think we should take this back to the main road and check in with the others," Ian said.

"Can't you check in with that?" Dean pointed to his walkie-talkie.

"I still think we should get back. What if there's news? It's better for you to be in a more centralized place."

"Okay," Dean said, barely mustering a shrug. It felt stupid to head back, but it was probably even stupider to walk aimlessly in the woods, hoping to find your child by trial and error.

"We're going to find him," Ian said. "He's a smart kid, and I'm sure he's taking care of himself. There's nothing dangerous in these woods. Just deer and squirrels."

The school director kept talking. He told Dean about Native American traditions in which boys Robbie's age were sent on weeks-long treks into the woods as a coming-of-age ritual. Then he told Dean about a quarry he used to go swimming in when he was a boy, a treacherous place where he and his friends could easily have drowned or knocked themselves dead with one false dive. Both anecdotes seemed meant as lessons of the dangers children naturally encountered in adolescence. And beneath them, Dean sensed a kind of romanticism, a lefty, back-to-the-land longing for a simpler life when children were free, more in touch with nature, and slightly wild. Never mind that quarries were manmade. Never mind that Native Americans had been decimated by disease, greed, and pure unadulterated aggression. Dean wanted to tell Ian that he'd watched kids burn their youth for him, tearing muscle and banging helmets. He didn't need examples of the dangers boys needlessly courted.

"I'm going to run," Dean said. He started without waiting for Ian's reply. His legs felt tight but quickly loosened up. Ian caught up and gave a thumbs-up, too winded to talk. Gravel crunched beneath their feet. Dean breathed deeply from his diaphragm, the way he'd taught the girls to do.

He kept thinking of the day he'd seen Robbie dancing onstage. The grace of his movements, his long arms white and slender under the lights, the way Nicole's had been. That was the day he'd seen who his son was—could be—in the world, the day he'd seen who Robbie was outside their family. It was a gift to see that, Dean knew that, but in the wake of it there was a sense of loss. He and his son were not alike, just as Dean and his own father were not alike. There had been a certain disappointment knit into Dean's relationship with Robbie, starting from the night he was born, when Dean witnessed the immediate intimacy between mother and son. He remembered Ed joking with him, "Step aside, you're useless the first two years." That was the beginning of Dean's closeness with Stephanie. She was seven going on eight, just a little younger than Bryan was now, a wonderful age, an inquisitive, optimistic age.

Dean's lungs ached. He was running fast. He ran harder.

He thought of Laura's face when she told him. As soon as he saw her at the track, he knew something was wrong. The school had called her when they couldn't get a hold of him in his office. *Why did they call you?* That was the first thing Dean could think to say. *Because he's under my care.* He saw in her eyes that she loved his son, and that her affection for Robbie was mixed up with whatever she felt for him. He saw her fear and he felt it.

And yet he could still locate the calm he'd felt before Laura had appeared, when the girls were racing on the backstretch, all of them hitting their splits, their strides long, their arms reaching. The pain was there, it wasn't disregarded, but it was transmuted. The drama was completely internal. There was something mysterious and joyous about the sport that impressed Dean. It was so true to life.

Dean had watched Megan sprint toward him, the others trailing her, closer than they'd ever been. He remembered thinking: *This is the start of a championship team.* And with that simple, childish idea came the possibility of happiness.

That was how happiness worked: it was simple, it was elusive, it was something to reach for but not to grasp.

And Dean had felt he could begin, again, to reach for it.

"That's the main drive ahead," Ian said. He paused to catch his breath. "I think I hear someone coming."

The two men hurried to the edge of the drive where two headlights appeared, casting everything around them into darkness. Ian ran into the middle of the road to flag down the driver. A police officer, Dean assumed. The car drew closer, and all at once Dean recognized it. Stephanie's car. She'd come back.

As THE OUTDOOR School's 1970s-style buildings came into view, Stephanie got an eerie and not entirely happy sense of déjà vu. Here was a place she had visited only once, but which had made such a huge impression that it existed in its own room in her mind. She felt as if she were driving into her memory.

The road forked as it approached the Outdoor School's main lodge, a sprawling, split-level construction with a large, round room at its center. This was the lounge, with its stone fireplace, round cushions, and a glass display case containing pebbles and rocks, fossils and shells, feathers, crystals, seed pods, arrowheads, bones, snakeskins, and birds' nests. Stephanie had a strong memory of looking carefully at each object in the case while she waited for a class to begin. There had been something so mesmerizing about the display, full of dead things and yet so evocative of life.

This evening, the windows of the lounge glowed softly, lit by firelight. A gray stream of smoke escaped from the chimney. Were the kids still awake? No, Stephanie realized, it was the teachers. It had never even occurred to her that they would stay up. You wore such blinders in childhood. But maybe they helped you to see more directly.

"Turn left here," said Mr. Knapp, the school's director.

He sat in the backseat, behind her father. He had introduced himself as Ian, but Stephanie could only think of him as Mr. Knapp. His beard and eyebrows were a faded brown instead of the deep reddish brown she remembered. He didn't recognize her, but then why would he? He met hundreds of eleven-year-olds every year—and then never saw them again.

They parked outside the mess hall, which stood at the end of two rows of cabins full of sleeping children. Everything seemed smaller. Stephanie remembered the cabins as quasi tree houses, raised high on stilts, with leafy branches brushing up against their wraparound porches, but instead they were only slightly raised, perhaps one story, and the porches were narrow balconies, barely wide enough for two children to pass each other. Only the trees were as impressive as in memory, even with their branches bare.

The local police had set up shop inside the mess hall, their equipment piled on one of the round folding tables. The room was small and shabby, with its wood-paneled walls, gray linoleum flooring, and the faded sheets of construction paper stapled to the bulletin board next to the kitchen. A chalkboard announced tomorrow's breakfast: French toast sticks, turkey bacon, and applesauce. Stephanie remembered eating at the round tables first thing in the morning, the intimacy of seeing her classmates right after they woke up, with wet hair and toothpaste residue in the corners of their mouths, the thrill of being able to excuse yourself when you were finished and walk outside in the open air. Stephanie had loved the freedom, or maybe she had simply loved being away from home, away from toddler routines, away from her exhausted mother, away from the pressure of always having to be the good older sister. She realized now that she had imagined college would be something like Outdoor School.

A couple of teachers emerged from the kitchen with mugs of tea. Stephanie didn't recognize either of them, but then her old sixth-grade teacher, Mrs. Davis, came in from outside, her gray hair in a ponytail and her cheeks pink with cold. She had not changed at all; in fact she was possibly wearing the same red down vest that she had worn when she accompanied Stephanie's class to the school seven years before. When she saw Stephanie, she hurried over to give her a hug. "Oh, my poor dear! I can't stop thinking about your brother. He's probably trying to make his way home right now. I've always said that they should retire this orienteering unit."

"I'm getting some coffee," Stephanie's father said, abruptly walking away. Stephanie knew he was irritated with Mrs. Davis, with Mr. Knapp, and possibly even with the police. He'd been radiating anger. But there had been a moment, when he first saw her, when he embraced her with dry, haunted eyes. And she had gone straight back to the morning her mother died.

"Are braids the style now?" Mrs. Davis asked.

"What? Oh, no, this is for a costume," Stephanie said, touching her Dorothy plaits.

"Were you a farm girl?"

"Yeah, basically." Stephanie didn't feel like explaining.

Mrs. Davis had the sense to leave when her father returned with two coffees and a stack of apple juice containers. Stephanie peeled back the lid of one of the juices, the gesture reminding her not of Outdoor School or school lunch but of visiting her mother in the hospital after Robbie was born. There had been two containers of apple juice included with her postpartum meal, and she had given them to Stephanie, who drank them while staring at her tiny baby brother with his red wrinkled face and his head leaning in the crook of his arm, which he held above him. Her mother said, "That's probably how he slept in the womb, with his arm up like that." And Stephanie remembered thinking that she wasn't alone anymore.

"The officers want us to stick around here," Stephanie's father said. "If he doesn't turn up by the morning, they'll alert the local news. They'll treat it like an abduction."

"Abduction? Jesus."

"Hey, it's okay."

"No, it *isn't*." Stephanie felt a surge of anger. "Robbie could be kidnapped, he could be dead. Don't say it's going to be fine."

"Honey, calm down. I only meant that abduction is the word they have to use to take it seriously. Right now they're operating from the assumption that he got lost."

"Of course he's not lost. He's too smart for that. He had a compass! He obviously ran away."

"That's what I think, too." Her father took a sip of coffee. "You know, he's been leaving school, playing hooky. More than just that one time."

"I know. He called me."

"When?"

"It was last month. He called from a pay phone. I don't know why. It was like he wanted to say hi."

"Maybe he'll call you again. Is there someone at school near your phone?"

"Where's he going to call from the woods?"

"If he's running away, he's going somewhere."

"Don't you think we'll find him before that?"

"I don't know."

Stephanie wasn't sure if she'd ever heard her father say he didn't know something. It scared her almost as much as the word *abduction*.

"Bryan is at Joelle's," he said. "In case you're wondering."

"I figured."

Her father finished his coffee. Stephanie still hadn't touched hers. She felt wired already.

"I can't sit here, waiting," he said. "You want to drive down the mountain? We can get on the lower trail. There's a road that goes around the other side."

"Okay."

Her father consulted with the officer in the mess hall and returned with a walkie-talkie. "He understood," he said. "He has a son about Robbie's age."

Outside, a few stray clouds crept across the night sky. The stars were bright pinpricks of light.

"It's colder up here." Stephanie shivered as she got into her father's car. "Is Robbie wearing his winter jacket?"

"I don't know. I packed it, but it was a little small." Her father got out his keys but didn't put them in the ignition. "I should have gotten him a new one."

"It's not that cold," Stephanie said. "There hasn't even been a hard frost yet."

He shook his head. Stephanie could tell he was trying to hold it together for her.

"Don't worry, Dad. We're going to find him, I know we are. He got in over his head, that's all. Remember when he was little and he ran away and he packed three cans of soup? And we all laughed at him because how was he going to open them?"

"Yeah." Her father grimaced.

"We're going to find him," Stephanie said. "Come on."

They got into her father's car and drove halfway down the mountain until there was a turnoff for what looked to Stephanie like a private driveway. But it was an actual road, narrow and patchily paved, tunneling through acres of trees. Every few miles there was a road sign warning of blind turns, or the occasional mailbox standing sentry at the end of an anonymous, unmarked gravel driveway.

"People live out here," her father said after a while. "It's not the wilderness."

"No," Stephanie agreed. But it was other human beings that made her nervous for her brother's safety.

"I guess we should pull over at some point and get on foot."

Her father slowed the car, pulling over onto the shoulder. There were power lines above; that was why the trees were cleared. When they got out of the car, Stephanie could hear the electricity crackling—a static, ghostly sound.

"This is pointless," her father said. "Let's keep driving."

"Let's walk a little. Do we have flashlights?"

"In the glove compartment," her father said, without making a move toward the car. He stood looking up at the power lines, listening to them.

Stephanie was disappointed by her father's lack of energy, even though she knew he'd been searching for hours. She'd only just arrived.

There was one flashlight in the glove compartment, along

with the paperwork for the car, an empty water bottle, and a paperback. Stephanie took the book, thinking it must be hers. But it wasn't. It was a romance novel with the author's name on the cover in a big swoopy font. A lavishly red flower bloomed beneath. Stephanie's first thought was that it was her mother's, but then she noticed a price tag with the name of a chain store that didn't have any locations nearby. All at once she knew whose book it was. Her anger toward her father, tamped down by Robbie's absence, returned all at once, like a bad memory. She felt exposed by the car's interior light and abruptly got out, slamming the door. Her father was startled from his power line reverie. She held up the flimsy paperback.

"Is this hers?"

It took her father a moment to recognize the cover in the dim light.

"Where did you find that?"

"In the car. Did you two go on a road trip or something?"

"No, I was borrowing it." He took the book from her. "It was sort of a joke."

Inside jokes were almost worse than a road trip.

"I don't understand. Are you dating her? Are you two together?"

"No, we're not together." Her father opened the car door and threw the book in the backseat. "We were never really together."

"How long were you seeing her?"

"Not when your mother was alive."

"But you knew her before?"

"We were friends. I needed a friend." Her father leaned against the car. "I don't expect you to understand."

Stephanie remembered her grandmother saying the same thing to her after she explained her petty resentments. *I don't expect you to understand.* But they *did* expect her to understand; otherwise, they wouldn't bother with their vague explanations. And why did they want her to understand? So she would forgive them. What Stephanie *really* didn't understand was why they thought she had it in her to forgive when they didn't.

"I *don't* understand," Stephanie said. "I don't understand how you could need a friend when Mom was so lonely. How you could have ignored her."

"I didn't ignore her. I was watching her all the time. You were, too."

Stephanie shook her head. "I pushed her away. At least I can admit it."

"You didn't push her away," her father said. "You kept an eye on her. You always did."

Stephanie felt tears coming on. She clung to her anger. "It didn't help."

"I know you want to feel guilty," her father said. "But you shouldn't. You didn't do anything wrong."

"Everyone keeps telling me that. But we must have done something wrong. Otherwise—" Stephanie couldn't speak. "Otherwise she just did it to get away from us."

Her father took a Kleenex from his pocket and wiped her eyes. The gesture reminded her so much of her mother, of childhood, that she cried even harder.

"You can blame me if you want," he said, wrapping his arms around her. His jacket smelled like cold air, dried leaves, dirt, and faintly, beneath all the outdoor scents, of their house. Stephanie thought of how many times her mother's cheek must have pressed against this jacket, and how impossible it seemed that she would never see her mother's face again. And she thought of her brother, out in the night, searching for their mother like a boy lost in a fairy tale.

"We have to find Robbie," Stephanie said.

"I know," her father said, releasing her. He looked down the mountain, down the sloping path cleared by the wires. Then he took a step back from her and started yelling her brother's name, really yelling, almost screaming: *"Robbie! Robbie Renner! Robbie! Robbie! Robbie! Where are you? Robbie! Answer me! Where are you? Robbie, come home! I won't be mad. I promise I won't be angry. All is forgiven. Did you hear that, Robbie? All is forgiven!"*

Stephanie stood there, watching him. It was like he was in a trance. He didn't wait for answers. He just kept yelling. After a while, he stopped. The wires crackled above.

"Probably no one heard that," he said.

"I did," she said.

Stephanie fell asleep in the passenger seat on the way back to the school. She was still so young, she still slept like a child. All Dean ever wanted was for her to be a kid. When he met her, she was on the verge of becoming her mother's keeper. Even at three years old.

Nicole had told him, once, that she would have killed herself if not for Stephanie. She told him once and he didn't take it seriously, so she told him another time, so that he would. It was important to her that he understood how low she could get. "You need to know this about me," she had said.

She told him on a sunny June day, a week before their wedding. The trees were in full leaf, the grass was overgrown, the gardens and farms were bursting with fresh green color, it was that time of year, right before pruning and weeding, when everything was allowed to bloom and grow without restraint.

Dean and Nicole were picnicking on her parents' farm. Just the two of them. Stephanie was with Nicole's parents; they could see the house from the grassy pasture where they sat on a blanket. Nicole was wearing a short-sleeved plaid shirt and a necklace that Dean had given to her, a gold chain with a gold heart and a tiny glint of a diamond. He loved her. They had packed sandwiches and watermelon and Geneva's oatmeal cookies, but he could hardly eat; he kept taking her arm and kissing it, and he put his head in her lap and closed his eyes as she played with his overgrown hair, in need of a trim.

Dean said, "I can die now, a happy man." A cliché but she had laughed. And then she startled him, saying that thing that had locked the scene into his memory for good, making it something more than just a lovely lovers' day.

"I can't believe I ever wanted to kill myself," she said. "Last year at this time . . . that's all I could think about."

"Not really," Dean said, his eyes still on the sky.

"Really," she said. She made him sit up. She took his hands in hers. "You need to know this about me. I don't handle . . . I don't handle things well. There was a time when I thought it would be better for Stephanie if I was gone."

"Stephanie adores you."

"I know," she said. "I know, I know."

"You're a wonderful mother."

"Dean, you don't have to say that. You don't have to reassure me. It was a kind of sickness. A kind of weakness. I didn't want to face my life. And maybe I was tired, too. I don't know.

You would never feel that way so you can't understand. But I want you to try."

"Okay," he said. But he didn't try. He didn't want to imagine her feeling those things.

"Dean, listen to me." She squeezed his hands. "These weren't just thoughts. I bought a gun."

"Okay." He searched her face for some change, some hint of bitterness or sorrow, but he could only see his beautiful fiancée with her gray-blue eyes and smooth, untroubled brow. "Do you still have it?"

She shook her head. "I got rid of it. I told myself it could still be a possibility; it just couldn't be that easy. That's how crazy I was. But then I started to feel better. And then I met you. And I didn't want you to know how I felt—how low I could get. I didn't want you to see me any differently."

"I don't," Dean said. And he didn't, in that moment.

"You don't have to say that. You don't even have to marry me. I just wanted you to know."

"But I want to marry you, that's all I want."

Did he want to save her? That was what Dean wondered now. Or was it Stephanie he wanted to save? And what was this thing in him that needed to rescue women? He saw Megan as someone in need of rescuing, he realized, trapped by Joelle's ideology. And maybe he saw Laura that way, too, as a woman who needed to be saved from marrying into the town that had trapped him.

He coaxed a drowsy Stephanie from the car and led her into the lounge, which was empty and dark. Dean turned on a small floor lamp near the fireplace. The coals were covered in bright gray ash; Dean blew on them and they briefly glowed orange.

Stephanie lay down on one of the sofas against the wall.

"I'll get you a blanket," Dean said.

"Mm-hmm," she murmured.

Dean found a large walk-in closet, but it was full of scientific equipment: scales, magnifying glasses, microscopes, water-testing kits, rubber gloves, and a variety of measuring instruments. On one of the lower shelves there was a box of compasses. Next to it was a pile of laminated maps. Dean took one out and unfolded it. It covered only a small portion of the mountain: the school, the fire tower, and the nature and fitness trails. The markings were cartoonish and not drawn to scale; it was more like the map you might find at the beginning of a children's story. Dean traced its borders with his finger, then pointed to a spot in midair, high above the map. That's where his son was. Out in the nothingness.

Stephanie was fast asleep when he returned to the great room. She had draped her coat over her, like a blanket. Dean imagined Robbie in the same prostrate position, somewhere in the woods. Fear gathered in his chest; it was a kind of tightening, a kind of pain. He went outside onto the deck where he could see the mess hall, the windows still lit. There was no news, no point in going over there unless he wanted the distraction.

He didn't want the distraction.

He noticed a telescope at the far end of the deck and went over to it. He knew nothing about the constellations, so he just looked at the moon.

Robbie had once asked him why the moon didn't fall out of the sky. That was one of his first big questions. Robbie asked more "why" questions than Bryan. Or maybe it was that he asked more specific ones. Bryan accepted life's constants more easily. You couldn't just say "the law of gravity" to Robbie. Dean had to set up a miniature solar system on their kitchen table. The moon was a blueberry. Earth was a Golden Delicious apple. The sun was the basket that held all the fruits. It took forever to explain how the moon could reflect the sun's light even as it was surrounded by darkness. Dean had to demonstrate how the moon could orbit the earth while at the same time the earth was turning.

"The moon is showing us that it's sunny somewhere else," Robbie eventually said. And then Dean knew he understood.

Now, as Dean gazed at the moon, he imagined that it held captive all the sunny moments of his life, starting with his childhood, when his mother was young and wore her hair long, tied back in a handkerchief when she was working in the yard and he would play nearby, bouncing his rubber ball against the walls of his small, sturdy house. And then, elementary school, catching the bus at the end of his dusty lane, playing flag football at recess with his friends, running home on the long dusty lane, talking to his father, helping him to brush the horses, carrying buckets of water to him and small hay bales, too, the twine cutting into the flesh of his palm in a satisfying way. Years and years of these wonderful hours of purely physical happiness, hours that began to break down during his high school years when a kind of willed determination crept in, hardening everything. But still, the sun beating down, the pain in his limbs, the excitement of growing up.

And then Nicole, a woman he remembered as doused in sunlight even though she was the saddest person he'd ever known.

Dean stepped away from the telescope. The moon was small and simple again, without contours, just a silver misshapen disc that looked like it could fall from the sky.

Where, thought Dean, *where, where, where? Where is my son?*

WHEN ROBBIE WAS feeling bored, or alienated, or out of his depth—when he was in gym class, playing soccer, for instance—he would narrate his circumstances, putting himself in the third person. *Robbie Renner stood near the goal in the fullback position, watching as clouds drifted by. He wasn't cut out for soccer, his thoughts were elsewhere* . . . It helped him see his life as a story, and he liked stories; you could hold a story in your mind in one piece.

When night first began to fall in the woods, when the moon came out and the shadows got darker and more mysterious, Robbie turned it into the setting of a story. He wasn't scared, or rather, he was scared, but he would appreciate his own bravery and nerve. He had done it! He was out late at night, on his own, in the world.

But as the night wore on, Robbie's sense of exhilaration faded. Fatigue and hunger began to creep in, and he couldn't be a narrator anymore. All he could think of was how hungry he was and how sore his legs were. He had eaten his other Snickers and two boxes of raisins. He had chewed all his gum and drunk the small apple juice he'd saved from lunch, earlier in the day. He was tired of sweet. He wanted something salty now—a grilled cheese sandwich or a plate of scrambled eggs. French fries.

Above, the tree branches creaked. Occasionally he saw the glowing eyes of a small nocturnal creature. He liked seeing them. He wasn't scared of animals.

He was going to be in so much trouble when this was over.

He could never explain himself to his father. Certain events would come back to him, and he would feel shame spreading through his body. Like the time his father caught him wearing his mother's clothes. Why had he done that? He couldn't say. But when he was crouched under his parents' bed, wearing his mother's clothes, feeling like the weirdest person in the world, he had heard his father say his mother's name out loud. And he clung to that.

He told Ms. Lanning about it. Not what his father said, but that he didn't think it was fair that Stephanie could take and wear his mother's clothes and no one said anything about it, because she was a girl. If it were the other way around, if his father was gone, not his mother, Robbie knew it would be okay for him to wear his father's old T-shirts. It would be encouraged, even. Sometimes he wished his father had died instead of his mother. Ms. Lanning said it was okay to have that as a wish. That it was normal, since he had been closer to his mother. Robbie thought it made him evil. Ms. Lanning said she didn't believe in evil, that it was a theological word. Robbie said it didn't matter to him if she believed it, he was the one who had to live with the word in his mind. Ms. Lanning asked him what he thought it would be like if his mother had lived, but not his father. But Robbie couldn't imagine his father dead. It was like his father was more alive than other people. Ms. Lanning said, *Yes, I know what you mean.*

Robbie's original plan was to walk until he reached the

main road, and then he would find a farm and sleep there, in a shed or a barn. But he had underestimated the distance. Or he had gotten off course. He wasn't sure at this point.

Ahead, the woods appeared to be getting darker, but he couldn't be sure. Probably a patch of underbrush. Maybe briars. He could usually walk around them, but at night it was hard to see where they began and ended, even with his flashlight.

A sharp, familiar odor reached his nose. Pines. There was a stand of white pines near his house; he liked to lie beneath them on hot days and listen to the branches whispering above him.

These pines were not white pines—they were something taller and hardier—but Robbie still felt protected as he sat down beneath them. He lay down on his side, resting his head on his arm. Then he changed his mind and gathered some pine needles and leaves into a pile, which he then covered with his scarf. His hands were cold and the tip of his nose was cold, but otherwise, he felt warm enough. He thought, *I'll never fall asleep like this.* He remembered his mother telling him it was okay to just rest on the nights when you couldn't fall asleep. And she would also say, *Joy comes in the morning.*

Robbie closed his eyes. Sleep broke over his exhausted body like a wave. When he woke up, six hours later, the sun was rising, a pale fragile light drifting through the trees. Birds sang noisily. So much more of the landscape was visible in daylight. He realized there was a field close by; he could see a break ahead in the trees. He hurried over to it; his legs were energetic again, and his body felt light. He was so hungry.

When he reached the edge of the forest, he found himself staring at a large, rolling field, freshly hayed with square bundles of straw deposited at regular intervals. In the distance was a line of telephone poles. The moon hung above the horizon, white in the pearly sky. Robbie checked his compass. Yes, he was heading west. That was good. The road he wanted was right ahead.

STEPHANIE WOKE UP to the sound of children's voices. She was completely disoriented; she couldn't remember falling asleep, or where she was or even what day it was. Large square cushions were scattered across the floor in front of a limestone fireplace with blackened logs in its hearth. A phrase floated into her head: *Death is the black door you walked through.* She didn't know where it came from, unless it was the residue from a dream.

Then it was as if some window was opened and reality could enter: she was at the Outdoor School, she had driven here last night, Robbie was lost.

"Dad?" She thought she smelled coffee brewing somewhere. She stood up and looked out the window and saw a group of kids lined up to go somewhere, their hats and coats bright against the fading autumn landscape. They couldn't stand still even as they quieted down; they kept shifting, touching each other, adjusting their clothes, scuffing the ground, and bending down to pick up pebbles, dried leaves, pine needles, clumps of dirt. Stephanie felt so full of longing as she watched them, it was as if she could reach out and touch her childhood. She didn't want to be a kid again, though. She just wanted her mother back.

She found a bathroom and washed her face and hands. She

took her braids out and pulled her hair into a ponytail. Her skin was pale, lusterless, her nose red around the nostrils, and there was acne emerging on her chin and in the space between her eyebrows. Her mascara had rubbed off beneath her eyes.

Outside the air felt especially cold on her damp face. The campus was empty of people, the trees bare of leaves. The children who had stood outside the window were gone, headed off to wherever they went on the last day. It was so quiet that she could hear the flags flapping and the little metal rivet banging against the flagpole.

"Stephanie! You're awake! I was just coming to get you." Her father was running toward her. He was coming from the mess hall. "They've seen him. Someone saw him!"

"Where?" Stephanie hurried to meet him. "When?"

"He was at a gas station—a Sheetz. About an hour ago. The guy working behind the counter saw his photo on TV."

"Robbie was on TV?"

"He was on the morning news."

"What time is it?"

"It's not that late, honey. Not even nine."

"I don't understand, why did he go to a gas station?"

"He was hungry." Her father smiled. "He bought powdered doughnuts."

"That has to be Robbie! Where is he now?"

"We don't know. But it wasn't that long ago that he was at that store. We'll find him." Her father kissed her forehead. "Come on, let's go get your brother."

Chapter 15

What seemed easy was difficult. The police had assumed Robbie was walking along Route 35, because that's where the Sheetz was, but he wasn't—or he was, but he somehow eluded notice. It was as if he didn't want to be found. Either that or something terrible had happened. He had hitchhiked and it had gone wrong. Or he'd stepped into oncoming traffic. Or he'd been bitten by a dog or hit by a combine or he had slipped, somehow, and fallen into a ditch. Or, or—what? What else? Dean tried not to let his mind go there, but it was hard when his house was full of worried family, and when the phone kept ringing with reporters, teachers, colleagues, and even two different lawyers who wanted Dean to know that their services were available should he choose to take legal action against the school system. Unbelievable. Dean felt assaulted by the world, with all its logistics, its pettiness, its demands and complications. He should have stayed up at the Outdoor School, up on the mountain, where it was nature and memories and waiting.

The kitchen phone rang again. "Goddammit!" Dean said.

"I'll get it, Dad," Stephanie said. She gave Joelle an apologetic look, but Joelle kept her eyes on the ham-and-cheese sandwiches she was preparing.

"I got it," Dean said. "Hello?" he barked into the phone. "Unless you're calling to say you've found my son, I really don't have time to talk. Okay?"

"Dean, it's Laura."

"Oh, God. Hi." He glanced at Stephanie, who he knew was watching him, and gave her a vague nod before taking the phone into the living room. Not that he could be alone there. Jenny, Megan, and Bryan were sitting on the floor, playing Parcheesi while they waited for lunch.

"Sorry," Laura said. "I know you need to keep the line open."

"No, no, I'm sorry. I'm glad you called."

"I wasn't sure if I should."

"You should, believe me. You wouldn't believe the scum that have been calling—reporters and lawyers. All the bottom-feeders."

"So there's no news of him yet?"

"Somebody saw him in a gas station around eight, and that's the last we've heard of him."

"You're sure it was him?"

"He was wearing the right clothes. It sounded like him."

"Well, look, how far could he get, right?" Laura said. Her voice was even, but Dean could tell she was scared. "He won't do anything stupid."

"I don't know," Dean said. It was such a relief to talk to her. "Even the smartest kid is a little bit stupid."

"Even if he did do something dumb, even if he hitchhiked, what are the chances—"

"I don't know, I can't think about that. I really can't."

"I'm sorry," she said.

"You warned me," he said. "I should have listened to you."

"It's nobody's fault."

"No, it isn't. But people only say that when they wish it was somebody's fault."

"I'm not trying to blame you."

"I know you're not." Dean looked up at the ceiling, trying to get a feeling of privacy in his house full of people.

"Can you think of a place he might want to go?" Laura asked. "He usually goes somewhere specific when he leaves school. Has he mentioned any place in particular?"

"He hasn't been talking to me much," Dean said. "Not that I noticed."

"Don't beat yourself up. Now is not the time."

"Laura, I need to change." It felt good to say her name. He didn't care who overheard.

"You need to find Robbie. That's all you need to do."

"I mean it. Nicole is gone. That's the truth. If Robbie comes home—"

"Don't say *if*; are you crazy? Of course he's coming home."

"I hate just sitting here, waiting."

"Is there anything I can do to help? Could I bring over some lunch?"

"Joelle's making lunch." Dean glanced at the kids. Megan was stretching, her legs in hurdler's position. Tomorrow was Regionals. He hadn't forgotten, but its importance had faded.

"Actually, there is something I need to do, but I might not be able to," Dean said. "The girls have a meet tomorrow. It's a big one. I'm supposed to be there." He glanced at Megan, who was openly listening. "Do you think you could go in my place? You would be a chaperone, you could leave all the meet logistics to Philips. I mean, if we don't find—"

"Of course," Laura interrupted. "Of course."

"You don't actually have to do that much," he said. "You just let the girls run."

AUNT JOELLE STARTED talking about dinner while she was cleaning up the dishes from lunch. Stephanie stood next to her, drying plates. Meal planning was clearly her aunt's way of getting control of the situation, but Stephanie couldn't think of a better subject of conversation. She stacked the plates and put them away. Uncle Ed came into the kitchen.

"I'm headed home, hon," he said. "Page me if you hear anything, okay? I'll come back as soon as I can."

"Okay, bye, sweetie." Aunt Joelle gave him a kiss on the cheek.

"Where's he going?" Stephanie asked.

Aunt Joelle gave her a look like she was playing dumb. "He has to do the milking in a couple hours."

"Oh, right." Stephanie glanced at the clock. It was barely two. The afternoon was dragging. "I guess it gets dark early."

There was nothing else to clean in the kitchen. Stephanie went upstairs to use the bathroom and to wash her face. She should have taken a shower as soon as she got home, but she kept putting it off, afraid of missing out on news.

What she really needed was a nap. She went into her bedroom and lay down on her quilt. She could tell her brothers had been using her room. Her television, her father's old black-and-white, was in a slightly different position, still perched on the windowsill but now closer to the bed. There were candy wrappers and an empty water glass on her bedside table.

"Stephanie?"

It was Bryan in her doorway.

"Hey, Bry. Come sit." Stephanie sat up and arranged pillows against the headboard for both of them. "Where's Dad?"

"He's on the phone with someone. I don't know what about."

Stephanie considered picking up the extension on her bedside table but decided against it. She was starting to feel hopeless. It had been six hours since anyone had heard news of Robbie. She kept trying to be rational, reminding herself that child abduction and kidnappings were extremely rare, that Robbie was sensible, that the police were good at their job, but it was getting harder and harder as the day went on. And yet she couldn't really go to the other side, she couldn't imagine the worst.

"Where are Megan and Jenny?"

"Jenny's watching *Brady Bunch* on Nickelodeon. Megan went for a jog. Dad told her to."

"Right, there's some big race tomorrow."

"We were supposed to go."

"Maybe you still will."

"Maybe." Bryan leaned against Stephanie. "I wish you lived here."

"Oh, buddy." Stephanie held her brother close. His legs looked long stretched out next to hers. He had on a pair of hand-me-down corduroys that she clearly remembered Robbie wearing.

"It's okay, I know you have to go to college."

Stephanie heard someone pull into the driveway, and her first thought was that somehow it was Robbie. Someone had found him and was bringing him back. She went to the window.

"It's Pastor Owen!" Bryan said happily. "He's from Aunt Joelle's church."

"Oh." Stephanie doubted her father had approved of or was even aware of this visit.

Stephanie reluctantly followed Bryan downstairs to the kitchen, where Aunt Joelle was welcoming Pastor Owen inside. He was younger than Stephanie had expected, probably in his late twenties. He had a broad face, large ears, ruddy skin, and short reddish-brown hair. His large, dark eyes radiated emotion. She couldn't help liking him. He reminded her of a big friendly farm dog.

He gave Aunt Joelle and Bryan long hugs and shook Stephanie's hand, holding it between his own two hands like it was a precious thing. His sincerity was almost overbearing.

"Jenny!" Aunt Joelle called. "Megan's out for a jog," she added apologetically. "I told her to be back by now . . ."

"I'm not in any rush," Pastor Owen said. "Is Mr. Renner around too?"

"He's on the phone," Stephanie said quickly. "Let me go get him."

Stephanie went up to her father's study, an alcove off the dining room, but he wasn't there. Then she checked his bedroom, but that was empty, too. The room had a slightly harder, cleaner look; it was missing all the fussy niceties her mother attended to: the runners on the dresser, the liners in the trash can, the flowers in the bud vase. Soon only the particular arrangement of the furniture would bear her mother's finger-prints.

Stephanie heard loud voices downstairs. Tension filled her body as she remembered what it had been like to live here when her mother was lost to herself. At the beginning of high school Stephanie would sometimes sit on the back stairs and listen in, monitoring the emotional weather, but eventually she grew to dislike the role of spy. It made her complicit, somehow. She learned to put on headphones and ignore.

She felt dread hardening in her chest as she descended the stairs. She heard her father saying, "What gives you the right?" And then Joelle saying, "I thought it would help!" A quieter voice intervened. Pastor Owen. Stephanie felt sorry for him. He was still talking when she entered the living room. Everyone was staring at him. Megan sat next to her mother and sister on the sofa, her bare legs mottled from running in the cold. Stephanie's father was in his chair, a worn-out lounger, while Pastor Owen sat in what was unofficially the guest seat, a semicomfortable velvet wing chair. Stephanie knelt on the floor next to Bryan, feeling helpless, like a little kid. But she couldn't interrupt a minister.

" . . . and I don't want to intrude, Mr. Renner," Pastor Owen was saying. "I'm happy to lead a prayer for your family or simply to sit with you, or to go. I won't be offended, whatever you choose."

"The issue is not with you," Stephanie's father said. "I'm not opposed to prayer. But you've walked into a situation with some history to it. To put it simply, my sister-in-law has been pressuring my family to worship in a certain way and it's led to a lot of conflict. And as you may know, my wife passed away earlier this year."

"You make it sound like the two things are related!" Aunt Joelle said.

"That's just your guilty conscience."

"So you admit it."

"What am I admitting? That you try to control everything? That you put your nose in everyone's business? Who invited you to come here today? Who told you to come into my house and invite strangers?"

"Pastor Owen is an important person to my family, he's an important person to your son."

"Don't tell me what's important to my son. I entrusted him to you and what do you do? You indoctrinate him in your pushy Christianity."

"You're rude and you're a bully, Dean. You always have been. Talk about trust. I gave my daughter to you!"

"Megan is fourteen years old. Like it or not, she's on her way to becoming an adult. She came to me, I did nothing to recruit her."

"Oh, you did nothing, of course, you're perfect, nothing touches you. Everyone loves you, everyone thinks you're so good. You walk on water because you're *Coach* and you *change lives.* But I know how selfish you are, I know how miserable you make people. I gave my *sister* to you. And now she's gone and you're letting her kids go. I'm trying to find a safe place for them. Pastor Owen is a good person, he has God with him, he could help you. But you don't want help. You want to do everything on your own."

"Mom, Mom." Megan put her arms around her mother and stroked her hair.

"I did the best I could with Nicky." Aunt Joelle was crying now. "I miss her so much, oh God in heaven, I miss her. I just want her to come back."

Pastor Owen looked stunned, his youth shining through. He reached out his hands, offering one to Stephanie's father and the other to Bryan, who was sitting closest to him.

"Let us bow our heads in prayer," he said. "But let it be a silent prayer."

Stephanie closed her eyes and listened to her aunt cry. She said a prayer not to God, but to her mother.

ROBBIE HADN'T ACCOUNTED for the wait at the bus station. He sat on a bench with molded plastic seats that were like the chairs at school. His seat was missing an armrest, as were many of the seats nearby. He was bored. At first it had been a relief to sit and rest his legs after so many hours of walking but now he was getting restless. He still had a half hour until his bus arrived.

He got up and did another lap around the station. He knew everyone who was waiting, or at least he felt as if he knew them, because he'd been staring at them for so long. Sometimes people would return his gaze, but most ignored or just plain didn't notice him. Periodically a group of three or four people would get up and go outside to meet their bus. Robbie was surprised at the variety of Pennsylvanian destinations on offer. There was a large group gathering for a Philadelphia departure, and it crossed Robbie's mind that he could change his ticket and meet Stephanie instead. But he couldn't give up his original plan.

There was time, he decided, to go outside. And it was late enough in the day that no one would ask why he wasn't in school. He left the station and walked down the street to a toy store that he used to go to with his mother whenever they made trips into Hagerstown. It was a very small toy store, not part of a chain, and his mother liked it because they carried old-fashioned chapter books, like the ones she'd read as a girl. Sometimes Robbie would ask her to buy him one, not because he really wanted one but because he knew she liked it when he asked for them. He always read them and usually enjoyed them, but they weren't the kind of books he preferred. They were too formal, with their hard covers and thick pages, the ends of the pages left raw so that they seemed to be torn from a large, grand sheet of paper. Sometimes the top and bottom edges of the pages were dusted with gold powder and it would get on Robbie's fingers when he first started reading them. Robbie preferred books that were small and portable—paperbacks that he could carry in his jacket pocket or in the back pocket of his jeans. He liked reading to feel a little bit secret.

A bell on the toy store's door jangled when Robbie entered, and a man in a sweater vest came out from a storeroom in the back. He waved to Robbie and then took a seat behind the cash register. Robbie made his way through the little shop, starting with the cascade of stuffed animals in the front, which spilled over into the window display, past the games and sports-related gear, past the dolls, past the Legos, past the drawers of plastic animals, rubber balls, erasers, stickers, and other doodads, and into the small room in the back that was devoted completely to books. Robbie was starting to feel too old for toys. It was as if he'd lost an appetite. Just last Christmas he had spent an hour circling Lego sets in the JCPenney catalog, but he couldn't imagine doing that again this year. He would rather circle items of clothing or books or video games.

The old-fashioned books his mother liked were in a special section called "Collector's Editions." Robbie already had several of them: *Charlotte's Web*, *Stuart Little*, *Grimm's Fairy Tales*, and *The Sword in the Stone*. Most of the other titles sounded too girly to him.

"Need any help?"

Robbie was startled by the voice behind him. He turned and there was the owner, watching him.

"No," Robbie said. He quickly took a book off the shelf, *Black Beauty*. "This is the one I wanted."

"Can't go wrong with a classic." The man smiled. "You look so familiar. Did you used to come here with your mother?"

Robbie nodded uncertainly. He didn't know what to say. He was so stupid to have come in here. He couldn't get caught now.

"I thought so! Where's your mother today?"

"She's shopping," Robbie said. "She told me I could come here while she shopped. This is actually a present for her. For her birthday. It's her favorite book."

"How nice of you! Would you like me to wrap it up?"

"Yes, please."

Robbie followed him to the register, where he stood awkwardly, fingering the bills in his pocket, praying the book wouldn't cost more than fifteen dollars, which was all he had left. If he didn't have enough money, the man would be annoyed. He might even charge for the wasted wrapping paper. It was fancy paper, a glossy blue with a gold, ribbonlike pattern. Robbie couldn't help thinking that his mother would have appreciated it. She always noticed if something was nicely wrapped.

"Twelve ninety-five," the man said when he was finished. He placed the book in a red paper bag with the store's logo on it.

Robbie handed him his money, feeling relieved even though he now had only two dollars left for bus snacks. He hurried out of the shop after promising the man that he would say hello to his mother and then cut through an alley to get back to the station. As he walked, he realized it was getting very close to the departure time, so he headed straight to the depot to look for his bus. He found it and boarded. He was worried the driver would not take his ticket, because he was so young, but the driver only examined the ticket, checking for the correct date and time. *Maybe I'm more grown-up than I realized*, Robbie thought as he headed toward the back of the bus. He'd just had two exchanges in the adult world and no one had questioned him, no one had told him to be careful.

As the bus pulled out of the depot and onto the street, Robbie noticed two police cars parked outside the station. He wondered if someone had committed a crime while he was in the toy store. The idea frightened him, but in a thrilling way that made him feel like he was really, truly in the adult world.

The bus drove through the poorer neighborhoods as it made its way out of Hagerstown. Bedraggled-looking row houses were tucked right up against the sidewalks. There was a church without a steeple or a cemetery or even a proper yard, only a large cross hanging above a regular-sized door in a plain, square building. As they drove farther out of town, the buildings were more and more degraded until suddenly they weren't; it was as if they'd passed over some invisible border and now the houses were new or semi-new or, at the very least, old with a new addition tacked on. These houses led to rolling suburbs with new construction, the houses all perfectly centered on their plots. Many of them had aboveground pools in their backyards, covered over with black tarps for the winter. Robbie began to doze off as they passed the views he liked best: the wide, open fields and split-rail fences that reminded him of his grandfather's farm.

GENEVA BROUGHT OVER dinner around six, knocking on the side porch door. "Joelle sent me," she said. "She said she's sorry she couldn't come over herself."

"I'll bet," Dean said, letting her inside. "Did she tell you what happened?"

"I got the gist." Geneva began to unpack everything she'd brought: green peppers, pepperoni, shredded cheese, tomato sauce, and a large premade pizza crust.

"Has there been any news?" she asked. "Any word from the police?"

"Nothing. Nada. Zilch."

"Don't lose hope, Dean," she said. "They're going to find him."

"They've fucked up two perfectly good leads," he said. "Excuse my language."

"No excuse needed."

"Someone calls from the bus station, says he's *sitting right there*, and then suddenly he's not sitting there? Where did he go?"

"Maybe he got on a bus."

"That's what I'm worried about. He could be halfway to D.C. or Baltimore by now. What the hell is he going to do there?"

"Take it easy." Geneva rubbed his shoulder. "You can't start panicking now."

Dean sat down at the kitchen table. "It drives me crazy that he's out there and no one can find him. What do they do when someone breaks out of prison?"

"Robbie's smarter than a criminal," Geneva said. "Here, help me with this pizza. It's a Boboli, I had a coupon."

Dean obeyed, finding a cookie sheet for the crust and heating up the oven. He wasn't hungry, but he recognized that food was something they could do. He spread the tomato sauce on the cold crust and then he called Bryan into the kitchen to distribute the pepperoni, because he knew Bryan would enjoy the task. And Bryan's presence would also force him to be optimistic.

"Stephanie fell asleep on the sofa," Bryan reported.

"Good, she hardly slept at all last night."

The three of them made the little pizza, assembling it quickly and putting it in the oven. Stephanie came into the kitchen while it was cooking. She seemed annoyed that she had been allowed to nap. She was obviously still tired; she had wrinkles around her eyes, the kind that emerge temporarily on the sleep-deprived. Dean got a glimpse of what she would look like when she was older, and for the first time, he could picture her in the world, the adult world, the one he sometimes felt he'd never lived in because he'd always worked in schools.

The pizza was tasty and Dean ate more than he thought he would. At the end of the meal the phone rang and Dean jumped to get it. But it wasn't the police. It was See-See.

"Hi, Coach. I'm sorry to bother you. I know you're dealing with a lot."

"It's okay, I was actually going to call you. Is everything okay?"

"I'm just wondering about tomorrow. We're still competing, right?"

"Of course. I'm sending over a teacher from the middle school to help out—Ms. Lanning."

"I know Ms. Lanning. I had her for English last year."

"Okay, good, good."

There was a silence, and Dean realized he had to say something coachlike. He felt depleted of advice, of the kind of optimistic and borderline-delusional things a coach had to say to get an athlete ready for a big event. And he felt self-conscious because his family was listening.

"Do you think I'm going to qualify for States?" See-See asked, finally. "Sorry, I know that's the last thing you're thinking of."

"See-See, I am always thinking about you girls," Dean said. And as he spoke, he realized it was true, that the girls had been running through his mind, pulling him along all these weeks.

"I'm nervous," See-See said.

"You should be. It's a big race. But you have the training for it." Dean struggled to find something else to say. A few words of encouragement were all that she needed. But they couldn't be generic.

"Maybe some other girl has more physical strength," Dean said, "but you have more mental strength. What I said the other day about you bringing this team together—I meant it. The team wouldn't exist without you, it really wouldn't. So when you get tired tomorrow, when you're in the last mile and you have to start passing people, ask yourself if the runner in front of you is as powerful as you are. If she's a catalyst, the way you are."

"I take it the answer is no, they aren't," See-See said drily—but sincerely, too.

"Exactly. Put a target on their back and reel them in. You're the leader, they're the followers."

"What should I tell the others?"

Dean heard a long beep, followed by two short ones, the call-waiting signal.

"See-See, I have to go, I'm sorry. Tell them to remember that it doesn't matter how fast they can run—"

"—what matters is how fast they can run when they're tired."

"Right."

Dean switched to the other call. It was the police lieutenant from Hagerstown. They'd gotten two new leads, one from the owner of a small toy store in town who'd seen Robbie's photo on the evening news and realized that it was the same boy who had come into his shop late in the afternoon. The boy had been alone but friendly. He had bought a gift for his mother.

"That doesn't make any sense," Dean said.

"Yeah, that's what we thought," the officer said. "And it kind of contradicts the other call we got."

The other lead was from a woman who had seen a boy who looked like Robbie on her bus. He had been traveling alone when she saw him. She'd thought it was odd for someone so young to be by himself, but she hadn't given it another thought until she returned home and heard something on the radio about a missing boy.

"The woman was on a five o'clock to Pittsburgh, so it's possible that your son went to the toy store and then boarded that bus shortly after. But that seems unlikely because we had sent officers to the station."

"You said the bus was going to Pittsburgh?" Dean asked. "What's the route?"

"It goes west through Allegany County and then into Pennsylvania."

"What are the stops?"

"Berkeley Springs, Cumberland, Frostburg, Meyersdale, Rockwood—"

"I know where he's going," Dean said. "I know exactly where he's going."

THE LANDSCAPE WAS hidden, the fields like dark quilts, with farmhouses set far back from the road. You traveled back in time when you headed west in Maryland and now, Pennsylvania. Old farms, old industries. They'd just crossed the Mason-Dixon line. There were very few lights; the road was illuminated only by passing cars and the occasional streetlight when they reached a significant intersection. Above, the sky was black as soot, with a wash of stars, some of them as fine as dust.

The radio was playing, tuned to an oldies station. People were sending out lovelorn dedications on Friday night. In the backseat, Bryan was quiet but awake. Stephanie's father had barely managed a sentence since they'd left. There was nothing to say now that they knew Robbie was safe. Still, it wouldn't seem real until they saw him.

Someone requested a live recording of the John Denver song "Sunshine on My Shoulders." It was one of the songs her mother liked best, and Stephanie remembered telling her that it was easily one of the cheesiest songs ever written. Stephanie didn't know why she'd needed to curdle such a sweet melody. It was as if she'd resented the song's simplicity. Listening to it now, at night, with her mother dead and her brother at the end of some secret journey, she wondered what the song had meant to her mother. She felt a twinge of guilt, the pinch of all the questions she'd been too angry to ask, and then she let the guilt go, just let it fly out through the windshield, let it rush past like the trees and the flat fields and the black road. She thought of riding in the passenger seat next to her mother when she was a little girl, of her mother's shoulders bare and freckled in a summer dress she used to wear that had string straps that tied in a bow around her neck . . .

The memory began to break into pieces, getting mixed up with the song lyrics, and before Stephanie realized it, she was falling asleep.

DEAN CAME TO a quiet stop at the end of his father's lane and opened his door carefully, so as not to wake Stephanie and

Bryan. The distinct smell of his father's farm drifted in, the smell of horses, dirt, hay, moss, mulch, and some other metallic, starry scent that Dean could never quite identify. This was where his wife had chosen to die.

His father came outside to meet him, wearing a heavyweight plaid shirt over his pajamas. His father was shorter than he was, with a narrower build, and Dean had to lean over, slightly, to embrace him. With his head bent, prayerfully, and with his father's broad hands on his back, he remembered how Nicole always described his father as having "a warm soul." And he realized how much he'd missed him.

"I'm so glad Robbie came to you," Dean said.

"When he knocked on my door, I thought I was dreaming. He walked here from the bus station."

"I have to see him," Dean said. "Let me wake Stephanie and Bryan."

"Go on inside," his father said. "I'll get them."

Dean's father lived in a different house from the one Dean had grown up in. It was smaller but newly renovated, a four-room, two-story cabin that was close to the barn and that had once been a servant's quarters to the farmhouse. Nicole thought it was adorable, and when they visited, she would always make a point of cooking dinner in her father-in-law's kitchen and eating it outside, on his little lawn. Now, as Dean passed the wooden picnic table, he thought of their last dinner there. She had been in such a good mood, she had made a pound cake for dessert, had put edible flowers in the salad. He couldn't make sense of what she did just two days later. He wasn't going to try to anymore.

As soon as Dean saw Robbie, his body covered by one of his father's old blankets, he felt his knees buckle and he had to grab hold of the door frame.

"Robbie," he said. "Robbie, Robbie, Robbie."

Robbie didn't stir. He was sleeping on his stomach, with his right arm dangling off the sofa bed and his face turned away from the doorway. Dean went over to him and knelt in front of him, carefully moving his arms back onto the cushions. Robbie moved slightly; Dean whispered his name and stroked his hair. Robbie rolled onto his back. "Mom?" he said, softly.

"It's me," Dean said.

Robbie turned toward him, his eyes opening slowly. His gaze was soft and dream-touched; Dean could see he was in a place where anything could happen. His mother could easily become his father; his father could be his mother.

"Dad," Robbie said, smiling, coming to the surface. He sat up and the blanket fell away. He'd fallen asleep in his clothes. "Hey, what's wrong?"

"Nothing," Dean said, wrapping his arms around his son. His narrow body felt taller, stretched out; it felt precious, living, growing. "I'm just glad you're okay. You have no idea how worried we were."

"I'm sorry," Robbie said. "I really am. I just wanted to come here."

"I would have taken you. We could have come here together."

Robbie nodded, acknowledging that this was what he should have done, but Dean could see that he didn't believe it.

"Why didn't you ask me?" Dean said.

"I don't know. I couldn't explain." Robbie tugged on the hem of his T-shirt, a gesture Dean recognized from his toddler years.

"It's okay, I'm not angry. I just wanted to know." Dean took his son's face in his hands, savoring the feeling of his soft skin. "You're my Robbie, you're my boy. You can't do this again."

"No, no, I won't. I promise."

Stephanie and Bryan came into the room. They climbed up onto the foldout mattress to hug their brother. Bryan cried, the tears coming effortlessly, almost joyfully. "You came to Grandpa's!"

Dean's father stood in the doorway, where Dean had been just a few minutes before. "I wasn't sure you'd ever come back here," he said.

"Neither was I." Dean couldn't look away from his kids, together on the bed, the sheets and blankets rumpled beneath them. Stephanie leaned behind her brother to turn on the lamp and the light filled the room.

Chapter 16

Stephanie awakened early, when it was still dark outside. She closed her eyes and tried to fall back asleep, but the floor was too hard, even with the three heavy wool blankets her grandfather had laid down as a makeshift mattress. She could hear her brothers' breathing, both of them asleep on the foldout. Outside the sky was a faded predawn black.

Stephanie changed out of her pajamas in the bathroom. The floors creaked as she made her way to the kitchen, where the stove clock said it was almost six. Her grandfather's lined plaid shirt hung on a hook near the back door and she pulled it on as a jacket.

Outside, the cold air felt like something bright on her exposed skin. The stars were still visible in the sky, and so was the moon. In the distance, the white barn where her mother killed herself was a pale gray. It looked peaceful, pastoral. The barn in her memory was different. It stood on a hill, it glowed white in the high summer sun. The road that led to it was hot and dusty, the fields that surrounded it were violently green.

It was November now. Winter was coming. Soon the whole landscape would be covered in layers of snow and ice, and on some days the barn and sky and ground would be almost the same shade of white.

Stephanie felt a sudden gratitude for the change of the seasons. It made life easier, somehow.

She began to run, the cold air spurring her to move. She jogged aimlessly, or what she thought was aimlessly, until she understood that she was following the horse trail down to the creek, the same trail she'd followed on that day.

In the summer, the trail was deeply shaded by the deciduous trees that grew alongside it, but now the gray end-of-night light shone between the bare branches. The trail had a steeper grade than she remembered, the road tipping down toward the creek. Stephanie heard the water before she saw it—a soft, rushing sound. There was a break in the trees above it, and when she reached the creek, the light was stronger there, and the clear water reflected some of it, like a dark mirror. Stephanie ran along the banks, stopping at the watering spot where she had stopped so many times before. The pebbly, muddy beach had hardened with frost, the shapes of horse's hooves and tire tracks preserved from the last warm days.

On the other side of the creek was the field of another farm. Stephanie often saw cows grazing there, but it was too early in the morning for them to be out. She looked upstream and noticed that a huge tree had fallen across the creek. A willow. The current was pulling its dead tendril branches downstream. It still had some of its leaves, and they were still faintly green. They'd never yellowed and fallen, Stephanie realized. The tree had plunged into the creek sometime over the summer. Stephanie remembered seeing it when it was alive, remembered her father saying it was going to fall over and stop up everything. She gazed at it, mesmerized by the way it disturbed the even current, and also by the water that continued to flow beneath it and over it and around it; there were dozens of miniature waterfalls spilling over the smaller branches that reached out across the surface of the water, and there were places where the water churned violently to get past the heavy trunk. The water was going to break down the tree, over time.

Stephanie stood and stared at the fallen willow for a long while before making her way back to her grandfather's house. The sun was rising, it was a bright orange spot of light low on the road. As it made its way up into the sky, shining between the tree trunks and then the higher branches, it seemed to be caught. But then it broke free.

EVERYONE HAD AWAKENED early, out of discomfort or exuberance or some combination of the two. They had to crowd to fit around the kitchen table, where Dean's father arranged two platters, one of toast and the other of bacon—the best breakfast he could provide on short notice. Dean had slept well, but he was still tired and looked forward to going home, to spending time with just his family, his boys, his girl, the four of them.

Dean's father turned on the radio to hear the weather. Rain was forecast for later in the morning.

"Do the girls still race if it rains?" Bryan asked.

"It's rain or shine," Dean said. "Let's hope Megan has spikes. I forgot to remind Joelle."

"We can bring them to the race," Bryan said.

"Honey, we're not going to the race," Dean said.

"Why not?"

"Because it's far away. We don't have time."

"We could make it. The race isn't until ten thirty."

"It's okay, the girls are still going to run it. They don't need us to be there."

"But don't you want to see it?" Bryan said.

"If we can make it, we should go," Stephanie said. "Why not?"

"Because we don't need to rush from one thing to the next," Dean said. "We've been through a lot. Right, Robbie?"

"I don't mind going," Robbie said.

"Robbie doesn't mind! Come on, Dad, let's go, please. I want to see if Megan wins."

"We'd have to leave really soon," Dean said, checking in with his father, who nodded his assent.

"That's fine!" Bryan got up from the table. "I'll go brush my teeth!"

"I guess that settles it," Stephanie said, with a funny smile on her face. She got up and began to clear the dishes.

The room was filled with new energy as they prepared for departure. Dean folded up all the sheets and blankets while Robbie changed into the clothes Dean had brought for him to wear. He frowned as he pulled on his sweatshirt, and Dean wondered if he had picked the wrong thing.

"What's the matter?" Dean asked. "Do you want to take a shower? You can, if you want."

"No, it's not that."

"Do you want to skip the race? We don't have to go. Bryan will understand."

"No, I want to go."

"Okay," Dean said. "Is it something else? Do you feel all right?"

"I feel fine, it's just that I wanted . . . I wanted to go to the barn."

"The barn?" Dean repeated. It was all he could think to say.

"Never mind." Robbie looked ill. "Forget it."

"No, it's okay," Dean said. "We can go."

"I just wanted to see it when it's normal inside, with all the horses there like they are in the mornings. So I can remember it a different way." His chin trembled. "I know it's strange."

"It's not strange." Dean knelt down to take his hands. "Hey, listen to me, it's not strange. Nothing is strange in this world."

Robbie nodded, taking deep breaths to hold back his tears.

Dean put his hand on Robbie's shoulder and led him through the kitchen where Stephanie and Bryan were sitting quietly with his father, aware that something important was transpiring in the next room. Dean signaled for them to follow him outside.

He didn't have to say where he was going; it was obvious. They followed the driveway up the slight hill that led to the barn. Dean remembered driving away from it to go to the hospital, seeing it in his rearview mirror and knowing his life had changed forever. But he hadn't really known. He wasn't the kind of person who understood things in an instant.

When they reached the barn, Dean's father helped him slide the heavy doors open. The horses stirred as light shone into their stalls. Dean could smell their bodies. There were only four horses; the white barn was the smallest of three barns on the property, and most of it was devoted to storage.

The rope swing had been toward the back of the barn, near the hayloft, but it had been removed.

Robbie stood still, and then he walked down the dirt aisle to a particular spot. He looked up toward the barn's vaulted ceiling and then he knelt down and he touched the floor with his hand flat on the ground like he was trying to make an impression. Dean wished he had a wreath or a flower or a stone to offer. He thought of his visits to the battlefield, the potent sense of lives lost. His wife had fought hard for her life; she had fought hard and she had been defeated. He had to honor that. Maybe that was all anyone ever meant by forgiveness.

THE RAIN HAD already passed over the valley and the sky was a rinsed blue. Dean stood on a hill, watching the teams line up on the field below. His legs and chest ached pleasantly from his sprint across the parking lot. He was too far away to identify his girls, and he had no idea of the course they were about to run. But he didn't care, he was just grateful to have made it to this spot.

Next to him, Robbie, Bryan, and Stephanie were yelling, "Go blue!" and trying to get the attention of the crowd of Willowboro spectators at the bottom of the hill. He felt an easy happiness, a desire simply to be near the people who meant the most to him.

The crowd went quiet as the starter walked out onto the field. He raised his arms and shot the pistol. A cloud of smoke appeared, floating like a ghost above the advancing runners. Dean watched it dissolve before following his children down the hill and across the playing field.

Acknowledgments

First, to Maura Candela and Courtney Knowlton, who coaxed this—and many other stories, essays, and novels—into existence. You are my first, most generous readers, and I can't thank you enough for your kindness, discernment, and insight—and of course, for all the gossip you've shared with me over the years.

To Emma Patterson, my agent: your support of and attention to my writing have made me a better storyteller. Thank you for everything.

To Margaux Weisman, my editor, and everyone at William Morrow: thank you for bringing this book to life with so much care and intelligence.

To Jennifer Acker, Kimberly England, and Krista Hoeppner-Leahy: your friendships have enriched my life in too many ways to list.

To Katie Bradley and Amanda Delong: you eased the loneliness of working alone. I couldn't have written this book without you two.

To my family, especially my husband, whose love and support have meant the world to me.

Andrew Solomon's *The Noonday Demon: An Atlas of Depression* was an inspiring and invaluable resource in writing this story.

I grew up in a beautiful corner of western Maryland. I am indebted to this landscape, and I tried to capture its essence in the fictional town of Willowboro. The events and characters in this book come from my imagination and should not be confused with real people or situations.

About the author

About the book

Read on

Insights,
Interviews
& More . . .

Meet Hannah Gersen

HANNAH GERSEN was born in Maine and grew up in western Maryland. She is a staff writer for *The Millions*, and her writing has been published in the *New York Times*, *Granta*, and *The Southern Review*, among others. *Home Field* is her first novel. She lives in Brooklyn with her family. ◡

Reading Group Guide

1. Aside from a pure and genuine love of the game, what do you think Dean gets out of his team that he doesn't get from his home life?

2. The author sets the story in 1996. How does this choice affect the tone and atmosphere of the novel? How did it affect your reading?

3. Both Stephanie and her brothers have an episode with their mother's clothing after her death. What do the differences in their responses mean to you? How are they using the clothes to cope with their loss?

4. Do you think Dean made the right choice in stepping down from his position? Why or why not?

5. Do you think Stephanie made the right choice in going to college right away? Why or why not?

6. Do you think Dean and Laura end up together? Why or why not?

7. A particularly evocative memory Stephanie has of her mother involves stopping by the side of the road to eat a peach. Why is this image so powerful? What does it signify?

8. Another very evocative memory is of Nicole being unable to cut a lemon and Stephanie pulling over to the side of the road to cry. Why do you think this is such a successful illustration of depression? How does it complement the moment with the peach? ▶

Reading Group Guide *(continued)*

9. Do you relate to Stephanie's experience in her first months of college? Why or why not?

10. One of the most heartbreaking moments in the book is when Jessica's mom is speaking with Dean and unwittingly begins talking about Nicole, referring to her as "that sweet woman." Why is this moment so powerful? What is the author trying to show us?

11. What are some of the leitmotifs the author employs in her writing and how do they work to advance the themes of the novel? ◠

Suggested Reading

Snow, by Orhan Pamuk

If there's any one book that inspired
this novel, it's *Snow*. It's the story of an
exiled Turkish poet, Ka, who returns to
Turkey to investigate a rash of suicides
among young, religious girls in a small
village. I love the mysterious, uncertain
atmosphere of this novel; it enveloped
me immediately, from the first scene
when Ka boards a bus that almost seems
to take him back in time. Although I
read *Snow* years before I started working
on *Home Field*, there was something
about its odd angles that got me thinking
about where I grew up and how I might
write about it.

Independence Day, by Richard Ford

I read this at the recommendation of my
husband, who doesn't read much fiction,
so when he likes a book I pay attention.
It took him several months to finish
it, and I teased him about that until
I started reading it. Even though the
story takes place over only a few days,
it's densely narrated by Frank Bascombe,
the protagonist of several of Ford's
books. I love Bascombe's narration,
especially his vocabulary, which is so
American in the way that he mixes
poetic language with regional slang,
technical terms with academic allusions,
and ten-dollar words with the simplest
endearments and place names. ▶

The Stories of John Cheever, by John Cheever

I discovered these stories when I was in my early teens and have been reading them ever since. My favorites are "The Country Husband," "The Death of Justina," and "Goodbye, My Brother"— a story I read pretty much every year. I love Cheever's sensibility: his jokes; his vocabulary; his feeling for landscape, mood, childhood, color, and light. His narrators are melancholy, dissatisfied, and ashamed, but they love life, and that mix of sadness and delight is what always brings me back to Cheever. I think of scenes from his fiction every time I go to the beach, take a walk in Manhattan, or board a train on the Hudson line.

The Autobiography of My Mother, by Jamaica Kincaid

I first read this at age nineteen and it floored me. It's the story of Xuela, a motherless child who grows up on the small Caribbean island of Dominica. Xuela is a survivor, a woman who finds her way in the world on her own terms, rejecting motherhood, daughterhood, siblinghood, and all kinds of inherited identity. At the same time, there's an embrace of the natural and material world that gives Xuela's writing an incredible vitality.

Sweet Talk, by Stephanie Vaughn

This is one of my favorite short story collections, simply because the stories are so full of emotion and evocative of childhood. My favorite story is "Dog Heaven." I still can't get through it without crying—and I'm not even a dog person.

A Home at the End of the World, by Michael Cunningham

I love the title of this book, I love the characters in this book, I love the warmth and elegance of the prose in this book, and I even love the movie adaptation of this book, which introduced me to the wonderful actor Dallas Roberts, whose performance I admired so much that I went to see him in a revival of Edward Albee's *The Zoo Story*. So, just read this book: it will enrich your life in unexpected ways.

Far from the Tree, by Andrew Solomon

As part of my research for this novel, I read Andrew Solomon's *The Noonday Demon: An Atlas of Depression*, which is an excellent and intensely personal nonfiction book about the history and treatment of depression. Around the time I finished *The Noonday Demon*, Solomon's next book, *Far from the Tree*, was published. It addresses what happens to families when a child turns out to be very different from his or her parents; for example, a deaf child born ▶

to hearing parents, a child prodigy born to parents of ordinary intelligence, or a transgender child born to cisgendered parents, to give just a few examples. Once I started this book I couldn't stop reading it. Every chapter brings a new family portrait, a new set of complications. It's like a series of linked novellas, except they are all founded in an extraordinary amount of reporting and research. Solomon's compassion radiates off the pages as he interviews families about their fears, joys, disappointments, and triumphs as parents of the children that they never expected to have.

Fun Home, by Alison Bechdel

I've been a fan of Alison Bechdel since the 1990s, when I started reading her syndicated cartoon, "Dykes to Watch Out For." But it wasn't until I read *Fun Home* that I truly appreciated her depth as a writer. *Fun Home* is a memoir, telling the story of Bechdel's complicated relationship with her late father, a closeted gay man who taught English and ran a funeral home, which was also the house Bechdel grew up in. Bechdel's childhood is strange, bookish, morbid, and haunted by her father's tormented identity. It isn't until she leaves home that she is able to come out as a lesbian; around the same time, her father dies suddenly in a possible suicide, leaving Bechdel with even more mysteries to unravel. Somehow, this is a very funny book, and also full of literary allusions and quick, sensitive pieces of literary criticism.

Americanah,
by Chimamanda Ngozi Adichie

This book showed me how to write the voice of Stephanie. I wanted her to be genuinely naive and lacking in experience, but I didn't want to condescend to her. *Americanah* follows two high school sweethearts, Ifemelu and Obinze, Nigerian students who are separated by war and by economic and social forces beyond their control. Ifemelu ends up in America, where she struggles with what it means to be black and African in a new country, while Obinze barely gets by in London on an illegal work visa. Both are unprepared for what life throws at them, and Adichie depicts their naïveté as well as their bravery and strength. It's a full, sympathetic portrait of youth and young love, and in general this novel is so full of life, so overflowing with observations, jokes, and dialogue, that I couldn't help feeling as if Adichie poured everything she knew into this book. That's always the kind of novel I like best. ⌒

Playlist

"Jesus Doesn't Want Me for a Sunbeam," by Nirvana

Which Nirvana song to pick for a book set in the 1990s? This is the one that immediately came to mind, even though it's not my favorite Nirvana song and isn't actually a Nirvana song—it was originally written and recorded by The Vaselines. But I like it for this story because it's a parody of Christian children's songs, the kind of music that Stephanie would have learned as a kid and rebelled against as a teenager.

"Violet," by Hole

At the beginning of the novel, Dean spots Missy wearing a Hole T-shirt and has no idea what it means. I probably never would have heard of this band if my older sister hadn't been living in Olympia, Washington, at the time and sending me mixtape dispatches. (My sister also got me a subscription to *Sassy* magazine—why, oh why didn't I keep the one with Kurt and Courtney on the cover? Why didn't I keep all of them?)

"Feel the Pain," by Dinosaur Jr.

I can't listen to this song without picturing the album cover, that sad-looking animal in a red jacket. I didn't even own this album; I didn't have to, because everyone I knew had it and this song played nonstop on the alternative stations.

"Basket Case," by Green Day

I was recently talking to my fifteen-year-old nephew about what music he likes and was surprised—and then not surprised—when he said Green Day. Their songs are so durable and catchy and unexpectedly timeless. As Stephanie observes, they're the one band that seemed to transcend all clique lines in her high school. That was certainly the case at my high school, which was divided between country music lovers, indie rock nerds, and hip-hop/pop fans. But everyone listened to Green Day.

"Walk This World," by Heather Nova

In college I had a mixtape with this song and a bunch of other Lilith Fair types. My work-study job in college was in the dish room and there was an old beat-up stereo where you could play your tapes while you worked. I remember bringing my Lilith mix one Sunday morning, slightly worried that my coworker, a guy I didn't know that well, would hate it. As it turned out, he loved Heather Nova in particular and said her voice reminded him of Laura Nyro, who I had never heard of. He ended up introducing me to a bunch of other female singers with gorgeous voices.

"The Bends," by Radiohead

I chose this song for the lyric "I wish, I wish, I wish that something would happen." There's no better description of what it feels like to be a teenager, ▶

especially a teenager in a small town.

"Hyperballad," by Björk

My boyfriend's twin sister introduced me to Björk. I remember when she played the CD for me because Björk's lush, emotional dance music was in such contrast to her spartan dorm room, which was really minimal with bare walls, all-white bedding, and hardly any furniture. Years later, one of my roommates lived in a similar fashion and blasted Björk whenever he felt depressed. "Hyperballad" was his favorite song and he had several different versions of it. I came to love it too, especially its dramatic and enigmatic lyrics.

"Marianne," by Tori Amos

Tori Amos had a huge influence on me as a teenager. Aside from Claire Danes in *My So-Called Life*, there was no one else who seemed to speak to the emotional and sexual confusion of being a teenage girl. She was a big influence on a lot of girls I knew; I remember my chorus teacher accusing soloists of "Tori Amos–izing" their melodies. To an adult with tempered emotions, Tori Amos can sound over-the-top, and in my twenties, I was somewhat embarrassed by my love for her theatrical, angsty, hyperfeminine music. Now I appreciate her again, especially the way that so many of her songs are stories with a female character at the center. "Marianne" is one of my favorite of her story-songs, and apparently it's based on someone Amos really knew.

"Man on the Moon," by R.E.M.

Is this my favorite R.E.M. song? No, but it's probably the most comforting one, which is why I chose it as the song that Stephanie hears when she's coming down from a really bad ecstasy trip. The lyrics are mellow and easy to understand, especially for an R.E.M. song. I read somewhere that Michael Stipe was trying to write lyrics with more "yeahs" than Kurt Cobain's.

"Who Will Save Your Soul," by Jewel

There was no escaping this song in 1996. The chorus was so catchy and sincere that you couldn't help remembering it. It played on both alternative and pop stations and it sprang to mind when I was thinking about what might be playing on Dean's car radio.

"Onion Soup," by Vic Chesnutt

I only recently discovered Vic Chesnutt. Unfortunately, it was his death in 2009 that brought his music to my attention. I wish I'd known about him when I was a teenager because I think I would have loved his lyrics, which are full of literary allusions. He's a southern oddball who was discovered by ▶

Michael Stipe, and like Stipe, he has a distinctive singing voice and lyric vocabulary, a regional sensibility that's part country and part art school—with a dash of Americana. I've just started getting into his music, but I thought this might be one of the songs that Stephanie would relate to, with its references to unsent letters and nostalgia for an old friendship.

"Castle on a Cloud," from *Les Misérables*

Les Misérables was touring the country when I was in high school, and my church choir got together a big group to go see it. I loved the music when I was a teenager, but I must admit that it has gone stale for me over the years. However, this song has a sweet melody that I remember singing in middle school choir, and I feel certain that Robbie would have learned it in school and perhaps taken comfort in it.

"Ghost," by the Indigo Girls

Indigo Girls rank right up there with Tori Amos as a Big Teenage Musical Influence. This heartbreakingly pretty song is the perfect one to listen to when, as my three-year-old likes to say, you need to "get the tears out."

"Sunshine on My Shoulders," by John Denver

I was recently listening to an interview with Nick DiPaolo on Marc Maron's

WTF podcast and was amused to learn that DiPaolo listens to *John Denver's Greatest Hits* when he's in bad traffic because it helps to calm his road rage. When I heard that, I thought, that's exactly why I disliked Denver when I was a teenager, but why, as an adult, I understand his appeal. When I was trying to think of the kind of music that Stephanie's mother would like but which Stephanie would think was unbearably cheesy, I chose Denver because his music would have been popular when Nicole was younger. I also thought Nicole would like his sweet voice and earnest lyrics— and that Stephanie might find them comforting after her mother's death.

"My Father's House," by Bruce Springsteen

I became a big Springsteen fan without even realizing it. It started in 2003, when I lucked into a ticket to see Springsteen at Shea Stadium. It turned out to be an incredible concert, with two long encores. I was surprised by how many of the songs I knew, because I'd never bought any Springsteen albums or given his music much thought. It was as if I had absorbed Springsteen's songs just by living in a small town and listening to a lot of rock music. After that concert I started listening to all his old albums. "My Father's House" struck me as a perfect song for this playlist ▶

Playlist *(continued)*

because of the imagery of forests and fields and ghostly voices. Thematically, it also covers similar ground; it's about a man who has lost touch with his father and dreams of being a child again and returning home. ❧